A..............
Story

ASSATTA

NEWMAN SPRINGS PUBLISHING
320 Broad Street
Red Bank, NJ 07701

First originally published by Newman Springs Publishing 2023

ISBN 978-1-63881-962-2 (Paperback)
ISBN 978-1-63881-963-9 (Digital)

Printed in the United States of America

To those who believed in me even when I did not believe in myself.

The story you are about to read shows that, in life, we all get A...............*Story*. Regardless of how gritty or grimy, it's yours!

As my sister and I entered the funeral home side by side, I couldn't believe all of the people seated mourning the death of Ma D. The pain I felt just seconds before I walked through the door, the pain of having to live life without the woman who took my sister and I in and treated us as her own, that was taking away and replaced with anger when I locked eyes with Peaches. I tried to shoot daggers through her with my eyes. How could God have been so cruel to have cursed me with a mother like her, not that I would ever call or consider her as my mother. The fact is she birthed and cursed me at the same time. Peaches pushed me out on May 27, 1980.

When the doctor handed me to her, she took one look at me and said, "Give her to her," and pointed to her youngest sister, Darlene, not even taking another glimpse at her newborn baby.

The nurse then looked over and asked Darlene if she wanted to hold me, afraid of her answer because of Peaches's response. She continued to play with the baby, awaiting Darlene's answer.

"Yes, I do want to hold my niece," Darlene stated in an excited tone.

From that moment on, Darlene knew she would have to look out for her niece, but never in a million years did she expect she would have to name and take her niece home from the hospital.

I looked over at Stormy as she grabbed my hand, and the pain I felt moments before resurfaced again. Stormy's eyes were watery and red. Her caramel skin had dried-up tear streaks along down her cheeks. Her eyes were a reflection of my pain. I could feel her hurt because I, too, had just lost more than an aunt—Darlene Marie

Lewis was our mother. Even though she would never let us call her mom, Ma D was what we referred to her as.

"Oh, God, why! Why you take my sister? God, no!" Peaches cried out hysterically.

I kept my focus on Stormy and tried to disguise the disgust I felt toward Peaches and her performance she's trying to win an Academy Award for. There were over 150 people in the funeral home; and for some reason, as we got closer to the casket, I felt like Stormy and I were the only ones in the room. The closer we got to the casket, the farther away it became. I felt Stormy squeeze my hand tighter as we stood next to the very end of the casket, tears falling from my eyes. Some man walked past us and led Peaches away from the casket as she was steady crying in the man's arms.

"Oh! I would do anything to have my sister here with me, Lord! Oh, Lord. Oh, Lord."

How ironic. She left two babies on her little sister and never even so much as picked up the phone to see if we were still breathing or if we needed one red cent, but here she stood in front of Ma D while there was not a piece of life in her left, telling her body that remained all of what she should have said when she was alive.

You would do anything to bring her back, but while she was living, you wouldn't so much as spit on her if she was on fire, I thought to myself.

A man and a woman stood in front of us. They appeared to be in their seventies and were very small in their physique. The woman, I had never seen before; but the man, I remembered coming over Ma D's house on holidays. She would always refer to him as "a good friend of the family." The women leaned over in the casket and kissed Ma D on the cheek. I couldn't concentrate on what the lady was saying because I could see Ma D's body from her chin down and I lost my composure. I knew that I was supposed to stand strong and firm for Stormy, but I couldn't hold in the tears. I couldn't hold in my cry for help. Stormy, who was at least five inches shorter than me, held me up as we stood face-to-face with Ma D. I felt so weak. I held on to the casket, and my tears wouldn't stop. Stormy just rubbed my back, not saying a word as the preacher went on to tell us to take our time. I silently spoke to Ma D.

"Ma D, please don't leave. Please! I can't make it without you. Please don't do this to me. Don't do this to us, Ma D."

For the first time in my thirteen years on this earth, Ma D didn't give me what I wanted; so I asked again, this time a little louder, as I bent down in the casket and whispered into her ear, "Ma D, please don't go."

"Come on, A," Stormy stated as she grabbed my hand. "Other people have to see her," Stormy said timidly.

I listened. As we took our seats, it felt like every eye in the funeral home were on Stormy and me. Everyone knew that Stormy and I were all that Ma D had, and with that said, she was all that we had. Our lives from this point on would never be the same.

CHAPTER 1

Do as I Say and Not as I Do

If there was one thing that Ma D taught me, it would be to stand up for myself. She often told me that no one had someone forever, so the best thing a woman could learn how to do was to stand and speak for herself. I always did just that. I always said what I meant and meant what I said. I understood that all you have in life is your word. Ma D expressed this over and over to Stormy and me, so how Stormy waited until the day we had to go to our foster home to decide she wanted to live with Peaches beat me.

"May I please go to the bathroom, Miss Eli?" Stormy asked our caseworker as we walked toward the car.

"Sure, you can, Stormy. We'll be waiting out here for you," Miss Eli stated in a pleasant tone.

"You want me to come in with you, Storm?" I asked her, sensing something was wrong.

"Nah, it's okay, Agape."

Agape? I thought.

In all the years I'd been around my sister, she had never called me by my first name, not that I could remember. She'd always called me A. Stormy couldn't pronounce my name when she was little. Knowing something just didn't feel right, I backed down and let my sister turn her back on me in a manner I never saw possible.

Miss Eli received a call. She then turned to face me with saddened eyes and informed me that Stormy would not be going to the

1

foster home. She had decided to go stay with Peaches, and if I wanted to, I could as well.

Not over Ma D's dead body would I go live with that woman, I thought to myself.

Miss Eli waited for my response, but when I didn't give one, she asked me if I was going to be okay. Miss Eli was a nice woman, but at the moment, I felt like she was only doing her job. I wasn't about to be a part of the parade of broken children confessing their problems to her. All I could do was look out the passenger side window and watch the rain flood from my eyes. I wanted so bad to get out the car and fight for Stormy to come back, to convince her to come to the foster home with me, but what would that do for me if she was willing to leave me for a woman she did not even know in such a deceitful way?

Miss Eli went on to tell me that, since my foster parent was expecting two girls, if I wanted, she could easily go pick another girl if I would like her to. I wanted so desperately to tell her "I think that's a good idea," but no words would leave my mouth.

But then Miss Eli said, "I'll even let you pick the girl," as she rubbed my back, trying to add as much as sunshine as possible to what was left of my cloudy life.

At this point, I knew Miss Eli wasn't just doing a job. She understood how I felt and what I was going through probably more than I did myself.

"Tameka Hoosk," I said flatly, still looking out the window.

Tameka was the only girl in the group home who didn't have a sibling that I knew of. We got along well the two weeks we were at Shawny Acres. I now understood how lonely she must have been in a group home with no form of foundation or family. That was why I chose her. Meaka and I both secretly thought we had it made as we pulled up to the two-story house that was painted a soft yellow. The house had yellow daisies surrounding it. The neighborhood was quiet and peaceful. Every house on the block was huge and had a two-car garage. Miss Eli introduced us to our foster parent, Sabrina McClure. She was very polite to us. Sabrina resembled Ursula, the girl Cleo went with in *Set It Off*. They had the same bleached-blond afro. Their skin complexions, just about the same. But Sabrina might have been a few pounds heavier than Ursula. It wouldn't shock me if she was gay. She asked us if we were hungry and if we wanted her to take our bags to our designated rooms. We both stated that we would do it ourselves, not wanting to lead Sabrina to believe that we were lazy. She showed us to our room, and I was thrilled when I found out that we had separate bedrooms. Each one of our rooms had everything a girl our age could ask for, like a computer, stereo, and a television with a DVD player. Soon as the redheaded White woman left her doorstep, she hadn't been as polite. We were nothing more than a check for Sabrina, and that day, she made sure she let us know that.

"Listen here, ladies," Sabrina stated with a serious tone after making sure that Miss Eli wasn't in eyesight by peeking through the curtains. "You are here for one reason and one reason only, and that's because no one else wants y'all asses."

I coughed to keep from laughing. I didn't know what she was about to say, but I surely didn't think she was going to say anything like that. Here she was talking to two teenage girls, and she looked us in our face and told us no one wanted us.

I couldn't even object because, no matter the pain that sliced through me after the words left Sabrina's mouth, that was my reality—no one wanted me.

"Do we have a problem, Miss Agape?" she said, pronouncing it *agupie*.

"My name is A-ga—"

Sabrina interrupted me, and those cat eyes of hers pierced right through me like a knife. "Look here, you little red orphan. I don't care what your name is. The only reason I even have you standing under my roof as we speak is because I need my bills paid." She turned to Tameka and whispered in her ear, "That goes for you too, so what I suggest for y'all to do as I say and not as I do."

As the years went on, Meaka and I learned how to deal with Sabrina. As long as we cleaned the house and her car, she was a happy camper. Don't vacuum, dust, or clean; and we would feel her wrath. Sabrina could be one mean lady on any given Sunday. She would torture us as a form of punishment. She wouldn't feed us for days. The only food we would have were our school lunches if the punishment took place during the weekday or whenever school was in, or else we wouldn't have anything to eat until Sabrina would allow us to eat. Sabrina sometimes looked over Meaka's half-cleaning antics, but for me, she seemed to be harder on me for some reason. She didn't let anything I did get by her. She constantly tried to turn Meaka and I against each other, but we shared a bond that couldn't be broken. We were both without our family; and our dreams were the only thing that brought us out of such a cold reality—the reality of knowing that we both had someone care for us and love us and, when it was time for them to leave this earth, no one else wanted us.

Peaches never wanted me or Stormy, and she did everything in her power to let us know that, never visiting us or never taking time to pick up the phone to see how we were doing—none of that. Even if we happened to see her out in public, she would only speak to Ma D. As we stood there begging for her to notice us, she wouldn't.

I could hear Ma D saying, "Peaches, don't you see your kids standing here?" secretly hoping Peaches would let us know how much we had grown and how pretty we were.

But not Miss Peaches 'cause all she would ever say was "How I see it, Darlene, those are your kids."

Yep, right there in front of us. I would never forget that, and maybe that was why I chose to go to a foster home over going to live with Peaches. It was something about all of the birthdays and holidays, as well as school programs, that she was never in attendance; for that made her somewhat of a stranger to me. In a way, Stormy as well, because she never even let me in on just the thought crossing her mind that she wanted to live with Peaches. As time went by, I was left with only memories of the sister I once shared everything with. I shared plenty ill feelings toward the actions that Stormy displayed, but despite those feelings, I wished nothing but the best for Storm.

Meaka, on the other hand, her grandmother raised her. By the time her mother was thirteen, she had birthed Meaka into this world, only to had run off a year later, never to be heard from again. Angie Hoosk, Meaka's grandmother, had the police looking for her. She put up missing posters of her only child, Megan Hoosk, but no one knew anything about Megan's whereabout. It was as if she had fallen off of the face of the earth. As time went by, Meaka was reminded of the mother she never saw from people in her neighborhood. Someone was always telling her that she looked just like her mother. Pictures of Megan told the same story. When I looked at Meaka's pictures, I wasn't sure if it was her or her mother. At the age of sixteen, Meaka was a spitting image of her mother. They both had smooth dark-chocolate skin and long, wavy hair, with the most amazing blue eyes. Meaka dreamed of the day she would have the chance to stand face-to-face with her mother, and if the day was to ever come, Meaka didn't know how she would ever forgive her mother for leaving her. She prayed that she would have it in her to forgive her.

I could feel Meaka nudge my arm for me to wake up, but I didn't want to leave my dream. I was dreaming about the time Ma D Stormy and I went out to Walmart to buy the new Martin Lawrence comedy special *You So Crazy*. We rode home in the car, anticipating on how funny it was going to be. Ma D loved her some Martin, often referring to him as her husband. We got out the car and ran into the house. After entering Ma D's room, we lay in the bed just a laughing away. We laughed so hard as Martin told joke after joke. Our eyes were watery; Ma D's face was red as mine was naturally. I was immediately awakened when I heard Sabrina hollering up the steps.

"Agupie, if you don't get your ass down these steps right now!" Sabrina yelled.

After slipping on my robe, I proceeded downstairs only to find Meaka on her hands and knees with a sponge cleaning the hardwood floors.

"Yes?" I said as nice as I could muster out but with much attitude.

Meaka noticed the attitude in my voice; she put her finger up to her mouth trying to calm me down as Sabrina's back was turned to her. I took notice and tried to shake the venom that had been, time and time again, ready to explode on her.

"Look, Agupie, I need for you to sort all of my dirty clothes—"

I interrupted. "Sort your dirty clothes? Now, don't you think that is a bit much, Sabrina?" I said sarcastically, knowing, if we could come on our menstrual for her, she would have us bleed two cycles a month for her.

There was nothing she wouldn't have us do. But I knew one thing I was not going to do, and that was sorting nobody's dirty clothes, until I looked down and saw Meaka's pleading eyes begging me to sort the clothes.

"Agupie, I don't know if you understand that I can have your ass shipped right out of here with just one simple phone call," Sabrina said with her hands on her hip.

This was nothing new. Sabrina always threatened me with calling children services. I made Meaka a promise that I would never do anything to get taken away from here, and since my word was all I had, some of the things I put up with were only because of that promise I made to Meaka the first night we stayed in this house. We'd built a family within ourselves. Meaka and I called each other sisters since neither one of us had a mother in our life. We'd made ourselves share the same mother, and in a sense, we do.

We're the same motherless daughters of women who chose one thing or another over us for whatever reasons.

"Okay, Sabrina, whatever you say. I'll sort your clothes if that makes you feel better about yourself," I said in a matter-of-fact tone.

I knew some of the things she had us do was because she felt bad about her own insecurities. What they may have been, I was not exactly sure myself because Sabrina was a pretty woman. She had a nice shape. She owned her own four-bedroom home, and she was no dummy by far because she was very good at manipulating the system. I just couldn't begin to understand why she treated us like slaves.

I mean, Sabrina could be sitting on top of the refrigerator, and she would call us collect if she had to, to come get her a Pepsi from the fridge. Sabrina always made sure she bought us the best of everything—name-brand clothes and shoes—and by the time we turned sixteen, we had a car of our own that we could only drive to and from school. That was the only time we were allowed to leave the house without Sabrina. Meaka was the best driver of the two of us. You would've thought she wanted to be a NASCAR driver. Meaka never drove under forty. I thought it was hilarious how she always got us home in ten minutes, and this was the very place we dreaded. She just couldn't help herself. On the outside, kids and social services were fooled into believing we were happy with Sabrina. If they were there to witness how she woke us up at three and four o'clock in the morning to dust the TV off, mop the floor, or, better yet, clean out the garage—it was as if nothing was ever clean enough for her—then they would know better than to think such a thing.

After washing and folding Sabrina's clothes, I placed her clean clothes on her bed. I could smell the breakfast cooking in the kitchen. Cooking was the only form of work it seemed like she did. After several attempts to teach Meaka and I how to cook, which only resulted to us nearly burning down the house, she gave up on us cooking anything. I headed for my room to try to get back to my dream. Then she called.

"Agupie and Meaka, come on down here and eat!" Sabrina yelled up the stairs.

Meaka came from her room with an exhausted look on her face.

"You all right?" I couldn't help but ask.

"Yeah, I'm good," Meaka answered, avoiding eye contact with me.

Before she could go downstairs, I grabbed her arm to let her know I was serious and, at the moment, very concerned.

"Meaka, you sure you all right?" I asked with much concern.

"Agape, I'm fine, girl. Just a li'l tired, that's all," Meaka responded with a slight grin, still avoiding eye contact.

Our plates were made on the breakfast table. I noticed Meaka had a lot more food on her plate than I. I had water; Meaka had orange juice. I had eggs, toast, and a piece of sausage while Meaka had eggs, toast, grits, and pancakes, along with sausage and bacon.

"Meaka, you keep eating like that, you going to be bigger than a house," I teased.

This was one of Sabrina's tactics to have Meaka and me at odds with each other. I saw through all the evil things she did.

"You want some?" Meaka asked, pushing her plate toward me.

"Nah, I'm cool. I'm trying to lose weight before homecoming. I'ma run for homecoming queen."

Sabrina spat out the orange juice she was attempting to swallow and laughed. "Homecoming queen?" she questioned. "Who would vote for you, Agupie? If you ask me, Meaka has a better chance at winning than you," she goes on to add.

"I think you would win, A," Meaka said very timidly while looking down at her plate.

"Thanks, Meaka."

"Well, Meaka, I want you to run too," Sabrina stated very sarcastically.

"I don't want to run up against my sister, Sabrina."

Sabrina laughed. "Your sister, Meaka? Now tell me how is it that you and Agupie are sisters when neither one of you know who your father is."

Meaka sat silently as she always did when we were faced with a dilemma regarding Sabrina. Meaka was no punk by far. She'd been in more fights than I could remember in the last three years we'd been here, some of which didn't even have anything to do with Meaka.

But for some reason, when it came to Sabrina, she would back down, not saying anything, literally.

"Well, we are sisters," I said adamantly, looking Meaka in her eyes, letting her know that Sabrina didn't instill the same type of fear in me that she did her.

"How, Agupie? Can you explain that to me? How the hell are you and Meaka sisters? Can somebody let me know? Huh, Meaka, can you?" she said.

Now she was taunting us.

"She is just as close to me as my sister would be, and since I have no sister, that is why I consider her my sister," Meaka stated timidly.

"Oh, so would you tell this sister of yours everything, Meaka?" Sabrina went on to ask Meaka but looked directly at me.

Meaka got quiet.

"Yes, she would," I stated, taking Meaka's side, staring right back at Sabrina.

"And how would you know that, Agupie?"

"'Cause Meaka know that, if she was to ever keep anything from me, we would no longer be considered sisters, and I know she would never do anything to jeopardize that," I said while staring a hole in Meaka.

She tried to avoid eye contact with me for what I didn't know. It was apparent there was something I didn't know about. Right now, I didn't know who to be mad at—Meaka or Sabrina for bringing the bullshit to surface. Meaka was still sitting there like a cat got her tongue. I mean, she wasn't saying shit.

"So is there anything you want your sister to know about, Meaka?" Sabrina asked sarcastically.

"No" was all Meaka said.

After another day of cleaning and more cleaning, even cleaning shit that was already clean, I lay in my bed, still thinking about what could it be that Meaka was keeping from me. It bothered me because I was sure that Meaka and I shared everything.

I lay there tossing and turning all night. I had to find out what was going on with Meaka. I got out of my bed, careful not to wake the warden. Meaka's door was cracked, and just as I was about to push the door open, I heard Sabrina's voice.

"You better put those handcuffs on, Meaka."

Handcuffs? I thought while still listening in on what was taking place behind the door.

"Either you gon' do it, or I'ma go in the next room and have that pretty little red sister of yours do it."

What the fuck is wrong with Sabrina? She has never referred to me as being pretty. It's always "You red bitch this" and "You red bitch that."

I continued to listen.

"Okay, just give them here. I want to put them on myself this time," I heard Meaka respond.

I was sure this had everything to do with what took place at breakfast the other day because it was obvious this shit had happened before, but why the fuck would she want to handcuff Meaka? I got lost in my thoughts or something because the next thing I heard was Sabrina calling Meaka a Black bitch and then a struggle between the two.

I couldn't phantom Sabrina hurting Meaka on my watch. I bust in the door, only to find Meaka and Sabrina both naked fighting on the floor. Meaka was on top of Sabrina, then Sabrina on top of Meaka. This was Meaka's fight, but I wasn't going to stand there and let Sabrina get the best of her. So when she got on top of Meaka, I kicked her in the side, knocking her to the floor.

"Oh, so you bitches want to jump me?" Sabrina stated while staggering to get up. "You bitches are out of my muthafuckin' house tomorrow."

Coming to grasp with what Sabrina had been doing to Meaka, I snapped. I didn't even know I grabbed the lamp until I busted it over her head. As she went down, she hit her head on the side of Meaka's dresser. Immediately we saw blood and lots of it. It felt like time had stopped as Meaka and I stood side by side, staring at the blood rushing from Sabrina's head. Meaka started screaming. She began stomping on Sabrina's lifeless body.

"I hate you, you fucking bitch. I hate you!" she yelled with each kick she took to her body.

I grabbed Meaka and pulled her to the bed.

She cried in my arms. "I'm sorry, A. I'm so sorry." She cried.

I couldn't help but cry because I didn't know what was going to happen. Within a split second, Meaka stood up and wiped off the lamp. I could no longer move; I had just killed Sabrina.

"Come on, A. You got to drive our car around the corner or something so you can have transportation."

Not paying much attention to what Meaka was saying, I was in total shock. I drove the car around the corner and jogged back. By the time I got back in the house, Meaka told me to go back in my room and put my MP3 headphones in my ears.

"You ain't seen nothing. You been 'sleep."

I caught on to what Meaka was about to do, and I pleaded with her not to do it.

"No, Meaka, hell no. I can't let you go down for something I did!" I could feel my eyes watering.

"Look, A, if I would have told you about this, none of this would have happened. It's just as much my fault as it is yours. Come on, A. You got to let me make this right for us. Go'n upstairs. The police are on their way."

Placing my earplugs in, I hit the play button, and instantly Jay Z's "Hard Knock Life" blasted through. I closed my eyes when I heard several footsteps come up the stairs, then the light from the hall seeped in my room. When Miss Eli opened my door, she attempted to wake me from my pretend sleep, lightly tapping my hand. I slowly took my headphones out of my ears just so that she could notice my ears plugged. Pretending my sleep had me disorientated. I acted as if I didn't recognize Miss Eli's face by squinting my eyes.

"Agape, something very tragic has happened, and I need for you to get dressed. You have to come to Shawny Acres with me," she stated with the same saddened eyes that I'd never forget she had when she had to tell me that Stormy was going to stay with Peaches.

"Where is Meaka?" I asked, knowing good and well Meaka was probably on her way to the juvenile detention center as we spoke, but I had to make it look good.

"Come on, Agape," Miss Eli stated as she pulled the covers off of me in an attempt to help me out the bed. "We will talk about Meaka later."

On the way to Shawny Acres, Miss Eli told me the same story that Meaka coerced over and over to me.

I didn't know what to think. I didn't know how to feel. I felt like shit that Meaka was sitting in jail right now because of me.

"Did you ever notice anything strange about Sabrina and Meaka's relationship?"

"No, I didn't. I mean, she treated us both like slaves."

As soon as the word *slaves* left my mouth, Miss Eli did a one-eighty. She was shocked to hear how Sabrina had been treating us.

"I gave you my number, Agape. How come you didn't let me know what was going on in that house?" The look Miss Eli had on her face let me know that she really did care about Meaka and I.

"I don't know, Miss Eli, really."

I had no answer as to why I would allow anyone to treat me the way Sabrina treated me, no reason other than I felt some sense of a family in that house, and without it, I had nothing.

"I'm so sorry, Agape," Miss Eli stated as she hit her palm against the dashboard.

I could see tears form in her eyes.

She went on to tell me, "I was supposed to protect you and Meaka, and I didn't."

I knew her reasons for feeling the way she did. That night, we both had guilt weighing heavy on our hearts, none of which we could ever voice. From that day forward, no words were ever exchanged between Miss Eli and me. Miss Eli felt like she had failed me and Meaka. She took personal responsibility for what had happened to Meaka and me, the treatment we both had received. She resigned to a lower position, in the mail room, but not before she approved me for the Independent Living Program. Miss Eli would personally deliver Meaka's letters to my room.

Shawny Acres is one of the biggest children services facilities in Dayton, Ohio. It housed over ten thousand children, even children who have had children. Since my birthday rolled around two weeks after the incident at Sabrina's house, Miss Eli saw me fit to enter into the program. The program was for any teenager that was in children services and at least eighteen years old. They would pay 85 percent of your rent and utilities. You just had to remain in school and stay on a good path toward becoming a productive citizen.

I kept the key to our car. After moving in my place, I went to pick up our car, and it felt so weird not to have Meaka on the passenger side with me. I felt my eyes start to tingle, and I couldn't help but cry as I pulled up to my apartment.

As I continued to beat my head on the steering wheel, some girl walked up to my window. She had short jet-black hair with a light-brown complexion. To say she was thick would say the least. With concern in her eyes, she began to speak to me.

"Are you okay? You need me to call somebody for you?" she went on to ask as she fumbled around in her purse.

"I'm cool," I stated, wiping the tears from my eyes, not sounding too convincing.

"You sure?" the girl went on to ask.

"I think so," I admitted.

Getting in the car brought back so many memories of all the people in my life I once loved and how they all mysteriously weren't here right now, and I felt so alone.

Maybe that was why I took this girl up on her offer when she said, "Well, how about you come over to my apartment? I stay right across the street, and if you want, we can talk about whatever it is that got you down."

I found out her name was Lyric. I learned that Lyric and I were very different. Lyric was very street savvy; and I, on the other hand, didn't know anything about the streets. Had I gone to live with Peaches, I'm sure I would be just as savvy as she was.

We talked for hours, me telling her only parts of my life that I wanted her to know, and I'm sure she did the same. I felt like I had overstayed my welcome when there was a knock on the door.

"Well, I guess that's my cue to leave," I joked.

As I proceeded to get up and leave, two guys entered the house. One had a rugged but sexy look to him. He wore a black tee with a pair of black Levi jeans and a chain hung below his chest with an initial C diamond-encrusted pendant. He was dark skinned. He had jet black hair and chingy eyes. He stepped in the room. His presence commanded my attention. It was obvious that he wasn't over there for Lyric because, when the other guy stepped through the door, damn near knocking me down, he immediately grabbed Lyric and put his tongue down her throat. Now he, on the other hand, was not so pleasant to look at. He was overweight and looked like he needed a training bra on. He was high yellow, with braids, and wore his jeans hanging down his ass. Just funky looking.

"Damn boy!" Lyric said in attempt to pull away from the kiss he was planting on her. "Y'all, this is my neighbor," Lyric stated, walking toward me in an attempt to introduce me. "Watch out, Todd." Lyric stepped in the middle of us. "This is Todd," she said, pointing to Fat Ass, "and this is Chance."

"I'm Agape," I stated while I eyed the dark-skinned man as if he and I were the only ones in the room.

As I stood there mesmerized, he spoke to me after pondering over my name.

13

"You know what, Ma? I need to holler at you."

The look that spread across Lyric's face was a look of disappointment, as if this was Todd speaking to me. I couldn't ignore the look that spoke volumes without words.

"Is that cool with you, Lyric?" I asked only because I felt like Lyric was a good person wholeheartedly.

She didn't have to come over there in the middle of my mini breakdown. She didn't have to invite me in, cook for me, and listen to all of what had transpired in my life over the past three years.

She disguised the look, then went on to say, "Girl, I don't care," and grabbed Fat Ass's hand and escorted him to the back of the apartment.

After realizing the coast was clear, he started to ask me a question.

"Do you know a Tameka? Um, I can't think of shorty's last name, but she locked up downtown in the juvenile detention center."

"What would it be to you if I do or don't know her?" I asked with much attitude.

"Look, she locked down with my sister. I been looking out for shorty on the strength that she cool peoples with my sister. She asked me to see if I could find a girl by the name of Agape, and when I just heard you say your name was Agape, I knew you had to be the one."

"How?" I teased.

"For one, the name Agape maybe common in other countries or some shit, but I knew that, when I heard the name, it had to be you," Dark Skin stated in a confident manner.

"And that's it?" I questioned.

"Oh, and it did help when your sister let me know you was a redhead, but if she had told me that you were red and as sexy as you are, because you are sexy, I would have started looking for you today instead of tomorrow as I planned." He smiled a sexy but sinister smile.

"Well, since you know all about me, can I at least know your name?"

"My name is Chance."

"Well, Chance, why is it that Meaka got you playing Inspector Gadget? Is everything okay? Please tell me nothing has happened to my sister," I went on to ask question after question, not even waiting on a response.

"You gon' let me answer you or not?" he said with a stern look on his face. "Your sister cool. She just needs you to know she goes to court in two days, and she wants you to be there, and oh, yeah, I got a ID for you to use so you can go visit her."

Tears came to my eyes when I thought about Meaka going to court for a murder she didn't even commit.

Just when a teardrop managed to escape my eyes, Chance wiped it away. "It'll be no need for all that, Red. I'm here for you. I'ma hold you and your sister down. You don't have to worry about nothing, all right?" he asked as he held my chin, looking me directly in the eyes.

"All right," I responded hesitantly.

"Come on. Let's go." Chance took me by the hand and pulled me up from Lyric's recliner and led me out the door.

"Where we going?" I asked.

"Do it matter?" was all he said as we hopped inside of a black Yukon truck with tinted windows.

I thought about his question; and I didn't have a response because, in all reality, it didn't matter if he was taking me to the devil's pit. Nothing could be worse than what I was already going through. As soon as the car started up, Jay Z's "Hard Knock Life" came blaring through the speakers. I just bobbed my head, feeling like I was in a trance with my eyes closed, rapping along with the lyrics. "Hard Knock Life" blared through the speakers, not even realizing Chance didn't pull off. The feeling of someone staring at me broke my trance.

I peeked open my eyes, so I asked, "What's up? I thought we were going somewhere?"

"Tell me what you were thinking about just now," Chance asked in a concerned tone.

"Do it matter?" was my response as we sat there looking each other eye to eye in the dark of the night.

Something about Chance felt welcoming. It felt like I knew him from somewhere, maybe in another life or something. It just felt like I knew him.

"So you staying the night at Lyric's?" Chance asked as he broke our stare by looking out the window.

"No. Lyric and I just met. I stay right there," I said, pointing to my apartment, not knowing if I just revealed too much information to this complete stranger.

Sensing what I was thinking, Chance pulled off. Swerving in and out of traffic, I pulled the seat back to enjoy the ride.

I was no longer sure where we were at as we pulled up to a house that sat on top of a hill with no neighboring houses within ten feet of the house. It was huge. I mean, it made Sabrina's house look like a shack.

"This is where I stay, Agape, so now you know where I lay my head. I can honestly say that you are one of few people and the only female outside of my sister that know where I live. You want to go in?" he asked.

"That's okay. I just want to go home."

It was a nice gesture, but I remembered the last time I pulled up to a beautiful home and how tarnished it turned out to be.

"That's what we'll do, but I need to let you know I'm spending the night because I'm not going to be able to make it back out here tonight."

"Says who? You better take your ass to Lyric's and spend the night," I said jokingly.

He lighted up one of the fattest blunts. After a few puffs of the blunt, he asked me if I smoked in between coughs.

"No, I don't smoke, but I wouldn't mind seeing what it feels like."

"Under one condition," Chance stated while holding up his index finger.

"And what's that?" I asked.

"You promise that you will only smoke this one time and never again."

Chance was only testing me. He knew that, if I promised such a thing, my word meant nothing and I would do and say anything; but what I said sealed his approval of me.

"Now, how am I supposed to promise you that I won't smoke again? And I never even smoked the shit before. What if I like it? I can promise you that I will only smoke with you as long as you allow me, and that's only if I like the euphoria."

"Good answer," Chance replied while passing the blunt.

After receiving coaching from Chance on how to hit the blunt, how to inhale and exhale the smoke, I could honestly say I never knew it was a technique to smoking; and Chance was going to make sure I mastered it because he kept telling me to "Hold it in, babe." But my virgin lungs wouldn't allow me. As soon as I inhaled, I was choking. Chance eventually grabbed the blunt and told me I was wasting his purp. I laughed to myself because I didn't feel like I was wasting shit. It felt like the car wasn't moving but the odometer read otherwise. The dash stated we were going seventy-five down I-75. I lay back in my seat, and all I remember was waking up in my bed the next morning.

How the fuck did I get in the bed? I thought to myself.

Then to see that I had nothing on but my panties and bra shook me because I didn't remember taking my clothes off. I stormed out of my room into the living room in search of the last person I remembered. No sign of him. I checked the restroom, then the kitchen. I looked out the window for the black Yukon. It was parked in my driveway. I ran, slipped some black leggings and a white tank top on, locked up my apartment, and headed for Lyric's. Fat Ass answered the door and had a completely different attitude toward me from last night.

"What's up, Agape? You want Chance?" he asked.

Now I couldn't tell if this nigga was being funny or if he really wanted to know if I wanted Chance.

"Where Lyric at?" I asked, not forgetting how he damn near ran me over and, not to mention, not once said excuse me.

So there was no small talk. I cut straight to the chase. He felt my attitude because he just walked away from the door yelling for Lyric.

I let myself in and sat on the sofa, waiting for Lyric to come out. When she did submerge from the back, she went in the kitchen without addressing me. So I just sat there and waited. After patiently waiting on her to come out the kitchen, I sensed that something was up, so I went in the kitchen.

"What's up, Lyric?" I asked.

"How are you?" she asked in a very sarcastic way.

"Is Chance here?"

The look she gave me was as if I just asked her if Fat Ass was here.

Just when I was about to confront her, I felt someone come up behind me a little too close. I felt someone with an early-morning hard-on on my back. I turned around and was faced with Chance. All the shit talking I had planned for him went straight out the window. All I could do was smile.

"Good morning, Red," Chance stated while touching a strand of my red hair.

"I need to talk to you."

"Well, we can talk. Let me holler at Todd real quick. What's good, Lyric? You up early," Chance stated, acknowledging Lyric as she stared a hole in my back.

When Chance left toward the back of Lyric's apartment, she had a whole new attitude.

"So tell me. Did y'all fuck?" Lyric asked with no regard for my personal life.

"Girl, no."

I was flattered. She thought Chance would go for me, but I was a little embarrassed at the same time because I didn't actually know what happened between us. I mean, I did wake up in only my underwear.

"Yeah right, girl. I know he smashed that," Lyric taunted on.

"You ready, Red?" Chance asked.

Used to everyone nicknaming me Red, I answered by second nature, "Where we going?"

"Do it matter?" he asked in a way that he knew it really didn't matter where we were going as long as his fine ass was there.

"As a matter of fact, it does 'cause I'm hungry, for one, and for two, I have questions for you, mister," I stated while poking him in the chest, not forgetting about the memory lapse I was experiencing.

"Well, what you want to eat? Denny's, McDonald's, Grandma's, what?" he asked.

"I don't care. Just feed me," I teased.

"Oh, I'ma feed you all right," Chance stated while looking very seductively at me.

It was then I realized that this man might have been interested in me a bit more than I thought.

"Can Lyric come?"

Chance damn near choked. "Can Lyric come?" he stuttered.

"Yeah, I'm sure she is just as hungry as you and I."

"Well, Lyric has a man that can feed her, ain't that right?"

Chance knew Lyric was listening no matter how she tried to clean the kitchen in an attempt to chameleon in on what was taking place right in front of her.

"What you say, Chance?" Lyric asked as innocently as possible.

"You not trying to go out to eat with me and Red, are you?"

"Who's Red? Some little bitch you done picked up out of the hood?" Lyric asked, knowing good and well that he'd been calling me Red since he submerged from the back.

"He talking about me, Lyric," I said as kindly as I could.

"Oh, nah, I'll pass," Lyric said, not giving it any thought.

"I mean, I think it will be cool, Lyric, if we go together. This would be a thank you to you for introducing me to Chance and looking out for me the way that you did yesterday."

Not knowing what I meant by looking out for me, he inquired, "How did she look out for you, Red?" with concern.

See, he knew Lyric and her sneaky, conniving ways; so he needed to know what was it that I considered looking out because that could come back to bite me in the ass messing around with Lyric.

"I was going through a thing yesterday, and Lyric came over and invited me in her home to talk. So I owe you, Lyric."

"Nah, you good, Agape. I mean, how could I just walk past, see you crying like that, and not see what was going on with you?"

Lyric knew firsthand how Chance felt about weak women. He hated them, couldn't stand them, despised them, and would, under no circumstances, fuck with a weak female.

Surely hearing that she was out in public crying would change his mind about her, Lyric thought.

Chance's mother was once one of the flyest females in the city until the day she let some young hustler turn her out on cocaine. Now she walked around with less than five teeth in her mouth. Her once-smooth dark skin was now ashy black, and her designer clothes she was once accustomed to was traded in for oversized clothes she found in the free clothes bins that sat out on corners near every hood. After Chance became of age to question his mother why she turned to drugs, she simply said, "I was weak." From that point, he made every attempt at making sure his only sibling, his sister, wasn't weak for anything. His woman had to be anywhere from a hustler to a CO, anything that showed she wasn't weak.

I couldn't believe she let the nigga know I was crying, I thought as I stood there with my head held low.

"Let's go," Chance said as he grabbed my arm and practically pulled me out the door.

"What the fuck is your problem? Why you grabbing me like that?" I said with much attitude.

"What were you out here crying for?" Chance asked with a serious look on his face.

"Do it matter?" was my response.

"Listen, Agape. Quit with the bullshit. Now tell me. Why the fuck was you out here crying publicly?"

It was obvious Chance didn't like the fact I was crying, but for what I didn't know, he was reacting like Lyric told him I was outside taking my clothes off or something.

"None of your business! Who do you think you are?" I yelled as I ran toward my apartment.

After getting in, I slammed the door and made sure I locked it because, at the moment, Chance seemed a little psychotic, the way he just went off on me about something that didn't concern him.

Knock, knock.

"No one is home!" I yelled at the door, knowing who it was.

No one knew where I stayed, not even Miss Eli.

"Man, look, I'm going to slide the ID for you under the door. Visiting hours are today from five to nine," Chance stated before sliding the ID under the door.

After hearing his music disappear within the air, I realized he was gone. After studying the ID of the redheaded chick named Kendra Williams, I found it quite strange how we looked almost identical to each other. Time flew past. Lyric and I ended up doing breakfast together. She kept bringing up Chance, but I didn't feed into the bullshit with her and him. But there was one thing I had to make sure I was clear on, and that was whether or not her and Fat Ass were in a relationship.

"How long you and Todd been together?" I asked as we waited for our food.

"Almost a year," Lyric answered hesitantly. "Why you ask that?" she asked, turning her face up.

"I was just wondering, was all," I said, basically wondering why the whole time we were having lunch she was busy talking about another nigga and not one time mentioning her nigga.

After we ate, I asked Lyric if I could use her phone because I didn't have one. I wasn't going to ask her for Chance's number because I was sure she had it. After scrolling her contact list, I saw Chance's contact information. I hit the send button.

He picked up on the first ring.

"You know you a dirty bitch, right?" Chance asked, thinking Lyric was calling him.

I was kind of drawn back by the way he was talking to me until I realized I was on Lyric's phone.

"I was trying to see if you were going to go downtown today. If not, did you have a message you want me to relay for you?"

Chance was quiet because he didn't know exactly how to handle me. Everything in him told him to take me and make me his, but under no grounds would he do that if I was a weak-minded woman. He couldn't come up with one reason I could have to be outside crying.

"Yeah, I'm going to be down there. I have to put some money on sis's books and your sister's as well. So I'll be down there, but I ain't gon' be doing no visiting though."

"How come? I'm sure she wants to see you," I stated to him.

"Nah, Armani good as long…as long as she got food to eat, money on her books, but you make sure you make it down there on time because, if your sister anything like you, she need a visit." Chance couldn't help but jab.

"And what's that supposed to mean? You don't know shit about me, Chance."

The mention of Chance's name, Lyric started to eavesdrop on the conversation at hand.

"Yeah, you right. I don't know shit about you."

Click.

After hanging up on Chance, I immediately handed Lyric her phone back.

When our food came, my appetite somehow vanished while Lyric, on the other hand, devoured her steak and potatoes. My cheeseburger and sweet potato fries were going home with me because I couldn't eat. As we pulled up to Lyric's apartment, she asked me if everything was okay with me and Chance. I simply stated there was no me and Chance.

"Well, girl, that's good. He ain't shit but a dog anyway," Lyric stated as she hopped out the car and I followed suit.

"What does that mean, Lyric? If he is so much as a dog, why didn't you tell me that the night you left him in the room with me?"

"Listen here, Agape. I like you, but we are all grown. You have to make your own decisions. Now, if I was to tell you how Chance brings a different bitch over my house each week, then you would be attracted to him, so I decided to let you see for yourself. I mean, don't get me wrong. Chance is my nigga and all, but he's just not your type."

Standing in front of Lyric's apartment, I was speechless, not at what Lyric just revealed to me, but because I could care less about how many females Chance had before me. That was his business. It was a vibe I got whenever Lyric talked about Chance, a vibe that she wanted him herself.

"Lyric, have you ever had feelings for Chance?" I asked.

"Girl, are you crazy?" She played it off with a simple laugh.

I joined her, but I wasn't laughing with her. I was laughing at her. It was obvious to me that she felt some type of way about Chance. I guess, since she was with his nigga, she couldn't admit to it.

"All right then, girl, I'll see you later. I'm about to go lay down for a minute," I stated as I walked across the street to my apartment.

"What you doing later?" Lyric asked, remembering the conversation she heard I had on the phone with Chance.

"I'm not sure exactly what all I have to do, but if I have some spare time, I'll come over and kick it with you if your man ain't there," I joked and walked in the door.

CHAPTER 2

How Well I Cleaned Depended on Whether or Not I Ate at One Point of Time

"If you have any change, cell phone, keys, or any metal in your pockets, put it in this cup and step through the metal detectors."

I kept a close eye on the door in hopes to see Chance coming in to put money on Armani's books. I hoped and prayed that I didn't get dressed up for nothing. I put my keys in the cup and proceeded to walk through the metal detector. I took one last look at the door, and there he was walking through the door. I swear the second hand on the clock stopped as our eyes connected, but he kept walking toward the clerk's desk, not even acknowledging me. I kept it moving, following the red line that the correctional officer instructed me to follow when I checked in. The room it led to had a class-setting desk and chairs, and the CO put you in mind of a teacher sitting up front, watching every movement that went on in the room. When Meaka walked through the door, I immediately stood up smiling from ear to ear. As she walked toward our table, she was doing the same. It had been months since I'd seen Meaka; and as strange as it sounded, Meaka looked happier than I ever saw her, something about the way her majestic blue eyes twinkled and the pep in her step as she walked toward our table.

I reached my arms out as Meaka did the same. Our hug spoke volumes, so many unsaid words between us. I missed Meaka in the same way I did Ma D. It hurt me deeply to think about why she was in a place like this. We both blamed ourselves, but the truth remained—it was my fault. I was the one who busted Sabrina in the head with the lamp.

"What's up, A?" Meaka asked, sensing something was wrong because I had my head down.

I just couldn't find it in me to look Meaka in her face. I felt so guilty.

"Nothing much. What's good with you?" I asked, head still down.

"You can't look your sister in her face no more, A?" Meaka asked.

I never meant to offend Meaka, so I explained the guilt I felt. "Meaka, I feel so guilty that you are locked up. This is no place for you. You are a good person, and it was me who killed Sabrina." I pursed my lips so that no one other than Sabrina could hear me. "I should be in here, not you."

Meaka grabbed my hand, and we sat there silently letting the vibrations from the atmosphere speak the words that we couldn't form with our mouths.

"I see he found you."

It was no question as to whom Meaka was talking about.

"Well, technically he didn't find me. I sort of found him."

I let Meaka know how Chance and I met up and everything else that led up to today, even how he just ignored me downstairs.

"I'm not sure why he ignored you, A. What I do know is that he's a stand-up type of guy. He doesn't know nothing about me, but I can call his phone and request anything I need, all because me and his sister cool. I was wondering what the nigga look like. I mean, Armani don't have no pictures of him. He probably a ole fat-ass nigga," Meaka joked.

I laughed. "You wrong, honey. That nigga fine with a capital F."

I looked behind me at a young girl that just came in with someone that appeared to be her father. The girl had on a jacket with some jeans despite the temperature of ninety degrees outside. I looked her

ASSATTA

in her face, and she had a scared look on her face. I was not sure if it was because she was in a vicinity where there were some of the most ruthless kids in Dayton or if she walked around with that scared look on her face every day.

Meaka took notice and informed me that the girl's name was Jaden. She was the little sister of a girl named Jennifer who was locked up with her. Jennifer walked in on her father smothering her mother with a pillow. Jaden watched from the closet door as her mother fought for her life. Jennifer then ran to the kitchen to get a knife. When she returned, her mother was no longer kicking and swinging on her father in an attempt to get him off of her. Jennifer said she ran toward her father while he continued to hold the pillow over her mother's lifeless body. She plunged the knife in his back, killing him instantly. Unknown to Jennifer, their mother had told Jaden to hide in the closet when she heard her husband yelling obscenities at her in a drunken state as he came through the front door; so from the bedroom closet, Jaden had watched both of her parents' lives taken away in a split second from their bedroom closet.

"Damn, that's crazy," I stated, still staring at the little girl.

The CO let us know that we had another fifteen minutes, then our visit would be over.

"Court start tomorrow, and they dropped the murder charge to a manslaughter. The lawyer that Chance got me did his thing with that, and I could be facing anywhere from a year and a half to eight years."

Tears came to my eyes as I tried to hide the pain of hearing Meaka could be locked up for eight years. Even though she told me that her lawyer told her the chances of her doing eight years was slim to none, that still didn't take away the guilt I felt.

After we said our goodbyes, I watched Meaka leave out the room, and I myself left out and began to follow the line I followed up here.

The daytime had turned to night, and as I walked down the street, I heard Jay-Z's "Hard Knock Life" playing from a distance. I mouthed the words to myself as I searched the night with my eyes. Downtown Dayton was filled with homeless people; so it was always

26

good to watch your back because, in a split second, someone was liable to pop out of anywhere. Just as I stuck my key in the car door, I felt a car pull up beside me. When I looked at the unknown all-white Lincoln with tinted windows, I clicked the unlock button, jumped in the car, and locked the doors as quick as one could. But the car just sat next to mine, blocking me in. I tried to start the car up, signaling I was trying to get out of the parking spot, hoping whoever the driver was, was trying to secure the parking spot. But the car still didn't move, so I blew the horn. The car still didn't move. As soon as I rolled my window down, the passenger side window of the Lincoln came down as well.

"Can't you see you got me blocked in?" I asked the driver, unable to see the driver's face and annoyed with how nonchalant the driver was with being in my way.

I heard a familiar voice say, "Come here, Red."

"Chance?" I questioned.

I got out the car and leaned on his passenger window to get a good look at him, and he looked just as good as he did the very first time I saw him.

"You riding with me?" Chance asked.

"Where we going?"

Knowing his answer before he said it thrilled me. I just stood there with a big smile on my face. To say I was cheesing would be an understatement.

"Do it matter?" was Chance's response.

I hopped in Chance's car after locking mine.

He already had a blunt rolled up. He handed it to me and asked if I wanted to light it up.

"Yes, sir."

I lit the blunt; and after a few puffs, I experienced the same euphoria as the first time I felt, like we were floating in the air, barely moving, only this time, when Chance pulled me out of the car, I woke up.

I noticed we were at Chance's house, and for some reason, it scared me to know what lay behind the doors of his home. Chance felt my hesitation and asked if I was all right. I told him yeah even though I felt like throwing up.

"I just want to go back to my car, Chance," I told him as I got back in the car.

"Man, what is your problem, girl? Get out," he yelled at the window.

"No, I want to go home."

"I ain't got no time for this kiddie-ass shit," Chance said under his breath as he hopped in on the driver's side. "You want to go home, Red?" Chance asked with pleading eyes, hoping that I would give in and stay the night.

It wasn't that Chance was desperate to be with a woman shit just before he came downtown he was at Lyric's, fucking her each way he saw fit, but the females he dealt with were not what he wanted. Chance felt like everything in him wanted to make me his girl. He never woke up to women in his house out of fear he might have been set up or robbed. With me, he didn't feel a need to protect himself; he felt the need to be a protector.

"Okay, Chance, I'll stay the night, but we're sleeping in separate rooms. No, matter of fact, I'm sleeping in your bed, and you, my dear, will be on the couch," I teased as I poked him in the chest.

I stepped out of the car, but for some reason, Chance remained in the car.

"You change your mind?" I asked as I cracked the door back open.

"Nah, just thinking," he said as he climbed out of the Lincoln.

As we walked through the door, I was amazed at how beautiful the inside of the house was. Chance's house wasn't immaculately clean, but it wasn't dirty either. Everything in the house was black, from the curtains to the furniture in each room; his kitchen was adorned with a black marble table. I hadn't even been in the bathroom yet or the bedrooms, but I could just about imagine that the color black was included in the decor.

"Why so much black?" I asked after receiving a mini tour of his home.

I was right. As soon as we made it upstairs, the restroom had black towels with the letter *C* embedded in them. The bath carpet was black. The only color that came from the bathroom was the red and orange toothbrushes that were placed in a black holder. Each of the bedrooms were decorated with some type of black ominous to them.

"What's in that room?" I asked, noticing that he showed me every room in the house except for the last bedroom.

"Oh, that's Armani's room. That girl will go ham sandwich if I let someone in her room." He laughed and then entered the room that he said was his.

I followed behind him cautiously. I sat down on the bed as he used the bathroom that was conjoined to his room. I searched the room with my eyes for anything that may have seemed strange. Nothing.

"Can I cut your TV on, Chance?"

"Girl, why you asking me? Can you cut the television on?"

So used to having to ask permission to turn the TV on at Sabrina's, I didn't realize how silly the question was.

"The remote is on the dresser," he stated as he left out the room.

After removing my shoes, I lay up on the bed, channel surfing and stopped when I got to Martin's *You So Crazy* comedy special. It was on HBO. It was like I never saw the comedy show before the way Chance and I were on the bed cracking up, laughing. We laughed so hard I was choking. I don't know if it was the Martin or the blunt we were smoking. As the comedy show ended, I could feel Chance stealing glances at me, but I ignored him, hoping he saw something he liked. I wish I could have ignored this somber feeling that was coming over me.

"What's up, Red? You all right?" Chance asked with concern in his eyes.

I tried to disguise the pain I felt, the pain that lay deep within me, and smiled and said, "Nothing. I think it's the weed."

"The weed, huh?" Chance questioned, not believing any of what I was saying. "Can I ask you something, Red?"

"Yes, Chance, you can ask me anything."

For some reason, I meant it. I was willing to answer any question he asked me at this moment. I felt vulnerable for someone to care—or at least act like they did. At this moment, there would be no big difference in the two.

"What is it that keeps you so sad all of the time?"

"Sad?" I questioned.

"Well, maybe it isn't that you're sad, but you always in deep thought about something. What is it that keeps you in deep thought?"

I sat and wondered, *How do I answer him?* Nothing came out.

"You can trust me, Red. You know that, right?"

There was something about this moment that I didn't want it to end, something about the tone that was set as we lay in the bed side by side, me fully dressed and Chance in a pair of plaid boxers and a beater, with the night air blowing in on us. I felt, for the moment, the happiest I had been in years.

"I have a lot on my mind, Chance. That's all."

"Well, tell me about it. Maybe I could help," Chance said as sincerely as possible.

"Can you change the fact I was born to a stubborn woman who never wanted me? Can you change the fact that the only woman who ever loved me left me in this world all alone after the only sister I had left me to be with the same woman who left us? Or maybe change the fact that Meaka is sitting in juvenile right now for a murder she didn't commit. Can you change any of that, Chance?" I asked.

Silence.

"Well then, you can't begin to help me."

Chance never would have imagined all of what I was going through. To hear my problems and to know there was nothing he could do to help me out with either situation did something to him. He realized that what I was dealing with was a lot more than he ever imagined. But he vowed to himself that I would no longer hurt as long as he had breath in him. I wouldn't have to be alone. I would always have someone on my side.

"I'm going to the living room and get me some sleep. You need anything, Red, before I go downstairs?"

I turned my back to him and faced the wall. "Can you hold me until I fall asleep?"

"I gotcha," Chance stated as he slid under the covers with me and held me till I felt the sun peeking into his bedroom.

When I climbed out the bed, careful not to wake Chance, I used the bathroom that was conjoined to his room. I wasn't surprised to see all black towels with *C*'s embedded in them—black carpet and a black shower curtain.

Remembering the house needed a little cleaning, I decided to straighten the house up for Chance. As he slept, I realized the house needed a bit more cleaning than I thought. I dusted and cleaned for hours and rearranged furniture, the whole nine. By the time I was done, Chance was coming down the stairs, shocked and amazed at how well I cleaned after informing him that, at one point in my life, whether I could or could not eat depended on how well I cleaned, so cleaning had become like a hobby of mine, almost an obsessive-compulsive disorder.

Looking at the clock, I realized I had only two hours to get ready for Meaka's court hearing.

"Why don't you take a shower here? I can run you up to Siebenthaler's plaza. There's a Wendell's up there. You can get you something from there."

Taking him up on the offer, I picked out an all-black Bebe dress and a pair of black pumps, remembering Chance's obvious fascination for the color black.

I tried the dress on, and after Chance's approval, I walked out in the dress. We had fifteen minutes to make it downtown.

The courtroom was packed. A lot of Sabrina's family and friends were in attendance, and Chance and I were the only people seated on Meaka's side. As soon as Meaka entered the courtroom, they had her handcuffed as tears rolled down her eyes.

It pained me to see Meaka cry. I sat there numb to what was going on around me until I felt Chance put his arm around my shoulder.

The prosecutor stated they want to make a plea deal, so they went to the back to discuss the terms of the plea deal.

The lawyer discussed the terms with Meaka, but she wouldn't agree until they ran the deal by me.

Her lawyer then asked permission from the court to let me know the full details of the plea deal. After, the lawyer let us know that the deal would give Meaka juvenile life, meaning she would be in jail until her eighteenth birthday. I looked at Chance and asked what she should do. He informed me of the pros and cons of taking a case to trial and, in his opinion, that was a slap on the wrist.

Meaka was sentenced, and I was a wreck. For the first few weeks, I couldn't eat or sleep. Guilt really took its toll on me. Chance stood by me, letting me stay at his place whenever I wanted. He gave me a key, which really set a different tone on our relationship because, at first, I wasn't exactly sure what Chance wanted from me until he handed me that key and asked, "You know what this mean, Red, right?"

Confused exactly what he was talking about, I let him know that I didn't know what it meant.

He said, "If I give any girl a key to my home, Red, she gotta be my girl."

My smile was wider than all outside.

"Don't smile yet 'cause looking good ain't yo' only job. I'ma need you to keep up the cleaning and start doing some cooking."

I actually thought he was serious until he started laughing.

"Hahaha, Chance, you were joking. I didn't find it very funny."

Then he reassured me that he was only joking about the cooking part, and I couldn't help but laugh.

I made sure Meaka had a letter to read every other day and cards every other week. I hated the Independent Living Program I was in because of the routine visits to Shawny Acres. Chance suggested I move in with him since I was at his place more than mine. I declined because then I wouldn't have the opportunity to kick it with Lyric.

I was not exactly sure what it was about her that Chance didn't like, but every time I mentioned Lyric, his whole attitude changed.

After accepting the collect call from Meaka, she was always in good spirits. I often wondered if she did that for me so that I wouldn't feel so bad.

"Hey, Meaka, how you been?"

"Girl, I'm good, just can't wait for these few months to go by. I been marking each day on my calendar."

"Listen to you sounding just like a convict," I joked.

We laugh.

Meaka asked, "Where was Chance?"

I informed her, "I stayed at my apartment last night, and he was upset that I went to the club with Lyric, so he didn't stay here with me."

"I don't get why you hang with that girl, A."

"Listen to you. You sound just like Chance. Lyric's a cool girl. You'll see when you get out. She remind me of you."

"Girl, please," Meaka went on to interrupt me. "I'm just saying you've only known her for a year, and you say her and Chance grew up together. Don't you think he know her far better than you do?"

I had to admit Meaka had a point.

"Girl, Chance just hates the fact Lyric be having me out partying and shit and not sitting in the boondocks out at his house waiting on him. I am a few months shy of my eighteenth birthday, and if it was up to him, I would be sitting with a needle and some yarn crocheting."

We both started laughing. The monitor let us know that we had a remainder of fifteen minutes left.

"I miss you so much, Meaka, and I'm going to throw you a big coming-home party."

"Girl, you don't have to do that. I just need me a hot bubble bath and some of them green trees Chance got you smoking. I wanna try some of that. But on a serious note, A, I ran into a woman named Peaches that's in here. She just got life for attempting to kill her daughter. I could be wrong, but the daughter's name is Stormy."

The monitor went on to tell us the fifteen minutes had turned into sixty seconds.

Silence. I didn't know what to say or how to feel.

I just simply said, "Some coincidence, huh."

After the phone hung up, I couldn't think of anything else but what Meaka just revealed to me. I couldn't see what would make

33

Peaches try to kill Stormy. I couldn't come up with one scenario that could have justified Peaches's actions. And if Stormy was no longer living with Peaches, than where was she? I didn't know whether to be upset or to be hurt. Both of them, at one point or another, turned their back on me. So the only thing I could do was put them at the back of my mind. For once in my life, I was happy as I once was growing up with Ma D. And I was not going to let anyone or anything take that away from me.

After several attempts at calling Chance's phone, I gave up and went across the street to Lyric's. As I was about to knock, the door swung open, and Fat Ass damn near ran into me, not paying any attention to what he was doing.

"My bad, Red," he said, calling me by unofficial nickname.

"Call me by my name please," I said as nice as possible and entered the house.

Lyric was sitting in the living room, polishing her toenails red.

"Girl, the club was jumping last night," I said.

"It was, and I know you gotta go to Gentle Lady's with me tonight, girl. It's gon' be all kind of balling-ass niggas in there. We gon' have a ball."

"I don't know, Lyric. Chance gon' flip if I don't have my ass at home tonight."

"Girl, fuck Chance. It's gon' be plenty niggas in there with money longer than Chance's. I don't know why you sweat that nigga the way you do. You be acting like he yo' daddy or something."

Some of what Lyric was saying made sense. I mean, Chance ran the streets night and day without hearing me complain, so why was it that he couldn't do the same when I felt like enjoying myself, which was not often?

"All right, I'll go, Lyric. You gon' get me killed."

We both laughed. Lyric lighted up a blunt, and I declined to hit it, holding true to my promise I made Chance the first night I got high.

"You be acting like you don't smoke or something," Lyric nagged.

I paid her no mind because I knew I wasn't about to smoke with her.

"So what you wearing tonight?" I asked Lyric.

"Girl, I got me this cute freakem dress," she said excitedly as she ran in her room to grab the dress.

She came out with one of the cutest dresses I'd ever laid my eyes on—a silver sequined minidress with a boat neck. To say the dress was bad wouldn't even tell the half of how the dress looked.

"I'm feeling that dress. That is cute."

"Thanks. I got it from Wendell's," Lyric stated as she put the dress up to her body, modeling the dress that was still on the hanger.

I checked my caller ID on my phone, and it was Chance. I picked up immediately.

"Hi, baby, I been calling your phone. Where you at?" Chance asked as if I hadn't said anything.

"Well, a hello to you too. I'm over Lyric's," I said, referring to Lyric as the nickname I called her.

"I'm on my way to pick you up."

Click.

I checked my phone to make sure I wasn't tripping, and I wasn't. He hung up on me. I went on to tell Lyric.

"That's 'cause he was probably with a bitch last night. You busy turning every nigga down in the club, and he got his old, tired ass out cheating. I tell you the truth. Niggas ain't shit, Agape. And the sooner you learn that, the better off you gon' be."

"I ain't worried about Chance cheating on me. He wouldn't do anything like that."

"Go to *Oprah* with that shit, Agape. Are you telling me you don't think Chance will cheat on you? Girl, are you stupid or just plain dumb? Let me know which one. Every man cheats, Agape. I don't care how good your pussy is or how good you can suck a dick. There is always a bitch with a fatter ass and bigger titties than you."

I just sat there quiet, then I heard the horn blow.

Lyric walked to the curtain and stated, "That's Chance, Agape."

"Oh, he must really be feeling his self this morning to be outside, blowing for me like I'm some type of hoe."

I called his phone. He didn't answer.

He blew again.

"Agape, I suggest you take your ass on out there before that nigga come up in here tripping, and I ain't got time for his shit today."

"You're right. I'll see you later, Lyric. Call me."

As soon as I opened the door, Chance asked, "What took you so long to come out?"

Knowing how to get under Chance's skin, I asked, "Do it matter?"

"Keep talking that slick shit if you want to, Agape. I'ma put my fist down your throat."

"Well, if you feel that way, you can turn this car around and take me back home!" I yelled.

"I'm taking you home, where you need to be, and I don't want you talking to that bitch Lyric no more either."

"You can't tell me who I can be friends with, Chance."

Lyric was my friend, and if he thought for a second he could just tell me that I could no longer talk to her without a reason, he was crazy.

"Yo' friend? What do you know about Lyric, huh? What you know about that bitch, Agape? You don't know shit about her. She is a friend to no one, and the sooner you realize that, the better off you will be!" Chance yelled at me as he continued to drive his Yukon recklessly through downtown.

Later that night, Lyric called, asking if I was still going out with her.

"Lyric, you know I would. It's just that Chance is in one of his moods, so I'ma have to take a rain check, but make sure you call me when you step foot in the house so I can know you got in safe."

"Will do. I just wish you was coming with me," Lyric said, trying to convince me to go out with her.

"Next time."

After saying our goodbyes, as soon as I hung up the phone, Chance questioned who I was talking to. Immediately I took offense because I never questioned him about who called his phone, and up until this moment, he hadn't either.

"None of your business," I stated as I attempted to leave out of the kitchen as Chance stormed behind me in a fit of rage.

"Agape, I'm not playing with you right now, so I'm going to ask you one more time. Who was you talking to on the muthafuckin' phone?"

I wasn't liking the way Chance was talking to me at all.

So I told him, "None of your muthafucking business, Chance."

And as soon as I tried to turn my back to go upstairs, Chance grabbed my arm and swung me back around. Now I faced him with a terrified look on my face because I didn't know what to expect next since the unexpected had just taken place.

"Do I need to ask you again, Agape?"

Chance was trying to make it clear to me that he wanted desperately for me to let him know whom I was talking to before things went too far. And a part of me wanted to let Chance know that it was only Lyric that I was talking to, but I was upset and hurt by the way Chance was squeezing my arm. I just stared blankly in his face as tears ran down my face as Chance held me by both of my arms, shaking me violently.

"Get off of me, Chance!" I yelled, trying to get him to let me go.

I tried my hardest to break free from the hold he had on me, but he wouldn't let go.

"Why are you doing this to me?" I cried out. "Let me go."

Chance didn't realize his own strength. What seemed to him as if he was just roughing me up was a completely different story when he let my arms go. His handprint was bright red around my arms. Chance immediately snapped out of his fit of rage and tried to console me, but the pain he just inflicted on me was more than I could bare.

"I'm packing my things, and I'm leaving," I stated as I ran upstairs.

"Baby, come on now. You know I wasn't gon' hurt you," Chance stated as he followed me up the stairs, realizing the damage he just had done.

He couldn't stand by and watch me leave him, so he tried everything from apologizing to practically begging me to stay. Not getting anywhere, Chance picked up his keys as well as mine. He took his key off of my key ring and locked me inside his house.

Hearing the door shut, I was somewhat relieved Chance left so I didn't have to look him in the face as I left out the house. I didn't know what that was all about, but I knew one thing for sure.

I'm leaving him. Next thing I know, he's going to be beating my ass, I thought to myself as I carried my last suitcase down the stairs.

Then it hit me. Chance had locked the door and took the key off my key ring, and being the fact the doors only open with the house key, he had me locked inside.

"Son of a bitch!" I yelled as I grabbed my cell phone.

"Hello."

"Chance, can you please come open the door so I can get out of here."

"Nah, Red, I can't do that," Chance replied.

"What do you mean? You can't just make me stay with you, Chance. You do realize this is abduction, holding me against my will," I stated as calmly as possible.

"Unpack your clothes, Red, and then I'll come open the door," Chance stated. "I don't want you to leave."

He was sincere. He had grown to love me over the past year that we had been together and had done more for me than any other female he had ever been with, but the bullshit that Lyric had been feeding him had him a little over the edge.

Click.

After hanging up on Chance, I beat myself up because there was no one to come and rescue me. I only knew how to get out here driving. I couldn't give plain directions to anyone, and then to whom? Lyric? She was the only person that I was cool with, and sure enough, Chance would really beat my ass if he found out that I let her know where he lived.

After the third ring, I answered the house phone, knowing it was Meaka. She was the only person who called the house phone.

"Hello?"

"You have a collect call from Montgomery County Juvenile Center. If you wish to accept the call, dial 0. If you wish to decline the call, dial 5 or just hang up."

"I hit the 0."

"What's up, A?"

Silence. I was torn between a rock and a hard place. I didn't know whether or not I wanted to let Meaka know what was going on with me and Chance. I didn't want her worrying about me, but I still needed someone to confide in.

"Nothing much, for real," I responded as normally as possible.

"What's wrong," Meaka questioned, knowing something was definitely wrong with me.

Not being able to hold anything from Meaka, I told her everything that just happened with me and Chance.

"So you telling me he has you locked in his house as we speak?"

"Yep. And I call this son of a bitch to come unlock the door, and he tell me to unpack my clothes, then he would unlock the door."

"Why don't you bust a window out?" Meaka asked.

"It won't do any good. He just got storm windows put in every window of the house. The windows are guaranteed not to break or open."

"I wonder why he reacted that way over you being on the phone. Girl, it ain't no telling if you ask me the muthafucka is crazy flat out. Is this his first time acting like that toward you? I mean, has he ever hit you?"

"No, he has never hit me, Meaka. Don't give me that *Dr. Phil* shit. I aint nobody's punching bag. Him grabbing me and shaking me is enough for me to see that he would eventually be blacking my eyes."

"Well, at least you realize that because a lot of women don't. A man putting his hands on them means that he loves them, as crazy as it sounds. I run into so many women that are locked up doing ten years or better all because they finally got fed up with they men putting their hands on them and struck back, only to have killed the man. But at the time, the abuse was considered a sign of love, so there's no police reports, no restraining orders, so it's left up to twelve people to decide what happens to them."

I listened carefully to what Meaka was saying because I felt bad for the women she was speaking of because life had to be pretty lonely or miserable to set standards that low for yourself to even consider that logic of thinking. Ma D always told me and Stormy that, if a man lied to you, he would cheat on you, and, if he puts his hands on you, he would kill you. And that's what I believe.

"You know, I love you, Agape, and I don't want to see anything bad happen to you. I don't want to tell you to leave Chance, but I do know there has to be a reason behind his actions. You've been with him for damn near a year, and he's never so much as got mad at you. Why would he just flip on you like that? I think it's more to it than what came to surface."

It was like Meaka to be a logical thinker. She always looked at things from every point of view. Me, I was an impulsive thinker. The first rational thought I came up with was the best thing to do, not caring about the ifs and whys.

After the monitor let us know that we had sixty seconds, I told Meaka to call right back. We talked for hours until it was time for Meaka to lock down.

By the time night fell, I was starving. Chance and I always ate out; so the only things in the fridge was days-old pizza, Chinese food, and red lobster. I was sure I wasn't gon' eat any of that, so I did what I always did at Sabrina's when she wouldn't feed us—I simply went to sleep.

In my dream, I could feel my Ma D brushing my hair while she told me that I had some of the thickest hair she had ever seen, and I laughed. But when I looked back on the dream, it was weird because Stormy wasn't in the dream. Never had that happened. I had never had a dream that involved Ma D and Stormy wasn't in it.

Ma D told me, "In life, Agape, you will have many enemies and few friends. See, it's not your enemies you have to worry about. It's the ones that call themselves your friend. You have to really watch the ones your closet to, Agape, because they're the only ones that have the power to hurt you."

Just as I was about to question her, the sun peeked in the living room, awakening me.

I jumped up to see if Chance had made his way in the house, and to my surprise, he didn't. Now I didn't know what hurt me most—him not coming to check on me or him damn near shaking the life out of me.

Immediately I picked up the phone to call his cell phone. The voice mail kept picking up every time I called back.

Chance's voice came over his voice mail, "Name and reason." *Beep.*

After several attempts at trying to contact Chance, I called Lyric to pick her and see if Chance had been over there.

"Hello?"

"Hey, girl, so how was the club last night?"

I didn't want Lyric to know I was calling her looking for my man, so I had to act as if everything was cool.

"All I'ma say is you should have been there. It was jumpin'. All the ballers was out last night. Even yo' nigga was in the club, which was shocking. You know, the club scene is not his scene. But couldn't tell how he was in each and every bitch's face. I tried to call you to throw one of yo' freakem' dresses on and come downtown and shine on that nigga."

So that's why he ain't answer his phone. He went home with one of them bitches, I thought. *Careful not to let Lyric know what she had just revealed to me.*

"I didn't know," I said. "Girl, you know Chance think he can have any bitch in Dayton, Ohio. What's new?" I laughed.

She laughed with me. "Yeah, that nigga of yours is something else."

It was as if Lyric knew more than she was telling me, not knowing that she had told me enough.

"What did you wear?" I asked Lyric.

"I had on a leopard one-piece with some red pumps and some red lipstick. You know yo' girl was turning all kinds of heads."

And I knew she was. I'd never seen Lyric in a one-piece, but Lyric had a big ole country ass that I knew a one-piece could only complement.

"Girl, you crazy. I'll be over a little later if you want to hang out," I stated, trying to get off the phone.

"You sure about that, girl?" Lyric asked in a sarcastic way.

"What you mean am I sure? I'll be over later, Lyric, or do your best friend need an invitation to come over now?" I joked.

"Oh, bitch, don't be brand new. I asked Chance where was you last night, and he said you were on punishment."

"No, that muthafucka didn't." I stayed on my toes, careful not to let Lyric know what I was thinking. "You know that nigga crazy. I'm a grown woman. How in the hell could I possibly be on punishment? And like I said, I'll be over."

"Okay. Well, call before you come to make sure I'm here. I came up on a few numbers last night. I wouldn't mind taking them up on a few of their offers," Lyric said, laughing.

"Where's Todd, girl?"

"Todd is yesterday's news. I need me a baller. I ain't got time to keep giving up this pussy for pennies, fucking with Todd."

"Bye, Lyric."

In walked Chance in all-white blazer with a white beater underneath some jeans and some all-white Air Force 1s on, definitely not the same black T-shirt and jeans he had on when he left from here. I looked at him, and he seemed like a stranger to me. I couldn't explain the distant feeling I felt. It was obvious Chance cheated on me last night, something I thought he wouldn't do, but now I stood in front of him with my head held low, begging for things to be the same between us.

Chance heard my silent pleas and walked toward me, wrapping his arms around me after placing my head on his chest. We just stood still in the middle of the living room.

Chance whispered in my ear, "I'm sorry, babe."

It's not that Chance never cheated on me. It was always unknown to me. As soon as I looked at him, it was clear to him that I knew he was guilty of infidelity. He didn't know how to make it up to me or even if I was willing to let him.

I knew it was never Chance's intentions to hurt me, but the fact remained. He did in more ways than one, and I didn't know how to hide that fact. Things would never be the same between the two of us no matter how much we both wanted things to be the same. It was obvious that we wouldn't be.

"I want to go home, Chance," I stated as I looked up in his eyes.

I could tell that he didn't want me to go, but I had to. I didn't want to take the chance of ending up like any of the women Meaka was telling me about yesterday. So I knew the best thing I could do for us both was go my way and let Chance go his.

"That's cool, Red. I understand, and everything I gave you, you can take with you."

"Even the truck?" I couldn't help but ask jokingly.

"Yeah, the truck too," Chance stated with a smile, trying to ease the queasy feeling in the pit of his stomach.

I left Chance's with a broken heart; and somehow, someway, here I was alone all over again as I pulled up to my apartment.

I saw Lyric hopping out of an all-black BMW with tinted windows. I got out of the car and proceeded toward her.

"What's up, girl?"

"Girl, come meet my new friend. Hey, Larry, this my best friend, Agape. Agape, this is Larry."

Something about the way this Larry character shook my hand didn't sit well with me.

I played it off and stated, "Nice meeting you, Larry."

I then turned to Lyric and told her to knock on my door when she was done entertaining her company.

"He about to leave, girl," Lyric stated as she grabbed shopping bag after shopping bag from the back of Larry's car.

As soon as we stepped foot in, Lyric took off running to the bathroom. Her cell phone rang.

"Answer that, Agape," Lyric yelled from the restroom.

I picked up after reading the name Big Daddy display across the screen.

I laughed to myself. *This girl is crazy.*

"Hello?"

"Aye, I was meaning to ask you. You trying to go to the Natti tonight?"

"Hold on. Lyric, it's for you."

"Who is it?"

"May I ask who's calling?"

"Is this the li'l red chick that was just outside?" Larry asked.

"Let me guess. This Larry?"

"Yeah, baby. This Larry."

"Hold on one second. It's Larry, Lyric. He wants to know if you want to go to the Natti tonight."

"Hell yeah. I don't see why not," Lyric yelled from the bathroom.

"That's a yes, Larry. She asked what time should she be ready."

"Y'all be ready around eleven. I got a somebody for you, Red."

"Oh, that's okay," I stated to Larry.

"Oh, my bad. You got a man or something?"

Remembering Chance and I broke up, I let him know I just got out of a relationship.

"Well, come on, man. Everything on us. All you gotta do is show off that pretty little face of yours and enjoy yourself."

The invite did sound tempting since I had no plans other than sit in the house and think about what just transpired between me and Chance. Not wanting to sound too anxious, I told him I'd think about it.

"All right. Tell Lyric to calls me once she's out the bathroom."

And I did, along with telling her that Larry said he wanted me to join them. Lyric was excited until I mentioned the fact that he said he had someone for me.

"Who could he have for you? He only hang with lame-ass nig-gas, girl. You be crazy to hook up with one of his niggas."

"Well, it ain't like I'm about to go to bed with the nigga, what's riding to the Natti with whoever he may be. You acting like we about to walk down the aisle together, Lyric."

We both busted out laughing.

"You right, girl," Lyric confessed. "We gon' have a ball, girl. Larry, he paid you. Seen all that shit he got me from the mall?"

"Yeah, I peeped that. How long you been knowing him?"

"Girl, I met him last night."

"So how is it he damn near bought you another wardrobe with only knowing you for a couple of hours? What did you do for him?" I couldn't help but ask.

"I didn't do anything. Shit, I barely shook his fucking hand."

"Okay, whatever, girl. I'm 'bout to go see if Mari can fit me in on her schedule so I can get my hair done real quick."

"All right then. Be here on time, Agape," Lyric whined.

"Will do."

Seeing all the cars that were parked outside the House of Cuties, I knew I could hang up Mari squeezing me in her schedule. But I still gave it a shot.

"Hello, do you have an appointment?" the young receptionist asked.

"I was wondering if I could speak with the owner."

"Well, she's kind of busy," the young woman stated. "Is there a message I could give her?" she went on to ask.

"Yes, there is. Can you tell her, her niece is out here in dying need of her services?"

As quick as the young lady disappeared behind the curtain, she came back out informing me that Mari stated that she didn't have any nieces with a grin on her face.

"Can you be so kind to tell her that her niece Agape is out here? I would appreciate it."

Out came Mari. "Hey, baby, I didn't know who was out here claiming to be my niece. You know I'll make room for you, but you gon' be here awhile."

"As long as I'm out by ten, Mari, I don't care how long it takes."

"Well, trust me. It won't be after ten 'cause yo' auntie got a date tonight," Mari stated, excitedly twirling her hands in the air about the date she had later. "Now don't you go telling Chance I got a date. You know Chance would have a fit if he knew I was dating anybody.

For some reason, that boy think I can't date anybody after his uncle June died. But little do he know, Mari got needs too."

I couldn't help but bust out laughing. "You are something else, Mari."

"Come on back here, girl, and let Janice wash your hair. What you trying to get done to that beautiful thick red hair, honey?"

"I want something different. Um, how about a short cut? You think that would look right on me?"

"You know, short is always safe because, if you get tired of it, you can always get some sewn in. It's only hair. It will grow back. But how my nephew take a liking to the new change?"

"I don't know."

"June never liked for me to cut my hair."

"Well, what Chance like really doesn't matter as of right now."

"Oh, y'all into it, huh? Well, I want to hear all about it soon as you get in my chair."

Everyone seemed to be indulging in their own conversation, but Mari and I knew better. At the salon, someone was always listening. Since I was the last person to get my hair styled, I waited 'til we were in the shop by ourselves to discuss all that had happened between me and Chance. She told me that she felt I did the right thing.

"Agape, I don't care if Chance is my nephew. He shouldn't have treated you like that, and you deserve a man that is going to come home to you every night and that's not going to cheat on you. I know Chance loves you a lot, but he just has a fucked-up way of showing it. You just remember that, if you don't stand for something, you will fall for anything."

Mari put the finishing touches on my hair, and when she swirled me around in the chair, I couldn't believe how good the short cut looked on me.

"I like it, Mari. It is so cute," I stated as I looked at the back of my hair by holding another mirror facing the big mirror in front of me."

"Come on, girl. Let's get on out of here. It's nine forty-five. You gon' make me late for my date."

I waited for Mari to lock the shop up. We hugged, said our goodbyes, and pulled off, going in different directions.

I stopped at the Mcdonald's on Gettysburg to grab myself a bite to eat, not wanting to go anywhere too hungry, and what if the guy that Larry hooked me up with didn't have any money to buy me anything to eat? I would be so embarrassed, so to kill the possibility of being humiliated, I ordered myself a fish meal to go.

After the third ring, I checked my caller ID; and to my surprise, it was Chance. I didn't know if I should answer the phone or not. I decided to continue getting ready for my night out. I lathered the soap on my body. As the water rained down on me, I couldn't help but think about whoever the guy Larry was going to bring for me. I hoped he was not lame like Lyric suggested he would be. The way Larry was spending money on Lyric earlier gave me reason to believe that Larry wasn't a lame, and I didn't want to be stuck with the loser.

Chance was my first everything—my first lover, boyfriend, and confidant. I didn't know how I was going to react if this guy wasn't half the nigga Chance was. I just hoped he could keep my interest at least for the night.

I stepped out the house ten minutes to eleven. I noticed a black Hummer sitting outside of Lyric's apartment.

As soon as my feet hit the street, someone called out my unofficial nickname, "Aye, Red."

Not knowing who was behind the window of the tinted vehicle, I continued across the street, trying to stare through the tint on the windows. As I hoped it wasn't someone Chance knew, the driver door opened, and I saw that it was Larry. I smiled only because of the devilish grin plastered across his face. Trying to ease the queasy feeling in my gut, I waved to Larry and proceeded to Lyric's door.

"Come here, Red. I want you to meet someone."

Ugh, I thought. *Lyric was right. This nigga must be lame. He got another nigga speaking for him.*

I played things cool, careful not to mess the night up for me or Lyric. I walked toward the passenger side door. But the back door on the same side opened up, and the guy that stepped out of the

Hummer proved me so wrong. I didn't know anything about the man. But what I could tell was that nothing about him was lame.

"How you doing?" he asked as he shut the door and leaned up against it.

"I'm good. How are you?" I stuttered to complete my sentence.

His response was "I'm fair. Your name Red, right?"

"You can call me Red if you want," I said, not really wanting him to call me the same name Chance refered to me as.

"I wanna call you by your name, if that's cool with you."

I looked in his eyes, and for some reason or another, it felt like I was looking in Chance's face. Why did they have to share the same facial features—same chingy eyes that I so loved and the same thick black eyebrows? The only difference was that he had a lighter skin complexion. He wasn't light skinned, more like the color of coffee that had cream added to it. To say that he was fine would be saying the least.

"My name is Agape."

"Agape?" he questioned. "Am I saying it right?" he asked.

"Yes, that's right. Now can I call you by your name?"

Silence.

"Look here, Agape. After tonight, I'll decide whether you can call me by my name or not, so until that time come, call me D or Al, whichever you like."

"That's cool. I think I like Al, so that's what I'll call you."

The smile he gave me sealed his approval of me. And the way he pulled me close to him let me know for sure he was no lame. Nah, the confidence he had let me know that.

And then my phone rang, and instead of Al letting me go as I tried to pull away before checking my caller ID, just my luck, I bet this Chance ass calling back. Al held me tighter, not tight, but held me just the way Chance did. It was Lyric.

"Hey, girl," I said excitedly as I answered the phone.

"Bitch, you better not set me up. Sounds like Chance is some-where around. That's the only time you all happy-go-lucky."

"I'm so sorry, Lyric. I changed my mind."

I put my finger up to my lips to quiet Al from saying anything, and he smiled and zipped his lips with his fingers.

"I just don't feel up to going out. But you guys have a good time."

"You know what, Agape? Sometimes I don't know why I fuck with you, and you always dissing me for that nigga."

I interrupted her before she said anything that just might have had me not wanting to go. "Girl, shut up. I'm outside. I was on my way over when I was introduced to my date," I replied by looking at Al.

"So is he a lame?" Lyric whispered through the phone as if the nigga was standing next to her.

"I don't know," I responded nonchalantly, not wanting to let her in on what I thought.

"Agape, I swear you act like you don't be knowing shit. I'll let you know if he lame or not soon as I get in the car. I'ma start coughing if he is a lame."

"Okay, and if not?" I replied while smiling as Al rubbed my sleeveless arms.

"Bye. I'm on my way out."

When I saw Lyric, I felt slightly overdressed. She was rocking a red halter leather dress; and I, on the other hand, had on a cream camisole on with a brown vest over it and some Victoria's Secret distressed cut-up jeans and some brown pumps and my brown-and-tan Gucci bag.

"Damn, should I change?" I whispered to Al.

He assured me I was fine. He said, "Baby if I didn't think you looked good, I would've told you. Look at us. You got the brown Gucci bag. I'm in all Gucci."

Not even noticing Al's outfit, I realized he had on an all-cream Gucci outfit. We definitely complemented each other.

Lyric began choking as soon as my back hit my seat. I thought Lyric was trying to signal to me that this nigga was lame. I didn't see how. I didn't want to entertain the thought that he was a lame.

"You all right, miss lady?" Al asked.

Lyric hadn't had the opportunity to see what the guy looked like. He didn't even pay her any mind as she twisted her ass toward the truck. He kept his attention on me.

So she took the opportunity to sneak a peek at him as she turned toward him in the back and stated, "Yeah, I'm good."

She didn't know anything about the guy. She never saw him in the city before and didn't know one way or the other whether he was lame or not, but that wouldn't stop her from leading me to believe he was a lame.

"Turn the music up, my nigga," Al requested.

But Lyric cut it up instead and asked, "Is that good?"

Al went on to ask me if I was cool with the volume.

Used to riding in the car with Chance, with the amps on full blast, I told him, "Yeah, it's cool with me."

"We good, miss lady," Al replied to Lyric.

Al and I sat in the back of the spacious Hummer, getting acquainted with each other. I found out that Al was five years older than me. He lived in CincinnatI with his three-year-old daughter.

Remembering that, for some reason or another, Lyric got a drift that he was lame, I asked, "So who do you live with?"

"I live alone, just me and my daughter," Al answered.

Curious as to what his daughter name was, I asked, "What's your little girl's name?"

"Her name Trinity. Why, you wanna meet her?" he questioned.

"Yep, as soon as I know her father's name," I joked.

"I see you have jokes, huh."

I laughed.

The forty-five-minute ride seemed like it was about ten minutes.

As we pulled in the parking lot of a club called Pinkies, I checked my eyeliner and my eyelashes I had Mari put in individually for me after she did my hair. Everything was good.

As we parked, Al whispered, "Don't get out until I tell you to."

Not sure what he meant by that, I sat in the car as I watched everyone climb out of the Hummer, then Al opened my door for me.

"Get out," he stated.

I smiled and grabbed his hand that he held out to me.

We walked hand in hand through the parking lot of the club as if we had been together for years. Lyric and Larry walked ahead of us. I was not sure why the line to get in was longer than the job center's line at eight in the morning. By the time we made it up to the line, Al kept walking ahead of the line. We passed up Lyric and Larry as we headed toward the front of the line. I could hear people saying, "Who the fuck they think they is?" and "They bet' not get in before me," and they were rightfully upset because here we were walking to the door as if there wasn't a line damn near wrapping around the building.

Once we got to the front door, the guy that was letting people in the club stopped everything he was doing and gave Al some dap. "What's up, my nigga? You in VIP tonight."

"You see this pretty lady?" Al stated as he grabbed my hand. "She with me and Larry in line, and he got a lady friend with him. Send him to my table."

Watching Al peel off four one-hundred-dollar bills and hand them to the security guard, I didn't care what Lyric thought. I was team Al as of right now. In the VIP section, I noticed a few girls that I went to Kiser with seated at a table together as Chance and I walked to our table, and the envy that they wore in their eyes was undeniable. Then it was the chick that was seated at the table next to them told the same envious tale.

"You have some admirers, don't you?" I yelled in Al's ear over the music.

He smiled, then kissed the back of my hand. Not saying a word, he escorted me to our table and told the waiter to bring back a bottle of Cristal.

"You drink?" Al asked as he was ready to fill a second glass of Cristal.

"I usually don't, really," I said, meaning I never did.

I never even tasted a Cooler before. I didn't want to pass up the opportunity of being able to say I drunk some Cristal. So I downplayed it like I was a social drinker.

After our second glass of the Cristal, I was starting to feel the effects of the champagne. I began to loosen up. The music started to control my body. I wanted to dance.

"You want to dance?"

Al looked at me with a seductive smile, and he replied, "I don't dance, baby."

"Come on. I want to dance, Al," I whined in a manner I knew was making him sweat.

I grabbed his hand and walked toward the dance floor, then it was like a blessing came down from the heavens when Usher Raymond and Lil Jon's "Lovers and Friends" blasted through the speakers. I hit the dance floor, rotating my hips and ass and rotating my hands in the air. I was in the zone as I sang alone to the words to the song. Any other time I heard this song, I thought of me and Chance, only at this moment I was imagining myself strip teasing for a whole 'nother man. I knew Al liked what he was seeing because he never took his eyes off of me as he stood outside of the dance floor with his legs apart, rubbing his chin. I, too, liked what I was looking at. I did the Naomi Campbell walk toward him. I turned around so that my ass would be up against him. I started winding my hips up against his dick. I could see how hesitant Al was. But he couldn't resist because, no longer after I put my ass up against Al, I felt our hips in sync with each other. Sensing Al wasn't much of a dancer, I kept it real clean and sweet, mind fucking Al the whole time we were on the dance floor.

After the song was over, we headed back to our table. Lyric and Larry were seated across from each other. I could feel that Lyric was slightly agitated, but for what, I wasn't sure.

"What's up, girl?" I asked as I sat next to Lyric.

"I'm good. I need to go to the bathroom," Lyric stated as she gave me the eye that could only meant one thing.

"I'm going to tag along because I need to freshen up."

We excused ourselves and headed in the direction of the ladies' restroom. Lyric grabbed my arm, pulling me toward the ladies' restroom. I was thinking this better be good because here I was trying to get better acquainted with Al, and she was signaling me to the bathroom.

"Bitch, Chance is here," Lyric stated with a serious look on her face. "And he in here with another bitch," Lyric added.

"Don't play with me, Lyric."

From the look on Lyric's face, I knew she wasn't joking.

"Agape, do I look like I am joking?" Lyric asked with an even more serious look on her face.

I then became paranoid, wondering if there was any possibility he might have saw me already. I started looking around the club in the many different faces of people, trying to avoid contact with Chance.

"I'm ready to go," I stated to Lyric.

"And how are you going to get home?" she asked with a stunned look on her face. "Because Larry is not about to take us all the way back home, and we just got here."

I understood exactly what Lyric was saying, but what had me feeling a certain type of way was the fact that she didn't even try to see if he would take me back home before she suggested that he wouldn't. Here I was in the club with a nigga, and my nigga I just broke up with a few hours ago was in the same club with another bitch. This would not be good. I already knew, and she was standing here like she could care less what popped off. I couldn't stomach Lyric any longer. She could be so heartless at times, and as of now, this was one of those times.

"I'll be in the car," I stated without a care.

I wasn't going to waste another minute with Lyric. As I walked off, I could feel Lyric staring a hole in my back. Luckily the door to the Hummer was unlocked. I climbed in, and a million and one thoughts soared through my mind.

I just hope Chance didn't see me on the dance floor with Al, I thought.

The only reason that I agreed to going out with Lyric and Larry was that I knew we wouldn't be in Dayton. I never thought Chance would be here, and I was guessing he thought the same.

When I heard the passenger door open, I was surprised to see Al slide in the passenger side seat.

"You all right?" he asked as he turned around toward me.

Silence.

"Yo' girl told me that you came out to the car because you wasn't feeling well, and if that is indeed the case, I'll keep you company out here, but if you just not feeling the club, I can see to it that we leave."

Hearing the words flow from his mouth, I realized he was genuinely concerned about why I left the club. I just didn't know what to say. Lyric had already collaborated a story, and I hadn't known this man long enough to owe him any lies. I didn't see how he had any power over whether we leave or not. I mean, he wasn't the driver.

"I guess we not the only ones who want to come out and have a nice time. Apparently my ex is in there with another girl. And it just wouldn't be good if I stayed up in there with you and see him and her."

Al remembered me briefly explaining my break up with my man. He knew that the breakup was still fresh and that, if he and I had just broken up earlier in the day only to find me in the club with another nigga, it wouldn't be sweet.

Al removed his Blackberry from his pocket. "Aye yo, Tubby, Agape ain't feeling too well."

"Oh, yeah?" Larry replied, knowing this meant the night was coming to an early end.

"Yeah, so grab ole girl and let's ride," Al stated.

"We on our way out, my nigga," he informed Al.

As Lyric and Larry walked up, Al hopped in the back with me. Lyric shot me a look that let me know she didn't like the fact she and Larry had to leave the club behind my bullshit.

Just as we were pulling off, I spotted Chance and his date hopping in his black Cadillac STS. I tried to strain my eyes to see what the girl looked like. It was too dark to see her face. I sat there in complete silence as a tear managed to escape my eye, and I wiped it immediately, hoping Al didn't see that. When I peeped over in his direction, he was looking ahead.

But Al did see me wiping the tear that fell from my eyes. He knew how I must have felt, and he didn't want me to be alone for the night.

"Aye, brah, let's go to my spot. We can stay out there and take these ladies home in the a.m."

Neither one of us objected, and quite frankly, I didn't care where they took me as long as I wasn't in eyeshot of Chance.

The way Al held my hand on the ride to his house was comforting. I just couldn't get Chance out of my mind, and the fact that Al came out to check on me when it should have been Lyric in the first place didn't sit well with me either because, had the tables been turned, I would've handled a lot of shit differently than she had.

We pulled in Greenview Condominiums' parking lot, parking next to the black BMW that Larry was driving earlier. I knew that from the personalized tags, DNTH8T. From the outside of the condo you would never imagine that it was so big. The living room had an antique theme with beautiful paintings on the wall. I liked this room the most.

I didn't know if guest were allowed to sit in the room. At Sabrina's, the living room was off-limits. We were not allowed sitting in there under no circumstances. So I asked if it was cool to sit down even though Lyric had already taken the liberty to sit down on the sofa.

"There you go with that silly shit, Agape. Why would the furniture be in here if you can't sit on it?"

I didn't like the attitude Lyric had since we left the club. I paid her no mind, but Al did.

"Just to let you know, miss lady, no one sits in this room."

Lyric sat there with a dumbfounded look on her face. I shot her a smirk as she proceeded to get up from the sofa with a frown on her face.

"Get your girl, man," Al warned Larry.

After getting a good look at the condo, I noticed that no room in the condo was made up for a little girl. The thought crossed my mind that Al might have been lying when he said that his daughter lived with him. I didn't see any sign of her, no pictures and no toys—nothing.

I liked the restroom. It had one of those toilets that cleaned your private areas when you were done using the restroom, and I just couldn't help myself. I had to use it, and it felt good.

Everyone was seated in the family room of the condo. Al and Larry were seated at the dining table across from each other while Lyric sat on the sofa, texting away on her Blackberry, visibly still upset. I was relieved when Al called me over to the table. I stood in front of him as he motioned for me to sit on his lap. I did. I looked across the table, at Larry, as he rolled up a fat blunt. I just looked on, making sure weed was the only thing he was rolling up. After the blunt was rolled, Al asked me if I smoked. I told him I did, and the promise that I once made with Chance went out the window. We smoked blunt after blunt. Lyric loosened up as the weed took its effect on her. She was back to herself. We all laughed and joked around till the wee hours of the morning. I sat on the couch with my head on the arm of the chair, ready to doze off at any moment.

"Red look like she 'sleep, brah," Larry said to Al.

Al looked back at me and could tell I was beat.

He took me by the hand and led me to the master bedroom of the condo.

I wasted no time. As soon as I entered the room, I stripped out of my clothes, only to have Al step in the room to see me in an all-white lace panty and bra set.

"Can I have a shirt to sleep in?"

Al stood there in pure admiration for what he was looking at.

"Hello?" I said while waving my hand in Al's face. "Can I have a shirt to sleep in?" I repeated.

"Oh yeah, here you go." Al threw me a shirt that was three sizes too big.

After putting the T-shirt on, Al complimented me, "It looks better on you than it did on me."

I laughed as I pulled the covers back on the bed. Lying in the bed, I looked up and smiled a tired smile and closed my eyes.

I hope he didn't think he was getting none tonight, I thought to myself.

"I'm down the hall if you need me, Agape."

"Thanks, Al," I whispered.

When he leaned over and kissed my temple, he sent shock waves through my spine.

He then whispered in my ear, "My real name is Dekalb."

I looked up and requested for him to come lie with me. Everything about Dekalb was pleasing to the eyes as he removed his shirt and shorts and got in bed behind me with only his boxers on. When he pulled me near him, I snuggled up in his warm embrace and fell right asleep, only to be awakened by Lyric's oohing and aah-ing. You could hear her moaning from whatever room they were in.

It was almost like they were in the room with us as Larry said all kinds of obscene things to her. "Get on your knees and suck this dick, bitch." Do this. Do that. Bitch this and bitch that.

You know, everyone likes what he or she likes; but when Lyric said, "Choke me Larry," it threw me through a loop.

Choke her, I thought.

"What the hell?" Al whispered. "Your girl is a super freak."

I whispered, "I see."

We shared a light laugh; then I heard Larry say, "Round two, bitch. Come ride this dick."

I put the pillow over my head and drifted off back to sleep.

"Agape, get up," Lyric stated as she tapped my arm, feeling like I just fell asleep.

I asked, "What time is it?"

"One o'clock," Lyric responded.

I slid out the bed and grabbed my clothes that I had previously placed on Al's dresser. Lyric handed me a washrag and escorted me to the restroom. After slipping out of Al's T-shirt, I placed my clothes on. After washing the sleep out of my eyes and giving my face a once-over wash, I held the rag on my face, trying to let the cold water wake me. I took a couple of deep breaths as I proceeded to check behind the mirror for some toothpaste. I put a dime-sized dab on my finger and used my finger as if it was a toothbrush. That would have to do for now. Just as I gave myself a once-over, I saw the restroom door open and Al's reflection behind me. I smiled.

"Hey there, Sleeping Beauty," Al stated.

"Good morning, or should I say afternoon?" I responded.

"Whichever you'd like," Al responded, stepping into the bathroom behind me.

I looked at our reflection in the mirror. Al talked to me through the mirror as I looked back at him.

"I think we would look good together, Agape."

I smiled to let him know I felt the same. Al went on to turn me around so that I was facing him.

"Listen here, Agape. I don't know what it is about you, but there is something about you that makes me want to get to know you."

Remembering the same words come from Chance's mouth made such a sweet phrase sour.

Al liked me in a way that he once liked Trinity's mother. They were together for three years. Al knew that he was taking a big risk on dating her because she was fourteen and he was twenty. Despite the age difference, she was very mature. Al often thought it was because of how her mother treated and talked to her. Al approached her, thinking that she was his age or maybe a little younger, not knowing the story behind her baby face. Her overdeveloped body had told a tale. She was only fourteen. Al walked off after apologizing to the young girl. It wasn't until Al was walking down the same street about a month or two later. The young girl and a somewhat-older lady were in the middle of a heated argument. Al was the type of guy who loved to see a fight, and in his younger years, he found himself in several fights with the neighborhood kids. Al stood next to a telephone pole and watched as the fight unraveled. The woman knocked the young girl to the ground. Why was she beating her unmercifully, yelling obscenities at the girl?

Al wasn't too sure how they were related until the lady told the young girl, "Bitch, I never wanted you anyway. You should have been like your sister and went in stayed in a foster home. At least she will have her money when she turn twenty-one. You bitch, on the other hand, ain't got shit. Everything I got, I bought with your money, ha!" She went on to laugh hysterically as she choked the young girl.

Realizing that the lady was going to kill the young girl, it took everything in Al not to intervene, but he just couldn't have the little girl's life on his hands if the women killed her right there in front of him.

"You actually thought I loved you. You ain't worthy for anyone to love you," the older lady continued as she kicked and swung at Al for pulling her off of the young lady.

"But, Momma," the young girl cried as she lay on the concrete balled up.

"Don't call me Momma now. You never called me Momma around that bitch of a sister of yours," the woman responded.

Al found himself wondering what the young girl could have ever done so wrong to not be worthy of her mother's love, let alone anyone else. The young girl sat on the curb.

Before the older lady pulled off, she yelled out of her passenger side window, "Don't show yo' ass up on my doorstep ever again unless you got some money with you."

Money, Al thought as he walked off.

He couldn't help but look back at the young girl. As she sat on the curb with her head in her lap crying, his heart went out to the girl. He turned around to let the girl know he lived around the corner and, if she needed somewhere to go, she could come over at any time. That night, she came over to Al's house. He tried to keep her at a distance and just help the young girl out of the streets, but there was just something about her that made him want her in more of an intimate way. Al didn't know how, but he knew one day what his actions would cost him.

He just didn't know that she would end up stealing ten thousand dollars from him. That day, he decided to take her life as payback for what she had taken from him. It wasn't the amount of money she had taken. At that time, Al was making that kind of money in a week. It was the act that he didn't take a liking to. She had everything at her disposal. Why she wanted to take from him, he couldn't come up with a significant reason for such a heinous act until he found out that she was back living with her mother. Al had an understanding of people in general. He understood that humans were habitual by nature. It was the only thing that kept a woman who was getting beat by her husband day in and day out committed to him. It was the only thing that allowed a child to continue to be mistreated by her mother. The only thing that saved her was the fact she was pregnant after the DNA determined that Al was 99.99 percent the father. He spared her life. In retrospect, he couldn't see himself allowing his child to grow up as he had—without a mother. She had everything at her disposal.

On our way back to Dayton, I decided to check my phone that I put on silent the moment we walked in to Al's condo. I had ten missed calls. All of them were from Chance. I couldn't understand what he wanted that was so important, as if he wasn't just at the club with another female. I couldn't deny I still loved Chance for everything that he'd done for me and Meaka. I just wished he just left me alone and let me get over him. I made a mental note to change my number. The ride back was a quiet one. No one said anything as we listened to 50 Cent's CD *Get Rich or Die Tryin'*.

I wasn't sure what Al was thinking about, but something had him in deep thought as he laid one hand on my left thigh while looking out the window, bobbing his head to the song "Many Men."

Al stared out the window to keep from being captivated by my beautiful hazel eyes. My smile had the ability to warm him on the inside, and when I spoke, Al felt at ease. I possessed an innocence about me that most women try to emulate, but for me, it was natural. Al liked everything about me. It wasn't until he watched me sleep most of the morning he knew I was special. Even in my sleep, he thought I was beautiful. The only thing that had him doubtful was that he saw the same qualities in Trinity's mother, only to had been deceived. Al told himself that he wouldn't allow another woman to get close to him. He didn't trust women and thought they were some of the most cunning creatures on earth, too emotional and indecisive and wanting only the things they didn't possess. If and when they did receive some of what they wanted, they became someone other than who they really were, willing to do anything to keep what it was they wanted, or there was a price they were willing to accept to leave what they'd always wanted. Al felt like it was always a price with women.

"What's on your mind, Dekalb?" I whispered in his ear.

He turned to me as our faces were only inches apart and stated, "You."

I could feel the inches between us lessen as Al kissed my lips ever so gently. I licked my lips to savor the taste. Lyric asked me if I wanted to hit the blunt.

"I'm good," I told her.

"What about you, Mr., um..." Lyric realized after all this time she didn't know Al's name.

"We good back here," Al responded shortly.

It wasn't that Al had anything against Lyric. He just knew her type all too well, the type of female that hung around a certain caliber of niggas for their own personal gain. He didn't know Lyric from a can of paint. But how he saw it, a spade is a spade, and there wasn't any going around that. That was why he got a kick out of letting her ride up front in his Hummer, knowing good and well she thought it was Larry's. If only she knew Larry just got out of the penitentiary last week and that he was the one who had been looking out for him on the strength Larry went to the penitentiary behind him. She would never be fucking him if she didn't feel like she had sat on a gold mine. All that loyalty, respect, and honor didn't mean shit to a female like Lyric if you didn't have no money to spend on her so that she could hide her insecurities behind Coogi, Prada, and whatever else they were liking these days.

Lyric thought Al was only hating, mad that he didn't have a Hummer to ride him and I around in, so she just played it off as if she didn't even notice how short Al was with her.

As we pulled up to Lyric's, Al told me to not get out until he told me to, just as he did when we were at the club. He got out, then opened my door for me. As he reached for my hand, he instructed me to get out outside the truck.

Al asked if it was cool if he got my number. I told him that he could give me his. He agreed only if I promised I would call. I promised. After getting Al's number, I said my goodbyes and walked over to my apartment.

Chance watched up the street as I interacted with Al. Chance remembered seeing the guy's face before, but he just couldn't recollect when or where. Chance waited for the truck to be out of eyesight before he pulled in my driveway. As he stepped up to the door, he turned the knob; and to his surprise, the door was unlocked. So he stepped in. It hadn't been a whole twenty-four hours since the last time he was with me, but he tried smoking blunt after blunt. He tried taking the girl that he had cheated on me with to a club out in Cincinnati just in case I decided to go out. He didn't want to take the risk of me seeing him out with another female if I just so happened to go out. He even tried lying up with her at her house, only to be reminded time and time again of me. He just couldn't get me off of his mind.

When I heard my door open, I immediately thought it was Lyric coming over to talk shit about Al. So I got up from my bed only in my panty and bra. Surprised to see Chance standing in my living room, I found myself covering my body as if this man had never seen me naked.

He then walked over to me. "Agape, baby—"

I interrupted, "Don't 'Agape baby' me."

"Just listen to me, baby, damn."

Not used to having to beg a female in his life, Chance wasn't good at making up, but he was giving it all that he had.

"Well, you better make it quick because you have two minutes."

"Agape, I tried to stay away from you, baby. I tried going out with a bitch. I just can't stay away from you. I'm sorry for everything I did. Just tell me how I can make this better."

Chance only told me that he went out with another female because he knew that I went out with another guy. After his call went unanswered last night, Chance caught himself riding past my apartment. He tricked himself into believing that he wanted to make sure I was all right. Just as he pulled up my street, he noticed me standing outside a black Hummer with the guy, and the way that I looked at him told him that I shared some interest in him.

Chance pleaded with me to give him another chance.

"Listen, baby," Chance stated as he looked into my eyes.

Chance could tell that I was warming up to him because the cold look I had in my eyes when he first locked eyes on me disappeared. So he then grabbed my hand.

"I love you, baby."

"I love you too, Chance."

I couldn't deny the fact that I still loved Chance. Yeah, he went outside of the relationship we had and, in a way, abused the trust he once instilled in me. But outside of Meaka, he was all that I had. The words escaped my mouth without a thought as I held Chance's hand. I wanted so desperately to send Chance on his way. Instead, I melted in his arms as he held me in his arms, telling me how sorry he was. I believed him, or at least the fear of being alone outweighed any other emotion that I could have been feeling.

Chance led me to my bedroom, and I couldn't find it in me to deny him of anything at this point. I allowed him to remove all of my clothes. I then lay on the bed and watched attentively as Chance removed his. He then removed his necklace that had the initial *C* medallion on it and placed it around my neck, placing the medallion up to my lips. He told me to kiss it. I submitted to his request as I looked him in his eyes and kissed his medallion softly. Chance then grabbed my legs and gestured for me to turn over and entered me from the back. I took every inch of him inside of me and enjoyed every minute of it, the sixty minutes we spent sexing each other. Chance thought for a moment that I may have cheated on him with the guy that was in the Hummer, but as quick as the thought entered his mind, it left as soon as he entered me. He knew I hadn't been. We both had a point to prove this afternoon, and I was sure the message was received subliminally as we both reached our third orgasm together.

CHAPTER 3

———◆●◆———

Birds of a Feather Flock Together

After I answered the phone on the third ring, the operator let me know that I had a collect call from Meaka. I hit the 0 on the phone. Meaka wasted no time singing happy birthday to me.

"Happy birthday to you, Agape. Happy birthday to you. How old are you? How old are you?" Meaka sang on. "How old are you?"

"Eighteen!" I yelled as we laughed together. "Thank you, Meaka. It was beautiful."

"Whatever, girl. I wish I was there to celebrate with you."

Silence. I wish more than anything that I could have Meaka here with me, and at times like these, I often wished it was me that sat behind those prison walls. I wanted to tell her so badly how there was not a day that went by that I didn't think about how I wished she was here with me. Instead, I minimized the situation by telling her that she would be home in a few months and that we would celebrate then.

I know I should be happy right now on this party bus with Chance and his friends, along with their girlfriends, but for some reason, the liquor I just consumed didn't numb how agitated I was. Here it was, my birthday; and Chance invited all of his niggas and they bitches, some of whom I never saw before, to party with us. Truth be told, I didn't have many friends. As a matter of fact, Lyric was my only friend. So one would think that, if no one else, Chance would have invited her; and the fact that he didn't did not sit well with me.

"Where is Lyric?" I asked in Chance's ear over the music.

The look Chance gave me told me that he didn't invite her. I sat back in my seat and played with my French manicure, trying hard to hide my anger and frustration.

Chance cut the music down as he passed the bottles of Patrón around the bus. "We 'bout to hit up the Trees, a night club that sat on the corner of an alley that some of the most ruthless individuals in Dayton partied at."

"The Trees?" I questioned.

"Yeah, bae, the Trees. Trust me, you gon' have a good time."

Chance knew firsthand that I didn't even like pulling up in the Trees' parking lot, let alone going on the inside, especially when they were on the Channel 7 news station every weekend for a homicide.

"Okay." I mustered out a smile, knowing good and well that the Trees was not a club that I would have chosen.

Hell, it was only one way in and one way out; so either way you look at it, someone was bound to get fucked up.

I looked at my phone, awaiting Lyric's call, as I had done all day. I hadn't talked to her. She didn't call and tell me happy birthday or nothing. I took it as she may have been in on the surprise Chance had for me, and since she couldn't hold water, I thought that was why she hadn't called. So I texted her come to the Trees.

Lyric responded, "Girl, since when you go to the Trees? Let me guess..."

"Yeah, you right. Chance's idea," I texted.

"I'll meet you up there," Lyric texted back.

Upon entering the club, Chance's friend Jabre's girl started throwing up all over the place. A li'l of the vomit got on Jabre's shoes, and he hollered off and smacked the poor girl. I thought that the liquor might have given her some courage, but not her. She just started crying hysterically. He then grabbed her by her hair and whispered something that had to be terrifying because she straightened right up as we entered the club. The club was jam-packed shoulder to shoulder. You couldn't move, and I could feel my curls falling. Beads of sweat had formed on my forehead as the music stormed through the club. Despite the Patrón we were just drinking, Chance and his entourage were ordering shot after shot of Patrón. His nigga's girls drinking right with them, but not me I was so desperately trying to shake the buzz I already had going on. Realizing I was in the belly of the beast also known as the Trees, I knew I had to be on point since no one else I was with was.

I looked toward the door, anticipating Lyric's arrival. It seemed like forever as I watched the entrance of the door as if I turned my head, it may have moved. In walked Lyric in a white strapless dress, the same kind I had on, only I had on the brown one.

"Look at you, birthday girl. You looking good, but I know I look better," Lyric stated as she turned around, showing off her most infamous ass.

We laughed, hugged, and headed toward the dance floor.

"Where Chance at?" Lyric asked.

"The same place he been at since we stepped foot in the door, at the bar," I stated.

"That's what he do, girl. He sit his ass at that bar and buy drinks for every bitch with a big ass."

I looked toward the bar. Chance had a dark-skinned girl seated next to him, and when he handed her a drink, I looked to the side of me to see if Lyric had witnessed what I just saw. She did.

"Girl, fuck Chance. We in the building. Look at us. We in our Hermès dresses with Jimmy Choos on our feet."

Lyric pulled me to the dance floor, and we did our thang. Lyric and I danced with each other in an almost-forbidden fashion. We could care less what anyone thought of us. We knew what it was. We were just best friends trying to have fun. Lyric knew that I would have never been bold enough to dance with another nigga even if my nigga was at the bar entertaining another bitch. But she wasn't gon' sit by and let me be drowned out by the other bitches. She was gon' put me right where I needed to be—in the spotlight. Lyric bent over in front of me as she twerked her favorite asset. I stood with my legs slightly spread, doing the same, shaking our asses to the beat of the

Ying Yang Twins' "Whistle While You Twurk." Niggas immediately surrounded the dance floor, watching me and Lyric.

Chance noticed niggas moving toward the dance floor, not just any niggas, but some of the most paid niggas in the city. This had to mean that it had to be a sexy female on the floor doing her thang.

He whispered, "Give me a minute," in his new friend's ear.

As he proceeded to the dance floor, knowing that his eyes weren't playing tricks on him because he picked out the dress and the shoes himself, Chance snatched me off of the dance floor.

"Get your hands off of me." I tried to loosen Chance's grip he had on my arm.

"We leavin'," Chance stated as we walked toward the exit.

Chanced gripped my arm tight with one hand, and with the other, he retrieved his cell phone from his pocket and called Jabre.

"We on our way to the bus. If y'all niggas ain't out here by the time we get on, consider y'all asses left."

Click.

"What the fuck did you think you were out there doing, Agape?"

"Do you have any idea how you made me look in there? As soon as you stepped foot in that club, it was as if you didn't even know me. You at the bar buying drinks for bitches, grabbing they asses. How do you think you made me look?" I asked as we waited for the driver to open the door.

The look that Chance had on his face was the same look I saw the day he had shook me. I would never forget that look. I got on the bus, not saying another word because I was scared of how Chance might have reacted. I felt somewhat relieved when everyone else started climbing on the bus.

It was when Jabre walked past me and said, "Damn, Red, I seen you out there working that dance floor out like it was a gym."

Then his girl said, "Yeah, girl, you did you thang out there. You and yo' girl had all them niggas' attention. I wish I can dance like that, girl. That's why I was at the bar."

I just looked at Chance to see if he still had the Michael Myers eyes, and he did. Just as I tried to look off, Chance smacked me so hard I could have sworn the bus got into an accident, I wasn't gon' just sit there and let him smack me in front of all of his friends. I jumped on him with my legs wrapped tight around his waist while I bit at his face. I bit him so hard I tried to tear the skin off of his face. He tried to pry me off of him.

His attempts had failed, so he yelled, "Man, get this bitch off of me."

I knew, when I let go of Chance, that this would be the end of him and me. I asked the driver to pull over and let me out. Everyone tried to convince me to stay, but I walked off of the bus and watched as the bus pulled off. I checked myself in the mirror and realized I looked like shit. I didn't want to let Lyric see me with this big-ass handprint across my face, but I didn't have anyone else to call.

"You okay, girl?" Lyric asked as she answered the phone.

A part of Lyric felt bad, but she didn't think Chance would react the way he did. Lyric secretly thought that it would pull him to the dance floor and he would then give me the attention that I deserve from him on my birthday. But instead he dragged me out the club.

"I need you to come get me. I'm downtown in front of the Schuster Center," I stated in a defeated tone.

"I'm downtown right now. I'm in the car with Larry. We was just about to get on the highway." Lyric didn't want to let me know that Al was in the car with them as well.

I was kind of relieved when Lyric stated Larry was in the car with her. Then she wouldn't have to pay me much of attention, so she just may not notice this handprint on my face.

When the BMW pulled up, I was relieved. I just wanted to lie down and not wake back up at that moment.

But when I opened the back door to the car and saw Al in the back seat, I almost shitted on myself. It felt like time stood still as I stood there with the door opened.

"Girl, get in," Lyric demanded.

I got in the back seat. I didn't know what to say to Al, so I said nothing. And he did the same.

"So where you going?" Lyric immediately asked, not showing any compassion whatsoever.

I didn't take it personally because this was just how Lyric was when she was with a nigga—heartless.

Al thought otherwise. He didn't care for Lyric and thought less of her than he had before. He could see the pain in my eyes. As soon as I opened the door, he noticed the red handprint that was across the right side of my cheek even though I desperately tried to hide it. And all Lyric could think about was taking me somewhere, not knowing if I would be alone or not, just so she could do her job so, by morning, she could be a few hundred dollars richer.

"I can go home. That's cool," I said, not really wanting to go home because I knew Chance would show up there.

I lay my head on the car door and tried hard not to let my emotions get the best of me. I couldn't help but wonder what things would have been like had I just called Al instead of trying to make things work between me and Chance. Now Al didn't have anything to say to me, and honestly I didn't blame him.

"Aye, brah, let's go to my spot."

I looked at Al as he looked back at me with a stern look in his eyes. I looked away, only because the look spoke volumes to me. I couldn't help but mouth thank you.

Al's condo was the same as I remembered it. I took a seat at the dining room table with my head in my hands, trying desperately not to look as miserable as I felt. Al walked in without looking at me at all.

"How you been?"

Al looked toward me as if he had not noticed me sitting here, then focused back on the movie collection he was looking at. After putting the movie in, Al sat on the seat, still not addressing my question.

I don't have time for this shit, I thought to myself as I entered the room I remembered sleeping in the last time I was there.

Not wanting to ask Al if it was okay to wear one of his shirts, I decided to sleep in my underwear, not wanting to be ignored like before. I fell asleep as soon as my face hit the pillow.

Al entered the room. The only light came from the light in the hall. Even with limited light in the room, Al maneuvered through the room trying to not look at me as I slept, in fear that the feelings that he felt for me would resurface. He just couldn't deny the beauty he thought I possessed even in my sleep.

I could feel Al staring at me. I tried to just lay there and pretend sleep. But my eyes started to blink uncontrollably. So I opened them slowly. Al scurried across the room when he saw my eyes open, apparently trying to avoid contact with me. I sat up in the bed and watched as Al moved throughout the room.

"Can we talk, Dekalb?" I asked as he searched the closet for something.

"We ain't got nothing to talk about, Red."

I wanted for Al to notice me, to see that I needed his attention more than I needed to be paid at this moment. I removed the covers and hopped out of the bed when I saw Al inching toward the door. I stood in front of the doorway, demanding the attention I wanted. Remembering how pleased Al was the first time he saw me in my underwear, I knew he would have appreciated how much I'd grown. Al stood back, taking me in.

"What you want from me, Agape?" Al whispered as I blocked his way.

"I want you to stay in here with me tonight, Al," I stated as I walked seductively toward the bed.

Then Al walks out as he pulls the door closed.

I lay there 'til I drifted off to sleep, praying that Al would return and take me up on my secret offer. I wanted to offer Al something that I had only offered one other man. I wanted so desperately to show him how much I appreciated him for not leaving me at home by myself tonight. I wanted to show him that I was over Chance and his bullshit. Though his handprint was no longer on my face, that inflicted pain was still there, and the only way for it to subside was for me to seek comfort in another man's arms.

I felt empty inside when I woke up. I stared up at the ceiling as if God himself was going to come through the ceiling. I couldn't help but think about what had transpired between me and Chance. I couldn't believe how he slapped me in front of all of his friends like

I didn't mean anything to him, then he just let me get off of the bus not knowing if I had a way home or not.

There was a knock on the door, and I was just hoping that it wasn't Al. With the way he rejected me last night, I couldn't fathom having to look in his face first thing in the morning.

"Come in!" I yelled, not knowing who was on the other side of the door.

"Rise and shine, sleepyhead," Lyric stated as she walked in the room with a big smile on her face that let me know she was up to something that I didn't know.

"What's in the bag?" I asked, referring to the Macy's bag she had in her hand.

"Oh, just a li'l something that Larry picked up for you."

"Larry?" I questioned.

"You know, Al wanted us to bring something back for you when we went to the mall. I'm guessing he didn't have any money because he surely didn't give Larry any to purchase yo' stuff. I picked this out for you," Lyric stated as she held up a zebra-print strapless dress with a pair of the cutest red pumps. I jumped out of the bed so fast. I couldn't wait to try it on. I slipped it right over my body. It fit just as I thought it would, hugged every curve of my small frame.

"I like it, Lyric," I said as I twirled around in the dress.

"We stopped in Vickey's Secret. I hope you don't mind me picking you out a thong. Al said he wanted us to stay out here for the day, and I know you needed a clean pair of undies."

"Nah, I don't mind," I stated as I pulled the dress off over my head.

I couldn't help but notice the victorious look Lyric had in her eyes just before she stated, "Oh and yeah, Larry bought those too. That nigga ain't even have no money to buy you a thong," referring to Al.

I asked Lyric, "So who do you think I should thank?"

"The person who bought the dress of course, Agape."

"But I was thinking just the opposite. I mean, it was Al's idea. Had it not been for him, Larry would've never brought me anything back."

Lyric looked at me with a disgusted look on her face. "Agape, you can be so naive at times." She left out of the room.

After getting dressed, I went into the dining room. All eyes were on me. I knew I looked good in the dress, and the way Al eyed me, I knew he thought just the same. I walked toward him despite what Lyric thought. I was going to thank Al for being mindful enough to think of me even if he didn't have the funds to purchase the items for me. The thought was enough to be thanked. Al sat at the dining room table.

I stood next to him and whispered in his ear, "Thanks for thinking about me."

He looked up and smiled. "You look good," Al couldn't help but compliment.

"Thank you," I stated.

Lyric noticed the way Al looked at me. She wished that Larry looked at her with the same admiration. Lyric couldn't help but feel jealous.

"I'm hungry, Larry," Lyric stated with an attitude for what was unknown to everybody but detected by all.

"Me too," I stated.

"What y'all want to eat?" Al asked.

"I want IHOP," I stated.

"IHOP?" Lyric repeated. "Who wants IHOP, Agape?" she went on to ask, and as of right now, she was just being difficult.

"You know how to drive, Agape?" Al asked.

I let Al know that I knew how to drive. He then grabbed up a set of keys and let Larry know that we were about to go to IHOP. I followed him out the door. He handed me the keys to an all-white Lincoln. As I hopped in the front, Al hopped in the back.

"Why are you in the back? Get in the front, Al. I am not pulling off until you get in the front. I am not your chauffer."

"Come on, Agape. I don't ride up front. Don't you think I would love to be up front with you?"

I could see the sincerity in his eyes, so I started the car up and put the gear in reverse. I didn't like the silence that loomed in the air between us.

I broke the silence by asking Al, "How have Miss Trinity been doing?"

I looked in the rearview mirror to see his reaction, and it saddened me, the look that came across him.

"She good," Al stated.

"When can I meet her?"

"She come up here next week. Me and her mother share custody of her, so she stay with me for six months, and she's with her mother for six months."

"Well, that's good," I stated, not understanding why Al sounded so somber.

"You only have half of the story, Agape."

"Well, tell me the whole story," I requested.

"This is how it is, Agape. I hooked up with Trinity's mom when she was young. We share a eight-year age difference. I looked out for her when she was going through a tough time with her mom. Her mom is a money hungry bitch that wanted her own daughter to trick for her."

I was stunned at what Al had just stated. I remained quiet because I wanted to hear the whole story about him and his daughter's mother.

"And when she refused, her mother beat her ass outside in broad daylight and told her not to return until she had some money. I had never witnessed a mother be so harsh toward her daughter. My heart went out to the girl. I couldn't let her just be succumbed to the streets, so I offered her a place to stay. She accepted. We were together for about a year until she stole money from me. I was gon' kill her, but she was pregnant with my seed, so I let it slide."

"What made her do something like that to you, Al?" I asked, concerned as to what kind of person would take from someone who had done nothing but help them.

"Trinity's mom was lost and still is. She longs for the love of her mother, and to be honest, she would never receive love from her mother, and it took for her to damn near kill her for her to realize that."

"Her mother tried to kill her?" I asked as we pulled in IHOP'S parking lot.

"Yeah, she stabbed her in her back when she walked in on her fucking her boyfriend."

"Hold up. Hold up. So your baby mother was fucking her mom's boyfriend?" I had to make sure I had this right.

"Yeah, but that ain't shit. That's how they get down. Her mother had her doing all kinds of foul shit. I can honestly say she tricked me. I thought so much of her, but she was made up, you know, not being herself. I thought, if I would be what she needed me to be, then I would get the same thing out of her."

Al had a defeated look on his face, and my heart went out to him.

"I hate that, that happened to you, Al. You really are a good dude," I stated, meaning every word of it. "So where do they live at?"

"Her mom in the penitentiary. Trinity and her mom live in a house off of Main Street in Dayton."

Al didn't let me know that the house Trinity's mom lived in, he bought her. Though he despised her mother, he just couldn't let Trinity grow up in the projects or not having anywhere to go. He made it his business to purchase a home for her; and he made sure she had lights, water, and food by paying all the expenses in the home. In a way, he wanted to make her mom suffer, but the love he had for his daughter wouldn't allow him to.

We walked in IHOP, and I could taste the pecan pancakes that I was about to order, along with some cheese, eggs, and sausage. Al ordered himself steak and eggs. We sampled each other's food. Al liked my pancakes just as much as I did.

He continued to say, "Let me get one more."

He damn near ate all of my pancakes.

"I enjoyed breakfast with you, Al."

I could tell that Al was still thinking about our previous conversation. I tried my best to take his mind off of what had taken place in his life.

I understand memories and the effect it has on you once they are brought to surface. Whether good or bad, you have no choice but to dwell on them. That's why I don't acknowledge my past memories. I've buried them somewhere in the back of my mind. And the pain that memories cause is what keeps me from discussing my past.

When the waiter left the bill, I picked it up to see the how much it was. I then pulled out three twenties. I didn't know if Al had the money to pay for the bill, but what I did know was that I didn't mind paying the tab.

Al liked the fact that I felt like I had to take the initiative to pay for the tab. Most women wouldn't, he thought, or if they did, they would complain about it. So now he waited for the complaints when we walked out the door. Without Al hearing one single complaint, he knew I was different.

"I want to show you something," Al stated.

"Like?" I questioned.

"Get on Interstate 75, south."

Al gave me directions to a beautiful home. I didn't know whose house it was, but it was nice—white house with a white picket fence, the kind I used to dream about.

"Whose house is this?" I asked as I parked the car in front of the home.

"Don't worry about that. Just get out," Al commanded.

I followed his orders.

Inside of the house was just as nice, white plush carpet throughout the house. The house was clean, but it needed to be dusted. A poster-sized picture sat on the wall of the living room of a little girl. She was caramel complected with two long pigtails and a birthmark on the side of her cheek. She had chingy eyes like Al's.

This gave me the indication to ask, "Is that Trinity?"

"Yeah, that's her when she turned three, and this is her on her second birthday." Al pointed to a smaller framed picture on his fireplace. "And this is her at age one."

That picture frame sat on top of a glass table.

"She is beautiful. She looks just like you."

I followed Al upstairs. He showed me a room that had to be as big as my whole living room. It had little pink furniture, a sofa and chair, with a plasma on the wall in front of the furniture; and off to the side was a canopy bed, which was also pink, with a pink-and-white quilt over it. There sat a dresser and chest near the bed, which had another plasma-screen TV sitting on it. There were all kinds of toys everywhere—stuffed bears, play ironing board, and kitchenette set.

"Who decorated her room?"

"I did. You needed to ask?"

"Well, I could tell it had your touch. The plasmas kind of gave you away. Only a man would sit two forty-six-inch plasma-screen TVs in one room."

"I stay at my condo when Trinity is with her mother. I just don't like walking past her room, and she's not in there. You know what I mean. It make me think too much."

"So this is your house, Al?" I asked for confirmation.

"Yeah, this is my home away from home. I spend as much time here as I do at my condo."

Well, that explains why the house is so dusty, I thought.

"Oh, and here." Al went into another room and came out with three twenties and handed them to me.

"What's that for?"

"For breakfast."

"You don't owe me that, Al, but you do need to grab Larry's money for this dress and shoes. Oh, and not to mention, this thong I have on."

Al laughed and walked back down the stairs. I followed.

I had a good feeling all over me, the kind of feeling you feel when you play the lottery. Even if the odds are, you have fun! I followed behind Al around his house. It was huge, and it put Chance's house to shame. Al rolled up some weed. We smoked. By the look in Al's eyes, I could tell that he was going to get personal, and he did.

"Where your parents, Agape," he asked.

"You could be my daddy. Neither one of us would know, and Mom was my aunt. Her name was Darlene Lewis. We called her Ma D. She died when I was thirteen. All I have is my sister, and she locked up right now."

"How old is she?"

"Seventeen."

"So you been out here on your own since your aunt died?"

"Nah, me and my sister went to a foster home after my aunt died."

I realized that I had just replaced Stormy with Meaka. I didn't mean to lie, but this was my truth. The thought of Sabrina brought me back to that night. I still could still feel the impact when I slammed the lamp on her head. Al must have read the sorrow plastered on my face.

Silence.

Al

"Agape, you know why I don't ride in the front seat? I…Because the only memory that I have of my mother is me begging her to let me sit up front. She was always weak for me. We were only going around the block to get some candy from the penny candy store, so she let me ride up front against her better judgment. After placing me in the passenger seat, Ma put my seatbelt on, walked over to the driver's side of the car. I can still remember her telling me, 'You better not tell your daddy, Dekalb.' I told her that I wouldn't, but she made me promise, and as if my promise wasn't enough, she made me pinky swear. I did. Her smile was just as big as mine. I always wanted to ride up front, but my dad wouldn't let me. We pull up to a stop sign. We stop. Ma put her foot on the gas while looking at me. 'Dekalb you tell your daddy about…'

"I saw the car coming. Honestly I did, Agape, but I couldn't get the words out of my mouth. Next thing I knew, I woke up in the hospital. I blamed myself for the accident. You know, she might have lived had she had her seat belt on, and since she didn't, her body was ejected from the car, and she was run over by another car traveling in a different direction. That's what killed her. I knew, if she cared enough to put my seat belt on, she would have put her's own on, but instead she had to make sure she drilled me about not telling my father that she let me ride up front. If only I let her put me in the back seat, like she insisted, I would have her here with me, and since then, I never wanted to ride up front."

Silence.

"You okay?" I asked.

"Yeah, I'm good. I just wanted you to know that you are not alone. We all have a...story."

I couldn't fathom the thought of how hard it had to be for Agape and her sister in the foster system. Now she was out here by herself and her sister on lockdown, my heart went out to her. I had a weakness for women. I blamed it on not having a mother around growing up.

"What you think about moving in with me?" I asked Agape.

She laughed. "Surely the weed got you tripping, Dekalb, because, just last night, you didn't want to lie in the same bed as me."

"I had my reasons, but that don't have anything to do with you moving in with me. You don't have to give me an answer right away. How about you stay with me for a month or so, and if you like it, you can move in."

Agape held her head low and informed me that the last nigga she moved in with put his hands on her. She wanted to know if I was capable of doing such a thing. As bad as I wanted to tell her that I would never lay my hands on her, I couldn't. I couldn't deny I was a man, and I know how us men react when we have our emotions involved.

"If I was to ever do such a thing to you, Agape, I would not only be a disgrace as a man. I would also be a disgrace to my mother as well. Moms taught me to never put my hands on a woman. I grew up watching my pops beat on my mom. My moms taught me at a young age that men that have control issues, men with low self-esteem, or men who have witnessed their mother beaten or been around a man that abuses women are prone to repeating the very same cycle. Not wanting me to be apart of the very same cycle, mom would make me feel the pain that a man can inflict on a woman by showing me her bruises instead of hiding them from me. She would make me promise her that I would never put my hands on a woman. I made my moms that promise long ago, and I have yet to break it, but I am my father's son, Agape.

"So your aunt that raised you, was she your mom's sister or your father's?"

"I don't know my father or anyone in his family," Agape stated.

"Was yo' moms on drugs, Agape?"

"What difference would it had made if she was on drugs or not? Would that be an excuse for her not wanting to touch me after she gave birth to me, for not taking me home from the hospital after she gave birth to me? Well, if so, I wish I could tell you that, that the evil bitch was on drugs, but the truth of the matter is my mother just never wanted children. Even after she birthed two daughters, she went on with her life as if she didn't have any."

"But you know, she still is your mother," I stated, trying to get Agape to realize that this was still her mother.

"You know what, Al? A dog is considered a mother, so don't give me that she-still-is-my-mother bullshit. That is the same shit Ma D would tell me when I would beg her to let me call her mom. She would say, 'Agape, I can't let you call me mom. You have a mother.' I never understood how anyone could consider her my mother only under the pretenses that she gave birth to me."

"You right. I apologize. Your aunt did a good job with you, Agape."

I noticed, every time she spoke about her aunt, she had a big smile on her face; and it was as if she was looking at something that I only can see.

"You really loved her, didn't you?"

"I did. She was the only one who was willing to show me and my sister what real love was. She meant so much to me, and I don't understand why she had to leave me, and now I have no one here with me."

"I would love to have a reason to come home, Agape, and with you being here, I would have more than enough reasons to come home instead of being cramped in that condo with Larry and whoever he bring there."

"Whose condo is that anyway?" Agape asked me.

79

As much as I hated to cramp Larry's game, I was on to something here with Agape, so I knew from this point on I had to be upfront and honest.

"The condo is mine. I rent it out when Trinity's home with me. Don't like being up here without her. When my homeboy came home from the feds, he needed a place to lay his head, so I let him stay there. Larry did ten years in the feds behind some shit I did. I will always be in debt to him, so giving him a place to stay, cars, money, and shit like that doesn't compare to that ten years that was taken from his life."

Agape was surprised, and the look on her face told me that.

"I think it would be a good idea to move out here. It's not nothing in Dayton for me for real, but if I do move out here, then I have to let you know that my sister will be getting out of the penitentiary soon, and I need to know you will be cool with her moving in with us, if need be."

"Don't worry about anything like that. As long as your welcome in my home, so is your sister."

"Sounds good," Agape stated. "I'll think about it."

"Well, I'm not sure how long the offer is going to stand. If I was you, I wouldn't keep me waiting long," I teased.

Agape stood up from her seat at the dining room table and walked toward me. She placed a single kiss on my lips.

"What do you want from me, Dekalb?"

As simple as the question was, I saw the complexity of it all in her eyes.

"Agape, I wanna see you happy as long as you are willing to see to it that I am happy. I'm a pretty easy man to satisfy, you know. A li'l cooking and cleaning does it for me."

We both couldn't help but laugh.

"I have to confess. I am a terrific cleaner but a terrible cook."

"Well, we shall see to it that you take up a few cooking lessons from Chef Boyardee himself."

"You saying you know how to cook?" Agape asked.

"Yes, I do. I have a little girl I have to cook for."

"That's cool. I would love to learn how to cook."

Larry and I dropped Lyric and Agape off at Lyric's apartment. I questioned Larry about what he was doing with Lyric. He had to know what time it was with a woman like her, but the more and more I see them together, it seemed as if Larry wishing it was so much more with them.

"What you talking about now, nigga?"

"I'm talking about how come you wasting so much time and money on that money-hungry bitch."

"Man, Lyric cool people."

"Yeah, sure, she is, long as she think you running in those dollars. The minute she get wind that you ain't no hustler and yo' shit don't stank like she thought it did, then what you gon' think about her then?"

"Can you get off of my bitch for a second and talk about that sneaky ass you sniffing behind? I know you would like to think her shit don't stank, nigga, but that bitch with Lyric more than I am. You know what they say. Birds of a feather flock together."

Larry had me on that one. The thought eased in my mind, that Agape just might have been like Trinity's mother, too good to be true. But just as quick as the thought came, it went when I thought about the way Agape reacted to me when I let her know who I really was. She treated me just the same as she did before she found out I wasn't some bum-ass nigga like I led her on to believe. Hell, she was even willing to pay for our meal. More than I could say for Lyric, I was more than sure, if a nigga take her ass somewhere and he ain't paying, that bitch would be willing to have the nigga go to the back and roll up his sleeves before she offer to pay. I knew her type.

"Yeah, whatever, nigga. You know damn well Agape ain't shit like Lyric."

Before I could even finish my sentence, my phone rang. After checking the caller ID, I saw it was Trinity's mom calling.

"Yeah?" I answered in a distracted way.

I could never disguise my disgust toward her no matter how hard I tried, but what I could say was that she hadn't been calling as much as she used to.

She might have found herself a nigga or something, I found myself thinking.

"Dekalb, Trinity is over here, crying for nothing. She keep on crying, talking about today is the day she is supposed to go with you. I keep telling her it's tomorrow, and she don't believe me."

The shit I put up with, I thought to myself.

"Put her on the phone," I said, not even acknowledging shit she just said because I knew how much of a liar she was and nothing she just said sounded too convincing to me.

I could hear her in the background coaching my daughter. "Tell him what I told you to say, T. T."

My nose immediately flared when I heard this, but I could feel my body calm itself down when I heard the angelic sound of my daughter's voice.

"Hi, Dada."

"Hey there, my Trinity. Listen up, all right?"

"I listening, Dada."

"Dada got a lot to take care of today, okay? But I'll come get you early in the morning, okay?"

"Okay, Dada. I love you, Dada."

Trinity knew how to make her daddy happy. She knew how much I loved to hear her tell me she loved me. It made me put up with all the bullshit that came with her mother just to hear those words.

"You know yo' Dada love you too, right?"

"Yes," Trininty said.

"Oh, and Dada got somebody he want you to meet."

Trinity eyes lit up. She loved surprises.

"Who is it, Dada? Is it my grandma Lynn?"

If she only knew how much she stabbed me in my heart, reminding me that my mother would never have the opportunity in this life to meet my firstborn.

"No, baby, not Grandma Lynn. It's a special friend of mine."

"Okay, Dada. I wanna meet yo' friend," Trinity went on to say. "Come get me early in the morning, okay, Dada?"

"Okay. Put yo' momma on the phone."

"Mom, my dada wanna speak to you."

"Hello."

"I'll be there to get her in the morning."

Click.

"Everything good with Trinity?" Larry questioned me as we hopped back on the highway.

"Yeah, she good. I heard that bitch trying to coach my baby into telling me some bullshit. I didn't even give her a chance to replay the bullshit to me. I cut straight to the chase and let her know I'll be there in the morning. Man, I hope my li'l mama don't turn out to be shit like her moms. That's why I gotta find me a good bitch to be a good example for my baby because her moms damn show ain't."

"Let me guess, nigga. You think Red gon' be a good role model for Trinity?" Larry asked.

"Yeah, nigga, you absolutely right. That's what I think."

After handling a couple of business deals, I had Larry drop me off at the condo. I made a few needed call. I had to get Maggie Maids up to my house by six in the morning so the house could be spotless by the time Trinity made it there. I had to call up my boy Emillio. He was the only nigga I knew to beat the drug game. He came out with over four million dollars. Now he's a chef in his own restaurant called Stallions. I had to have him come over and teach my soon-to-be woman how to cook. When everything was in place, I had to make sure that everything was cool on Agape's end. I gave her a ring. She picked up on the first ring.

"Hello?"

"What's up with you?" I asked.

"I'm lying down on the bed, bored."

"What you doing, bored?"

"It ain't nothing down here to do but the same ole' shit. I went to the mall with Lyric and spent up all of my birthday money. Now I'm lying here broke without a clue."

She laughed, and I just listened. I liked how she laughed so open and free.

"Why you ain't call and let a nigga know you needed some bread?"

"I'm good."

"You coming up here tomorrow and spend some time with me and Trinity?"

Agape was stuck. She didn't know what to say. Silence. Of course, she wanted to meet my daughter and spend time with us both, but how would Trinity's mom feel? She wasn't ready to cause any tension in the little girl's life.

Just as she was about to decline, I said, "You can't say no because Trinity is expecting to meet you."

"Well, what can I say?" Agape asked.

"Just say yes."

"Yes…"

My smile spread across my face when I lay in bed thinking about the next day. I hoped everything went as planned. As soon as I opened my eyes, I realized the day wasn't going to go as planned. Larry was nowhere to be found. I called his phone over and over again. These were the times I hated this phobia I had about being up front in a car. At times, it felt like a handicap. And I knew this was Trinity on the other line telling me she was ready. Usually I was pulling up to her door when she called on her day to come with me for her six-month stay. I didn't know how she was going to feel when I told her that she had to wait a little longer.

"Hello?" I answered.

"Where you at, Dada? I'm waiting on you in front of the door. I don't see your car, Dada," Trinity rambled on.

"I'ma be there. Give Dada a minute."

"No, Dada, I want you to come now. You told me that you would be here in the morning."

At times like these, Trinity reminded me of her mother. These were the only times that I wanted to discipline my daughter. I didn't want Trinity to grow up and be anything like her mother or her grandmother.

"Watch your mouth and how you speak to your father, Trinity."

Silence.

"You hear me talking to you, Trinity? Is that how you talk to your father?" I questioned her.

"No, Dada. Trinity's sorry."

"You not sorry, baby. Don't ever say that. Dada will be there in a minute, all right?"

"Okay, Dada. Dada, Momma want to speak to you."

I could feel the hairs on my back stand up. I loved my daughter, but I hated her mother.

"Dekalb, what time you coming to get Trinity?"

"What difference do it make? When I get there is when I get there. What, you got a job or an interview to go to or some shit I don't know about?"

I resented the way I felt about my daughter's mother. But she stood for nothing, so she would fall for anything. I didn't respect that aspect of her life.

"Fuck you, Dekalb. Who the fuck—"

Click.

I never wanted my daughter to witness me and her mother arguing. That was why the only time I would cuss her mom out was when Trinity was in my custody. I would make sure she was out of ear distance or sound asleep before I would call her every trifling, dirty bitch I could think of. She, on the other hand, was so scared by all of the shit her mother had done to her she didn't see anything wrong with cussing me out while Trinity listened on. I made damn sure Trinity knew who put a roof over her and her mother's head and who bought the food, clothes, and whatever else that she needed and wanted.

I continued to call Larry's phone, only to have my calls go unanswered. Then it clicked to me. He might have been off with that money-hungry bitch Lyric. I then called Agape. She picked up the phone on the first ring.

"Hello?" Agape answered groggily.

"Agape, I'm sorry to awake you. I need to get your girl's number."

"Whose number?" Agape questioned, hoping she heard me wrong.

"I'm looking for Larry. I think he might be with Lyric."

"Hold on. Let me see if I see the car outside." After peeking out of the blinds, Agape saw the black Hummer sitting outside. "Yeah, he with Lyric. Your hummer outside."

"Agape, can you do me a favor? I promise to make it up to you. I need you to go over there and knock on the door, beat that mutha-fucka down if you have to, and put that nigga on the phone."

"All right, I'm slipping on some pants now. What's up? You okay?"

"I'm good. Late going to pick Trinity up, and she having a fit."

"Aw, is she?" Agape questioned. "I'm walking out of the door right now."

After a few knocks, Lyric came to the door.

"Where Larry at?"

"Larry?" Lyric questioned.

"He in the back. What's up?" Lyric questioned with a puzzled look on her face.

"Here," Agape stated, handing her phone to Lyric. "Al want to speak to him."

"I don't believe this. Who the fuck do y'all think that nigga is. You running over here at the break of dawn talking about he want to speak with my nigga?"

Lyric didn't grab the phone. Instead she started talking shit because she didn't like the way I looked at her. She didn't know how it was that a nigga who didn't have no money could call shots as if he was a boss.

"Tell that nigga, unlike him, Larry fell asleep in some pussy last night. He 'sleep, and he will call him when he get up."

"Lyric said he 'sleep and he will call you when he get up."

"Agape, do you have a car?"

"Yeah."

"Is it tinted on the windows?"

"No, there's no tint on the windows of my car, but I have a truck with tinted windows."

"How much would you charge me to come get me?"

"Where you at?"

"I'm at my condo."

"I'm on my way."

I left Lyric standing there, looking stupid in the middle of her living room floor.

Agape

I knew that Dekalb was pissed when he grabbed the handle on the front door. I guess he realized what he was doing because he went straight for the back door. When he got in the car, he didn't say one word. I took the initiative to drive toward Dayton.

"I need you to stop by Lyric's place."

I didn't know if that was going to be a good idea. "How about we go pick up Trinity first? You already late. You said she live on Main? That's right on our way. Just tell me the address. Your baby momma will never know I'm in the car," I added that to seal the deal because I knew, as a man, he had to prove to me that his baby momma wasn't an issue, which I didn't think she was.

When we hit Main Street, Dekalb let me know what house was Trinity's. He got out, and I took note that he had a key to the house. As quick as he went in was as quick as he went out. I watched as Trinity kissed her mom on the cheek. I tried to see her mother but couldn't.

CHAPTER 4

Stupid Is as Stupid Does

As I sat outside of Marysville, I couldn't imagine what it was like for Meaka to spend two years in a place like this. Meaka told me that, no matter how hard things got, it was my letters that kept her going. She said the visits and money orders from me and Chance helped in the beginning, but my letters meant the most. How could a few pages of paper and ink empower a person so much? I could only hope and pray to never find out. I watched as Meaka walked out of the prison doors, sitting behind tinted window in an all-white Mercedes.

Al wanted me to tell Meaka the Mercedes was a gift from me. Just like him to not want to take any credit. But I declined. I felt like it was only right for Meaka to know that it was from Al. I wanted him to accompany me to pick up Meaka. He insisted that I go alone, stating that he felt like we have a lot of catching up to do and we couldn't do that with him in the car. I didn't fight with him on it. I just hopped in the Benz and pulled off, going seventy down the highway.

Meaka now stood on the curb, searching the parking lot with her eyes. I sat back and smiled. I loved Meaka. A smile spread across my face. As I watched her, I tried desperately to find the right words to say to her, how I could thank her for what she had done for me; and I couldn't think of one. I watched Meaka walk off toward the exit of the parking lot. I immediately pulled the Benz up on the side of her.

"Where you think you going?" I asked as I parked the car.

Meaka let me know there was no need for thank yous from the look in her eyes and by how she embraced me when we hugged.

"Where was you going?" I asked Meaka.

"Girl, look, I was going to start walking. I couldn't stand to be outside of this place a minute longer."

We shared a nervous laugh. Neither one of us knew if it was the proper response for what was said. I ran to the passenger side of the car. Meaka just stood there.

"Come on, Meaka. You driving." I smiled.

It felt like the first day we were able to ride to school together as Meaka closed the driver door. Meaka just sat there, staring out of the windshield. I could tell something was bothering her.

"You okay, Meaka?" I asked as I put my arm around her shoulder.

She just sat very still as tears rolled down her eyes as she just stared off at nothing in particular.

"I'm scared, A," Meaka stated.

"It's gon' be okay, Meaka. I promise you, coming to live with me and Al and—"

"I'm talking about driving, A. I'm scared to drive."

Silence.

"I'll drive," I stated as I tried pulling Meaka toward the passenger side of the car.

"I'll ride in the back, A," Meaka stated somberly.

Not you too, I thought.

Meaka didn't know why she reacted that way about driving. She loved to drive, but she couldn't deny the paranoia she felt being behind the wheel of the car.

"You okay?" I asked Meaka as I pulled on the highway, careful to go the speed limit and not a notch faster.

"Yeah, I'm good," Meaka lied.

In all reality, it didn't sit well with her how scared she was to drive, to hop in that driver seat, and to take off in this M-series Mercedes-Benz. She remembered seeing an M-series Mercedes in a magazine I had sent her to Marysville. Meaka had bragged to her bunky that, if she ever had the opportunity to get behind the wheel of one of the cars, then she would push it to the max. But instead she couldn't even attempt to put it in drive.

I called Al as we pulled up to the house. He came out to greet Meaka.

"How you doing?" Al asked as he locked eyes with Meaka.

He was taken aback by how pretty Meaka was. Her navy-blue prison jumpsuit and two braids that were braided to the back didn't disguise how beautiful she was. He was mesmerized by her cold blue eyes. He thought she looked like something out of the magazine.

Meaka took notice at the lust in Al's eyes. Locked up with women who were doing life in prison without the possibility of parole for two years, Meaka knew that look all too well. She ignored it and answered the question at hand.

"I'm good. Happy to be home."

"That's good because home is where you need to be. We gon' make sure you stay out of trouble." Al grabbed on to my hand after almost forgetting I was standing there, captivated by Meaka's presence.

Meaka didn't know how to respond. *Surely he couldn't know what I was in jail for because, if he had known, he would've known that I didn't do anything wrong, but why wouldn't Agape let him know that I was innocent instead of making me appear to be troubled?* Meaka thought.

The blank expression Meaka had on her face let Al know that Meaka's incarceration might have been more than what appeared on the surface. Al never asked me what Meaka was in jail for. He always thought, when the right time presented itself, I would disclose that information. But what he did know was that I was loyal to Meaka throughout her bid, so what she was in jail for really didn't matter to him. He automatically assumed that she might have done something petty in a nigga's eyes but punishable by law. It was now obvious to Al that he may have been wrong. And since he might had been, Al thought it was foolish of him to go against his better judgement when he didn't inquire about what Meaka was locked up for or about my life. Al realized that all he knew about me was that my aunt raised me and my sister. We were sent to a foster home, and now that sister stood before him, he almost wished that I wasn't. Not that he loved me any less, he would be stupid to act on such an impulse, especially with me being the best woman he had had as of yet. I showed him how to love again, but you know how the saying goes—stupid is as stupid does.

Meaka

I just wanted to run when I saw that look in Al's eyes. He looked like he wanted to fuck me right there while Agape stood there. I just hoped Agape didn't notice. I could be wrong, but I had never been before. Every time I saw this particular look in someone's eyes, it always reminded me of how my foster mom, Sabrina, used to look at me before she started making advances at me and threatening to send me back to Shawny Acres if I didn't allow her to have her way with me. Reluctantly I agreed, only because I made Agape a promise that I wouldn't do anything to get sent away from our home. I meant that, and I guess Sabrina knew I did too. Unknown to us, Sabrina had been eavesdropping on us outside of Agape's bedroom when we made the pact. Sabrina told me about it after I began to allow her in my bedroom in the middle of the night.

The women in Marysville had the same look in their eyes, and just whenever I would ignore it and push it off as a friendly gesture, they would begin to tell me how pretty I was. It always resulted in a fistfight because, when it boiled down to it, they wanted more than my friendship; and at the time, I gave off the wrong impression to some of the inmates by helping them with items they may not have had, whether it be clothes, food, stamps, paper, or envelopes—whatever I had. I was willing to give a hand to someone that was also in need. I knew what it felt like to be alone. I wouldn't place that burden on my worst enemy. If I could help, I was willing, but this was taken as a weakness for some and a sign of a lesbian for others. Neither being correct, I found myself practically fighting to basically keep them off of me.

I felt relieved when Agape stated, "Come on, Meaka. I want to show you your room and get you out of this jumpsuit."

I myself was ready to change into anything. I didn't care what it was as long as it wasn't blue. I told myself that, when I got out, I would never where the color blue again! Agape hooked me up with a closet full of clothes and shoes.

I took a two-hour bath. I had to keep adjusting the water by running hot water in the tub whenever the water got cold. It had been so long since I took a bath I didn't want to get out. I dipped my head underwater, wetting my hair and all. I didn't care. I just knew that the water felt so good.

When I heard the knock on the door, I prayed Agape didn't leave the house and that was not Al at the door.

"Who is it?" I asked.

"Who else, Meaka?" Agape questioned. "I was just making sure you ain't drowned," Agape went on to state.

"Funny," I stated. "I'm about to get out."

In all reality, I would have stayed in had it not been for her coming to the door. I immediately dried off and slipped into my clothes. With the weather getting cooler outside, I chose to wear a pair of True Religion jeans with a gray True Religion T-shirt and a pair of all-white Air Force 1s. I loved the way the jeans hugged my thighs and butt. I stepped out of the bathroom. Agape called me from her and Al's room.

I was impressed to see that Agape still had all of our pictures that we took when we were at Sabrina's. We went through the bag of pictures, laughing at how we had captured so many memories with a flash of a camera. It felt good to be home. Two years behind bars was a lot of time, but as of right now, it felt like yesterday to me when Agape rode to Bluecrest Street with Miss Eli.

I asked Agape, "What's been up with Miss Eli?"

"I think she still work at Shawny Acres," Agape stated nonchalantly as she passed pictures to me.

"What you mean you think? I thought you kept your apartment with the Independent Living Program."

"I did, but Miss Eli is not a caseworker anymore, so I don't see her. As a matter of fact, I think I heard something about she resigned."

Silence.

I wondered if Miss Eli felt guilty for sending me with Agape that day instead of making her go alone. I hoped she didn't because, no matter the consequences of her decision, I was happy with the outcome of things. Agape and I were back together, and nothing was ever going to separate us again. She was the sister that I never had. I wouldn't have changed things even if I could. I could feel a sadness come over me that I was not ready to face, so I shook it off.

"You all right?" Agape asked.

I smiled, trying to cover up the sadness that so desperately wanted to escape.

"Yeah, I'm fine," I lied.

But in all reality, I was taken back to all the nights Sabrina made me do explicit sexual things with her and different men. I always prayed for the day it would stop, but instead her request just became more and more explicit.

"I'm about to take a walk," I stated the quickest thing that came to mind because I could feel the tears of my true feelings ready to pour down.

I knew that the tears were going to fall, and the one place I didn't want them to fall was right there in front of Agape. I'd cried almost every night of my life as a little girl. I cried for the day my mom would come back, then when I was in Shawny Acres, I cried for the death of my grandmother. I cried for someone to love me, for someone to care. Then there was the night Sabrina first had her way with me and the countless nights thereafter, even nights of praying for the strength to kill myself. I cried from those thoughts as well.

I immediately left the room, heading for the staircase with tears in my eyes. I felt victorious to had not broken down right there in front of Agape. I grabbed for the doorknob, but the door flew back. Al was on the other side. I locked eyes with him, and there went that look in his eyes again. I hated the way he looked at me, as if I was Agape or an orangesicle in the summertime.

"You okay?" Al asked, concerned.

"I'm okay. I'm going to go take a walk."

"A walk?" Al asked, puzzled. "Well, how about I walk with you? I would hate for you to get lost," Al stated jokingly.

We shared a laugh, and that look went away and was replaced with a look of genuine concern.

"That's cool," I stated as I walked out of the door.

What was I going to say? I mean, it was his house that I would be staying in, and I wasn't trying to be on his bad side.

"So tell me, Meaka. What is it that you like doing?"

"Well, since I been away, I spent a lot of time reading and writing. I was young when I got sent to juvenile, then from juvenile I was sent to prison. So I never got the chance to go out and experience any type of recreational activities. I'm sure Agape told you how mean our foster mom was, so you could just about imagine all the shit we missed out on."

The puzzled look on Al's face told me that Agape hadn't told him about our foster mom. I just hoped that she told him that we lived in a foster home because, if not, I done opened up a can of worms, I think.

"Honestly, Meaka, Agape doesn't like to talk to me about her past, and I don't force her to. It will come a time she let me know about her past."

Silence.

We walked in silence for a couple of blocks.

Then Al asked, "If you don't mind me asking, what were you locked up for?"

I smiled because I knew it was only a matter of time Al asked me this question. Even though the question was posed toward me and about me, I just didn't feel like I should be the one answering the question.

"My charges were murder, but the judge knocked it down to involuntary manslaughter."

Silence.

Al's phone rang and interrupted the awkwardness in the air between us. When I heard Al say, "I'm walking with Meaka," I knew it had to be Agape. Al went on to let Agape know I was cool and that we were on our way back. We turned around and proceeded to walk in the same direction we came.

"Meaka, I just want you to know that I think you are a wonderful young lady and you are very beautiful. If you need anything—I mean anything—please don't be afraid to ask."

"Thank you, Al."

As innocent as Al tried to make things seem, the look in his eyes said something totally different. I ignored it, and we proceeded to the house. Agape was sitting out on the porch.

"Baby, you going out to eat with us?" Agape asked Al as we walked up.

"Yeah, that's cool with me," Al stated.

"You cool with that, Meaka?" Agape asked.

"Yeah, that's cool. I just wish I had someone with me. I ain't trying to look like the third wheel."

Al knew just the guy to hook me up with, but for some reason, he was hesitant to but decided that he would hook me up with Emillio. He hopped on the phone and set things up for Emillio to meet them at Sake's in an hour. Emillio let Al know that he could meet me and hang out, but he only had an hour to spare because his flight for Miami was at three. That wasn't a problem for Al. He gloated over the fact that Emillio wouldn't have that much time to spend with me. For some reason, he didn't want to see anyone with me since he couldn't have me.

When it came time to leave, I hopped in the back seat and was thrown back when Al hopped in next to me. And what surprised me more was that Agape didn't say anything.

"How come you not sitting up front with, A?" I asked.

"Probably the same reason you not up there," Al responded.

Silence.

"Al don't ride up front, Meaka."

The ride to Sake's was very awkward for me because I had to sit in the back seat with Al and try to act like I didn't notice him stealing peeks at me.

"What's yo' boy name again, Al?" I asked.

"His name is Emillio. We gon' grab something to eat. Y'all can get to know each other, and whatever happens happen."

I didn't exactly know what Al was insinuating, so I asked, "What does that mean?"

"Loosen up, Meaka," Al stated. "Emillio is a good dude. If he wasn't, I wouldn't even set you up with him."

I guess he sensed the tension that I felt.

Outside of the restaurant, I took note that Sake's was a Japanese hibachi.

I hope that I can read the menu, I thought to myself. *If not, I'll have Agape order for me.*

The restaurant had a lot of customers. Good thing Agape had made reservations. Otherwise, we would have been waiting to be seated, along with the other people seated alongside the entrance. The tables faced a flat grill. The table across from us had already ordered the food, and the chef stood in front of them and cooked their food while putting on a fire show.

I think I'm going to like this place, I thought as I looked on with excitement.

I caught myself looking at every guy that entered the room, trying to see if I could guess who Emillio was. Never in a million years would I have thought that this dark-complected guy with braids was Emillio. Soon as he entered the door, Agape gave me a light bump with her elbow and let me know that he was Emillio. I was shocked, and it wasn't that the brother didn't look good. I just didn't peg for him to be Black with a name like Emillio. If you could have seen how many Mexicans I would have sworn was Emillio. But not one time did I suspect any Black men. I found that hilarious. Talk about not judging a book by its cover. Emillio greeted Al first, then Agape, who sat next to me. Then when it came time for him to greet me, he pulled my chair from the table, gesturing for me to get up. He introduced himself to me and kissed my hand. To say that he was a gentleman would be saying the least as he slid me back to the table, just as I was before. I couldn't quite tell Emillio's nationality. I knew that he couldn't be all Black by the grade of his hair. He had a curly, thick texture, and his braids hung down the middle of his back.

To my amazement, I was able to read the menu. Of course, there were a few words I couldn't pronounce. Even if someone offered to pay me to, I wouldn't be able to. I didn't have to worry about that because they had my favorite shrimp and rice. After everyone placed their order, Emillio slid his chair closer to me. I locked eyes with Emillio.

He whispered in my ear, "Tameka, I think you are truly beautiful."

I couldn't help but smile. "Thank you," I replied, "and you don't look too bad yourself."

We shared a laugh. He and I both knew that I was down playing how I really felt because, hands down, I thought he might have been one of the finest men in Dayton, Ohio.

"So where you from, Meaka?" Emillio asked.

"I'm from here," I stated, puzzled. I went on to ask him, "Why you ask me that?"

"I mean, you are so beautiful, baby, you look like you could be from the islands."

"Now you playing," I stated. "What is so beautiful about me?" I couldn't help but add.

"Look at you. That skin, smooth black skin that's beautiful, and those eyes are like the icing on the cake. They are even more beautiful. I bet you got a lot of niggas wrapped around your pretty little finger."

I blushed, and then I blushed some more. I'd always received compliments on how pretty I was, but no one had ever taken the time to explain just what they thought was so attractive about me. Emillio had done just that without even knowing the magnitude of his answer.

"How old are you, Tameka?"

"I'm eighteen."

Emillio knew I was young, and truth be told, he didn't really care how old I was. He wanted me, so he was going to have me.

"And how old are you?" I asked.

"I'm twenty-eight, baby," Emillio stated.

"How is it that you are my man's girl's sister and, as long as they been together, I haven't met you?"

I felt beads of sweat form on my forehead. I didn't know how to tell him that the reason he hadn't met me was because I was in prison. Then out of nowhere, the chef came to the table and prepared our food right there in front of us. That was close. After the chef served our food, Emillio slid his chair back in front of our plate. No one said another word other than complimenting how good the food was because it was good. I noticed Emillio kept checking his watch as if he was not trying to be late. I took that as a form of boredom. I didn't know what to say to him, so I started conversing with Agape.

"You think I can stay at your apartment tonight?"

I didn't even know why I just asked her that. It was the only thing I could think of to keep from dealing with the fact that Emillio, all of a sudden, lost interest in me. For what, I didn't know.

"Why? You wanna go over there?" Agape asked. "I thought you were going to stay with me and Al," Agape stated disappointedly.

"I just think you and Al need y'all privacy."

I needed some type of distraction from what was taking place.

The way Emillio placed his napkin in his plate just after he slurped up the rest of his pop, I could tell he was about to leave. I was floored. It felt like we just got here, and here he was leaving. I wasn't ready to go, so that meant I'd be stuck here as the third wheel just like I didn't want to do in the first place. Then his phone rang.

"I'm headed that way now" was all he said before hanging up the phone. He turned to me and said, "It was a pleasure meeting you, Tameka," and kissed my hand.

He then said bye to Agape, and Al excused himself from the table and walked out with Emillio.

"So what do you think about Emillio?" Agape asked.

"He seem like a nice dude," I stated, not wanting to get into how dismissed I felt at the moment, so I just downplayed it with that.

"I think y'all would look good together. Emillio really is a good dude," Agape stated.

"What do you know about him, Agape?" I asked.

"Not much other than, every time I have been around him, he's always respectful. I know for sure he is a very busy man. He travels a lot, um, um..." Agape strained to think of what else she knew about Emillio. "Oh, yeah, and his money longer than W. Second Street."

We both laughed. I eased up, thinking that maybe he had something important to take care of, but couldn't he put that on hold? He was only here for thirty minutes, tops. I couldn't help but still think his departure was very rude, and if ever given the opportunity, I would make sure I let him know that.

After dropping Al off at his condo in Cincinnati, we headed back to Dayton so Agape could show me her apartment. I liked it a lot. It was a nice one-bedroom apartment, very spacious and clean. Agape let me know that she still came out to the apartment every week to clean. I was then reminded about how much we used to clean Sabrina's house. It gave us both some sort of obsessive disorder when it came to cleaning up. I used to clean my cell every day. My cellmate would often tell me that we had the cleanest cell in the whole prison. I would clean the walls and sweep and mop the floors with a T-shirt. I didn't care. I just couldn't stand to see anything dirty. Agape took me over to her friend's that I had heard so much about— Lyric's house. After Agape knocked a few times, she came to the door and welcomed us in. There was a guy sitting on the sofa. I could feel his eyes all over me, and I had to look to make sure I wasn't tripping. I was right. When I gazed in his direction, I saw his eyes glued on me like I was a lighter to his cigarette. I rolled my eyes and said hello to Lyric as Agape introduced us to each other.

"So what's jumping tonight? We going out?" Lyric stated excitedly about me being home. "I'm telling you, Meaka. We gon' have a ball tonight," Lyric continued to say.

I was ready to explore what the night was going to be like out in a club since I had never been to one before. Lyric seemed like a cool person. She asked me if I had anything to wear because she had a couple of small dresses with tags still on them I could wear if I wanted to. She was cool. I could see why Agape took a liking to her. I appreciated that Lyric but A hooked me up with a nice wardrobe. I was sure I had something to wear tonight. We said our goodbyes and let Lyric know that we would be back around eleven.

"So be ready," Agape jokingly demanded.

"Have you seen Stormy?" I asked, beating around the bush.

"Nope," Agape answered.

Just as always, anytime it came time for Agape to talk about her sister or her mother, she would show no emotion nor interest in the conversation. I never pried, but now I had to. I had to let Agape know that the woman I once told her I thought was her mother really was her mother. I didn't know how Agape would react to Peaches trying to kill Stormy or if she would even care. I just felt like she needed to know.

"What's up, Meaka? You got that look in your eye."

I tried to play it off with a light laugh. "What are you talking about?" I went on to ask.

"You know exactly what look I'm talking about," Agape stated.

"I'm sorry. I don't." I tried my hardest to make light of the situation.

"Meaka, I know when you keeping something from me," Agape stated playfully.

"You remember that time I told you that I think that your mom might be locked up with me?"

"I remember you telling me that you thought Peaches was locked up with you. As far as my mom go, she died years ago."

I found this out when we were at rec together. Rec was when you had the opportunity to leave out of your cell, work out, and go outside. Not that there were many things we could do, but you had the opportunity to interact with other people other than the bunky you are assigned. I went outside to the yard. That was when I saw Peaches. I knew her only by name and her charges. I never saw any pictures of Peaches, and she never visited Agape when we were at Sabrina's. Therefore, I didn't know what she looked like. All I knew her name was Peaches. I wanted to ignore that matter, but something told me that this was Agape's mother. She was charged with attempted murder on her daughter, so if this was her mother, then I was sure she needed Agape right now.

I walked over to the lady named Peaches. I didn't start a conversation up with her quickly just because, at times, your intentions could be misinterpreted. Not wanting to appear interested in her in a gay kind of way, I waited for my opportunity to spark up a conversation. But I didn't need to. As soon as she looked me in my eyes, she walked over to me and asked me where I was from. I let her know that I was from Dayton, Ohio. She went on to ask me if I knew who Meagan Grise was. Silence. Just when I thought I was going to do all the questioning, she turned the tables on me.

"No, I don't know anyone by that name," I lied.

I don't know why, but when someone asked me if I knew her, my answer was always the same: "Yeah, my mother's name is Meagan Grise." But in all actuality, I didn't know who she was. I never saw her, and I didn't know nothing about her. So in a way, I didn't.

"Girl, when I tell you, you look just like this girl I used to be cool with back in the day. I mean, y'all look alike down to the T. I thought she might have been your mother or something. Y'all look so much alike. You look like you could be about her daughter's age. I remember because we were pregnant at the same time. I had my first daughter before she had her daughter."

This was going to be easier than I thought.

"How many kids do you have?" I asked her.

"I have two daughters, and I cannot stand the ground. Neither one of them bitches walk across," Peaches stated in a joking but serious tone.

"Surely you're joking, right?" I questioned, hoping she was.

"What's your name, baby?" Peaches asked me.

"Meaka."

"Meaka, do you have children of your own?"

"No."

"Okay, then you will never know where I'm coming from, so I'm going to speak for myself. When I had my first daughter, the doctors pulled her out of me. She didn't cry. She didn't holler or scream, which is unusual for a child just being born. You have to understand that this baby is being taken from a place where it's been nurtured. So by nature, the baby cries because it can't understand the distress that it's being placed under. But not my firstborn," Peaches went on to say. "That bitch didn't cry or nothing. The doctors thought she was dead until they checked her pulse. The doctor told me the only babies he ever delivered that didn't cry, they all were stillborn, dead. I wished that I had been that lucky," Peaches said to me with no remorse.

"You wish that your daughter had died?" I questioned, hoping that I didn't hear her right, but in my heart, I knew I had. If looks could kill, I would have had yellow tape surrounding my body.

"Yes, I do wish she had died," Peaches boldly stated to me.

I asked why, not even knowing if there was an answer as to why a mother would wish death on her child. I just had to ask.

"So I wouldn't have to abandon her the way that I did. I didn't name her on her birth certificate. It just states Baby Lewis."

I instantly tensed up when I heard Lewis. That was Agape's last name.

"What did your sister name her?"

"My firstborn name is Agape. She told me she named her that because it meant love. My other daughter name is Stormy."

By the time the name Stormy left her mouth, I felt as if I was standing there facing the woman who birthed and left me. Peaches just stood there, and I myself felt nauseous. Peaches must have felt the conviction I had in my eyes.

"Meaka, I'm not shit, and I'm not going to ever be shit. My mother instilled that in me a long time ago. She put me out of her house at the age of twelve to fend for myself because she didn't want to believe me when I told her that her husband had been coming in my room at night molesting me. She swore up and down I was jealous of her and I just wanted her man. He told me she wouldn't believe. He told me she would take his side," Peaches said as if she was that twelve-year-old girl again. "Momma turned a blind eye to her man coming in my room at night fucking me and eating my young pussy. It wasn't until she found out I got my period she put me out on the streets, telling me she only had room for one bloody pussy in her house. I never had the chance to tell her that I was pregnant.

"I hid the baby from everyone, but my friend Meagan, Meagan never judged me, and she believed me when I told her that my momma's husband had been fucking me. Her mother moved me in their place. When her mom found out that I was pregnant, she told me that I had to go back home. Miss Marilyn told me that she didn't want to be held responsible for nobody's kids coming up pregnant. I understood where she was coming from. I didn't want her to know what had been happening to me because I didn't want her to think I wasn't shit like momma did. So I left. I left Mrs. Grise's house and went to the streets. I stayed from house to house.

"It was so hard for me during my pregnancy. I hated the seed that grew inside of me. I didn't want the baby, and I tried everything, from starting fights with the neighborhood girls and boys to drinking bleach, pushing my body down the steps face forward. I did everything you could imagine to get rid of that baby. As soon as my mom got word that I was in the hospital having a baby, she called out to the hospital and told me she left Harry. She wanted me to come back home. When it came time for me to push her out, when she didn't cry, I felt relieved because I thought she was dead. But when the doctor told me she weighed 6.3 ounces, I knew she didn't die, and I couldn't take one look at her, too afraid that she might look like him."

I watched as Peaches looked off in the thinness of the air. I couldn't see what she was staring off at, but I could see the tears form in her eyes. Something inside of me, I felt sorry for Peaches and Agape the same because she never knew why her mother left her the way she had.

"Can I ask you a question?" I went on to ask Peaches.

"Yeah."

"Why do you dislike your other daughter?"

After a deep breath, Peaches stated, "What can I say? Momma let Harry come back."

"I just think it would be good if you look for Stormy. I mean, she might need you, A. I mean, she is your sister."

"How I see it, Meaka, you are my sister. When I needed Stormy, where was she at, huh?"

Silence.

"Right. She was nowhere to be found, off somewhere enjoying her life with her mother. That is all she was concerned with. So she is no concern of mine, flat out."

I understood what Agape was saying, so I left it alone.

"So where we headed?" I went on to ask Agape.

"We gon' go to the Cincinnati Bell store to get you a cell phone, and then we gon' head back to the house so that we can get ready for our night."

I had butterflies in my stomach. I was anticipating our night out. I couldn't wait to see what the club scene was like.

I went to get some rest before our night out. I went to my room, and in walked Agape just as I lay my head on the pillow.

"Do you mind if I give Emillio your number?"

"No, I don't mind. I think Emillio is cool. Honestly I didn't think he was interested in me, the way he left the restaurant."

"Girl, trust me. It had to be a reason he left. He might had some business to attend to. I don't know. But he would have been a fool not to be interested in you."

I appreciated Agape's compliment. I wasn't sure why. When I looked in the mirror, I didn't see what others saw in me. After Sabrina's, I didn't like the reflection that looked back at me. I grew to hate the way I looked despite what others thought. No sooner than Agape left the room, my phone started ringing.

"Hello?"

"Tameka?"

"Who is this?" I asked, knowing good and well who was on the other line.

"Who do you want it to be?" he jokingly asked.

"Ed McMahon with a whole lot of money."

"Well, this ain't Ed, and I got enough of money. Will that do?"

"Depends," I carried on.

Emillio laughed.

I listened for his comeback, and when he didn't give one, "Hello?" I said into the phone.

"I'm waiting on my answer."

"How you doing, Miss Tameka?"

"I'm cool, lying in the bed, trying to catch some rest," I said, blowing him off just the way I felt he had done me at Sake's.

"Am I interrupting you?" he asked innocently.

"Well, I can't get any rest with you on the phone."

I wanted him to know that I was upset with him. I also wanted to know how he reacted under pressure.

"All right, Tameka, I'ma let you get some rest. You got my number. I want you to use it whenever it's convenient for you."

"Why should I call you after the way you dissed me earlier?" I teased.

"Dissed you, Tameka? Never. Why would I want to diss someone as beautiful as you?"

"I don't know. You tell me."

"I didn't do anything like that."

"You left me."

"Baby, listen. I want to apologize for that, but I had prior engagements when Al gave me the call to come out and meet you. I let him know that, and I'll apologize again if you were not aware of that. I should have made sure you were. You know what they say about assuming. I had a flight at three thirty. I left you at three. I almost missed my flight."

"Where are you now?" I asked.

"In Miami."

Silence.

I felt like a ton of bricks had been thrown on top of me. I thought I was going to have the opportunity to see him tonight. My chances of that were slim to none, him being in Miami.

Emillio broke the silence. "Have you ever been to Miami?"

"To be honest with you, Emillio, I never been out the city of Dayton."

"I plan on being out here for a week. I can arrange for you to. Come down here if you'd like."

There was a smile came across my face. "Surely. I wanted to go to Miami."

Missy and Marisole were Latino twins from Florida I was locked up with. They would constantly talk about how beautiful it was there, how the sun was always shining, and how beautiful the water was. I wanted to see for myself if the water was as beautiful as they said it was. I couldn't see how water could be considered beautiful unless you were stranded in the desert.

"Are you serious?" I asked, maybe a little too excited.

"I would love if you could come down here. I really want to get to know you, and you know me, so you can decide if I am the type of nigga you want to be with."

Inviting me to Miami without even knowing me? Oh, I can tell you are the type of nigga I want to be with, I thought, but "Okay, that sounds good to me" came out of my mouth. "Is this your number?"

"Yep. You gon' call me when you ready?"

"Yeah, I'll call you," I said, smiling from ear to ear as the words rolled off of my tongue.

Emillio heard the excitement in my voice. He could hear me smile through the phone. He found that it was contagious. He himself smiled. He knew he had made the right decision inviting me out to Florida.

I lay there thinking what I did to make him want to invite me out to Florida. I didn't know what it was, but I was happy I did it. I didn't want to get any rest now. I hopped out of the bed, anxious to let Agape know about my invitation.

"Agape," I called out from my doorway.

"I'm downstairs, Meaka."

I took a seat on the sofa next to Agape. Al sat on the love seat across from us.

"Guess what?" I didn't give Agape a chance to guess anything. "Emillio just invited me to Florida."

"Oh, I'm happy for you, boo."

Agape could see the excitement in my eyes. She felt like I deserved a vacation. She knew that Emillio would make sure I was safe, so she gave her blessings.

"When you gon' leave?"

"I was thinking tomorrow."

I couldn't help but notice the disappointed look on Al's face even as he tried to hide it, but he said nothing, staring blankly at the television.

"You gon' be okay on the plane by yourself?" Agape asked.

"Plane…Oh, nah, I didn't even think about that. I'm not getting on no plane," I stated.

"Well, how else are you gon' get there? That's like an eighteen-hour drive."

Now I was the one who wore the disappointment across my face. I had never flew on a plane a day in my life.

"Girl, it will be over before you know it. I'm not going to go. I'll just tell him I'll see him when he get back. I ain't getting on no plane," I stated adamantly.

"What if I went with you?"

I blushed. "Would you?"

"Al, can we go to Florida?" Agape repeated what I just said to her as if he wasn't just sitting here when I told her about my invitation.

Al said he had no problems with it. We were geeked. We both ran upstairs, yelling like the house was on fire.

Agape showed me several different bathing suits with tags still attached. I liked them all, but neither one of them I wanted to wear. But beggars can't be choosers, so I chose a yellow one-piece with the sides cut out. Agape eyed me when I went through the swimsuits. Being in prison gives you a sixth sense. You can always feel when a person is looking, staring, or contemplating against you. I acted like I didn't notice.

"You don't like these, do you?" Agape stated, reading me like a book.

"They cute," I lied.

"Well, how is it that it's over fifty bathing suits and you choose one?"

She had a good point.

"We can just go shopping for bathing suits when we get there."

The club was packed. I, Agape, and Lyric were the center of attention. Every nigga that walked past wanted ours. Agape let them know she had a man. Since I and Lyric were single, we collected numbers, but never at one time did we give ours out. Lyric taught me that during her Club 101.

"Now, Meaka, don't give yo' number to these niggas. Get theirs," she told me as we walked in the club.

I listened and took note to what Lyric said.

"Don't dance up a sweat, and if you feeling a nigga, just keep giving him the fuck-me eyes."

I was drawn back with this one. "What is the fuck-me eyes, Lyric?"

The girl turned around and put a top-model look on, and when we locked eyes, we both busted out laughing. Lyric was cool. We partied all night until they called last call. We stumbled to the car, intoxicated from the endless shots of Patrón we consumed. The parking lot was full of big rims lined up outside of the club. Niggas were trying to holler me, and Lyric walked over to a black Avalanche that was desperately trying to get our attention. Agape continued to walk to her car.

"See, that's why I ain't got no man," Lyric stated. "You can't have no muthafuckin' fun." Lyric almost stumbled over her own feet.

We laughed. The guy from the passenger side of the truck walked around and led Lyric on the other side of the truck. The driver gestured for me to come over to the truck. I complied.

"What's up, Ma? How you doing?"

"I'm good."

"You look like you a little fucked up. You need a ride home?"

"Nah, I'm good. I'm riding with my sister."

"Oh yeah? Well, is you and your sister trying to go get something to eat?"

Me knowing good and well how Agape had been dissing niggas all night, there was no way she would be willing to go out to eat with them.

The passenger yelled over the driver and asked the most ridiculous question, "Aye, baby, is them yo eyes? Excuse me. Is them you girl eyes?" I heard him go on to ask Lyric.

"Nigga, you trying to be funny. When have you ever seen a bitch that black with blue eyes?"

She and the passenger began to laugh amongst themselves.

Driver looked at me to ask, "Are those your eyes?"

I turned my back on them and proceeded to Agape's car.

"We on our way home, baby," Agape stated into the phone.

Soon as she hung up the phone, I let her know what Lyric had said.

"Meaka, come on. Lyric didn't mean any harm. Trust me."

The passenger door opened, and Lyric hopped in. I gave her a slow roll of my eyes, making sure she saw me.

"Oh, bitch, do we have an attitude?" Lyric asked in a drunken state.

Not one to hold my tongue, I said, "Yes, I do. Don't ever call me out like that."

"Hold up, bitch. I know you ain't popping off because of that shit back there with them niggas," Lyric stated, upset.

"Hold up. Hold up, everybody. We done had a goodnight tonight. We not gon' start this shit," Agape stated, looking in the rearview, eyeing Meaka.

"Well, don't look at me. You need to check that sister of yours. She mad a mufucka ask her was them her eyes, and when I let the nigga know basically there was no way in hell that them were her eyes, this bitch get mad."

It wasn't that I had never been called a bitch. Agape and I referred to each other as bitches. It was just something about the tone in Lyric's voice I didn't like, and Agape knew it.

"Lyric, those are Meaka's eyes."

"Oh, so you want me to believe that?"

Secretly Lyric had noticed how every nigga in the club gave me their attention. Niggas had been buying us drinks all night in hope to holler at me. Some of the most paid niggas in Dayton were trying to get at me. And Lyric didn't like it one bit. She didn't like how I downplayed everything, almost as if I wasn't interested in the niggas. Had it not been for the blue contacts Lyric swore I wore, I wouldn't have been receiving so much attention. To hear that they were her eyes, Lyric wasn't trying to hear that because that would mean that I looked better than her.

"Just take me home, Agape," I stated because I was fed up with Lyric's bullshit.

Lyric didn't know me that well, so I spared her from an ass kicking.

Then my phone rang.

After checking the caller ID, I saw that it was Emillio.

Just in time, I thought.

"Hello?"

"Hey, Miss Tameka, what you doing?"

"Just left the club with my sister," I said, not even acknowledging Lyric in the car.

"I know them niggas didn't know how to act when you stepped in there."

We shared a laugh.

"Yeah, right," I stated. "They wasn't paying me know mind," I lied.

"So what time you plan on taking your ass in the house?" Emillio stated playfully.

"I'm on my way home now."

"Do you know when you want to come down?"

"Hold on real quick. A, this Emillio, do you know what day we gon' leave?"

Agape responded, "We gon' leave tomorrow."

"Yo' sister coming out with you?"

"Yeah, I didn't want to fly by myself. She and Al gon' fly with me. Is that cool?" I asked sensing the hesitation in Emillio's voice.

"Yeah, that's cool. You got some bathing suits?" Emillio asked.

"I only have one," I stated in a disappointed tone.

"Leave that one bathing suit at home. When you come down here, I don't want you to bring anything with you."

"Not even my toothbrush?" I asked jokingly.

"Not even your toothbrush."

We shared a laugh.

"Meaka, Im'a let you go. Be careful and take yo' sexy ass in the house. I don't want them niggas looking at what's soon to be mine."

I blushed. "I will. Good night, Emillio."

"Good night, Tameka. Be safe."

"Trust me. I will."

I was delighted to hear Emillio claim me as his. I couldn't wait to fall asleep, to get up, and to leave for Florida.

"Where y'all going?" Lyric asked, interrupting my thoughts.

Agape let her know we were going to Florida.

"Nobody asked me did I want to go to Florida," Lyric whined.

"Emillio invited Meaka. She's afraid to get on the plane alone, so we decided to go with her."

"I want to go," Lyric playfully begged. "Can I go, Meaka? Please, I promise to be good," Lyric stated with a fake puppy-dog face. "Please, and I promise to not mention a thing about your contacts."

We all busted out laughing. I liked Lyric. I couldn't deny that she was a lot like me and Agape.

"Okay, Lyric, you can come," I gave in.

Lyric jumped in the back, hugging me and thanking me. We were excited. We watched Lyric walked in her door, and we headed back to the house.

Agape handed me two small blue football-shaped pills before we stepped in the airport.

"Take these," she stated as she handed them to me.

"What is this?" I asked, looking at the pills in my hand.

"Trust me, Meaka. It will help you relax."

I popped the pills. My nerves were already shot just by watching the planes in the sky from the car. Knowing that I would be on one in a matter of minutes had me nervous. Lyric and Agape had so much luggage it looked like they planned on being in Miami for a few weeks. I myself carried a Louis Vuitton overnight bag even though Emillio said for me not to bring anything. I couldn't help bringing along a clean pair of underwear and a toothbrush along with some toiletries. I felt carefree walking through the airport with my bag. It was amusing to see Agape and Lyric tugging their luggage. Al had to carry his and Agape.

"Damn, Agape, did you have to pack your whole closet?" Al stated in reference to all the suitcases she had.

Then some airport worker pulled up a rack for them to place their luggage on. After going through security, I could feel the effects of the pills Agape gave me take their course. All of a sudden, I felt relaxed. I took my seat on the plane. I was not sure if it was the pills or what, but it didn't seem like we were on a plane. I was seated next to Lyric. Al and Agape were seated behind us. The flight attendant told us to put on our seat belts. We would be taking off soon. She let us know that we might feel the turbulence as the plane moved above the cloud. I lay my head back on the headrest, and that was all I remember.

"Meaka, Meaka." Agape nudged me.

I peeled my eyes open and realized that it was time to exit the plane. Lyric, Agape, Al, and I were the only ones left on the plane.

"Damn, Meaka, we thought you were dead. We been trying to wake you up for the last hour," Lyric stated.

I wiped my eyes trying to pull it together, for some reason or another, it felt like time had stood still. I didn't recall the plane taking off. The last thing I remembered was the flight attendant instructing us to put on our seat belts. My legs were a bit wobbly when I stood up to exit the plane. I pulled it together when I saw Emillio standing in the airport, and if he looked good the first time I saw him, it didn't compare to this time. Emillio had his hair pulled back in a ponytail. His hair was thick and curly. He had on a white-green Gucci shirt with the khaki shorts to match along with the tan Gucci visor and belt. His feet were adorned with some tan Gucci flip-flops. I felt like a child again, trying to find the words to say to this man.

"How you doing, Miss Tameka?" Emillio asked.

"I'm good now that I'm here with you." I smiled.

Emillio took me under his wing as he wrapped his arm around my shoulder.

I introduced him to Lyric. "Emillio, this is our best friend, Lyric."

"Emillio knows Lyric," Agape stated as she walked up and gave Emillio a friendly hug.

He and Al gave each other a dap.

I couldn't wait to see what the sun looked like this far down south. It was beautiful. The sun sat bigger in the sky to me. I guess that was why it got hotter here than in Ohio. The temperature had to be a hundred easy outside, and here I was in a Hollister jogging suit burning up. I decided against my decision to not bring anything. I sat in the back seat of the three-row Cadillac truck that some unknown White guy drove. Emillio gestured for us to get in, and we followed. I still felt somewhat tired. Emillio slid in next to me after he helped Al with Lyric's and Agape's luggage.

"Damn, how long ya'll plan on staying?" Emillio teased Agape and Lyric.

"As long as we need to," Lyric responded. "Y'all better hope I don't come up on one of these Miami niggas. I ain't lying. I ain't coming back."

"Yeah, right."

"Meaka, you see this face?" Lyric asked, putting what she considered her serious face on. "Consider me *left*," Lyric stated, stressing the word *left*.

I and Agape laughed, but it was weird that Al and Emillio didn't find any humor in what she just said.

Emillio took it upon himself to reserve a room for Agape and Al. He also reserved a room for Lyric and I.

"That is, unless you want to share a room with me?" Emillio stated in a joking way.

"I plan on sharing a room with you," I responded, but I wasn't joking.

Emillio handed the keys to Agape and Lyric, and I followed him down the hall to our suite. The suite was humongous. I had never been in a hotel, but I would have never thought they'd look like this. Shit, this one suite was as big as somebody's one-bedroom apartment. Emillio carried my bag in and set it on the bed.

"I thought I told you not to bring anything with you."

"Well, I needed clean underwear," I state, embarrassed.

As he looked through my bag and pulled out a pair of my panties, he went on to taunt me some more. I guess he could feel the embarrassment spread across my face when he sniffed my panties.

"What are you doing, nasty?" I asked. "Don't let me find out that you go around sniffing females' panties."

We shared a laugh.

"You won't." Emillio then looked at the tag inside of my panties and stated, "You a eight?"

"Yup."

"You ready to do some shopping?" Emillio asked.

"What you want me to say? Yeah, I'm ready to do some shopping!" I stated excitedly.

I took my jacket off to my jogging suit and laid it across the bed.

It is too hot for that damn thing, I thought to myself.

As we walked out of the room, Emillio stopped at Al and Agape's room, and I stopped at Lyric's room. She came to the door in a towel.

"We about to go shopping. Do you have any fashion tips for me?" I asked, smiling from ear to ear.

One thing about Lyric was the girl had style, and being the fact I just got out of the penitentiary, I had none. Agape dressed with a nice style, but her wardrobe screamed "I got a man."

"Now this is going to cost you, Meaka. I can't just keep letting you soak up all of this game for free. Now, honey, you know the saying 'The game is to be sold, not told'? That goes for you too, sweetie."

I stood there like a deer in headlights because sometimes you just couldn't tell if Lyric was serious or not.

"Girl, I'm just messing with you. Damn, you always so serious. Lighten up a li'l." Lyric ran down what was hot and what was not to me in a matter of seconds. "And if you really want to see if the nigga's trying to spend some bread, take his ass to the Gucci store or Chanel bitch. All they sell is shoes and bags, and ain't shit in that bitch under a stack."

"It doesn't matter how much he spends, do it?" I questioned, just figuring the invite was enough.

Lyric spoiled that thought. "Yes, it does matter. Who want a cheeseburger when you can have a steak, Meaka?" Lyric questioned.

Well, shit, I don't even like steak. I would have the cheeseburger, I thought.

"Thanks, Lyric. I'm about to say my goodbyes to Agape."

"I'll see you later, and don't you forget about your best friend," Lyric stated sarcastically.

"I won't. I promise."

We laughed, and I headed toward Agape's room. Agape greeted me with a hug. Al and Emillio were seated on the sofa. Agape and I entered the bedroom of the suite.

"So what's up? I hear you and Emillio are about to go shopping."

"I guess, when he finish talking to Al."

"Tameka, you ready, baby?" Emillio called from the other room.

"Here I come," I responded as I eyed Agape. "What?" I asked.

"Nothing. Enjoy yourself, Meaka. You deserve it."

"Thanks."

I don't know why. I just felt the need to give Agape a hug.

"Y'all in here talking about me?" Emillio asked playfully as he entered the room.

"All good things," I stated.

Emillio reached for my hand. I gave it to him. He pulled me up from the bed, and off we went. After the parking attendant handed Emillio's keys to him, I stood there like a deer in headlights. I had forgotten all about my paranoia about being in the front seat, but as soon as I grabbed the handle on the door, it came to me again.

"You okay, baby?" Emillio went on to ask.

"I'm cool. Do you mind if I ride in the back seat?" I asked while looking through the passenger window.

"The back seat," Emillio stated.

Maybe the look in my eyes told the paranoid feeling I felt about riding in the front because Emillio stated, "Nah baby, hop on in the back. I'll be your driver," he kidded. "Where to first?" Emillio questioned.

I heard about a store called Alpine. You ever heard of that?" I asked politely.

"Yeah, I heard of Alpine." Emillio punched the name in his GPS system.

Shopping was so fun with Emillio. He got me everything that I requested. Lyric was right. It did matter how much was being spent. I didn't think we would have had this much fun had there been a budget. I let Emillio pick out my bathing suits. He picked a baby-blue Victoria's Secret two-piece and a leopard string bikini that I didn't think I would have the confidence to put on.

I might have to give that to Lyric, I thought.

We stopped in a hat store called Hat World. They had all kinds of hats, from baseball hats to Kangols. I mean, they had any kind of hat you could think of. Emillio had me pick a few hats out for him. I did. He liked the ones I picked out. He chose a few of his own. I watched in astonishment as he paid a stack on a few hats. Emillio carried all of the bags. I assisted him as he placed them in the trunk. I hopped in the backseat of the car. I was tired. I had to let Emillio know that I was beat in case he wanted to do anymore shopping.

I called out to him over the music, "Emillio."

He turned the music down and responded, "What's up, babe? You good back there?"

"Yeah, I'm good. I'm a li'l tired though."

"You wanna head back to the room?" Emillio questioned.

"Would you be upset if I said yes?"

"Nah, babe. Just let me know what you wanna do. I can't be having you out if you tired," Emillio stated.

"I am." I blushed as he turned around to look at me.

I lay my head down on the seat and was off to sleep. Emillio woke me up just as the valet parker got behind the wheel of the Mustang. He tipped the greeter one hundred dollars for bringing our bags to our room. I wasted no time lying in the bed. I still felt sleepy.

We lay there on top of the covers fully clothed.

Emillio caressed my face. "You know you are beautiful, Tameka."

"You keep telling me that." I laughed.

Emillio didn't. He stared deep in my eyes. I turned my head to the side, afraid that he might have seen the things that I have seen. I was a firm believer in "The eyes never lie." I had no choice but to break his stare. I didn't want him to see all that had happened to me. I didn't want him to be turned off by what he saw. Emillio tried to turn my head toward him. I resisted.

"What's wrong, baby girl?"

Silence.

Emillio didn't press me, and I appreciated that. He kissed me on my forehead and went into the other room. I drifted off to sleep.

Lyric

I woke up from my nap, feeling rejuvenated. I slipped into an indigo-blue halter dress that would turn a few heads.

I don't see how Agape brought her nigga. I would have left his ass in Cincinnati and took the flight out to Miami by my damn self, I thought to myself as I admired my figure in the full-length mirror.

Happy with my appearance, I stepped out of the hotel and headed for Meaka and Emillio's room. Emillio opened the door and invited me in. I swished my ass all the way through the door only because I knew he would be watching. I mean, why wouldn't he? Meaka was nowhere in eyesight, and I didn't have any panties on. I marveled at the thought of Emillio lusting over all of this ass while Meaka lay in the next room.

"Where's Meaka?" I asked innocently.

"She's in the back, 'sleep," Emillio stated.

I couldn't help but notice the Chanel shopping bags lined up against the wall. I wondered what Meaka did to this man. Here he was, bringing us to Miami, putting us up in the Sheraton, and splurging out at Gucci and Chanel on Meaka. Damn, I might have needed to take pointers from Meaka—not!

I went in the room and woke up Meaka, and to my surprise, this bitch slept in them damn contacts.

"Hey, Lyric," Meaka greeted me groggily.

"Hi, Blue Eyes," I joked.

"Ha-ha!" Meaka stated.

"Get up, bitch. What you plan on doing, sleeping the day away? You slept the whole flight, so I know you ain't jet-lagged."

"Okay, okay," Meaka stated, "I'm getting up."

"I see yo' nigga came through like a real nigga suppose to."

"What you talking about now, Lyric?"

117

"I'm talking about all those Gucci and Chanel bags in the front room."

Meaka smiled, remembering her shopping spree with Emillio.

"Look at you, bitch, all in love," I stated after seeing the lust in Meaka's eyes.

"Whatever," Meaka attempted to blow me off.

But I knew what I saw, so I pushed for the truth. Emillio was eye candy, and if she wasn't feeling him, I sure as hell didn't see how. I wouldn't pass up the opportunity to put it on him.

"Girl, you feeling that nigga?" I kidded around, hoping she would deny any emotional attachment toward Emillio so I could use that to my advantage.

I had always had a thing for Emillio, and Agape knew this. But not one time did she ever try to hook me up with Emillio. So what if I used to fuck with Larry? Larry was my trick. He paid me for what I did for him, but after he started snorting coke, the money wasn't even enough to keep me around. The nigga was straight-up crazy.

I met Emillio out one night I was with Agape. He wanted to get at me, but Al put a bug in his ear by saying God knows what. All I know was he never called, and when I called him, I got the voice mail. I didn't care if he had his head up Meaka's ass right now.

Meaka don't know how to handle a nigga like Emillio, I thought.

Emillio walked past the room and peeked his head through the door. "Wake up, Black Beauty," he said to Meaka.

"I'm woke," Meaka stated, still sounding like she just woke up.

I took note that Meaka lay on top of the covers fully clothed. How? Had I been sharing a room with Emillio, I wouldn't have known what clothes were. I would be up in this room prancing in front of him, asshole naked every second of a minute.

"I like that dress," Meaka complimented.

"I got it at the Tri-County Mall."

"Where is that at?"

"You don't know where the Tri-County Mall is?" I asked in astonishment.

"I don't," Meaka responded.

"It's not far from Al's condo."

"Oh, you know what? I think I seen that mall. Do it sit off of the highway?"

"Yeah, that's it."

"I'm about to get dressed. What's up for the night?" Meaka asked.

"You know me. I'm trying to find me a victim."

We laughed, and I left out of the room.

Meaka followed me to the door. "Don't leave without me."

"I won't be all day, Meaka," I demanded.

I was ready to get the day started.

I dreaded going to Agape's room. Al and I didn't quite see eye to eye. I knew he didn't care for me, and really I would have had more respect for him in the beginning had I known he wasn't a broke-ass nigga like he led on to be. But oh well.

I knocked on the door.

Agape greeted me with a smile, "Hey, miss thang, you sho' looking good."

"Don't I always?" I joked.

But that was more than the truth. I was always at my best. I didn't care if I was grocery shopping. I had to look good. My motto was "You never know who's looking"; and where I was from, there was always somebody looking, believe it or not. The way I look was how I advertised myself. I mean, who would want to spend money on a bum? I know I wouldn't.

"You going out tonight?" I asked, noticing the look Al shot Agape from across the room.

"Yeah, I'm going. I'm sure Al and Emillio have plans for tonight," she said, shooting him the look right back.

That was what I liked about Agape. She respected her man's wishes but valued her own as well.

"Meaka across the hall getting dressed now," I informed Agape. "I'm about to take a walk and see what I can see." I winked my eye at Agape.

She smiled. "You are so bad, Lyric," she whispered as she walked me to the door.

"I mean, what am I supposed to do? Y'all bitches all booed up and shit."

"I'll call you when I'm dressed."

The sun was shining bright. I took off walking up the block, shaking everything that my momma gave me. A black Cadillac truck pulled up alongside of me.

"Hey, baby," a guy called from the driver side of the truck.

I kept walking, trying not to appear too desperate.

"Baby in the blue," the driver called out.

I turned to the truck as if he had called out my name.

"Come here," the light-brown-skinned dread head requested.

He wasn't what I would call fine, but I never had a dread head. I twisted my ass over to his truck. My sixth sense was working. I could just smell money.

"What's up Ma? You need a ride?"

"I'm just sightseeing," I stated innocently.

"Well, I'm liking the sight I'm seeing, so why don't you let me show you around?"

I put on a look that made him think I was contemplating on whether or not I was going to go with him when, all along, I knew good and well I was getting up in this truck.

"It's okay, Ma. I ain't gon' hurt you, only if you want me to," he added while we shared a smile.

I grabbed for the door. "Only if you promise me to drop me back off when my sister calls. I'm waiting on them to get dressed back at the hotel."

He promised and pulled off.

"So what's your name?" Dread Head asked.

"Lyric, and yours?"

"My name Rico. How long you in Miami?" Rico asked.

"Until tomorrow," I lied, knowing good and well I would be out here for a week.

But I didn't want to spend my whole week with him. Whatever we were going to do, we had to do it quick because, by the time his money was in my hands, I would be on to my next victim.

I was a lot different than your average female. Most females were taught to believe in the marriage and the children with the picket fence. Me, I wasn't taught that. Instead, my mother taught me how to manipulate any situation. Yolanda Dame taught me how to shake my ass before I was five. She would constantly tell me, "Lyric a woman walks like this." She would show me what her version of walking was, a twist of the hip along with throwing her ass from side to side. My momma had one of the meanest walks. Ever since I was little, I always wanted to have a walk like her a walk that commanded attention. Every time we would walk to the Parkside store, a store across the street from the projects we used to live in, the hustlers would always compliment her. "Shake that thang, Mama," "Look at all that ass," and "Goddamn!" were some of the things they would yell out as we walked past. I never had a daddy, so my momma taught me what she knew about men, which was "Every man will pay a price for pussy and not attention."

By the time I was in middle school, Momma told me that it was time for me to lose my virginity.

She started off by saying, "Now, Lyric, you getting older. It's time for you to let one of these niggas have that virginity of yours."

I looked stunned when Mommy sat me down to tell me that one day after school. Most parents were trying to see to it their daughters were virgins until marriage. Not Yolanda. she thought thirteen years on this earth was well enough time to have your virginity taken. I, on the other hand, was scared to death of having sex. The way Mommy would holler and scream when she was having sex, I thought I would never have sex in my life.

"Mommy, I don't think I'm ready for anything like that. I'm scared" was my response.

"I should have known you would say some shit like that. You're a punk, just like that punk-ass daddy of yours. You know that, Lyric."

I was confused as to why Mommy always felt like I knew these things about my father, being the fact I never even saw my father. The only time she talked about him was when I did something she didn't approve of, then she would mention him like he had been an active father figure in my life.

"You aint shit like yo' mama," she ranted on while I sat there wondering if she was trying to play some sort of trick on me.

I hoped and prayed she was, but she wasn't.

I knew that, when she went on to ask me, "You know why I say you ain't shit like me?" in my mind, I didn't want to respond.

But the words "Why?" escaped my mouth.

"Because when my momma sat me down and had this very same discussion with me, I ain't think twice about what she said. You want to know what my response was?"

For some reason, my mouth obeyed my mind this time because I just sat there staring at this woman whom I had been calling mother for the last thirteen years as if she was a mere stranger to me. Mommy stood over me with a look of pure disgust in her eyes. I lost my virginity that night. I didn't want to question Mommy's authority, so I did what any little girl who didn't want to disappoint her mother would do—I said okay. And as soon as the word left my mouth, I saw a sparkle in her eye, and I felt better now that the disgust she just had was nowhere to be detected.

Mommy wasted no time laying down the law for me when it came to having sex with a man. Yep, a man.

Mommy said, "Rule number one was to never fuck with any nigga under the age of eighteen. They ain't got shit to offer you, Lyric. All you gon' come home with is a wet ass, and ain't no child of mine gon' be out here fucking for nothing. You don't live off of air alone. If the nigga can't buy you what you want, then fuck him too. Number two, never fuck with the same nigga over ninety days. That's all they get, Lyric, a ninety-day trial period. And the last rule but the most important of them all, keep your eye on the prize. If you spot a nigga that got money and you want him, that's all you think about, not if he have a girl, a wife, or kids. That's his business. Keep it as such, so with that said, you better never have no bitches as your friends because, if they nigga got money, he is not off of limits. And that's the game. You better thank God yo' mama ain't no hater. Shit, I just gave you the three hoe commandments."

I lost my virginity that night to some man Mommy brought home. She said that his name was Marcus. He was a nice-looking

Black man. He looked like he could have been my mama's age. He was dressed in a suit and tie. To see this man out on the streets, you would never suspect him to be attracted to young girls. When she opened my bedroom door and he walked in behind her, I knew what time it was, and the only thing I could do was comply.

"Lyric, this is Marcus. I was telling him about you, and he wanted to come meet you," Mama stated with a big smile on her face.

I put on a nervous smile, trying to ease the queasy feeling in my stomach.

"He knows that you are a virgin, and he is more than willing to take it easy on you. I mean, that is, if you want him to," Mommy added.

I was glued to the bed. I didn't want to move. I felt like I was in a movie, and sooner or later, the film would stop. I was hoping it would stop before this Marcus guy got the opportunity to touch me.

"Lyric, let Marcus take a look at you."

I slowly removed the cover from over my body. I stood next to my bed.

"Come over here, girl," Mommy stated. "He can't see you from over there."

I walked over slowly, anxiously, waiting for the film to end.

"Hi, Lyric," Marcus greeted me as if he knew me.

When I didn't take his hand that he held out for me, Mommy asked, "Lyric, is that the way you treat someone that is willing to pay you a thousand dollars for that virginity of yours?"

A tear escaped my eye.

"Come on now, Lyric. Let your big sister help you get ready for Mr. Marcus."

Sister? I thought as I followed Mommy out of the room.

She led me to the restroom. I watched as Mommy turned on the shower.

"Get in the shower."

I followed her orders. When I was under the water, Mommy left out of the bathroom. She came back in with what she wanted me to put on. She handed me a razor along with some shaving cream. Mama taught me how to shave my pussy that night, and the black lace leotard was like wearing nothing at all. Mama sprayed her favorite perfume over me, the same perfume that, up until this moment, she had prohibited me from touching. I felt a sense of pride at that moment. The fear I felt evaporated in the air as the perfume hit my skin.

"Now gon' in yo' room, Lyric."

I searched my mother's eyes with mine. I tried to tell her in so many ways that I didn't want to do this, but she ignored my silent pleas. I walked back in to my bedroom to find Marcus on my bed naked with a penis the size of a horse's. I felt like throwing up. I thought I was going to faint when he motioned me to come toward him. My feet were planted in the floor. I couldn't move.

"You look so good in that lace, baby. Come here. Let Daddy see you. Come model for me," he requested.

A light went on. I dreamed of being a model. That had lightened me up. I modeled straight to him.

"Oh, damn, baby, you look good."

The compliments had me feeling good about myself. I always tried to show Mama my signature runway walk. She would never pay attention, and now this man lay here telling me I looked just like a model. He then grabbed me and pushed me down on the bed. He quickly pushed my leotard to the side, wasting no time placing his face in between my legs. I liked it! I liked how my pussy tingled when he licked on my clitoris. It wasn't until he stood up and pressed his penis up against my tunnel. The reality of what was taking place hit me like a ton of bricks. The pressure was more than I bargained for. I thought he was ripping my vagina apart. I could feel his horse penis going in and out of me. The pain was crucial. It had to be the worst pain my body had ever felt. I screamed out in agony.

Marcus continued to pummel inside of me harder and faster. I thought I was going to die, then after a loud moan, he fell on top of me. I slid my body from underneath his. I needed his scent off of me. I ran to the bathroom naked. I locked the door and proceeded to scrub Marcus's scent off of me with scalding-hot water. No matter how hard I scrubbed, I could still smell him. Tears wouldn't stop rolling down my face. My private area felt like it was swollen. How could

Mama do this to me? How could she let that man come in and fuck me while she sat in the other room? How could she ignore my cries? I could no longer take the hot water that was now freezing cold, so I cut the water off and lay down in the tub. I convinced myself that what took place with me and Marcus was normal. I told myself that this was the way all little girls lose their virginity. I cried myself to sleep.

I was awakened by Mommy banging on the door. "I need to use the restroom, Lyric."

I didn't know how to look at Mommy, so I shifted my eyes away from her even though my body stood right there in front of hers. I was determined not to let her see me cry. I walked out of the restroom and into my bedroom. I noticed there was blood all over my sheets. I had the slightest idea where the blood came from, so I pulled the sheets off of my bed and threw them to the side. When I went to lay down on my bed, I could smell Marcus all over again. I jumped up from the bed and lay down on the floor.

Mommy came in and handed me eight hundred dollars of the one thousand Marcus gave her. "You did good, Lyric. Trust me. It gets easier, and soon you'll start to enjoy it."

I looked at the eight hundred. This had been the most money I ever held at one time, and it was mine. I didn't like the fact that Mommy kept two hundred of my money. She didn't do anything. It was my virginity that was taken. It was then I realized everything had a price. And from that day forward, I made sure any nigga who wanted some of Lyric Dame, they had to see to it that they paid their fare. Mommy became jealous of all the niggas I was fucking and the money they were giving me. She started charging me money to fuck in her house. She started stealing money, clothes, and jewelry from me. The night of my sixteenth birthday, I brought home an older man I met downtown. I did as usual. I introduced Mommy to him as if she was my sister.

"Lonnie, this is my sister, Yolanda. Yolanda, this is Lonnie."

Lonnie and I headed for the bedroom.

Mommy called out to me, "Lyric."

"What's up?" I asked as I stepped into the living room.

Mommy had a cigarette dangling from her mouth. "Get that nigga out of my house."

I stood there like a deer in headlights. "Huh?" I asked, puzzled.

"Get that muthafucka out of my house, and you bet' not fuck that muthafucka."

"Mommy," I whispered, "he is about to pay me a thousand dollars."

Surely that would change her mind, I thought.

"Lyric, I don't care if that nigga is willing to pay you a hundred thousand dollars. Get him out of my house!" Mommy raised her voice.

I knew she never did this unless she was serious, but I was serious about getting that thousand dollars from him.

"Mommy, I can't do that. I'll make it quick," I tried to convince her.

She got up from the sofa and marched to my room. Lonnie was on my bed, jacking his dick off. I noticed the smile on his face when Ma stepped in the room. She wasted no time telling Lonnie to get the fuck out of her house before she called the police on him. Lonnie was the oldest man that I ever brought back to the house, but I didn't see how that went against the rules. I stepped in the middle of Mommy and Lonnie, trying to diffuse the situation.

"All right, Yolanda, we leaving."

"No, you not going nowhere." Mommy pushed me on the bed.

Lonnie left standing there, confused. One thing that was for certain, nothing or no one was going to keep me from that stack that Lonnie had in his pocket for me. I stood back up, challenging my mother with my eyes as we looked at each other eye to eye. Lonnie slipped on his pants.

"Lyric you staying or what?" Lonnie asked.

"I'm coming," I stated as Mommy stood in front of me with her hands on her hips. "What is up with you, Yolanda? If I didn't know any better, I would say you acting like you my mama."

Ma understood underhandedly what I was saying to her. She had no choice but to let me go and do what she showed me how to do. I left with not a regret in this world—that is, until I came back home—and Jay Baby gave me the suicide note Mommy left.

Dear Lyric,

It wasn't until I looked into Lonnie's eyes I realized my demons that I had subjected you to. I apologize for exposing you to such a trifling life. I apologize for taking your innocence away from you. I apologize for not telling you that I once had the same dreams of becoming a model. That's why I never wanted to watch you model or register you for any modeling classes. It was too much for me to come to grips with all that was taking away from me. Lonnie is the man that your grandmother introduced me to when I was twelve. Please find it in you to forgive me, and forgive me for not letting you know the last hoe commandment, "Once a hoe, always a hoe." I marked you for life, Lyric, and it's nothing you or me can do about. But before I watch you instill in your child what I instilled in you, I would die first. So I am willing to break the cycle with my life. Know that I always loved you and I only wanted what was best for you. Please don't blame me for not knowing any better, but I'll give you the best gift a woman could give their daughter. I'll make up for this with my life.

Love,
Your mother/sister

"Lyric, you want to go downtown?" Rico asked.
"Yeah, that sound cool. I want to see every inch of this beautiful city."
"This your first time in Miami?"

"Sure is," I answered.

"Well, let me show you around."

Downtown Miami had a lot of traffic. We had a hard time finding a parking spot. We eventually found one. We exited the truck and walked downtown.

"I want to show you something."

We walked to the beach. I was ecstatic.

"Y'all have a beach downtown?" I asked in amazement.

As we got closer to the beach, I could see the sand and the water that looked like it didn't end. Rico gestured for me to sit down. He pulled off my sandals and carried them for me as we walked across the sand. I wanted to see the water. Meaka talked about her prison friends from Florida. They told her that the water didn't look like the water that was in Dayton. I told Meaka she was a damn fool if she believed that the water looked different.

"Meaka, water is water," I went on to tell her.

Meaka rolled her eyes at me and remained quiet, not even putting up a fight about it.

From a distance, I could tell that the water didn't look like the water in Dayton because the water in Dayton had, like, a tint of green to it whereas this water was the color of clear blue. As I stepped in the water, I could visibly see the fish swimming in the water. The water was beautiful. I stepped in the water and spun around in circles with my arms stretched out in the air. I felt like a kid again.

"Take your shoes off, Rico," I requested.

He smiled and complied with my request. He swung me around in the air.

"This your first time at the beach?"

"Is it that obvious?" I asked, embarrassed.

Before Rico could answer me, my phone rang.

"Hello?"

"Where you at?" Meaka asked.

"I'm at the beach downtown with my new friend, Rico," I stated, smiling at the fact I knew already what Meaka was thinking.

"You don't waste no time, do you?"

"Now, now, now, Meaka."

I had to remind her that she shouldn't be so quick to judge. I was sure she and Emillio would soon be knocking it off if they hadn't already.

"When you coming back? I thought we were going to kick it. Emillio and Al are already gone. We got Emillio's Mustang drop-top. Need I say more?"

I was excited all over again. "I'm on my way."

"I hate to bring this to an end, but that was my sister. They're ready."

"No need to explain, Ma. I enjoyed your company. And maybe we could hook up later. What you think about that?"

"That sounds good to me."

I explained to Rico that Meaka and Agape were with their significant others and I was the only single one, so I was sure we would be hooking up later.

Meaka and Agape sat outside of the hotel in the drop-top. I couldn't wait to hop up front of the cobalt-blue Mustang. I was so happy Meaka didn't like riding in the front seat. I didn't know why and cared not to know as long as I was up front. Rico and I pulled up behind them. I told Rico to get out and meet my sisters.

"Hey, girls," I greeted them with a big grin on my face. "Meaka and Agape, this is Rico. Rico, these are my sisters." I pointed to each as I said their name.

Rico extended his hand. Meaka and Agape both shook his hand.

"I see you've met my little sister," Agape stated.

"I hope you were on your best behavior, Lyric," Meaka added.

"And I was. Rico and I had a nice time together."

"Your sister was an angel, sis," Rico stated.

I watched him closely interact with Agape and Meaka, trying to pick up on any vibe that he might have been feeling to either one of them.

"I'm let y'all go. Y'all be careful. This is a beautiful place, but like any other city, it does get ugly."

"We will," we all chimed in at the same time.

I gave Rico an innocent kiss on the cheek and let him know I would be calling him.

I threw my body over the door, hopping in the front seat.

"So where we off to?" I questioned as Agape pulled off.

"Let's just ride around," Agape stated.

I was floored. "Ride around?" I questioned with my nose turned up to the sky.

"Yeah, what's wrong with riding around?"

I turned to the back to catch Meaka's reaction. She had a neutral look on her face, so I had to see where her head was at.

"Meaka, you hear this bitch? We ain't trying to ride around. We trying to kick it, Agape. What the fuck? We can ride around when we get back to Dayton."

"Lyric, please don't start. Can we just ride?" Agape stated before she turned the music up.

I might have been cool if she had drowned me out with some music I wanted to hear, but here she was playing some fucking Keyshia Cole.

I immediately turned the CD player down. "Well, if we gon' be riding, shouldn't we at least be listening to some riding music?"

I flipped through the CDs and stopped when I got to Yo Gotti's *Cocaine Muzik #1*. I politely ejected that bullshit-ass Keyshia Cole. Not that I didn't like Keyshia Cole, I loved her music and how she set the hair trend short-angled bob. Keyshia had every broad in Dayton, Ohio, wearing that hairdo. I just wasn't in no Keyshia Cole mood now.

"Why you taking the CD out, Lyric? Nobody want to listen to that shit."

I turned to Meaka. "Tell this bitch we are not trying to listen to that lovey-dovey shit."

"I really don't care what we listen to," Meaka informed us. "I just want to get out of this car," Meaka stated.

I knew she would speak up eventually. Meaka didn't like being in the car. Agape knew this.

Finding a way to get my way, I fed on what Meaka stated. "See, even Meaka not trying to just ride around."

"Okay," Agape stated, turning toward me, agitated. "Where we going, Lyric? Since you want to call all the shots."

It wasn't like that. I didn't want to call all of the shots, but since she mentioned it, the thought didn't sound too bad.

"How about we go back to the hotel, get our bathing suits, and go to the beach?" I stated with excitement.

I didn't forget about the many different faces I wanted to be acquainted with. Had it not been for Rico, I would have been all over them. Meaka's eyes lit up like I knew they would. Meaka firsthand wanted to see the water.

"That sound like a plan," Meaka agreed.

Agape hesitated. "Al wants me to go with him later."

"Now this is getting to be a bit too much for me to bear. If I knew this, I would have stayed with my friend and let you, Thelma," I said, referring to Agape, "chauffer Louise around town," referring to Meaka.

"I think you taking it too far, Lyric," Agape stated as she went through a red light.

"Lyric right, Agape. We are in Miami. We looking good. Why wouldn't we put our bathing suits on and show out? Al out with Emillio taking care of business. What could it hurt?"

"I'm with you, Meaka," I agreed.

Agape drove silently; and I sat on the passenger side even quieter, awaiting her response, because, if she didn't come up with something and something quick, I was calling Rico...I think.

"Put the CD in," Agape stated as she did a U-turn in the middle of the street.

I could tell we were headed back to the hotel. At least I hope we were. Yo Gotti stormed through the topless Camaro.

"It's that cocaine music, homey. Don't you confuse it. Lames gon' talk it. D-boys gon' move it," I and Agape rapped along to the lyrics.

Meaka smiled in approval to my choice of music. "I like this song. Who is this?" Meaka asked.

"Yo Gotti," I answered.

We pulled up to valet parking. Agape told the driver we would only be a minute. We entered our separate rooms. I couldn't decide on what swimsuit I wanted to wear, so I tried them all on. I wasn't feeling either suit at the moment. I was frustrated with the fact I went and purchased each swimsuit for this trip and, here it was time to go to the beach, I didn't want to wear any of the swimsuits I had. I felt defeated, then there was a knock on the door.

"Come in," I stated from the bedroom.

I was envious as Meaka pranced through the door with a baby-blue Victoria's Secret two-piece bikini.

"Here you go," Meaka handed me a swimsuit.

I held it up and didn't know whether to be appreciative or offended. The swimsuit was a G-string, my favorite. It had a leopard print I knew I would look good in, but I had to get one thing understood before I accepted the swim suit.

"What, you didn't think I had a swimsuit?" I asked, looking confused at the swimsuit, then back up to Meaka.

"Nah, I told you I would get you something for putting me on to the hottest stores out here."

I immediately tried the swimsuit on, and I loved the reflection that looked back at me.

"Damn, bitch, you rocking that swimsuit," Agape came in the door complimenting me.

I blushed. I knew I looked good. I didn't need their compliments to confirm that, but the attention did more for me than flattery.

"You look good, Meaka," Agape complimented.

She had one of them exotic looks to her. She would be my only competition tonight. Agape carried herself like an old lady now that she done snagged Al. She stood before me in what looked like a halter dress. It was her cover-up. I couldn't even tell if she had on a bathing suit. Meaka pulled out her cover-up and wrapped it around her waist. I grabbed my glasses off of the dresser and headed out the door.

"You not gon' put on a cover-up?" Agape questioned.

"Do I look like I'm putting on a cover-up?" I responded with much attitude.

Clearly she had me mistaken with her man. I didn't see nothing wrong with what I got on. It was one hundred degrees out there.

"I wish I had that confidence to wear some shit like that," Meaka stated as she eyed my body.

"I think you should wear a cover-up," Agape stated as we waited for the valet driver.

All eyes were on us. If it wasn't my ass they were looking at, it might have been Meaka's breast. Meaka had a set of 36 double Ds. She didn't have much of an ass, but what she lacked in that area, she made up with those tatas. Agape stood there covered up, so I was not sure what they could be looking at if they were looking at her. I noticed how she was standing there with an attitude because I was not putting on a cover-up.

Cover-up for what? Because it was a G-string? And I bet I ain't gon' cover up this five-hundred-dollar swimsuit, I thought to myself.

The valet driver couldn't help but admire the beauties that stood before him.

"Can I have the keys?" Agape asked as he stood speechless looking at my ass.

"I'm sorry, ma'am," he stuttered and handed Agape the keys.

I didn't like the way Agape was carrying me and Meaka as if we were her children. I kept quiet because she was the driver.

We made it to the beach, and I watched in amazement at the scenery. Women and men skated down the street. I paid close attention to how the guys turned their heads toward every ass that walked pass them. I laughed to myself as we climbed out of the Mustang. Crossing the street was a task. Cars came from everywhere. We ran across the street and walked toward the beach. The beach was as beautiful as I remembered it. I strutted toward the water, Meaka was ahead of me.

"This shit is so beautiful. Lyric, look at this fucking water," Meaka stated excitedly as she splashed the water.

"I know. I said the same thing when I saw it. It is beautiful."

I walked up and splashed some water on Meaka. She returned the favor; and there we were, splashing water all over each other, laughing and playing like kids.

I forgot Agape was at the beach with us because her goody-two-shoes ass was up on the beach as if she was not even with us. I didn't pay her no mind. I and Meaka were having a ball.

"Let's go over to that concession stand," I stated while pointing at it.

Surely I wasn't hungry. I could go for a drink, but in all honesty, I was more interested in the niggas that were at the concession stand. I had no twenty-twenty eye vision, but I did know money when I saw it.

"Take off that fucking cover-up, Meaka," I stated as we walked toward the concession stand.

"You think I should?" Meaka questioned, grabbing on her cover-up.

"Yes, I do. I mean, what is the point of having on the swimsuit if you only gon' cover it up?" I asked.

"Well, you right," Meaka stated as she unwrapped her cover-up.

"Where y'all going?" Agape yelled.

Meaka turned around as if she forgot Agape was with us. "We going to the concession stand."

"You want us to bring you something back?" I asked, clearly not wanting her to tag along.

"I'm cool. Just don't get lost," Agape sarcastically responded.

"We will," I stated as we headed toward the concession stand.

I made sure I shook everything that my mommy gave me. As we waited in line behind what smelled like niggas with money, I put on my charm.

"Excuse me." I tapped a brown-skinned dude that I was sure had those dividends.

"What's up, Ma?" Brown Skinned questioned as he turned around, eyeing Meaka and me.

I don't know what done it for me, whether it was the way he licked his lips after the word *ma* left his mouth or if it was the way he rubbed his hands together in confidence that he just came up on something good.

I put on my innocent smile. "Do you know some clubs that's jumping tonight?"

"Well, baby, pretty much every club out here jump. Where y'all from?" Brown Skinned asked.

"Dayton."

"So this here is your sister?" he asked, referring to Meaka.

"Yeah, I'm Lyric, and this is my sister, Meaka."

It was obvious that Brown Skinned was attracted to Meaka when he extended his hand to her. She gave him hers. I watched as he kissed her hand and told her his name was Tookie.

"Can I get a number or something, Meaka?"

"Um..." Meaka looked from me to Tookie and from Tookie to me. "Well, I have a man," Meaka told him.

I appreciated Meaka's humbleness to the matter at hand. I smiled, and she returned the gesture.

"Well, you have to give me credit for trying," Tookie stated. "You ladies be easy, and, Meaka," he called out as he walked away, "you tell that nigga he better be good to you, and if and when he don't, hit a real nigga up." Tookie walked off.

Meaka and I ordered lemonades. I suggested we order Agape one.

"Agape don't drink lemonade."

"She don't?" I questioned.

"Nah," Meaka responded, ordering Agape a fruit punch.

We strutted our way over to Agap. Niggas were loving Meaka and me, and we knew they were. Every time we turned around, some nigga was trying to holler at us. We came up on several numbers. We were enjoying ourselves, me especially, until I saw the sour look plastered across Agape's face.

"What's wrong?" Meaka asked.

Good thing she did because I wasn't going to begin to entertain the bullshit.

"Nothing. I'm good," Agape responded flatly.

"I got you something to drink," Meaka stated while handing Agape her medium-sized cup.

"Are we going to just stand in the sand?" I questioned to no one in particular, but I was sure Agape was going to speak her peace.

"What should we be doing, Lyric?" Agape questioned, just as I suspected.

"Enjoying our fucking selves however we see fit," I responded and walked off.

I wasn't on Agape's shit, and if Meaka wanted to stand around with her, that was her business. But I bet I would not.

Meaka

"Just look at her. I cant believe she came out here in that string bikini, with that big ass of hers swinging all over the place," Agape stated as Lyric walked off.

"You sound like you hating, A," I stated.

"Hating?" Agape questioned. "I could never find myself hating on Lyric. For what? I mean, she ghetto as fuck, for one, and for two, she don't have shit going for herself. All she want to do is sell pussy. Lyric ain't shit to be hating on. I just want to go back to the room," Agape went on to say.

"You want to go back to the room?" I questioned, hoping I didn't hear her right.

"Yes. I'm not trying to be out here with this bitch looking like a fucking slut," Agape responded, upset.

I didn't like the way Agape was talking about Lyric. Emillio had brought the bathing suit for me. Had I worn it, I, too, would have had to eventually take my cover-up off; and then she would be feeling this same way about me, I think. I felt somewhat responsible for the tension between Agape and Lyric. I was the one who gave Lyric the swimsuit.

"Can you go get Lyric? I'll be in the car," Agape stated as she headed toward the car.

She left me standing there like a deer in headlights. We just got here, and since she had a problem with what Lyric had on, she wanted to go. Not only leave the beach, she wanted to go back to the room. Now I was mad. Then my phone vibrated.

I checked the caller ID and saw that it was Lyric.

"Girl, I was just about to come looking for you. I'm up in the clubhouse."

"Where is that at?" I questioned.

"It's over there by the concession stand. Just keep walking past the concession stand. You can't miss it. You would never believe who up in here."

"Who?" I asked, not sure whom she thought I knew. I was sure I didn't know anyone in Miami.

"Chance."

I hadn't heard anything about Chance since he and Agape called it quits. When I walked in the clubhouse, I spotted Lyric in the corner talking to a guy that I assumed was Chance. I walked toward the two, only to find out that this was one of Chance's friends. Chance was at the bar ordering us a bottle of champagne. I looked toward the bar to see if I could tell who Chance was. I couldn't. As soon as I saw one guy that looked like he may had been Chance, then there was another one that I could have sworn was him. It wasn't until a dark-skinned brotha with chingy eyes walked toward us with a bottle of Moët in his hands and diamonds in his ears that could blind you.

"Meaka, this Chance. Chance, this is Meaka," Lyric introduced.

I stood there not knowing what to say. I should have reached out to Chance. Things may not had worked out with him and Agape, but Chance looked out for me even when he and Agape broke up. He continued to send money on the strength he made a promise to Armani that he would make sure I was straight during my bid. He didn't want me to mention any of it to Agape, and as hard as it was to keep something from Agape, I chose to because then I would feel like a crutch to her when it came time for me to have commissary and hygiene condiments. Chance wrote to me from time to time. Agape never sent pictures of Chance. She said that he didn't like taking pictures, and I didn't know why. As fine as he was, you would think that he would like having his picture taken at every picture booth.

"Hello," I stated, breaking the silence between us.

"So we finally meet," Chance stated with a smile on his face.

I tried to ignore the lust in Chance's eyes, and I tried my hardest to disguise the lust that seeped through my thoughts. I stuck my hand out for a handshake. Chance went in for a hug.

"Is that how you greet your peoples, Meaka?" he asked as we embraced each other.

I laughed and told him, "My bad."

"Don't worry about it. Look, I got y'all a bottle of Mo just to get y'all started. Lyric told me y'all were here. You don't have to let Agape know where the bottle came from. I'm sure, if she know it came from me, she wouldn't take a sip."

"What's up with Armani?" I asked, realizing that I hadn't written to her since I had been home.

"You know how it is, Meaka. Out of sight, out of mind. She told me she haven't heard from you since you got out, yet and still she let me know that, if you needed anything, to make sure I look out for you."

I could feel a lump in my throat. No words would form. I felt like shit for not reaching out to Armani when I came home.

After hearing the CO call out my prison number, I hopped off of the top bunk. The moment I had waited two years for had finally came. I was on my way home, but there was a feeling of fear that lingered over me. The last time I was on the streets, I was a child. Now I had grown, I didn't know how I would adapt to the outside since I had become accustomed to the life in what we called the third world. Armani stood up and embraced me in a loving hug, the kind of hug that a mother gives her daughter when she sends her off to school on her first day.

"I'm going to write you tonight, so you should have a letter from me in two days."

Armani insisted that I wouldn't. "Meaka, it's a whole world out there!" Armani exclaimed. "You expect me to believe you gon' take time out of your life to write me?"

I looked at her in disbelief as a tear escaped my eye. I didn't know what hurt me more, her words or the fact she was right.

"Don't worry about it, Meaka. You know, as long as I have breath in my body, Armani is going to be good," Chance stated.

"What did you say you were looking for me for?" Lyric interrupted as she handed me a glass of Moët.

The discreet wink of her eye made it clear she was trying to come to my rescue, and I was so happy that she did.

"I almost forgot," I stated. "Agape in the car. She wanted me to let you know she ready to go back to the room."

"Oh, hell nah," Lyric stated in a slur.

The Mo was taking its effect on her. I could tell. I myself was not ready to leave and entertained the thought Lyric put forth.

"Call that bitch and let her know we will find our way back to the hotel."

I felt like a rock in a hard place as I stared at the phone, contemplating whether or not I was going to make the call. I decided what the hell.

After the first ring, Agape answered, "Hello?"

"A, I was calling to let you know that Lyric and I are going to stay. We'll get a ride back, so you don't have to worry about us."

I was hoping that A would reconsider going back to the hotel when she realized that we were staying.

"You could have told me. I been out here waiting on y'all," Agape responded with an attitude and hung up.

Who was I fooling? Agape left us, and we hung out with Chance. He told us that he brought out a female friend to Miami with him. She was tired after the flight. He, on the other hand, couldn't wait to hit the beaches; so he left her at the hotel, letting her know to call him when she was up and ready. He had just received the call. The beach had been so entertaining, when we got in the car, I realized I hadn't spoken to Emillio since earlier. I tried hitting up his cell. All three calls went unanswered.

I was surprised to see that we were staying in the same hotel as Chance. That worked out perfectly. Lyric and I discussed as we rode up on the elevator to the fourth floor.

"So what's jumping for the night?" Lyric asked me.

"You know, I'm trying to kick it," I responded.

"Good, because that's just what we're going to do. I don't know what's up with that sister of yours, but she ain't gon' fuck up my night," Lyric demanded in joking way. You crazy girl, we gon' have fun tonight, trust me."

"I'm about to go get in the shower."

"I hope Emillio ain't in that room," Lyric whispered as we walked down the hall to our rooms.

"Why you say that?" I questioned, confused.

"Because, bitch, it's a chance you ain't coming back out."

I laughed it off and entered my room.

I smiled. I came face-to-face with different-colored roses decorated all over the room. I noticed a trail of rose petals on the floor leading to the bathroom. The door was closed. I opened it, only to feel my smile spread wider. As I eyed the bubbles in the hot tub, chocolate-covered strawberries sat on a plate near the hot tub with an envelope next to them. I entered the bathroom slowly. I took off my clothes right there and hopped in the hot tub. The water was just right. I picked up the envelope and opened it. It was a blank card that read:

> I hope you are having a wonderful time. I got back to the room, and you were not here. I know that you are safe because your sister told me you were at the beach with Lyric. I just want you to enjoy yourself. For some reason, I think you deserve it, Miss Tameka.
>
> Emillio

A tear dropped from my eye. I never had anyone go through all of this for me. Emillio's generosity only made me feel inferior because I had nothing to offer him in return. I never had a boyfriend, so I wasn't sure how to respond. But I sure as hell had to find out. I hopped out of the hot tub to retrieve my cell phone. I dialed Agape's number as I slid back in the hot tub. I got the voice mail, so I tried again. This time, Al answered.

"Can I speak to A?" I asked in a pleasant tone.

"She in the shower, Meaka. You good?" Al questioned.

"Yeah, everything good. Lyric and I just got back. I was trying to see what A was doing tonight. Do y'all have plans?"

"Nah, we ain't got no plans. Me and Emillio have to make a run to Tampa, so we gon' be there for the night. She a li'l upset, but after all this business is attended to, we gon' all get together and have a good time."

"Okay, well, I look forward to that. Tell A to hit me up when she get out of the shower."

"Will do," Al responded before he hung up.

I hopped back in the hot tub and soaked my body. I heard the door open, but I didn't even have to open my eyes. I could smell Emillio's Versace cologne as he stood in the doorway.

"Did you like your surprise?" he asked as he stepped in the restroom.

"Did I like it? I loved it," I stated as Emillio poured himself a glass of champagne.

I found myself trying to cover up with the water to no avail. Emillio took a seat on the rim of the tub. He poured another glass of champagne, took one of the strawberries and dipped it into the glass, and fed it to me. As I bit the strawberry, the juices dripped down my chin. That was when Emillio went in and licked my chin. It felt a li'l weird but in a good way. I smiled to let him know I liked what he was doing. I felt the need to let Emillio know that I was a virgin. Don't ask me why. I just didn't want to get caught up in the moment, and he was expecting me to do something that I didn't know anything about.

"Emillio, I need to tell you something," I requested in between kisses.

Emillio pulled back. "What is it, Miss Tameka?" Emillio asked with lustful eyes.

"I just want to let you know that I am a virgin."

The innocence in my eyes let Emillio know I was telling the truth. Up until this point, this was the first kiss I ever had with a man.

"Come on. Get out that tub. Let me see you," Emillio stated.

I didn't expect that. I pleaded with my eyes for him to take things a little slower, but Emillio was persistent. As he reached for my hand, I looked around the candle-illuminated room and was reminded by how I felt the moment I walked through the door. I reached for Emillio's hand. He took my hand in his and gently pulled me out of the tub. The water dripped from my body. With a simple pull of his hand, my body followed him into the bedroom. I stood there like a helpless child as Emillio grabbed a towel. He then dabbed the towel over my neck. The plushness of the Ralph Lauren towels against my neck felt soothing. He then dried my shoulder blades, front, then back. I stood there with a look of nervousness spread across my face. I searched for his approval of me. I then felt the towel go down each of my arms, underneath my armpit. I wasn't sure what he was doing this for instead of letting me dry myself off. After he dried my breast, I realized that I myself would have never dried myself ever so gently. After the outer shell of my body was dry, Emillio motioned for me to get on the bed. I did. He spread my legs and began to dry off my inner thighs, then the bottom of my feet. I lay there with my eyes closed.

"Open your eyes, Meaka. I want you to watch what I am about to do."

I then opened my eyes slowly as I felt Emillio's warm breath on my pussy. He opened my pussy up with one hand, then commenced to licking and sucking my pussy. I had never felt so much vibration inside of my body. Emillio kept up the pace.

"This noonie, Tameka, and this li'l noonie belongs to me now," Emillio stated, referring to my vagina.

My body soon couldn't take any more. I started to shake and had what I knew now as my first orgasm. I saw the approval I was looking for plastered across Emillio's face when he came up and kissed me on my forehead. The next thing I remember was waking up to the door being beat down.

When I opened the door, Lyric and Agape stood on the other side, grinning from ear to ear.

"What are y'all up to?" I questioned.

"Don't give us that innocent girl shit now," Lyric stated as she marched past me. "Oh, and look at this," Lyric stated as she eyed the arrangement of roses throughout the living quarters of the room.

Agape followed the beeline Lyric created and chimed in, "Oh yeah, this is nice."

"So are you going to get dressed, or did Emillio beat that pussy sore?" Lyric couldn't help but jab.

"Funny, Lyric, very, very funny," I said sarcastically.

"By the way, you looking good. *You* know that, Meaka. You wasting time. Please hurry up and get ready," Lyric rushed.

My mind kept rekindling what had just taken place between me and Emillio. As I laid my clothes out, we hadn't had sex, but I felt the same closeness that I'm sure sex brings in a relationship.

Agape

I tried desperately to get the bartender's attention, but my five-foot-five frame didn't stand a chance next to the other five feet sevens and over patrons that were also trying to consume some liquid courage. Then out of nowhere, some guy handed me a bottle of Cristal. Not only was that what I was about to order, but how did the guy know what bottle I was trying to pop? I couldn't accept such an expensive bottle of champagne from someone I did not know. If there was a time I needed Lyric on my side, that would be now. She would have snatched the bottle out of this guy's hand so fast that it would not have been funny. But here I stood looking dumbfounded, not knowing how to accept the bottle of Cris. I dug in my purse for my money just to let him know that I could buy my own bottle.

"No need for that, miss," the high-yella brother told me. "This is a gift for you from a friend."

I didn't know who he thought I was, but I was sure this was some sort of mistaken identity because I had no friends in Miami. I tried to hand the bottle back to the guy, but he turned his back on me and walked off.

I took the bottle back to our table in the VIP area of the club. Before I could even set the bottle down, Lyric had grabbed it up and poured herself the first glass.

I hate when she does that, I thought.

But then she passed the glass to Meaka.

"What is this?" Meaka questioned.

"This some of that fine shit, Meek," Lyric answered as she poured another glass and handed it to me.

She then pours herself a glass. "Let's make a toast to a good night amongst some bad bitches," Lyric stated.

"What kind of toast was that?" I questioned.

"Agape, just drink your drink please," Lyric whined. "Do you always have to have something to say?"

I did just as told. I put my glass up to my lips, and the bitter-sweet taste I loved reminded me about the guy at the bar.

"Some dude gave me that bottle," I stated, referring to the bottle of Cristal.

"What did he look like?" Meaka asked.

"Fuck what he look like. Where the nigga at?" Lyric questioned as she stood up pretending like she was looking for the nigga.

All three of us started laughing.

"For real, A. I mean, what did he say?"

"Nothing much other than it was from a friend of mine. I feel bad for the girl the bottle was for because I'm sure it wasn't for me."

"Uh-huh," Lyric teased. "See, A? I knew there was more to you than what meets the eye. You let me find out you stepped out on Al when you called yourself going back to that room earlier," Lyric teased.

"Lyric, you think it might be from Chance?" Meaka questioned.

"Oh yeah, that's who might have sent it."

"What make y'all say Chance?" I questioned the both of them.

"My bad. I told Lyric that I would call and let you know that Chance was down here, but when I called your phone, Al picked up. He said you were in the shower and that he would tell you I called."

I searched Meaka's eyes for the truth, and for some reason, I felt like there was something she wasn't telling me. Al never answered my phone, and if he did, he never gave me any message. I went along with what she was saying even though I knew she wasn't telling me everything.

Meaka knew she hadn't been completely honest with me. In all reality, if it hadn't been for the guy giving her that bottle, she would have never mentioned that Chance was in Miami. She didn't see any reason to. But she couldn't let Agape know she was willing to keep it from her.

Lyric stood from her seat and asked, "Is y'all bitches ready to hit the dance floor? 'Cause I know I am."

I sat there with a queasy feeling in my stomach. These two bitches thought I was either blind or just plain stupid. I saw the wink Lyric gave Meaka.

"Y'all go on. I'ma finish my glass. I'll meet up with y'all."

As soon as they were out of my vision, I pulled out my cell phone and dialed Al's number because I had to know whether or not Meaka called me.

"What's up, bae?" Al answered on the first ring.

"I have a quick question for you," I asked, trying to make this call as quick as possible.

"What's that?" he responded.

"Did you answer my phone any yesterday?" I questioned, trying not to make it look like I was hiding something from him.

"Nah, I didn't answer your phone. Why you ask me that?" Al went on to question.

That bitch, I thought. "So Meaka didn't call my phone when I was in the shower?"

Preparing for his answer to be no but hoping for a yes, I could feel anger rising from the pit of my stomach.

"Oh, my bad, baby. I forgot all about that. Yeah, she called. She said she was trying to see if you were going to go out tonight."

The steam I felt on the inside released itself through my ears. I was happy that Al recalled the call because, had he not, Meaka would have been taking her ass to go live with Lyric. I should have known that Meaka wouldn't keep anything from me. It was Lyric and that wink that sent me over the edge. I still had questions for Meaka about what went on yesterday with Chance because I could only imagine what tricks Lyric had up her sleeve.

When I made it to the dance floor, Lyric was on the floor doing her usual, shaking her ass up on some nigga. I couldn't see his face, but I could tell from standing behind him slightly to the right. I could see his facial expression, but I looked on as I bobbed my head to the music as he rythmically grinded up on Lyric. I could feel someone staring at me. I looked to the left. There were Meaka's eyes on me. I walked toward her. She continued to stare at me as some guy whispered in her ear.

"Excuse me. I need to speak with my sister." I smiled as I pulled Meaka across the room.

"Whew, thank you. That nigga's breath smelled like *Dayton Daily News*."

"The look on your face said it all."

We laughed.

"What's so funny?" Lyric questioned as she walked up, wiping sweat from her brow.

"You and that sweaty face of yours," I responded.

Lyric eyed me with a devilish grin. "Look who came out to play," Lyric stated, looking behind me.

I immediately turned around in the direction she was looking in, and I liked to shit on myself when I stood face-to-face with Chance.

"Hello to you too, Lyric, Meaka," Chance greeted with a nod of his head. "What's up, Red?"

I don't want to sound cliché to say the cat had my tongue, but how else do I explain not being able to say one word?

"What's up, Chance?" Meaka responded.

"Out enjoying myself, me and my mans," Chance stated, referring to the high-yellow guy that gave me the bottle of Cristal.

I noticed how close Chance and Meaka seemed as they stood there holding conversation with each other, and I didn't like it a tad bit. I walked off toward our table. By the time I sat down, Lyric was walking up.

"This party is jumping," she stated, full of glee.

I looked on as Meaka and Chance conversated. A cloud of jealousy surrounded me. I hadn't thought about Chance since the night of my birthday. All the hate I felt for him went out the window the second I turned around and saw his face. And there Meaka stood talking to who was now an enemy. How could she be so disloyal?

"When they become so cool?" I questioned to Lyric.

"Meaka fucks with Chance, A. I don't see how when he put his hands on her fucking sister. The nigga looked out for her from what I understand..." Lyric responded. "And that ain't got shit to do with what happened between you and him," she just had to add.

I rolled my eyes at her.

As I searched my purse for my phone, I saw that I had a three missed calls from Al and a text message that read "I been calling your phone. Not sure what's going on, but you or Meaka not answering y'all phones. I'm on my way back to Miami."

I immediately dialed Al's number, only to receive the voice mail on the first ring. I tried again. Voice mail.

"I need to get Emillio's number from Meaka. Al not answering his phone."

"You know, A, you come with a lot of bullshit. Why don't you let that girl enjoy herself?"

"And what's that supposed to mean, Lyric?"

"She not thinking about Emillio. Why are you?"

"Fuck you, okay, Lyric?"

"Nah, dat's what you have Al for, or did you forget?"

I turned around at the mention of Al's name. "And what would you know about that, Lyric, since no nigga ever fucks with you over ninety days? Bitch."

Lyric stood up from the table with venom in her eye, and I returned her stare.

"Look, Agape, you don't want to fuck with me. You should rather want to fuck with seven wild horses, bitch, than to want to fuck with me. I'm not ever going to forget the shit you just said either, bitch," Lyric threatened.

It didn't go under deaf ears. I knew Lyric was a beast. I knew firsthand how she could whoop a bitch's ass. I turned my ass around and headed toward Meaka and Chance.

"What's up, A?" Meaka asked, sensing something wasn't right.

"What's Emillio's number?" I questioned.

The look Meaka gave me was sorta like the one Lyric gave me. I was baffled. I mean, damn, could I get the number or not?

"All right, ladies," Chance interrupted, "it was a pleasure seeing the both of you," and disappeared in the crowd.

"It's not a problem giving you his number, but my thing is, what it look like you call Emillio's phone for? Al and I haven't even called Emillio."

"Meaka, I'm not thinking about all of that. I'm just trying to see if my man is cool."

"Meaka dialed the number from her phone and handed the phone to me. I started to snatch it out of her hands but opted not to. I could hear the phone ring over the music. I walked toward the exit, then out of the door. Emillio's phone went straight to the voice mail. I tried again and got the voice mail. On my way into the club, Chance was coming out. I tried to push past him. But he grabbed me by my waist. He pushed me back outside of the door. He came in close, taking in my scent.

"I miss you so much, Red," Chance stated sincerely.

I could never deny Chance. This was what I hated most about him. As his back was turned to me, his arms was still wrapped around me. Somewhere in the night, Al appeared, standing directly behind Chance with a gun to the back of his head. The look of shock was presented through my eyes was what broke our embrace. Chance put his hands up, apparently thinking this was a stickup.

"Why don't you let the lady go back inside of the club?" Chance stated to his unknown assailant.

"This what it is, Agape?" Al questioned with gun still pointed to the back of Chance's head.

I felt lost. I didn't know what was taking place before my eyes. I knew there wasn't anything I could say in my defense. Chance looked at me with fury in his eyes.

Unknown to Al, the reason why Chance was coming out of the club in the first place was to check on his mans that was outside getting serviced by a female that was in the club. High Yellow had watched the whole thing unfold from behind tinted windows. High Yellow didn't know how to respond when he saw his man being held up behind some bitch. He warned Chance to stay away from Agape, and he didn't listen. High Yellow crept up behind Al and fired one shot to his head, killing him instantly.

"No!" Agape cried, pushing past Chance. "What did you do? What did you do?" Agape cried as she held on to Al.

Chance looked at Agape, and he couldn't understand how things panned out this way. He hated to run like a coward, but he didn't need the heat that this shit would bring.

Emillio

Seated in the parking lot, I heard the sound of a single gunshot. I immediately pulled the car from around the corner where I was parked waiting on Al. I was heated when Al suggested that we turn around so that he could check on Agape because she wasn't answering her phone. I respected the fact that he loved his lady. That was the only reason I was willing to turn around.

"You know, sometimes business has to wait," Al tried to reason with me when I told him he was having a sucka attack.

In my line of business, business was the only thing that should never wait. I gave in. How could I argue with a man that wanted to ensure the safety of his lady was enforced? I couldn't do anything but respect that.

When I pulled up, I noticed people huddled up in a circle. I jumped out of the car, and the sight placed before me almost made me drop to my knees. I saw what once was Agape's pink dress now bloodstained as she held on to Al as if her strength alone could save him. I made my way through the crowd. My heart went out to Agape as I tried to pull her up from under Al's body. She fought with all of her might to get me off of her, but my strength was overbearing. I picked her up from the ground and hugged her in a bear hug as she kicked and screamed.

"Let me go, Emillio. Let me go please, Emillio. I can't leave him, Emillio, please."

It hurt me to keep her away from the same man that couldn't be away from her, but I had to do something. I could feel her body shaking.

"Where's your sister?" I hated to ask, but I needed to get us up out of here.

Agape continued to cry, then I heard what I now saw was Meaka's cry.

I grabbed her hand and whispered in her ear, "I need you right now, Ma. I need for you to pull yourself together for your sister. She's about to really need you."

I met her eyes, and she knew how serious this was. I explained to Meaka that I had some shit in my trunk that I could not risk getting caught with. I carried Agape against her will to the car. She clawed, kicked, and screamed.

"Why are you doing this to me, Emillio? I want to be with Al. Please let me be with him."

After placing Agape in the back seat, I hopped in the front. Meaka hopped in the back with Agape.

I started the car up. "Oh, shit, where Lyric?"

Meaka questioned, "We don't have time for that, Meaka. We gotta get out of here now."

"Well, leave then. I can't leave her. She rode with us."

Lyric always made it clear to Meaka, "We come together. We leave together." "No bitch left behind" was Lyric's motto. She couldn't find it in her to just leave Lyric. When she felt me put the car in drive, she hopped out of the car in search of Lyric.

I yelled out to Meaka to get back in the car. She ran back toward the club. I hoped Meaka knew what she was doing. In my heart, she did. I heard the sirens get closer, and I had to make a decision and one quick. I pulled off with Agape in the back seat crying. I tried to maintain my manly stance. But a tear managed to escape my eyes as I headed toward the hotel. I couldn't get the sight of my mans laid out on the ground like that. Al was a good dude. He ain't deserve that shit. I have to get to the bottom of what happened.

I carried Agape to me and Meaka's room. She continued to sob in my arms. My heart went out to her. I plugged my cell on the charger and dialed Meaka's number. No answer. I tried again. No answer. I was torn. I usually was an impulsive thinker, but something in me wouldn't allow me to think impulsively. I had three ladies I had to see to it made it back to Ohio. I had to get back to the club, but how would I do that without leaving Agape? I could not let her go back to the scene of the murder. After I paced back and forth, the door swung open. Meaka and Lyric walked through the door. Both of them looked like they had seen a ghost.

"Where A?"

"She in the back."

They both entered the room. I sat back in the living quarters of her room. I could hear Lyric comforting Agape.

"It's gon' be okay, baby. Don't you worry about shit, A. We got you. Do you hear me, A? We got you." Lyric repeated, "It's gon' be okay, baby."

I heard the sorrow in Lyric's voice, and I guess hoes really do have hearts. I never perceived that I would witness someone as gritty as Lyric be so gentle and concerned about someone other than herself. Meaka stepped in with red eyes. She sat down on my lap and curled up like a little baby. I didn't mind one bit. The innocence that she possessed was what captivated me.

"What happened out there, Emillio?" she asked.

I wish I had an answer, but I honestly didn't know shit. I explained to Meaka how we were on our way to West Palm Beach when Al asked him for the number.

"I gave him your number, but you didn't answer. He felt like something might not be right with Agape, so he wanted to turn around. We did. When we pulled up to the club, there wasn't any parking spots, so I parked around the corner. I let him know I wasn't trying to cramp yo' style, so I suggested he run on in an' see if everything was good with his lady. I was more than sure, with the music banging, you guys just didn't hear the phones going off. My nigga got out. I sat in the car. No more than two minutes later, I heard a single gunshot."

Tears rolled down Meaka's face. "I felt so bad for Agape. Had she not dragged Al out here, he would still be alive."

"That's not true, bae. Don't think like that."

"Yes, it is. I was too scared to get on the plane by myself, so they decided to come with me."

I looked in her eyes and tried to differ with her, but she didn't want to believe it.

"If it make you feel any better, Al was only trying to surprise Agape. That's why she didn't know, so either way you look at it, they would have been. If that takes the guilt out of your heart, you had nothing to do with what took place tonight, Meaka. Don't beat yourself up about it, all right?" I stated as I kissed her forehead.

Then what she asked me stirred something up inside of me. "Why you not sad, Emillio? How can you be so calm when your friend is laid out, outlined in the concrete with yellow tape surrounding him?"

I thought about Meaka's question, and it brought me back to when I was thirteen. I and my best friend, Reggie Braces, started selling drugs in the projects we grew up in. We came from homes where it was either get some money or don't eat. No father around the streets raised us, so before we knew it, we was out of the door without a clue to how vicious the streets could be. We were getting on with quarters, then ounces. Before we knew it, we got on with our first brick by the time we was sixteen.

Braces's moms was a dope fiend who happened to be eavesdropping on a conversation that I and Braces had the previous day. She knew her son was dabbing in the dope game, but she thought he was small time. Any time she searched his room, she only found crumbs or a couple of hundreds of dollars. Unknown to her, all his money and dope he kept up to me. But when she heard how excited we were, the dope fiend in her told her to eavesdrop on her son. She went to his door and stood quietly next to the door. She overheard us indulge in a deep conversation.

"Nigga, you know this gon' change a whole lot of things in the game. Young niggas with a brick, you know niggas gon' be hating," she heard her son mediating the conversation.

When she heard him say a brick, she felt like she could taste the crack in the back of her throat. She then pressed her ear up to the door, desperately trying to see if she could hear where the brick of coke was. She fantasized how long she could get high off of a brick of coke.

That was when Braces stated, "So it's on, nigga. Tomorrow at three, meet me at the top."

Beanie, Braces's mom, knew when a conversation was coming to an end. She had heard all that she needed to hear.

Three o'clock the next day came, and we got on. We ran all the way to my grandmother's house. We discussed everything, from how we were going to cap up the dope, who was gon' cook the dope, and who were potential apartments we could use as dope spots. We decided to use my grandmother's house as the stash house since Braces moms was on drugs. He decided it would make sense if we used his house as a spot. I didn't agree. I didn't trust Braces's mom. We dealt with crackheads from day in and day out. I had seen first-hand what crack does to an addict. I didn't think it would be good for business. Braces acted like he knew something I didn't.

All he said was "Trust me on this, my nigga. Ma know all the dope fiends. She gon' bring us that money, and in return, she getting high, so everyone gets what they want."

Braces walked out of the door with his book bag that concealed his half a brick. The next time I saw him, he was laid out on his bed with his whole stomach shot out.

When I knocked on Braces's door, something just didn't feel right. No one came to the door. I twisted the doorknob, and the feeling that I felt standing outside of the door intensified when I stepped in the apartment and saw Braces's backpack on the floor. I ran to his room and opened the door, and there he lay. I knelt down beside his lifeless body, and as hard as I tried to fight back the tears, they flowed freely from my face. That was my mans.

"Meaka, death can only show up so many times before you get used to it. I have much respect for Al. He was a real stand-up guy, but see, Meaka, in the line of work I'm used to, you see a lot of guys like Al six feet under for all kinds of reasons. I don't question it. I don't respect it, but I can't question the laws of the universe. It's bigger than me. So if you think, because I'm not crying, then that mean I'm not hurting, you're wrong. Al got a three-year-old daughter that's left without a father, and her mother so fucked up in the head she just might rejoice in his death because, more than likely, Trinity will be left with everything that Al owns."

"He has a daughter?" Meaka questioned, then there were more tears.

Lyric

As soon as Agape fell asleep, I gently got out of the bed to let her sleep. I pulled the door up behind me and entered the room Meaka and Emillio were seated in. I put my head in my hands. I could feel a migraine coming on.

"You all right, Lyric?" Meaka asked.

I couldn't deny the sight of Al laid out on that concrete had me shook. I somehow couldn't get the image out of my head no matter how hard I tried.

"I'll be better if I had some green to smoke."

"Say no more," Emillio stated as he stood from his seat.

I followed him with my eyes. Before I knew it, Emillio was lighting up some green that stank so good.

When Meaka passed me the blunt, she asked me, "Did A tell you what happened?"

"Nah, I didn't want to badger her with questions. She just cried herself to sleep."

I wish I knew though. Al didn't deserve that shit. I know I and Al didn't see eye to eye. But I would have never wished his death on my worst enemy. I just didn't know how A was going to go on from here. Al had become Agape's everything.

The green felt good seeping into my lungs I choked so hard from the potency of the weed. The room became cloudy as Emillio lit up another blunt and then another. The weed took its effect on all of us. We sat quietly. The only noises in the room were the sound of deep inhalation from each of us. It was obvious to me that we were looking for some form of amnesia and we hoped the weed would provide us with it. After the three blunts, Emillio excused himself and left out of the hotel room.

Meaka curled up next to me on the sofa.

She placed her head on my shoulder and asked me, "What are we going to do, Lyric?"

I didn't have an answer. I wrapped my arm around Meaka and let her know, "We are going to get through this, Meaka."

I saw the uncertainty in her eyes, and I wondered if she could see the same in mine. Honestly I had know clue of what life would be like for her and A now that Al was dead. I mean, they did live in his house, and everything that they had was provided by him. So for them to no longer have him left them where? That place I didn't want to acknowledge until the time came. And I didn't need Meaka to worry about that as well. I was not sure what Emillio would do for them, but if he was the stand-up type of nigga that he seemed like he was, then he gon' look out for them. If not, I guess back to A's apartment they would have to go.

I'm so happy A was smart enough to keep her apartment, I subconsciously thought.

"Look, Meaka, everything gon' be all right."

Tears formed in Meaka's eyes, and I was aware that it was apparent she looked for the same sympathy in mine. Unlike her, I was hardened at a young age, and it would take more than a dead body to bring me to tears. Where I was from, you could find a dead body. It hurt me that I couldn't show a more vulnerable side at such a fragile moment.

The sound of the door closing behind Emillio snapped me out my trance. The weed was giving me a real beatdown. I yawned and then let Meaka know that she and Emillio could sleep in my room and that I could stay in here with Agape. Meaka searched my eyes. I let her know that it was okay.

"I'll call you when she get up, Meek," I stated with a smile, desperately trying to avoid eye contact with Meaka; so I pleaded with Emillio with my eyes to take Meaka in the room and comfort her because I didn't know how.

After my mom's suicide, I had no feelings. It was like I couldn't feel anything. Of course I wanted to cry. But the truth of the matter was I couldn't.

Emillio pulled Meaka up from the sofa. I walked them to the door. Meaka turned around and gave me a warm, heartfelt hug. Not knowing how to respond to such compassion, I pulled back.

"I'll call you as soon as A gets up." I put my game face on, adorned with a smile.

I was aware that my smile didn't match how I felt inside, and the truth was I hated myself for not being able to empathize with my friend. Would it have killed me to have at least shown an ounce of sympathy for her and her situation? I guess it would have because I pulled the door up as Meaka stared in my eyes. I placed my back against the door, and for the first time in a long time, I shed a tear.

*****

Meaka

"Do you think Lyric is okay?" I asked Emillio as he lay down in bed next to her.

"Yeah, she seemed good to me. Why you say that?"

"I don't know. She seemed a li'l weird to me. You didn't notice how, when I tried to give her a hug, she pulled away from me?"

"Meaka, that don't mean nothing is wrong with her. Everyone is not open with their feelings and emotions. That's what I get from it. In her line of business, it comes with the territory," Emillio added as he wrapped his arms around me. "Now get some sleep," he stated just before he planted a kiss on my forehead.

I remained silent and soaked in the words that just left Emillio's mouth. I get what Emillio was trying to say, but I expected more from Lyric. I expected her to comfort me the way a friend should.

Agape

How the fuck did I get in Meaka's room? I questioned myself as I got up out of the bed.

We must have really got fucked up last night. Then when I saw Lyric asleep on the sofa, I knew we had to got fucked up. Lyric opened her eyes just as I was about to wake her up to see if she could recollect any of the night's events because I couldn't remember shit. Lyric looked at me as if she had seen a ghost.

"Come sit down, Agape," Lyric stated to me calmly, a little too calm for my liking. "You okay?" she went on to ask.

"Yeah, I'm good," I responded. Baffled as to why she and I are in Meaka and Emillio's room, I asked, "Where Meaka and them at?"

"Oh, they stayed in my room," Lyric answered.

Call me crazy, but Lyric was acting kind of weird. Keep on asking me if I was okay.

"Should I not be okay, Lyric? Why you keep asking me am I okay?"

Lyric dialed a number on her cell phone, informing someone that I was up.

"Who was that?" I asked.

"That was Meaka."

As soon as Meaka's name left Lyric's mouth, Meaka entered the room.

"Hey, A, how you feeling?" Meaka asked as she hugged me.

"All I want to know is what happened last night. You and this bitch keep asking how am I doing like I'm sick or something," I stated, referring to Lyric.

The look the both of them gave me left me speechless. It was apparent that something had happened that I had no recollection of. No words left either one of their mouths, and in walked Emillio.

"Emillio, can you please tell me where my man at? These bitches over here acting like they on something."

Emillio had the same look in his eyes. Emillio grabbed me, and I knew that something wasn't right. Under no circumstances had he ever held on to me the way he had, then what he whispered in my ear, I couldn't have heard him right.

"Al gone, A. He died last night."

"That shit ain't funny, Emillio."

If looks could determine one's honesty, I would have known right then and there that Emillio was telling me the whole truth and nothing but. I looked from Meaka to Lyric and from Lyric to Meaka. The silence in the room was very disturbing to me. I felt like the walls were closing in on me as the reality set in, but I wouldn't allow it.

"Y'all are sick as fuck."

I left from the room and proceeded down the hall to me and Al's room. There was no sign of Al. The room was just as we left it. I ignored the cold feeling that desperately tried to enter in my heart. I felt empty in the stillness of the room. I walked briskly back down the hall to Emillio and Meaka's room.

"Can somebody please tell me what's going on?" I pleaded.

The saddened look Emillio wore on his face let me know all that I needed to know. But I couldn't accept what he was trying to tell me.

"Where is my phone? I needed to call Al."

I searched my purse for my phone. I couldn't find it. I looked on the bed and under the bed. I pulled the sheet off of the bed. I tried not to acknowledge Meaka and Lyric as they stood in the doorway.

"Who got my phone?" I questioned Meaka.

"I don't know, A," she answered.

"Lyric, you seen my phone?" I asked while I looked under the bed for the second time.

Everything that was there before was still there. I hated myself for not memorizing Al's number.

"Meaka, do you have Al's number in your phone?"

"A, listen," Meaka stated as she stepped in the room, leaving Lyric in the doorway. "There was a terrible accident last night. Al is dead."

"Bitch, why would you want to play like that? What the fuck is wrong with y'all? I can't wait to tell Al how y'all in here practically wishing death on him."

"It's true," Lyric whispered, looking down at the floor.

"Oh, how you wish, huh, bitch? You wish my nigga was dead, don't you, Lyric?" I taunted. "You think I don't know you wanted to fuck Al, you gold-digging bitch, just like you wanted to fuck with Emillio? I bet you ain't tell Meaka that, did you?"

Lyric put on her infamous devilish grin. "Fuck you, you crazy bitch," Lyric responded with no remorse before she exited the room.

I looked back at Meaka to see if she wanted to quit with the shenanigans. I didn't know if she was mad at the fact Lyric wanted to fuck with Emillio or not, but she handed me her phone and left out of the room. I searched the call log for Al's number and hit the send button when I located it. After two rings, the phone picked up, and I was relieved when it did.

"Hello?" I said into the phone.

There was no response.

"Hello?"

"Hello, this is Detective Flemming. Are you trying to reach Mr. Dekalb Williams?"

"Yes, I am," I stated as a matter of fact.

"And what is your relationship to the victim?"

Victim? I thought. "I am Dekalb's wife. Can I speak to my husband?"

"Well, ma'am, your husband has been murdered, and we need someone to come by and identify his body."

"No, you must have this all wrong. Dekalb isn't dead. I just was with him last night, or was I? For some reason, I couldn't remember shit that happened last night, but I had to have been with him."

My subconscious allowed me to think.

"Well, ma'am, apparently between the hours of one and two o'clock this morning, Mr. Dekalb was shot in the back of the head and was killed instantly."

I dropped the phone out of my hand. I went in the living quarters of the room. Emillio sat on one sofa and Meaka on the other.

"Emillio, is it true?" I asked as I stood over him.

He closed his eyes and nodded.

I fell to my knees. "No! Please, no! Please don't tell me he gone, Emillio."

Emillio picked me up off of the floor.

"Who did this to him? Who did this, Emillio?" I cried on his chest.

Emillio didn't respond. He just held me. I held on to him as if he could bring Al back to me.

"They want me to come down and identify the body."

"Don't worry about that, A. I got somebody on top of it, but in the meantime, I need to get y'all on the next flight out of here. Meaka, I need you to go pack up A's things. I don't want her back down there. Can you do that for me? And I'll handle your things."

I looked on like a lost puppy as Emillio handed out orders.

"Stop by Lyric's room and let her know what's up."

"Okay," Meaka stated before she left the room.

Lyric

I ran around my room frantically packing my things. The nerve of Agape to front me out like that. I had never looked at Al in any way that I shouldn't have been, at least not while they were together. Truth be told, I broke my code of ethics for her because at no time would a bitch's man be off of limits until I got cool with Agape. Okay, I was fucking Chance every chance I got. I had been fucking Chance before Agape came into the picture. I had enough of respect for her to send his ass back home to her. Chance was the only nigga in the world that the money wasn't the motive. But Al, on the other hand, was her man; and I had never even constructed up a plan to get his attention. That was my first sign that I had grown to have love

160

for Agape. And to think, all this time, she thought that I wanted her nigga. That didn't do nothing but made me wish I had fucked him.

I hoped it wasn't Agape knocking at the door because I really didn't need her shit and I was sure we would come to blows. I didn't want anything from her—no apology and no mediation, nothing. I looked through the peephole and allowed Meaka into my room.

"Emillio want us to start packing so he can take us to the airport," Meaka stated as she looked off in the thinness of the air.

I stared off in space. I knew I owed Meaka an explanation about what Agape had just said.

I took a deep breath. "Look, Meaka, for what it's worth, my attraction to Emillio was way before I met you. I never thought it was a need to tell you that I was somewhat attracted to him, being the fact he didn't share the same feelings about me."

"It's cool, Lyric. I'm not even on that. I don't know why A reacted like that to you. I just think she going through a thang."

"Yeah, and that I do know, but it doesn't excuse her or her attitude she has been having toward me since we been out here."

I noticed how Meaka screwed her face up when I mentioned Agape's attitude toward me.

"You can't act like you ain't noticed how she been playing me, Meaka. That's your sister and all, but that's the truth."

I'm not denying that, Meaka thought about when they were at the beach, the shit Agape was saying about Lyric and how she didn't like it; but she decided to play mediator to the situation.

"Lyric, you have to excuse A. She going through a thang right now. You know she didn't mean none of what she said. She need you right now."

"But the bitch thought I wanted to fuck her man, Meaka."

Meaka saw the hurt on my face, and she couldn't tell me that she thought there was some truth in the words I spoke.

But she said, "I don't think she thought that. A always speak highly of you, Lyric. You have to understand she just lost her everything and don't think there is anything in this world worse. She is just lashing out. That's all, Lyric."

Meaka stood from the bed and let me know that she was about to go too.

I sat on the bed with my head held low. I knew me and Agape's friendship was over after A's outburst. But that wouldn't stop me from being there for Meaka, so if it took for me to put up with Agape, I would do that out of respect for Meaka.

Meaka reminded me so much of myself before her innocence was taken away from her. I'm not sure how Meaka held on to her innocence. Shit, she was the only one of us that had done jail time, and I'm sure she went through just about as much as Agape did. I don't know, but it was the one thing that I liked about Meaka. I was just so over this. I wish I had kept my ass in Dayton. I ain't even get a chance to get ratchet down here. This was absolutely a waste of my time. As hard as I tried to shake the shit Agape said to me, I couldn't get her words out of my head, nor could I forget the look she had on her face.

Yep, that's the end of me and that bitch, I concluded.

We got on the plane, and there was not another word exchanged between me and Agape. Meaka babied her like she always did. I plugged my ears with my iPod and was off to sleep. I had had enough of excitement for two porn stars.

Agape

I knew what today was. That was why I locked my door the night before. I was aware of how Meaka would try to make me go through with going to Al's funeral. I couldn't see myself seated in front of Al's casket. It was like witnessing him being murdered all over again even though I couldn't remember anything from that night. I lay there trying to block out Meaka's beating on my bedroom door.

"Agape, I know you hear me!" Meaka yelled through the door. "Al's funeral is in, like, an hour, A. You have to come."

I heard Meaka's pleas. I honestly wish I could get up out of this bed and be there for the man that had done nothing but be there for me since the first day he met me. I smiled as I thought about the first night I met Al and how we instantly clicked.

162

"Agape, come out here. You know my boy gon' be real upset if his lady ain't out there for his going-home party," I heard Emillio say through the door.

I had no words. I lay there silently looking up at the ceiling with tear-filled eyes.

"Come on, Agape. What Trinity gon' think if you not there?"

I felt selfish. I had not thought about Trinity the whole time I was grieving. After Emillio told me that Al didn't have a will and that all of his possessions were going to the city of Dayton and Cincinnati, his house was now Trinity's slash her mother's, I was left with nothing. I buried Al in my mind that day. I cursed him for not having a will. I cursed him for leaving me that day when he promised that he would always be here for me. I hated Al for leaving me out here like this, but not one time did I take time to think about Trinity. I don't think there is any bond that's stronger than a little girl's bond with their father. I never knew what it was like to have a father; but I imagined, if I had my father in my life, that our bond would have been like the one Trinity and her father shared. If Trinity was strong enough to show up at her father's funeral, it left me without the option not to.

"Trinity's going to be there?" I questioned.

"Yeah, and she asked were you going to be there."

Emillio was lying about that. He was aware of the promise she made to her father never to utter a word about me to her mother, but the look in her eyes each time he interacted with her, he knew it was something she was dying to ask. But her mother would always be around. Emillio wanted to get Agape out of that room. And if he had to tell a little white lie to do it, he would do it again.

Hearing Em say she asked about me, I eased myself out of the bed and politely unlocked the door. I knew my existence worried them. Shit, I worried myself I had to have lost a good twenty pounds within the last two weeks. When I opened the door, I felt naked. I felt so vulnerable. I felt like that little girl who screamed for her mother's attention, only to have never received it.

"You okay, boo?" Meaka asked as she stepped into the room.

"I'm good. I have to go through some of my things to try to find me something to wear," I stated as I tried to busy myself with going through my boxes.

I took as much of my things as I could from Al's home—portraits of me and Al and clothes as well. I'd been staying at Emillio's with Meaka.

Meaka could always feel my frustrations.

She walked over and placed her hand on my shoulder. "Here, A, I got you something I think you might like." She pulled out an elegant floor-length black Hermes dress and a black hat with a lace veil that hung from it.

"It's beautiful, Meaka."

I couldn't hold in my tears as I tried so hard to do. I cried because I knew Al would have loved to see me in this dress. He always told me that he loved me in long dresses.

"Come on. No time for those tears, A. You have to get ready before we be late."

I went in the restroom, hopeful that, by the time I got dressed, I would come back out ready to attend the funeral.

When I held the dress up, I realized it was a size 6, and I slid comfortably down my once-size 8 frame.

I need to start eating, I thought as I stepped out of the restroom with my head held low.

I appreciated the lace veil more than I realized. Emillio escorted me outside. There were three white Navigator limos lined up. Emillio led me to the first limo. He opened the door for Meaka and me. I slid in first, and Meaka followed. I was surprised to see Lyric in the limo. She and Larry were in there. I was not sure if they were back kicking it or what. A few of Al's other friends were in the limo as well. Lyric came and sat next to me. I didn't know how to take Lyric. In some ways, I wished she had died that night instead of Al. I don't know why; I just felt that everyone had someone to lose other than her. She grabbed my hand in an attempt to console me. I gently took my hand out of hers and folded my hands on my lap. I hoped, for Lyric's sake, no one witnessed what took place between us; but when

I looked up and witnessed the confusion on Meaka's face, I knew she had seen what I did.

The ride to the church seemed like a hop and a skip. We were there in no time. Emillio stepped after the doors to the limo were opened.

"Where's Trinity?" I asked Emillio as if I was the child and she the adult.

"She should be in there already."

Emillio intertwined his elbow with mine and escorted me in the church. I hid behind my veil. I thought of myself as being invisible as I walked down the aisle leading to Al's casket. My small steps created a line behind us. I didn't want to break down in front of everybody seated at the funeral. I could just feel my self getting weaker. Meaka walked up and took Emillio's place; and despite how rude I was toward Lyric, she stood to the right of me, holding me up. I noticed the casket was closed, and I didn't understand why.

"Why is his casket closed?" I whispered to Meaka.

But Lyric spoke up, "His last wishes was to have a closed casket."

Meaka mouthed thank you to Lyric behind my back. She didn't know how she was going to tell me that the reason the casket was closed was that they couldn't close the hole that he had in his head from the bullet going through back of his head and out of his forehead. There were life-sized pictures of Al surrounding his casket. I felt Al's presence within my soul. I smiled because I remembered some of the memories that took place of what the flash had captured.

I could hear Al telling me, *It's all good, Agape. Let the law of the universe take its course.*

Emillio walked up behind me. "Agape, look what I got for you."

I didn't know what he could have had for me at the funeral. I turned around, and I felt like Al had died all over again when I looked into Trinity's eyes. She was so beautiful.

"Hi, miss lady," I greeted her as I took her out of Emillio's arms.

"Hi, Mom," she whispered in my ear.

Her tearstained face had the biggest smile on her face.

"You remember our secret?" I asked.

"How could I forget?" Trinity questioned.

I held her so close as if her small little body could absorb my pain.

"My mommy said I have to stay with my uncle Emillio, but I want to go with you."

"Well, we gon' have to see about that."

I never liked to hear the preacher preach at a funeral. They always said things that didn't sound anything like the person they were speaking of. I think that was because, most of the time, they didn't know anything about the person they were speaking of. I zoned out with Trinity on my lap. I thought about all the good times we shared with Al, and I wouldn't allow myself to cry with Trinity on my lap. Me and Trinity went and sat in the limo when they were about to take the casket out. I didn't want Trinity or myself to sit through that.

"Do you miss my dada, Mom?" Trinity questioned.

"More than you can imagine."

"Mama said that he dead and he ain't coming back and it ain't nothing I can do about it."

I never met her mother and didn't know anything about this woman other than what Al told me. To explain death that way to her own child, she had to be a product of a mother who did her just the same.

"Well, listen here, Trinity. Your Dada will always be there for you. You can talk to him anytime you want, okay? Your daddy loved you more than anything, and he will always be with you."

Trinity eyes lit up. "So I can talk to my dada whenever I want to?" Trinity wanted confirmation.

"Yes, baby, whenever you want to."

Trinity sat in silence for a brief moment. Then she said, "Dada, me and Mom miss you, and I'm not talking about my mama. I'm talking about Agape. We miss you, and we love you. Did he hear me, Mom?" Trinity asked.

"Yep, he heard you."

"Come on, Trinie." Emillio reached for Trinity. "Your mommy wants you."

"I don't want to go," Trinity said. "I want to stay with Mom."

Emillio looked from me to Trinity and from Trinity to me. I knew he was in a hard position and he was trying to do what was right for his best friend. I pulled Trinity out of the limo.

"Where is she at?" I asked Emillio, referring to Trinity's mom.

"She in the limo behind us."

I walked toward the limo with Emillio behind me. I stood at the limo as she and Emillio exchanged words. My back was turned as I leaned up against the limo.

"Come on, Trinity. Your friend is not going to the burial, so you can't go with her."

I didn't know how to take her calling me her daughter's friend. I left it alone. She, too, wore a veil covering her face. She stood in front of me and lifted her veil in hopes I would do the same.

Stormy did too. She wanted to know who this mysterious woman was that no one ever talked about. All she knew was she was Meaka's sister.

I didn't lift my veil. I had already seen too much. At that point, I could have cared less about Trinity or Stormy. Emillio didn't know what was up. He was left with no choice but to follow me to the limo. I got in and snatched my veil off of my head. I kicked and screamed at the air. I was letting go of all what had been bottled up inside of me. Emillio desperately tried to figure out what was going on until everyone started climbing in the limo. Meaka sat next to me. I rested my head on her shoulder.

"You gon' be okay," Meaka consoled.

I let Emillio know that I wasn't going to the burial, as if I hadn't already told him, so they detoured and dropped me off at the house. Meaka stayed with me. I explained to her that Stormy was Trinity's mother.

Meaka understood just how devastating that was, but she had to ask, "Did she say anything to you?"

"Nope. I didn't take my veil off. She didn't know who I was."

"What you plan on doing?" Meaka asked.

"I don't know, Meaka. I really don't. I just want to lie down."

"Okay."

Meaka walked me into my room, and I asked her if she had some Xanax, something that I had been requesting regularly. I saw the look in her eyes, but she didn't question me.

She said, "Hold on."

Within a few minutes, she was back in my room with two of the football-shaped blue pills.

I placed the two pills in my mouth and let them dissolve underneath my tongue. The taste was yucky, but the effect was quick. Before I knew it, I was knocked out.

Meaka

I was delighted when Emillio walked through the door. It felt like a weight had been lifted off of me. I greeted him with a kiss as I sat down on his lap.

I then went on to ask him, "How did Lyric get home?"

He told me that she rode home with Larry.

I had to laugh. *She gon' kill me*, I thought.

"I got something that I need to tell you," Emillio said.

"Please don't tell me that you are leaving me, I joked.

Lord knows I was serious but wanted to appear as if I was joking.

"Nah, baby. You know it ain't nothing like that, but I learned something from what has taken place. When you love someone, you need to let them know just how you feel. What I'm trying to say to you is, from the first time I laid eyes on you, I knew that you were special to me."

"Oh, listen to you trying to get all sentimental on me," I joked, trying to make it easier for him to say whatever else it was he wanted to say.

"Come on, baby. I'm serious right now," Emillio said as he eased me off of his lap.

He kneeled down on one knee. I just wanted to scream, but I held my composure. In walked Larry and Lyric and a few of Emillio's family and friends.

"Tameka Hoosk, I know we haven't been together that long, but I want to be with you till the end. Will you marry me?" Emillio asked as he opened up a red velvet box.

What I saw after that blinded me. It was the same five-carat princess-cut pink diamond ring I pointed out to Lyric. One day, she came and got me talking some crazy shit about we were going shopping for our own engagement rings. We laughed and joked about marrying ourselves.

I looked right at Lyric, and she mouthed sorry. I smiled to let her know that it was okay and got back to the matter at hand.

"Yes, I will marry you."

Emillio slid that ring on my hand, and I liked to have fainted. He stood up, and I jumped up in his arms.

"I love you so much."

Larry and Juan, Emillio's brother, brought in cases of champagne. I couldn't remember being this happy. Of course, when I was let out of jail, but this is a different type of happy. I was so wrapped up in meeting Emillio's family I liked to forgot about Agape. I excused myself from the room to go get her. I hoped that my joy would somehow channel joy into her. I called Agape's name from the doorway. She still slept. I hated to be selfish and wake her up, but I was to ecstatic not to. I tried to shake her, and she woke up for a brief moment, only to shoo me off.

"What, Meaka? Damn, can I just sleep?"

I wasn't going to allow her to steal my joy. She could join my happiness when she woke up. I went downstairs and enjoyed my engagement party.

Then next morning, I was up bright and early despite me and Emillio all morning lovemaking. I wanted to cook my man up something since he had been giving me lessons in the kitchen. I nailed the waffles, eggs, bacon, and potatoes. Emillio and I thought that he was going to have to do all the cooking. He was going to be so happy I made all three of our plates, and I headed upstairs so I could wake up Emillio and Agape. To my surprise, Agape was already up. She had a li'l pep to her that I had been missing. She walked out of the bathroom.

"You gon' eat breakfast with us?" I asked.

"Yes, ma'am. I miss another meal, I'm afraid I might disappear."

I laughed. "Well, your plate is made. I'm about to go wake up Em."

Agape and I sat at the table and began to eat. Agape reached over and grabbed my hand.

"Well, damn, look at you. What you do to deserve this?"

"You know what? I asked myself that last night."

We shared a light laugh. I dug into my plate.

"Who cooked this?" Agape asked.

"I did. You like? Please tell me you like it."

"Girl, you know your ass ain't cooked this food. You ain't got to front for me. I ain't none of your man. I know your ass can't cook."

"I did cook. Emillio been trying to teach me for the past couple of weeks."

"Well, Emillio did a good job."

"What you talking about? Them five carats?" Emillio asked, assuming that Agape was talking about my engagement ring, "because I was gon' say that got y'all girl name all over it."

Emillio laughed when he thought about how he and Lyric snuck out together so she could show him the ring that I wanted. When they walked up to the case, Lyric showed him the ring, and he saw the price. He knew that Lyric had my name stamped on this. Somehow, someway, he didn't think I would go to the galleria and pick out a $1.5 million ring.

"I should have never trusted that girl to take you looking for an engagement ring."

"Engagement ring?" Agape said, astonished.

"Yeah, we're engaged, Agape. I tried waking you up last night to attend the li'l gathering we had last night, but you wouldn't get up."

"You tried to wake me up?" Agape questioned in a way that told me she didn't believe I did.

"Yeah, I tried waking you up twice, and when you cussed me out, I left you alone. Why wouldn't I wake you up? You my sister."

Maybe because you know that I buried my man a few hours ago, and how dare you and this nigga spit on his grave like that? And then to top it off, Lyric goes with you to pick out the ring, Agape thought. "I don't know. I just don't remember you waking me up."

"Well, I did."

Agape knew me good enough to know when she was lying. *I knew that Meaka was telling the truth. I just chose to think otherwise.*

I played over my food, awaiting on a "Congratulations," "Meaka, I'm happy for you," or something; but instead Agape got up from the table. I tried to be there for Agape, but my patience was running very thin with her. Before she left the kitchen, I called out to Agape.

"A, I want you to be my maid of honor," I said sincerely.

"Oh, that's so sweet," Agape stated as she left out of the kitchen, leaving me and Emillio sitting there with blank expressions on the both of our faces.

I cleaned the kitchen in attempt to ignore what just took place between Agape and me. I couldn't think of one reason why she couldn't find it in her to be happy for me. I didn't understand why she didn't accept my request for her to be my maid of honor. But I know, in the end, she would be there for me.

Emillio would never voice his opinion on how he felt about Agape disregarding my newfound happiness. That was his fiancée's sister, so he felt like there was no need to get into it. But he decided to take me house shopping. He wanted to get me away from Agape, even if that meant giving her the house they lived in now.

House shopping was fun and tiresome. I was drained when we got back to the house. I called for Agape, and when she didn't answer, I went up to her room and noticed all of her boxes were missing. There was a letter on the her bed that read:

Meaka,

I am writing you this letter to let you know that I decided to leave. I'm not sure where I'm going, but I know it's nowhere fast. I feel like I'm losing myself, and in order not to do that, I feel I

need to just be alone. Don't come looking for me.
Let me do this on my own. I'll be fine. Trust me.

Signed,
A

I couldn't have dialed her number fast enough. I wanted to say so much to her, and the universe must have known it because I kept getting her voice mail. But that didn't stop me from calling her day in and day out, updating her on my wedding, what I did that day, and what I will be doing the next; but there was no answer nor response to my messages. I was beyond worried about Agape. I was supposed to be happy, but instead I walked around as if I had just lost my best friend. When in reality I had, I had lost the person closest to me. As the months went, Agape and I had become distant while my relationship with Lyric had blossomed into a friendship.

I was lying in my bed when Lyric's name and number popped up on my phone.

"And what pleasure did I provide to receive a call from you this early in the morning?"

"Hahaha," Lyric teased. "I just thought I would let you know that I see a truck like Agape's sitting outside of her old apartment."

"Are you serious?" I questioned.

I had been past there numerous times looking for Agape, and not one time did I see any sign of her.

"Well, don't sound so excited, Lyrie," I said, referring to Lyric as her new found nickname by me.

"That's your sister, bitch. Holla," Lyric said right before she hung up on me.

I immediately woke up my sleeping king. "Guess what, baby?"

"What's that?" Emillio questioned groggily, rubbing his eyes in an attempt to wake up.

"Lyric found Agape."

"Oh yeah?" Emillio questioned, trying his hardest not to show his disinterest on the topic at hand. "So what's up?"

"I'm going to go over there and see what's up with her."

"You need me to go with you?"

"Nah, that's cool. I just miss her so much, and I need to make sure she's okay. I know she misses me, but she been through a lot, you know."

I saw disappointment written across Emillio's face. I needed for him to look at things from my point of view.

"All I'm saying, baby, is this. When a person shows you who they really are, you have to believe them. It ain't no going around that."

"I know. I know, baby," I said, slipping on a pink heather gray Victoria's Secret jogging suit.

"I love you," Emillio said to put an end to the conversation.

"I love you more," I stated before I walked around and planted a kiss on Emillio's cheek.

"Don't be gone long."

"I won't."

Agape

"Wake up, Red," Chance said as he shook my shoulder. "Meaka want you."

"Didn't I specifically ask you not to answer my muthafucking phone!" I yelled.

"She in the living room."

I should have been hoping that she didn't hear me say that, but I didn't give a fuck.

"What do she want?" I asked.

"I don't know. Go see," Chance said as he lay down in the bed.

I guess the time had come for me to finally face Meaka. I just hoped she didn't stay long. I looked in the mirror. I looked liked shit. This I knew, but it didn't stop me from trying to pat my hair down.

I didn't like the way Meaka looked at me as if I was a fucking disease.

"Hi, girl, how you doing?" she asked as if I was a stranger to her and her to me.

I laughed sarcastically. "Meaka, what is it that you want with me? Can you make it quick? I was up all night, and I'm tired."

"Huh, do you realize I been looking for you for the past six months, A? You missed my wedding. I been calling you every day, leaving you messages after messages, and you have yet to return any of my calls."

It pained me to see Meaka upset, and I wish that I had an excuse for my actions. But truth was I had no excuse, and I couldn't find it in me to sympathize with her either.

"Girl, please you ain't been thinking about me. You think I don't know how you and that bitch Lyric been running around the city like Thelma and Louise? You think I don't know you made that bitch your maid of honor?"

"A, you know you were supposed to be my maid of honor. I still have your dress hanging in my closet. I called you every minute of the hour, begging you to come to my wedding. What was I to do? Not have a maid of honor?"

"Is that all you want?" I questioned with much attitude as I stood there with my hands on my hips and screwed-up face.

"How about we go out somewhere tonight and kick it? We always have a good time when we go out."

"We who?" I questioned.

"Me, you, and Lyric."

"Oh, hell no. I'm not going nowhere with that hoe. Fuck her. That's your friend."

"Agape, did you forget that I wouldn't have known Lyric had it not been for you?"

"Well, I won't be going. Sorry," I said as I walked toward the front door, hinting to Meaka that this meeting had come to an end.

"You're putting me out, A?" Meaka asked with tear-filled eyes.

I avoided eye contact with her, but the monkey on my back needed her out of here and fast.

I had been going to the projects hanging out with one of the hood rats from the Bass. How I figured it would get under her skin if she saw me with her. I had become addicted to Xanax, and Chance didn't like how I lay around and slept all day. I was expressing this to Donna, and she told me all I needed was an upper to balance the downer of the Xanax. I tried, and I couldn't enjoy any other drug other than that white girl. The first time I felt the high, I fell in love with that bitch. It haunted me that I couldn't remember what happened to Al. I often found myself thinking that Lyric had something done to Al. Tried to replay that night over and over in my head, but everything was like a blur. I just couldn't remember anything. That was until I started going to someone who did hypnosis, and it was then I found out that the man I was in bed with was the reason that the love of my life was killed. By this time, my recreational cocaine use had turned into an all-out addiction. I couldn't turn my back on Chance the way that I should. He was the only way I would be able to cop my drugs. With every dollar he gave me, I gave to Jay Baby, Donna's drug-dealing boyfriend.

Chance didn't know that I didn't have any memory of the night of Al's murder. He honestly thought that I had forgiven him. Shit, it was my man that had a gun pointed to his head. He knew that Al was rolling around in his grave with that fact that he and I had gotten back together. Chance had noticed the change in Agape. He blamed it on me having my man's head blown off in my face. My once-crazed addiction to the finest of everything had changed to my walking around half the time like a zombie. My figure was slowly diminishing, so he sent me to a psychologist. But I went to see a hypnosis instead.

"Well, I just want you to know you can call me whenever you like. If you ever need me, then I'm here for you."

"I'll keep that in mind, Meaka, but the help I need, only God can give it to me."

With that said, Meaka left out of the door, and I slammed it right behind her and proceeded to the bathroom. I retrieved my girlfriend from my hiding spot and went to town snorting line after line.

If only Chance had known that I wasn't sniffling from crying—instead, I was behind the door snorting lines as big as the Eiffel Tower—he would have got up and left out the door right behind Meaka.

Lyric

I hated pulling up to the Bass, the very same projects I grew up in. It was there that a lot of memories haunted me from my past. It was this very same housing project that I lost a lot of friends to the graveyard or to drugs and my mother to suicide, and many of the same girls I grew up with, they now were tenants of their own apartment with three and four kids running around with their mommas practically living next door. But this was the only place in Dayton, Ohio, you could come to, to find some grade-A marijuana. And Jay Baby was my supplier, so as long as he had it, I was coming to get it.

Jay Baby was the first nigga I saw on the corner out of the five niggas standing on the corner.

If this nigga would only leave the corner alone, he could make him some real money, I thought to myself.

He must have spotted me as well because he started walking toward my car.

"What's up, sexy?" he greeted.

"Nigga, you know what I want," I said jokingly.

Soon as I stepped out of my new Mustang, I could feel the stares, and I loved every minute of it. Most of the females in the Bass didn't like me because I was sleeping with either their nigga or their baby daddy. Whichever it was, they couldn't understand why their nigga was willing to not only fuck with a bitch like me but also pay my bills and pay for my car and whatever else I wanted. But that was for me to know and for them to find out. It ain't my fault their mommas were too stupid to teach their daughters the game.

When I walked through Donna's door, she screwed her face up. Donna never liked me since we were younger. I remember that fat bitch used to chase me home every day after school until the day my momma caught me running home from her. She sent me right back outside to fight her, and after Donna whooped my ass, I went in my house and realized that was nothing compared to the ass whooping my momma put on me. She stomped me in my stomach and in my face, vowing to kill me if she so much as thought I was running from any bitch.

Her words? "I don't care how big a bitch is, you better pick up something and knock the shit out of that bitch with it!" Momma yelled as she beat me unmercifully.

Momma told me that the only way she would leave me alone was unless I fought her back, but that wasn't enough for Donna. She wanted to fight every time we saw each other. I was willing to because, no matter how bad she beat my ass, each time we had a fight, it was nothing compared to how momma beat my ass. The whole hood watched the ass kickings I would take from Donna. No one would break it up or anything. I didn't take it personal because it was like that in the hood. No one broke up fights, especially not a one-on-one fight. The last ass kicking I took from Donna, after I picked myself up off the ground, I dusted off my brand-new pair of Jordache jeans. That was when some dude walked up to me.

"How come you keep letting that big bitch beat you up like that?" he asked.

I held my head low. I felt defeated. I felt like, no matter how hard I fought her, I just couldn't beat her.

"She too big," I said.

And that she was. Donna was at least fifty pounds heavier than me, and the blows she threw, I felt each one of them.

"Man, it ain't no such thing as a mufucka being too big. You just don't know how to fight. Come over to my house. I'll teach you how to fight."

The thought of learning how to fight sounded like music to my ears. I was tired of getting my ass beat by Donna.

"Where you live?"

"I stay up top," he said, referring to the front of the projects.

The Bass had a one-way entrance and a one-way exit.

"What's your name anyway?" I asked.

"Chance."

I couldn't remember where I had heard the name from—that is, until the day I took him up on his offer teaching me how to fight.

When Amira came to the door, it clicked to me where I had known Chance's name from. He was Amira's big brother. Amira and

I were in the same class. Nobody fucked with her because she was Chance's little sister.

"Is Chance here?"

"Chance!" Amira called out.

He came to the door and asked, "What's up?"

"I thought you was going to show me how to fight?" I questioned.

He laughed. "So you ready to learn how to fight?"

"Yes, I am." And I was more than willing to learn how to fight.

"Okay. Here I come. Wait outside. Amira, get the boxing gloves."

Boxing gloves? I thought.

Chance and Amira came outside with a set of boxing gloves each.

"Here, put these on," Chance said, throwing me a set of boxing gloves.

I put the gloves on and noticed Amira putting on the set that she carried out the house.

"Come on. You and Amira gon' box."

We stood facing each other.

"You ready?" Chance asked, looking directly at me.

"Yeah, I'm ready."

"Box!" was all he said, and I felt a punch right to the face.

The impact from the glove stunned me. I couldn't believe Amira. She had hit me in the face. I ran up on her and swung the gloves widely. Bink. Bink. I felt two hits to the face. I backed up and ran up again. Another two hits to the face. I felt I had to be doing something wrong. Amira never left off of her square. I was the aggressor and still didn't land one punch. I looked over at Chance. He and his friends were laughing. I felt a hint of embarrassment. I threw the gloves off. I felt pity in Amira's stance.

"Put the gloves back on," she demanded.

"No, so y'all can stand out here and make me the laughing-stock? I think not."

As I turned around to walk toward my apartment, Chance said, "Hold up, shorty. We not laughing at you. We were reminiscing about the time we had to teach Amira how to fight. Imagine me standing in your position."

I questioned what he was saying.

"I will never forget that shit. Chance kept dinging me in my muthafuckin' face," Amira said, reminiscing.

"Don't give up. Just watch."

I watched on as Chance and Amira boxed it out. It amazed me how she ate his punches as well as landing her own.

"Put 'em back on," Chance demanded, handing me the gloves. "Hold 'em like this." Chance demonstated how he wanted me to put the two gloves up in front of my face. He said, "It don't matter how many times you swing if none of them land. Keep your head up and watch where you swinging. Keep your arms straight in front of the target, pull back, and connect."

It can't be that easy, I thought.

I stood there with the gloves in front of my face. I focused on Amira's mouth and her right eye, just where she had hit me at first. I pulled back and connected with much force. I made the mistake replacing Amira with Donna and hit a li'l too hard. Boy, wasn't I brought back when she uppercut me and sent me straight to the ground. I got up a li'l shaken.

Chance scolded Amira. "You supposed to be helping her learn how to fight, not trying to knock her out."

Me and Amira continued this up for about a month. The next time I came in contact with Donna's big ass, I ran circles all around her and bust her head to the white meat.

I looked at the permanent war wound she wore to this day. I followed Jay Baby's lead, stepping over kids' trash and pit bull puppies. It had to be about five puppies living in that apartment with them.

"So when you gon' let me hit that, Lyric?" Jay Baby whispered.

"When you get your money up," I responded.

"What you trying to get?"

"Give me a ounce of that kush."

I peeped the pounds in the cabinet. It had to have been about seven or eight of them, just maybe Jay Baby getting some money. Jay

Baby grabbed a few handfuls of weed from the pound and stuffed into a plastic baggie and handed it to me.

"That's on the house."

I smiled as I grabbed the kush-filled baggie.

"So what's been up with you?"

"You know me, Jay Baby. Same shit, different day."

Donna sat on the couch in the same spot she was in when I came in. I threw her my most infamous grin as I proceeded to the door. I knew she hated me, and if I was her, I would hate me too.

Donna didn't like the way Jay Baby looked at me. She didn't like the fact, whenever the three of them were in the same room, Jay Baby never said one single word to her. She felt that she was invisible to her man when I was around. And she hated it.

"You seen your girl, Agape?" Donna asked Lyric.

It was not what she asked me that bothered me. It was just the mere fact she was talking to me that rubbed me the wrong way. The bitch had never attempted to say anything to me, so I knew she had to have been on some bullshit. I should have just pushed open the screen door and ignored her like my instincts told me to.

"Nah, I ain't talked to her," I said out of respect for Jay Baby.

I was aware of his relationship with Donna even though he'd been sniffing behind my ass since I could remember.

"Well, she been over here kicking it with me," Donna rubbed in, trying to make me feel like their friendship was something other than a mutual addiction to the same white bitch.

Agape was damaged, and so was Donna. They shared one common hatred—that is, for Lyric.

"Oh, that's good, being that fact you ain't got no other friends," I joked, just before I said my goodbyes to Jay Baby.

There goes that look again, Donna thought.

When she saw nothing but lust in her man's eyes for another woman, that pained Donna. That was why she wanted to bring pain to me.

"You know, she on that shit."

The look I gave her let her know she had struck a nerve.

I had heard this before about Agape, but I didn't know how true it was. Now here was the person that I heard she had been getting high with confessing Agape's addiction to me for her. It was like a smack in the face, but I'd be damned if I let her know that.

"Well, if A want to run around getting high, that's her mutha-fuckin' business, and if you got yo' big lazy ass up off of that couch, then you might have some to tell of your own."

Jay Baby understood my position. He knew why I reacted the way I did, but what he didn't understand was why Donna put it out there like that. She knew that Agape and I were cool, and he also knew that he had better got me out of there fast before I whooped Donna's ass.

"You better watch your bitch, Jay Baby. That shit wasn't cool, what she just pulled. Had her kids not been in that house, I wouldn't have been so forgiving."

"That shit ain't about nothing, Lyric."

I slid in my Mustang, and the question that was lingering in my head I had to bring to existence.

"So is it true?" I asked, hiding behind my Tiffany's sunglasses with watery eyeballs.

Jay baby's hesitation to answer the question sent a sharp pain in my head. I placed my forehead on the steering wheel.

"You all right, Lyric?"

"How do you know that shit is true?" I asked, making it apparent that, without words, he told me what was up.

"Man, listen, Lyric." Jay Baby paused as he tried to find the right way to use words to describe a very complex but common situation to me. "Agape come through here from time to time and copped from me."

"How could you do that, Jay? How could you sell that shit to Agape?"

Out of all the mothers, sisters, nieces, and daughters he had sold cocaine to, he never felt no kind of remorse about handing them their drug of choice. That was until the first time Agape stopped by his apartment to purchase some cocaine. When he looked out of the peephole of the door, he recognized her as Lyric's buddy she had been rocking with. Despite the three o'clock unannounced visit, Jay Baby let her in automatically, assuming she was there to cop some green, just not knowing what grade she wanted.

"So what's it gon' be? Reggie, purp, kush? I got some of that sour diesel too."

"Nothing like that," Agape stated with a light laugh, trying to make light of the situation.

"Well, what you looking for?"

Surely this young, beautiful sister not here to purchase no crack or powder, Jay Baby thought to himself as he awaited Agape's answer.

"I need some powder."

It was then that Jay Baby saw the coke fiend in her. Who was he to judge her? He himself snorted powder from time to time, so he did what any drug dealer in his position would do.

"How much?"

"A eight ball."

My cheeks were tearstained. Jay Baby felt blessed I had on shades because he couldn't see the tears but could feel my hurt.

"How could you do that, Jay Baby? Why would you even sell her that shit?"

"Come on now, Lyric. You from around here, you know how it goes. If I wasn't selling the shit to her, then somebody else would."

"You know what? Fuck you, Jay Baby," I stated as I started up my engine.

"It's like that, Lyric."

I put the car in drive and hit the gas, not looking back.

I knew that the word on the street had been true. Miracle had told me that the word in the street was that Agape was out in the Bass getting high with Donna in the wee hours of the morning. I wasn't going to just take her word for it. As close as Me and Miracle were, I also knew that Donna and Miracle shared a friendship as well and was well aware of how a pair of lips would say anything. I didn't want to trouble Meaka any further than she already was regarding Agape, so I decided to keep the whole Agape getting high to myself.

Chance

I reached over to grab Agape in my arms. I wanted to feel her close to me. I wanted to rekindle what we had once shared, but something about her seemed different, borderline weird. I opened my eyes to make sure no one else had jumped in my bed. I was sure that the body I was holding on to damn sure was not that of Agape's. I saw her eyes flickering when she turned her back to me. I knew she wasn't sleep.

"Wake up, Red."

"Huh?"

"Why the fuck you so damn skinny?" I asked, cutting straight to the chase.

"Chance, what are you talking about?" Agape asked, eluding the question.

I knew that there was only one way that a woman could lose so much weight in such a short period of time. I couldn't ignore how rough her once-soft skin felt. All the signs of a drug user were sitting right in front of me. It wasn't until I arose from the bed, cutting the lamp on, that it was apparent what Agape had been doing. When the light hit her eyelids, Agape instantly opened her eyes, and I was looking right in her glossy, bulging eyes. The fiend in her told her that I wouldn't be able to tell that she was high, so she tried to remain as calm as possible.

"Chance, I've been dieting, baby. Lie back down."

I felt humiliated that Agape would try to insult my intelligence. I laughed a sinister laugh. Had it not been for the cocaine she had been snorting, she might have been scared, but the powder gave her courage.

"You think I don't know when I'm in the presence of a mutha-fucking dope fiend?" I asked as I pulled Agape's body out of the bed by her hair.

"Get your hands off of me, muthafucka. Fuck you."

"Fuck me, huh? No, fuck you, bitch," I stated just before I punched Agape in her nose.

Instantly blood came gushing from her nose. The impact should have knocked her out, but the powder made her numb to the punches I dished out at her. I dragged Agape's naked body out of the house. I knew she was on something, and I was determined to find out just what drug she had become succumbed to.

"Why are you doing this to me, Chance?" she asked. "Please stop, Chance, please."

Each blow sent Agape flying to the ground, but she didn't feel a thing. She just continued staggering her way up on her feet as if she was the underdog in a heavyweight fight. I couldn't believe the sight before me. How could she do this to herself? It reminded him of his mother and her addiction to her drug of choice. I didn't know how to take the woman whom I spent so many years loving was just like the one woman whom I despised most of my life—my mother. I knew me and Agape were over, and I hoped that this beating would do her some good.

Agape

Naked and beat up, I banged on Chance's door, hoping that he would let me in.

"Chance, please let me in. I have nowhere to go."

And I really didn't. Chance talked me into letting my apartment go completely. It was hard because I just wanted to get him out of my face so I could run off and get high, so I did. I didn't have my truck because I rented for some powder to one of the drug dealers in the Bass. I told Chance I had to put it in the shop because the transmission went out on it. He gave me the $1,800 to get it fixed, but I snorted that up too. I avoided Chance a lot, pretending that I was so busy trying to get my thoughts and my life together. In all reality, I was cooped up in Donna's apartment getting high. I even stopped going to Mari's shop. Even in the midst of getting my hair done, I wanted to get high. When Mari told me that she'd been noticing a change in me, I quit coming because I would hate for her old nosy ass to put any kind of ideas in Chance's head.

"Just give me something to put on, Chance. I can't go anywhere naked."

Chance then threw out a sheet. I wrapped the sheet around me and began walking to his closest neighbor's house, which was about twenty minutes up the road. My guess was the drugs had worn off because, all of a sudden, I felt weak, too weak, to walk any farther. Then a sharp pain went through my spine.

Meaka

I told myself that I would wait on Agape when she was ready to talk, then she would reach out to me. I just wish I knew the reason as to why she was treating me like a stranger. It bothered Emillio the way Agape's been acting toward his wife. He didn't want to intervene, but he did need to try to straighten things out between us before I started growing gray hair.

"What's up, blood?" Emillo greeted me with a hug. "What's got you down? Don't answer that." Emillio could feel that this somehow had to do with Agape. "It's A?"

Silence.

"I just don't get it, Emillio. I don't understand why her attitude has changed so drastically. I have done nothing but be there for Agape, and she treat me like the enemy."

Emillio looked on as I ranted on and on about Agape's shenanigans. Tears formed in my eyes. I wanted to cry, but this time, I was determined not to. I pushed the tears back somewhere. I didn't care where as long as they didn't slide down my face. I was tired of focusing on Agape. I had to get my marriage in order and be the woman my man needed me to be. I'd noticed how Emillio's business trips were lasting longer and more frequent. Emillio used to always ask me to come along on his trips. I would always decline because I was so engulfed in finding Agape. Business was business with Emillio. He felt that he had done enough to mend Agape's broken heart. That didn't bother him. Her willingness to not address what the problem was, was what bothered him, and her not showing up at his wife's wedding was a low blow. So he pretty much avoided any conversation regarding Agape.

Emillio saw that my eyes were no longer filled with sadness but filled with resentment. He was lost.

"Meaka, you know that I love you. Shit, I love you for better or worse, but this whole Agape thang, it's really fucking with me. I don't understand why you let her handle you the way you do. Shit, I'm your husband, and when I joke with you about your cooking, you're down my throat, and this bitch—Pardon my French." Emillio was caught up. He never wanted to disrespect his wife's sister, but he had a point to prove. "That's your sister and all, but I feel like she might as well be your husband." Emillio wanted to get my attention once and for all. "I wish you would chase behind me the way you do her because then maybe you could see how you're neglecting to be here for your man. I constantly come home and you soaking in misery. I give you everything a man is supposed to give his wife, and that's not enough to make you happy."

I listened to Emillio confess his heart to me. those very tears I held in flowed profusely.

"What makes you hold on to such misery? And when I say misery, I'm speaking of that sister of yours. I know that's you sister A, but today you have to choose between me and your sister. You choose me, I'll promise to be there for you for better or for worse. You choose to continue to run behind someone who doesn't have your best interest at heart, then I'm leaving."

Emillio hated to put it to me that way, but he had to put his foot on her neck. Otherwise, he feared he was going to lose his wife. He didn't like coming in his home finding his wife like this and couldn't stand another night of it.

"How could you ask me to choose between you and my sister? I love you both just the same, and I am not willing to do such a thing. Matter of a fact, I won't choose. And if you love me the way you say you do, then you should understand," I cried out.

"Is that your final answer? I'm not bullshitting with you," Emillio stated as he walked to the door.

He didn't want to have to make me choose between himself and Agape. He just wanted to know where my loyalty lay, and obviously it wasn't with him. Emillio wanted me to realize that I had already lost my sister and choosing him was opportunity to be taken away from the pain of not having Agape around.

"I love you, Emillio. Don't do this to me," I begged.

The thought of him walking out the door on me, I couldn't bear. I wanted to tell him to walk the fuck out and fuck him for trying to make me make such a selfish decision.

Instead, I said, "I choose you, Emillio."

Hearing the words flow from my mouth brought satisfaction to his soul. He knew this was his soul mate sitting before him. He just had to get me to see that.

Emillio walked back and sat on the sofa with me.

"I have something to tell you," I confessed.

I never wanted my husband to feel inferior to Agape. It was apparent that he did.

"Agape is not really my sister. She is actually my foster sister. I have no siblings."

Emillio looked just as confused as I thought he would. We shared a common bond. We promised each other that we would never do anything to mess up the sense of family that we had created within ourselves. When I made that promise to Agape, I meant it. That was why I took the rap for her when she killed our foster mom. Emillio sat there and listened to my story, and by the time I was finished, he loved me more than he had before. Not only was his wife a woman of her word, but I was his. Emillio knew that I had a wall put up. He just didn't know exactly what the wall was built of.

I felt that there was a ton of bricks pulled off of my heart. It had been hard walking around with so much on my heart. Agape and I never talked about that gruesome night. That night changed my life forever. That night was the reason for many nightmares I had after that night. The nightmares stopped the first night Emillio held me to sleep. Emillio was my comfort, and in me, he saw so much innocence. I didn't understand how anyone could look at my tarnished past and consider me as a prized possession. That was why I hid the things that I had been through. I was willing to accept who I was. I felt it wasn't fair to not give the man that married me the opportunity to choose, to choose whether or not he was willing to accept all that there was to me.

I shied away from him as he held my chin.

"You know what, Tameka? You don't have to hide from who you are with me. Everything that you told me, that's you."

I brightened up.

"I hate that you had to go through those things, but I look at you no less. Matter fact, I love you more. You are the best thing that has happened to me in a long time. Now come and give me some of my noonie."

Agape

"Do you have anyone that we can contact for you, Ms. Lewis?" the doctor asked as she handed me my discharge papers.

I didn't know how I was going to get from the hospital. I wasn't dealing with Chance anymore. The way he beat my ass, I could never forgive him for that, so I let Dayton's finest deal with his ass. They picked him up on felonious assault. Fuck him. I hoped they lock the door and throw away the key on his bitch ass. I missed Meaka so much, and it pained me how I'd been so inconsiderate. I was happy that Meaka was the type of sister she was. She never let me down. She was always on my side. I didn't know how to make up for the pain and confusion that I had been placing before our life.

That's who I'll call.

Ring. Ring. Ring.

"Hello?"

"Hi, Meaka, this is Agape. I was just wondering. Would you mind picking me up from the hospital?"

"Right now?" was Meaka's only question.

"I'm ready whenever you are, if you not busy…"

"I'm in the car with Em. We can come now if you want."

"Please."

"Which hospital?"

"I'm at Miami Valley."

"We'll be there," Meaka stated.

I hopped out on my crutches. All thanks to the handywork Chance put in on me, I had a fractured leg, two black eyes, and a fractured rib. Meaka helped me into the car, demanding that I tell her who did this to me.

"Chance..."

"What happened, A? What would make him do some shit like that to you?"

"I don't know. He just came home from the club, tripping. I woke to him punching me in my head. He dragged me out of the door by my hair asshole naked, beating the shit out of me. He left me out there for dead, Meaka. I can't believe that muthafucka Agape I lied."

I was too mad to cry and too hurt to show my pain. My body ached from all the fractures I sustained.

"Do you mind carrying her in the house, Emillio?" asked Meaka, referring to me.

"No, baby. That's a good idea because it would be hard for her to get up all those steps."

Emillio parked the car and gently pulled me from the car. As gentle as Emillio tried to be, the bruises were everywhere. The pain was all over. Emillio's steps quickened as I squirmed with discomfort in his arms. I missed Em and Meaka, and as much as I didn't want to admit, I needed them.

Emillio and Meaka nursed me back to good health. I put on a few pounds, but I still was nowhere near my size 8. Yet and still I was no longer a two. Meaka thought I lost weight because of not being able to eat good because of stress. I was even back speaking to Lyric, but the tables had turned tremendously. I was now on the defense, and she on the offense. Every time I made an attempt to speak to her, she made me feel as if I was two feet tall.

"What's up wit it?" "What's good?" and "What pop'n?" would be her response. No actual "How are you?" or a flat-out hello. She and Meaka were inseparable. I kind of found myself jealous of their relationship. Anytime I was in the room with them both, I found I would excuse myself from the room. I felt like a stranger in Meaka and Emillio's home.

I guess I really had no one to blame but myself. I placed the boulder that was placed between Meaka and me. It wasn't until we were alone in a room together that the void between us was apparent. I wanted to fill the void by letting Meaka know that I appreciated her and everything that she had done for me. I wanted us to go out and have some fun. It had been a while since we did something together.

"How about we do something tonight?"

"Yeah, that's cool," Meaka stated. "It sounds like fun to me. Lyric invited me to an all-white party. We can go see what it's like."

We went to Macy's to find us something fierce to wear to the party. I took the time to ask Meaka if Lyric knew I was coming to the party.

"Yeah, she know your coming. She's excited that you gon' come out with us tonight. Matter of a fact, this is her on the phone," Meaka announced as she checked her caller ID before answering her phone. "What's up, girlie?"

"Nothing much my way in traffic. I was just trying to call you and remind you that the party starts at ten and there is no need to be fashionably late."

"Girl, I know you ain't talking, Miss I-will-be-late-to-my-own-funeral Ass Bitch."

Lyric couldn't help but laugh because she was always late. "You got me on that one."

I couldn't help but chuckle as I eavesdropped on Meaka's conversation. I knew all too well how Lyric's excuse for being late was "Don't take it personal. I'ma be late to my own funeral."

"So are you gon' ride with me and Agape, or we riding with you?"

Lyric hesitated. "I'll ride with y'all."

"Okay then. It's on…Peace."

By the time we picked Lyric up for the party, it was already ten. Lyric was dressed in a white strapless dress that hugged her like a hustler embraces the block. I noticed that Meaka and Lyric shared the same taste for clothes just as well as shoes. Shit, they had the same pair of shoes on; and if you weren't looking hard, you would have thought they had on the same dress.

"Aren't we looking mighty good?" Lyric complimented to no one in particular. "I like that suit, A."

"Thank you."

I rocked an all-white Capri pantsuit. I didn't feel comfortable to wear a dress with these chicken legs. I had a few more pounds to put back on before I pulled out my "freak em dress," in Lyric's words. Lyric sat in the back rolling up some loud-ass weed that stank so good. As soon as the blunt was in rotation, I was a li'l hesitant to hit the blunt because I hadn't had any drugs in my system, but I said fuck it. Who was I fooling? This was my first drug of choice. I hit the blunt and immediately started choking.

"Damn, you all right?" Lyric asked. "If I ain't known no better, I would think that you had virgin lungs."

I continued to choke on the weed as I inhaled the smoke. I was high after the first round. I didn't understand how I ever made the decision to put powder up my nose when weed was so much friendlier and easy to cope with. I felt a sense of guilt come over me. I had told myself that I wouldn't get high anymore, and that meant any drug, or so I thought. By the time we made it to Club Lola, it was jumping. Everybody that was somebody was out. I was feeling myself. I walked in the club with the attitude like I owned the club. Lyric and I were taking numbers. Meaka even accepted a few just for fun. I warned her that it wasn't a good idea to be taking anybody's number especially since she was married.

"Meaka, girl, you good? Do you we know ain't none of these niggas fucking with brah brah?"

"Ain't shit wrong with taking a number," Lyric shot back.

I got up from the bar and walked toward the exit. The liquor and the weed had me feeling suffocated in the club. Soon as I hit the door, I bumped into Jay Baby.

"What's up, Red?"

"Oh, I'm good. How you doing?"

"I see you doing good," Jay Baby complimented.

"Why, thank you," I said.

"Who you up in here with?"

"Meaka and Lyric," I responded.

Jay Baby hadn't seen Lyric since their dispute. She hadn't been by to cop no green from him or nothing.

"Oh yeah, let me get on in here."

Jay Baby didn't want to be in the presence of me any longer. The longer he conversated with me and realized how much beauty I possessed, the more he kicked himself for playing such a vital role in my demise. I noticed the guilt written all over his face, but I didn't want him to feel like he had wronged me in any type of way. Before I let Jay Baby walk into the club, I grabbed his hand and pulled him toward me.

I whispered in his ear, "I came to you, Jay. Remember that."

The burden he carried was lifted right then and there. It was clear the message I was trying to send to him, and when he kissed my forehead, I knew he understood exactly what I meant by that.

Donna had been following Jay Baby's every move. Ever since she and Lyric had their falling out, he hadn't been staying home; and when he did come home, it was only to shower, change his clothes, and see his kids. Donna didn't understand why Jay Baby felt so strong about her telling Lyric about me getting high. She forced herself into believing she had it wrong when she thought that Lyric and Jay Baby were creeping. From the kiss she had witnessed Jay Baby gave to me, a kiss on the forehead, to Donna, it was the ultimate sign of disrespect.

"I should go over there and beat the red off of that bitch," Donna said to Miracle, who sat seated on the passenger side of the car.

"Girl, fuck all of that. Let's go in this party and have a good time."

Miracle didn't want any problems with me. She knew that I was Lyric's girl, and to her, any friend of Lyric's was a friend of hers.

I walked back in the club and caught Lyric tearing the dance floor up.

That girl know she can dance, I thought to myself.

Meaka was standing on the outside of the dance floor doing a two-step. I took the initiative to hit the dance floor. I wasn't sure whom the pair of hands belonged to that were planted on my hips;

so I continued to wind my hips hoping, whoever it was, they were enjoying the view. I was full of intensity and ready to find out who was behind me, so I did a slight turn, only to find out it was Jay Baby.

"We gon' slow it down for a minute, fellows, so grab on to one of these sexy ladies and do yo thang," the DJ announced.

Jay Baby held his hand out to me, requesting this dance. I took his hand and stepped in his space, and we began slow dancing. All the guilt Jay Baby felt, he expressed it through the dance they shared.

"Can I butt in this dance?" someone asked, tapping me on the shoulder.

It was Lyric. She had a smile spread across her face that I couldn't deny her of the dance. As comfortable as I was, I had to break free from Jay Baby's embrace.

Lyric

Look at Jay Baby getting his groove on with Agape. It was a good thing that A decided to come on the winning team because that was exactly what Meaka and I were doing. We were loyal to each other and only wanted the best for each other. Therefore, everything that we'd wanted so far, we'd received. We were true to ourselves. That was why we never let anyone or anything penetrate our circle or take us off of our square. We were alike in so many ways, but on the surface, we were different. I guess that was why we were so tight.

My friendship with Agape, it was kind of forced. When I went out of my way to see why she was outside of her apartment the very first day I met her, shit, I was just being nosy. I had no one else to kick it with. My only female friend was Miracle and Amira.

Amira had just caught a case for stabbing a girl with the rat-tail of her comb. Amira was defending herself against four girls. Chance had one of Dayton's best attorneys fighting Amira's case, but unknown to everyone, the girl who got stabbed was a family friend to the judge on her case. They gave her juvenile life.

Miracle was a girl that reminded me too much of why I fucked and sucked any and every nigga I thought was worthy of some money. Miracle was a product of her environment. She was a single mother of three girls. She had her first daughter at the age of thirteen. None of the kids had an active father in their life. Miracle didn't work. The system fed and supported her children. Each one of the girls got an SSI check, including Miracle. Don't ask me what was wrong with any one of them because they didn't appear to have any disabilities that I was aware of. She lived in the Bass and had been living there since she was a kid. Miracle fucked a lot of niggas with money. Only thing was they never gave her shit. She was busy moving the niggas in, cooking and doing laundry for them, completely forgetting about what mattered—getting some money. I tried to school Miracle, but talking to Miracle was like talking to the wall.

"I ain't no hoe, Lyric" would be Miracle's response when I would tell her she needed to be getting money from them niggas if she was fucking them.

And my response would be "I know you ain't because you ain't getting shit."

That's what I just don't understand about females. They feel like, as long as money is not exchanged, then they are excused from being a ho. If that's how they want to look at it, then that's cool too; but I would rather be a paid hoe on any given Sunday rather than a fuck bitch because, if you're getting just as much of dick as a hoe and you're not getting paid, then you're nothing more than a fuck bitch. But what do I know?

When I noticed that Chance was checking for Agape, I kept her close to find out the ins and outs to their relationship. I and Chance had an understanding between each other. We weren't in a relation-ship. He was open to be with whomever he wanted to be with, and so was I. But if and when he felt like he needed or wanted him some of me, I was willing. It started off as a sick game. I would sex Chance and then send him home to Agape. I might have even given him head while he checked in on her at home. This came natural for me and Chance. The day he showed me how to fight, I was *forever* grate-ful. We were around each other so much she started to grow on me, then I felt guilty.

"May I please butt in this dance?"

"Go'n 'head, girl," Agape said just before Jay Baby grabbed and let her know that she looked good and he wanted to keep seeing her that way.

The understatement was read by all of us. He gave her a friendly hug, and she walked off.

"You know, I got love for you, Jay Baby," I had to admit.

I knew why he displayed the actions that he did. He only knew the code of the streets. Jay Baby was born and raised in the Bass, never leaving the bricks, not even to go to school. Jay Baby's moms never so much as enrolled her son in school. He couldn't tell you what the inside of a school looked like. All he knew were numbers.

"How about I take you up out of here so I can show you just how much love I got for you?"

"I keep telling you, Jay. You got to get yo' money up," I whispered in his ear before I laid my head on his chest.

And we grinded innocently to the Adina Howard's "T-Shirt and Panties."

Jay Baby hated when I assumed that he wasn't getting money. *If she would only pay close attention to the thousand-dollar Akoo jean outfit I got on and the two-thousand-dollar manis on my feet. Shit, I got ten thousand on my neck up, but Lyric knew better than to judge a book by its cover. I didn't even know that Lyric was going to be in here. Otherwise, I would have never even wore this chain.*

"Lyric, why you always talking that get-your-money-up bullshit?"

Is that sincerity I hear? I thought. "Jay Baby, get out. Your feelings?" I said, trying to make light of the situation.

I pulled back, ready to end the dance, but Jay Baby wasn't finished. He pulled me near aggressively. I didn't know why I was enjoying this.

"You saying you won't fuck with me unless I'm paying?"

I used to tell myself, if I was to ever give this up on the humble, I would give it to Jay Baby; but I wasn't gon' tell him that.

"Jay Baby, you know what type of bitch I am. Who you kidding?" I asked as I turned my back to him and looked back to see how much he appreciated the dance I was giving him.

It wasn't until he pushed up on me and I felt that monster of his. I smiled.

"Why the fuck you all up on my man like that?"

I turned my head, only to see Donna, and Miracle stood to the side of her. But when I locked eyes with her, she showed whom her loyalty was to when she walked off. I appreciated that because otherwise I would have given her the same ass whooping I was threatening to give to Donna with my eyes.

"Get your girl," I warned Jay Baby.

As I walked off, leaving them to pick up their relationship, Meaka had already peeped what was going on; so she walked toward the three.

"What's up, Lyric?" Meaka asked.

"Girl, fuck that dumb bitch. Let's enjoy this party."

I was not about to mess my night up over some tired-ass bitch or her broke-ass baby daddy.

I walked toward the bar. I took note Agape was at the bar talking to Jody, some nigga I knew to have money.

Just like that bitch to snag a baller, I thought.

"What's up, A? You good?" I asked, not really caring, just letting Jody know she ain't up in this club solo; so hopefully he had some of his balling friends with him.

"Yeah, I'm good."

"I thought I was about to have to beat Donna's fat ass, girl. That bitch—"

When I turned to Agape to finish my sentence, it looked like she damn near shitted on herself.

"What's your problem?" I questioned, knowing good and well she and Donna were just getting high together and now came the time her little secret might be exposed.

I didn't give a damn either way.

"Nothing. I'm just shocked she up in here. I've never known her to go to clubs."

"Girl, it's a lot you don't know about Donna. Well, let me let you entertain this eye candy."

After giving Jody a wink, I ordered me another drink. Boy, I needed one.

Meaka

Lyric would kill me if she knew I snuck to the bathroom to call Emillio.

"What's up, wifey?"

"Hi, baby, what you doing?"

"Sitting here trying to figure some shit out."

"And what's that?"

"Nothing for you to worry your pretty little head about, so tell me. How many of the niggas up in there trying to get at my wife?"

I giggled. "Only a few," I said.

"Well, when you done gassing them niggas up, bring your ass home."

"I love you, baby, and don't wait up."

"I will."

We shared a laugh, then I ended the call.

I love him, I thought to myself.

I walked out the stall only to be pushed by the girl I saw up in Lyric's face along with a high-yellow girl with some of the pinkest lips I'd ever seen.

Word is excuse you, I turned and said as she hurried her big ass in the stall.

"She just drunk. It's all good," Pink Lips said.

I turned around and mouthed, "Yeah, it is, but if her fat ass bump me like that again, I ain't gon' let her being drunk stop me from whooping her ass."

This was the prime reason I didn't drink. You never know what the fuck gon' jump off, and a drunk bitch is easily a beat-up bitch fighting with a sober bitch.

"Hold on now, you Black bitch. Wait till I finish my business in here, and we'll see if you talking that bullshit."

Who does this fat-ass bitch think she is? I thought. "Oh, bitch, I'm waiting."

Before I knew it, Pink Lips ran off.

Lyric

"Lyric!" Miracle called out as I sat next to one of Jody's friends from Virginia that Agape had him introduced me to.

I turned around, and from the look on Miracle's face, I knew something was up.

"Yo' girl in there about to bang with Donna. I don't know her or if she got hands or not, and I didn't want her to get fucked up in there."

"Who is my girl?" I asked, looking around the club in hopes that Miracle didn't know what she was talking about.

"Dark-skinned chick with the big-ass *E* and the *M* on her back."

I was stunned for a minute, taking in what Miracle was saying.

"You know, that girl with the blue contacts."

"I hopped off of the stool and floated to the restroom. By the time I was in there, Meaka had Donna in a headlock. I ran up and kicked the bitch dead in the mouth. I snatched her out of Meaka's headlock and rammed her head into the sink. She fell instantly. Miracle walked in and began pushing us out of the bathroom.

"Y'all need to get out of here."

I looked back and noticed Donna struggling to get up. I felt relieved. I mean, I wasn't trying to kill the bitch.

I laughed so hard once we were in the car.

Meaka started going off. "Can you believe that fat bitch? Who the fuck she think she is?"

I continued laughing as Meaka ranted on.

"Girl, that's Donna. Jay Baby's baby momma."

"Donna?" Agape questioned.

I couldn't have told you if she was mad or shocked.

"Yeah, Donna's fat nasty ass." I rubbed in the fact I didn't like Donna because I knew she did.

"What happened?" Agape asked.

I wanted to hit the roof. "What happened?" I repeated. "What happened don't even really matter. Just know that bitch is beat the fuck up. I need a smoke. That bitch had blown any high I had left."

As soon as I lit the blunt, my phone rang.

"Yeah," I stated when I saw that it was Jay Baby.

"What happened, Lyric?"

"Yo' bitch was on one all night. Come on now, Jay Baby. You know that."

"I hear that too, Lyric, but did y'all have to jump her?"

"As a matter a fact, we did that bitch two of Meaka. What do you mean did we have to jump her?"

"That shit wasn't cool, Lyric."

"All right then, Jay, I know that bitch sitting right next to you and you had to make this call, but know that bitch had it coming to her."

Click.

Agape

I was lost as to why Meaka and Lyric had a fight with Donna. I sat on the passenger side of the car on pins and needles. I hoped that their fight didn't have anything to do with me. I could only imagine the way Meaka would look at me if she got word that I was getting high with Donna regularly.

"What happened?" I asked.

Then Lyric went on to say some fly shit out of her mouth about it didn't matter what happened and to just know she got her ass kicked. Lyric shot me a nasty look and began to roll up a blunt.

I walked through the door with Meaka on my heels. Emillio was seated at the table with a guy that looked familiar. I couldn't place my hand on where I knew him from.

"In so soon?" Emillio greeted us.

"Yeah, your girl and Lyric showing out, we had to flee the club."

Meaka looked shocked I had let Emillio know that she was showing her ass. I didn't care. Someone needed to put a light up under Lyric's ass. Hopefully after this, Emillio wouldn't let her hang out with her. I resented how close Meaka and Lyric were. I felt like Meaka was slowly but surely replacing me with Lyric just the way I had done Stormy. When Emillio got up from the table, he looked over Meaka. When he noticed that she had a busted lip, he became enraged.

"Who did this to you Tameka?" Emillio spoke calmly and slow.

He wanted to know how was it that his woman left the house only to return with a busted lip.

"Some bitch."

"Who was she?" Emillio continued to interrogate Meaka.

"I don't know her. I think her name was Donna. Ain't that her name?" Meaka turned around to confirm her name with me.

"I think so," I stated, trying not to appear as if I knew anything about her or the fight.

"How the fuck is it that you in the club not only fighting with some bitch, but you don't even know the bitch's name?" Emillio asked Meaka.

Emillio was very upset because he was aware that Meaka had no enemies. He knew that Lyric had a laundry list of bitches that could have and should have had beef with her. He knew Meaka's loyalty to Lyric, and he could see her jumping into some shit that had nothing to do with her and everything to do with Lyric. Meaka didn't like the way Emillio was going off.

"Don't talk to me like that. Why are you yelling?"

"Why am I yelling?" Emillio chuckled. "You just don't get it, do you?"

Emillio couldn't help but notice that I seemed to look just about the same as I did before I left out the door—not a piece of hair out of place, no bruises, and damn sure not a busted lip.

Emillio then turned to me. "What happened, A?"

"I'm not sure exactly what happened. I just know that Lyric was beefing with the girl before the fight. I think it was because Lyric was dancing with her man." I used my words carefully because I wanted to place Lyric in the worst light. "Next thing I know, I see them running out of the club. It still didn't click to me what was going on until one of Lyric's friends tapped me on the shoulder and let me know what just took place."

Meaka stood there and listened in as if she wasn't one of the people I was talking about. From the look on Emillio's face, I could tell that this was going just like I wanted it to.

Emillio then turned to Meaka. "I'll be back." Emillio said to the guy that was seated at the table, "Let's roll, brah."

Meaka tried to block Emillio's path. "And where do you think you are going at three in the morning?"

"Go put some ice on your lip," Emillio said as he walked to the door.

The guy followed Emillio's path, and they left.

"What is his fucking problem?" Meaka asked no one in particular.

She dug in her purse and pulled out her phone. This was the first night I had ever witnessed Meaka and Emillio dispute with one and another. I hid my satisfaction. I was sure that Emillio was not going to be happy with Lyric's presence any longer. And with that, I was satisfied.

I woke up in my bed fully clothed with a headache out of this world. I went into the bathroom to see if there were any kind of pain relievers in the medical cabinet. There were none, not an Advil or Tylenol—nothing. After washing my face and brushing my teeth, I went up the steps to the third level of Emillio and Meaka's trilevel home, where their bedroom was. As soon as my foot hit the top step, Emillio walked out of their bedroom completely naked. I was amazed at the sight before me. My feet was planted in the floor and my eyes on his manhood.

"My bad," Emillio stated as he attempted to cover up his body parts to no avail.

Damn, I thought, *what a sight.*

I waited for a moment to call out to Meaka. I didn't want her to know that I was aware of the reason she was so in love with her man. She was not here. I was taken aback. Meaka never left the house without me.

"Where she at?"

"She went out to Lyric's," Emillio yelled from the room.

"Do y'all have any pain pills?" I asked.

"Uh…uh," Emillio stuttered as he tried to recollect if they had any pain pills. "Nah, A. All I got is some Xanax."

My eyes lit up. It had been a few months since I had one of the blue footballs.

"Can I get one, Emillio? My head is killing me."

"Yeah, come on in."

"Are you decent?" I asked, knowing good and well I didn't care whether or not he was decent.

I could stand to see him naked again. Shit, I hadn't been in the presence of a man in months. Looking ain't hurting nobody.

"Yea," he called out. He went in his drawer to retrieve the pills. "How many you want?"

"Let me get two."

Meaka

I turned the knob to Lyric's condo.

This girl never locks her door, I thought as I headed toward Lyric's bedroom.

I heard the moans coming from her bedroom. Don't ask me why I continued to walk toward the room.

"Lyr—" I began to call out and was shocked as hell when I saw her on top of Jay Baby, riding his dick like a jockey.

She didn't skip a beat as I stood in her doorway. I turned around and walked toward the living room of her condo. I needed someone to talk to, and if that meant waiting on Lyric to finish sexing Jay Baby, I was willing to do that. I took in the condo. I never paid much attention to how coordinated and stylish Lyric was until I looked at how impeccable her condo was decorated. Her zebra-printed furniture had bright yellow throw pillows on it with a huge life-sized portrait of Lyric when she was younger with a girl that looked like she could have been her older sister. To say they looked alike would be saying the least.

"What up?" Lyric asked as she walked in the living room wrapped up in a white towel. She had that sneaky grin that she always put on.

"Was that Jay Baby?" I asked, already knowing the answer to the question.

"Girl, we'll talk about that in a minute. Now why is it that you come over here this early in the morning killing my action instead of being laid up with that sexy-ass husband of yours?"

Lyric was my friend, and I knew how she could be when it came to men. But for me, I never thought she would cross me in any type of way, so I took what she just said about my husband as a compliment.

"Girl, he mad at me."

"Don't tell me because of the fight?"

"Hell yeah, because of the fight," I confirmed.

"What did he expect for you to do? Just let the bitch hit you in the mouth and you not do shit? What type of bitch do he think he got?" Lyric questioned, clearly upset.

"I didn't even get a chance to let him know what took place. He saw my lip was busted and just got to going off. Girl, he left with Juan, and as I'm pulling down the driveway, he pulling in."

"Hold on, so he didn't come back home?" Lyric asked for clarity.

"Nope."

"Ew!"

I know one thing for sure. It wasn't that fucking serious. Lyric was upset because she felt that, in a sense, it was her fault for me and Donna's altercation. She knew that Donna's beef wasn't with me but with her.

"Well, I feel like you at the wrong place. You need to go back home and work that shit out with Emillio."

Lyric knew I had a good man and that I needed to make things right with him before things got out of hand.

"I'm not thinking about that nigga. How he just gon' walk out on me like that?"

"Meaka, you have to understand his position. You are his wife, and you came home from the club with a busted lip. And a female did it, so that leaves him no room to protect you. I mean, what can he do? Go beat Donna's ass for you? You know that nigga don't play over you."

I kind of sided with what Lyric was saying, but I didn't understand why Emillio just left me like that. All kinds of shit ran through my mind. Was he with another woman? Had he been cheating, and had I been so consumed in my own bullshit that I hadn't noticed? I didn't know what to think. We went out to breakfast—me, Lyric, and Jay Baby. Jay Baby apologized for Donna's actions. I let him know that his apology wasn't necessary. We ate good, and for the first time in my life, I smoked some weed. I didn't see what Lyric got out of smoking weed because, by the time we got back to Lyric's, I was knocked out, only to be awakened by Lyric. I felt that I slept for about twenty minutes when, in all reality, I had been asleep for hours. The once-bright sun was replaced with a dark sky and a full moon.

"What time is it?"

"Time for you to take your ass home. Yo' man been calling and calling, and I can't find it in me to keep lying to the brother," Lyric joked, knowing good and well she would get on the stand and lie for me if it came down to it.

I stood up from the sofa. I was laid out on to stretch. Lyric retrieved my shoes from the back room. I didn't even remember taking my shoes off.

"Where's Jay Baby?" I questioned.

"He in the back, watching the Lakers and Miami game."

"So what you gon' do with him?" I questioned, smiling from ear to ear.

"You let me worry about Jay Baby." Lyric walked to the door and opened it. "Come on, miss lady. You have a man that you need to go home to."

I sat on Lyric's chaise lounge stubbornly, not wanting to move.

"Come on, girl." Lyric pulled me up off of the chair. "You ain't got to go home, but you got to get the hell up out of here," Lyric joked.

I walked toward the door and looked back at Lyric for certainty.

"That's your husband, Meaka, and he loves you. You know that. Don't let something so small come between y'all."

I would be forever grateful for Lyric's advice because, as soon as I got home, Emillio was in the kitchen with a suit and tie on and with an apron around him, cooking something that smelled so good. As soon as I walked in the door, he stood in the doorway of the kitchen looking good enough to eat. He walked toward me and grabbed my oversized Lucky purse off of my shoulder and set it on the table. He then walked me to the kitchen. He sat me on top of the island that was in the middle of our kitchen. Emillio grabbed a spoon and had me taste test his Alfredo sauce.

"Taste this?" he asked as he held my chin.

I seductively opened my mouth. "It taste good, baby," I complimented.

Emillio then kissed my lips ever so gently.

I then began working on my neck. "You know that's my spot, Emillio."

"I know."

Emillio placed his finger up to my lips to silence me, and I didn't protest when he lifted my shirt over my head. When he pulled my tatas out of my bra and began to lick and suck on my nipples, I subconsciously began rotating my hips on the surface of the island. Emillio saw just how heated I was, so he picked me up from the island and turned me around and pulled down my Bebe jogging pants along with my pink lace boy shorts. When my panties came down, I felt a chill go up my spine.

In the back of my mind, I thought, *Where is Agape?*

But my body needed what was getting ready to take place, so my mouth couldn't began to ask. I bent over and grabbed on to my ankles. As I looked back at my husband, "Give it to me," I whispered.

"Oh, I'ma give it to you, all right," Emillio teased.

When I felt the deep penetration of Mr. Bobby, my official name for Emillio's mandingo, I gasped with air as I continued to match the rhythm of his hips. I had never shared another lover, but I don't think it got any better than this. My body began to shake as Emillio hit the spot I loved the most. We came together.

After showering, we got dressed. I asked Emillio where Agape was.

He simply stated, "Agape grown, Meaka. She said she would be back in the morning."

I felt bad for asking where Agape was at such an intimate moment for me and my husband. I wanted to make it up to him, to show him my appreciation for all that he had done for me.

"I want a baby, Emillio," I stated as I kissed his ear.

"You want my baby?" Emillio questioned.

"Yes, Daddy," I purred in his ear.

"Come on. Let's eat," Emillio stated as he stood from the bed.

I took note how Emillio tried to elude the matter at hand.

"Emillio," I whined behind him, trying to see where his head was at.

"Let's eat, Tameka," he turned to me and said before he walked down the staircase.

I followed. Emillio lit the candles that were placed on the table. He hit the lights and then made our plates. I sat there thinking about how Emillio was trying to act as if I didn't just tell him I wanted to have his baby. After he poured me a glass of wine, I took two gulps and began to eat my food. Emillio was an excellent cook. He knew I loved his food but not enough to address what was before us. As good as the chicken Alfredo was, I found myself picking over my food.

"You don't like it, babe?" Emillio asked.

"Yeah, it's good." I put on a fake smile, trying not to kill the tempo of the room.

But the harmony wasn't there. The air became thick, and I found myself voicing all that I was thinking.

"Emillio, you don't want me to have your baby?" I couldn't help but to ask.

Silence.

Emillio looked up from his plate and asked, "Where is all this baby talk coming from, Tameka? We ain't been talking about no babies. I just don't understand why we have to right now."

I was appalled at what he just said. I was stunned. Surely I thought, if I wanted his baby, he would want me to have his child.

But as of right now, I was severely questioning that. I got up from the table. I felt defeated. Emillio kept his head in his plate. I went to bed and was surprised when Emillio didn't follow.

Emillio sat downstairs watching the flickering of the lit candles. In the darkness of the room, he knew the time would come, that I would bring up having a baby. Women always do, and anytime Emillio was presented with the proposition, he would walk out. In this matter, he had fallen in love with me and took my hand in marriage. He couldn't just walk out on me as he had on the other women before her. Emillio thought that, by me being so young, I wouldn't put any pressure on him about having kids anytime soon; and by the time I did want children, he hoped that he would have dealt with the skeletons in his closet.

Lyric

I answered my phone for the upteenth time, only to have gotten hung up on. I didn't know who the fuck was this playing on my phone. I looked over at Jay Baby and questioned if it was Donna playing on my phone.

"I think that's your bitch playing on my phone."

"Man, now how would she get your number? You buggin'."

"Nigga, ain't nobody been playing on my phone. Now I let you up in my space, and a mufucka keep calling, breathing in the phone, and hanging up," I hollered as I threw a pillow at Jay Baby's face.

"Watch that shit, Lyric. You think I'm playing you?"

"Let me find out that's Donna playing on my phone. I'ma beat her ass."

"Man, yo can't beat Donna," Jay Baby instigated jokingly. "Why u and yo' girl have to jump her if yo can beat her?"

"Nigga, if don't nobody know, you know that I would put a Nike sign in Donna's face."

"Nah, though, what's up with yo girl? She good? Her nigga was a little heated about her fighting in the club."

I went in the living room to check on Meaka. She was sound asleep. I slid her shoes off and slid her purse from under head. She woke up briefly to adjust herself on the chair. I went into her purse and retrieved her phone. I knew that Emillio was worried sick about Meaka. I fought with myself to stay out of Meaka's business, but I didn't want her to mess up her relationship acting out of emotions. I scrolled through her phone and dialed Emillio's number.

"Man, where the fuck are you at?" Emillio questioned as he answered the phone.

"Aye, look, Emillio, this Lyric—"

"Where Meaka at?" he interrupted.

"She at my house. She been here since this morning. She had a lot on her mind. We talked it over. Now she's on my couch 'sleep. I'ma see to it that she get home as soon as she get up."

Emillio was silent.

At times, Emillio questioned my loyalty to Meaka. He didn't know how to take me. I was always around Meaka. He just didn't know if any of it was genuine. That was up until now because I could have kept Meaka's whereabouts to myself, but the fact I gave up this info showed him that I was real.

"Good looking, Lyriee," Emillio joked, calling me by the name Meaka called me.

"It's all good. You just better treat my girl right if she ever come up over here in the early a.m. and it's not to take me to breakfast. But to talk about you, I won't be so nice, *comprende?*" I joked.

"I got you. All right."

I went back in the room and smoked some kush with Jay Baby.

"You know I want you, Lyric," Jay went on to say.

I rolled my eyes up in my head.

"What?" Jay Baby questioned as he passed me the blunt.

"Nothing"

"What's wrong with me telling you how I feel?"

"I don't deal in feelings, Jay. You wanted some pussy, I gave you some, so now you can be up."

"Hold up. You putting me out."

"Yes, I am. I need to get me some beauty rest, and it's about time you gone home to Donna," I stated sarcastically.

"Come on. You know I would leave Donna for you."

Is this nigga serious? Of course he would say this to me, but would he say it to Donna is the question. "Call her and tell her that."

"What you want me to say?" Jay stated with no hesitation as he pulled his phone from his pocket.

"Boy, I'm just fucking with you. For real though, Jay Baby, it's time for you to go before you get too comfortable. Next thing I know, you'll be moving your clothes and shoes in," I joked.

"All right, I'm out," Jay Baby said as he planted a kiss on my forehead.

I walked him to the door and decided to wake Meaka up and get her out of here because I needed some me time.

After Meaka left, I went through my mental Rolodex and dialed Emillio's number. "She on her way, brah."

Click.

I curled up in the bed. Out of nowhere, I began to think about my mother. Yolanda wasn't the best mother. Yet and still she was my mother, and I missed her dearly. I often thought about her when I was by myself. I thought that was one of the many reasons that I kept plenty of male company, to hinder myself from thinking about Mommy. I don't think nothing in the world could make me forget about the night of my mother's suicide. I often thought that, too, would be my own fate. Mommy was a strong woman. I guess all the wrong she had done with raising me had caught up to her. I struggled with whether I should blame my mother for the way I was now. Of course I could blame her, but I sympathized with Mommy. I didn't think she intended to trap me in a web of promiscuity and prostitution. She didn't know any better. She simply showed me what her mother showed her. I know, if she knew any better, she would have done better when it came to raising me.

I guess, in a way, Mommy saved my unborn daughter from being subjected to what I was subjected to. Ma broke the cycle with her life, so that was a life-learned lesson. I found myself thinking what life would be like if Mommy was still here. Would she be proud of me for being just like her; or did she know that, when she looked at me, I was a mirror image of what her life was? Maybe that was why she killed herself. She saw herself in me. A tear flowed freely down my face. As much as I resented my mother, I was just like her in every way. Only difference was I didn't have a child around to be succumbed to my madness. I wanted to change my life around. Only thing was I didn't know how. I had too much pride to ask. I entertained the thought of giving Jay Baby a chance and dismissed it just as quickly as it came.

Agape

"Do you know where Lyric live?" Donna questioned.

"She stay in Englewood. Why?" I asked.

Donna called me over talking about she missed me and she was happy I was clean. After a few compliments from Donna, she invited me over for dinner. I decided to go. I was tired of being cooped up in the house with Emillio. Meaka was gone. I needed something to do.

Since I stepped foot in the door, Donna kept asking questions about Lyric. Even while we were sitting here eating, she was asking about where Lyric stayed.

"Where Jay Baby?" I asked, hoping to sway Donna to talk about something else other than Lyric.

"I don't know where that nigga at. He ain't been here all day."

Damn, I thought, *Jay Baby's her man—shit, her kids' father—and she hasn't seen him all day. How much sense does that make?*

"You sure he ain't in jail?"

"Nah, I called down to the county. That nigga ain't in jail."

Donna got up from the couch and came back with a plate full of cocaine. She immediately put her nose to the plate. And before I knew it, I was grabbing the straw Donna held out to me. I and Donna snorted line after line for hours until all of the powder was gone off of the plate. I immediately felt guilty. The guilt ate away at me as I sat on Donna's sofa, hoping that Jay Baby didn't bring his ass home. It seemed like, as soon as I thought about Jay Baby, he came through the front door. I saw the pity Jay Baby had in his eyes.

I wasn't sure if the pity was for me or Donna until he asked, "What you doing over here, A?"

"I'm just chilling." I tried to avoid eye contact with him and played with some lint on my Victoria's Secret hoodie.

"Chilling, huh?" Jay baby questioned suspiciously.

"Yeah, chilling," I stated.

Jay Baby knew that I had been doing a lot more than chilling. My bulging eyeballs told him that. And my constantly picking at my jacket didn't help but confirm his suspicions of what I had been doing. Jay Baby went upstairs dialing Lyric's number.

"What's up?" Lyric answered.

"Your girl over here on that one way."

Lyric knew what Jay Baby was insinuating. "Jay, she grown. Ain't nothing I can do for her. You feel me?" Lyric questioned. "Peace."

Click.

Jay Baby looked at the phone, realizing Lyric just hung up on him. Jay Baby went in his son's room and lay down on his twin-size bed with him. Jay Baby couldn't get why Lyric wouldn't give him a chance. He could provide her with everything she wanted, but he wasn't willing to do that and hold the title of being one of her tricks. He wanted Lyric exclusively to himself. He knew a night of fucking, licking, and sucking would surely make her his; but Lyric had the heart of a nigga. Jay Baby felt like he had the weight of the world on his shoulders trying to figure out a way to snag Lyric. He knew she was well worth it despite what anyone else thought.

"You think he know I'm high?" I asked Donna.

"Nah, girl, he don't know shit."

As much as I wanted to believe Donna, I knew she was feeding me bullshit. I got up nervously and left out of the door, not uttering another word.

The drive to Meaka's seemed like forever. I was drowned with so many thoughts. When I pulled up to the house, I hoped Meaka and Emillio were asleep. When I stuck my key in the door, I noticed Emillio sitting at a candlelit table by himself. The lights were off. The setting was beautiful.

But where is Meaka? I couldn't help but think.

As much as I wanted to make sure Emillio was all right, I just couldn't chance him seeing me high, so I proceeded up the stairs to my room. I leaned up against the door, inhaled, and then exhaled deeply.

Meaka

I didn't feel Emillio climb in the bed with me. I looked over and couldn't help but admire how fine Emillio was. As mad as I wanted to be with him, I found it hard to be mad at him as he lay here sleeping peacefully.

"Em," I whispered in his ear.

Emillio opened one eye sleepily. I stared back at him.

"I love you, Tameka," Emillio stated sincerely.

I turned my head. I couldn't look him in his face. It saddened me that I questioned the love my man had for me.

If you love me so much, then why don't you want me to have your baby? I couldn't help but think.

Emillio knew what was bothering me. He just couldn't address the situation. It had been four years since the death, and he still couldn't face what happened. So he got up from the bed and proceeded to get dressed.

I watched Emillio pull his pants up, all the while trying to figure out if he was trying to hurt my feelings, and if so, he was doing just that.

"Emillio," I called out. "I wanted to get this out of the air between us so we could go back to the way things were."

"Not now, Meaka," Emillio said. "I'll be back." And out the door he went.

I grabbed my phone off of the dresser.

"What's up?" Lyric answered.

"Lyric, he don't want me to have his baby," I cried into the phone.

"What's going on?" Lyric questioned.

"Emillio don't want me to have his baby."

If it ain't one thing, it's another with these two girls, Lyric thought, referring to Meaka and Agape. *I thought I had problems, but damn.*

I began telling Lyric about the current events that took place between Emillio and me.

"Meaka, what are you tripping for? If the nigga don't want you to have his babies, then good for you. Shit, you' too young to be having kids anyway. Do you first."

I understood what Lyric was saying. I was not sure if she would ever understand where I was coming from. A place where you're good enough for marriage but not good enough to have your spouse's child? How does that work?

"Have y'all ever discussed anything about kids before this?"

"Nah, I never thought to interview him on whether or not I would be able to have his child."

"The only thing I could think of is that it has to be a reason for him to act like that. Maybe he can't have kids. Did you ever think about that?" Lyic went on to ask.

I paused for a moment. That didn't even cross my mind.

"Oh my God, Lyric, that's it. He can't have kids. That has to be it."

How come I didn't think about that? I questioned myself.

"Call that man, girl, and get off my line. I need some sleep. I got a date," Lyric informed me.

"With who?" I asked.

"That's for me to know and for you to find out, miss lady."

Click.

"Hello?"

That heifer hung up on me. I laughed.

"Wake up, sleepyhead," I called out to Agape from the doorway of her room.

She turned over and ignored me.

I stepped in the room and tapped her leg. "Get up, A. You wanna go to the mall with me?"

"I don't want to go anywhere. Can't you see I'm 'sleep?"

I noticed Agape was still fully dressed as she lay on top of the bed. That was weird because she never lay down in the bed unless she stripped down to her underwear.

"Well, I guess you are pretty tired since you have your clothes on."

Truth was Agape had been up all morning. The coke she and Donna was snorting had her tripping. The wind hitting up against the window sounded like someone was trying to get in the window, so she sat up all morning monitoring the window. When she heard someone coming down the stairs, she hopped on top of the bed and played possum.

"Well, damn, you didn't have to be so nasty about it. I'll go by myself."

The mall was crowded as always on the first of the month. Females were everywhere hanging on to three and four pairs of small hands. I never understood how could a woman go shopping with three and four kids. Shit, three or four bags was a distraction for me. I walked in Macy's and picked up me some True Religion perfume. As I stood in line, I turned toward the back of the line, and I saw a lady and a man holding hands. All the while, he held a little boy that resembled him. My mind went back to me and Emillio's dilemma. I dialed his number, only to receive the voice mail. I hung up without leaving a message. I thought Emillio was taking it too far, this whole baby situation. He better not let me find out that he had other kids or some shit. Something just told me that it was more than him not being able to have kids, but what?

After stopping in few more stores, I decided to leave the mall. I guess I was in the mall longer than I thought because, when I left out of the mall, I couldn't recall where I had parked. I looked around the parking lot. I looked at the girl that walked toward my direction. She held on to the hand of a little girl that looked familiar to me. I couldn't put my hand on where I knew her from. I looked back up at the woman whom she was walking with, and she looked familiar as well. But when the little girl took off running toward me, yelling my name, I knew just who she was.

"Hi, Trinity." I gave her a big hug.

She had grown so much, and she looked just like her father.

"Where my uncle Emillio?"

"I just tried calling him, but he didn't answer. What you been doing?"

"Nothing. I miss you." Trinity turned around to see how close her mother was. When she saw she was a few steps away, she asked, "Where Mom at?"

I knew about Trinity keeping Agape and her father secret; so I whispered, "She lives with me and Emillio," as I eyed Stormy as she walked up.

"Hello," Stormy greeted.

"I'm good, and you?"

"I can't complain, girl. About to go to this mall and spend some of Al's money," she joked, only I didn't find it too funny.

I knew, had Al had a will, he would have left everything to Agape. I knew this because he often said that, if anything was to happen to him, he wanted her to have what was his only because he knew she would do right by his daughter. He told Agape that on several occasions right in front of me. Agape was always afraid of discussing death, so she would never want him to make out a will. I saw why he said he didn't trust his baby mama, whom I now knew as Stormy, because here she stood with a ten-thousand-dollar purse on a pair of six-thousand-dollar shoes.

It was obvious that Stormy didn't remember me from Shawny Acres. She'd never said one word to me even though she came to our wedding. She made it clear that she was only there to support Trinity. She was our flower girl.

"How's Em?" Stormy questioned, referring to Emillio by his nickname he got from Al.

Then it clicked to me that Stormy was with Al at the time when he and Al were running the streets. I was sure she knew whether or not Emillio could have kids.

"He good. We trying to have a baby," I lied with a slight grin.

Stormy looked like she had seen a ghost. "Well, that's good. I didn't think ole Em would go down that road again," Stormy stated.

"Again?" I questioned, confused because I was sure this bitch wasn't telling me that he was willing to try to have a baby with someone else and the nigga was against me having his child.

"Oh, my bad, you don't know?" Stormy realized that she had just let the cat out of the bag. She looked at her Movado watch and stated, "I…We have to go. Come on now, Stormy."

"Don't do that to me." I grabbed her arm desperately. "Who did he try to have a baby with?"

"I don't want to get in the middle of that. Why don't you ask Em what happened with him and his baby mama?"

Baby mama? Surely she had this all wrong because my husband had no kids. I looked in her eyes, and I didn't see the least bit of sympathy. I was kind of insulted by her actions, and I couldn't take it.

"Well, that's cool, I guess. We both don't want to be in the middle of something. I told Agape the same damn thing," I stated as I walked off in search of my car.

"Meaka!" she yelled out to me.

I didn't turn around. Fuck her.

Agape

Soon as I heard Meaka pull up, I hopped on the phone and dialed up Donna's number.

"Hello, what's up Donna?"

"Shit, girl over here about to party."

That was Donna's way of telling me she was about to snort some powder.

"Where Jay Baby at?"

"Girl, how come you always asking about my nigga? If you keep that shit up, I'ma think something is going on between y'all."

"Girl, you know it ain't nothing like that. I just don't like getting high in front of people. You know that."

Donna knew I wasn't lying. Jay Baby had just come in the house from being gone all night. Therefore, she knew firsthand that he wasn't leaving anytime soon.

But that didn't stop her from telling me, "Girl, he ain't here."

"Can I come?" I asked, sounding like a child who wants to fit in.

"Bitch, you better hurry up. You know how I do."

I couldn't have hung that phone up faster. I made it to Donna's in record time. I needed to get high.

I knocked on the door. Instantly I was heated when Jay Baby pulled opened the door. I stepped in and gave Donna an evil eye.

What? she mouthed with powder all over her nose.

"What's up, A?" Jay Baby questioned.

"Nothing. Just came over to chill with Donna," I answered, avoiding eye contact with him.

I sat down next to Donna as she sucked line after line up her nose. The monkey on my back was kicking my ass. The sound of Donna snorting the powder up her nose seemed to be satisfying to me. I hoped Jay Baby was on his way out the door, but all bets were off when he closed the door and sat down on the opposite couch from me and Donna. Donna passed me the straw. I stared at it and then back at Jay Baby. Even he couldn't witness what I was about to do. He left out the door, and I began snorting line after line.

"Damn, bitch, pass the straw."

I was so high all I could think about was getting higher, so when Donna said that we had about four lines, I was floored. Donna saw the disappointment in my eyes. We both didn't want the morning to end. We had been getting high for hours. So Donna suggested we cook the powder up to stretch it, and we would just smoke it. I didn't see anything wrong with it shit we had been snorting it all night. What's smoking it? I convinced myself it was the same thing.

Donna cooked up the powder. We now had a few crack rocks. Donna run upstairs to retrieve a crack pipe. She brought it back downstairs and instructed me on how to hold and hit the pipe. When I hit the pipe, I felt an instant gratification. I could feel myself floating in the clouds.

Bennie, a crackhead from the Bass, had showed her a few days ago. Donna had been hitting the pipe secretly. She couldn't live without Jay Baby. He had been her everything, and now all of a sudden, he was not coming home. When he was at home, he was not paying her the least bit of attention. He was constantly complaining about the house being dirty. She knew he was fucking with someone. She just didn't know exactly who. First she thought it was Agape. That was why she called her up in the first place. Then she thought Lyric, so she got Lyric's number out of Agape's phone. She would call and listen to see if she heard Jay Baby in her background, but she never did.

Donna was pleased that I was hitting the crack pipe. She felt like she just found herself two new best friends—me and the crack rock in her hand. She didn't need Jay Baby. Fuck him. It was his fault she started snorting powder in the first place. He pressured her into snorting, telling her that, if she loved him, she would do it with him.

I sat in the corner of the apartment with my eyes bulging out of my head. I could feel my heartbeat. It was then that I realized that I might have bitten off more than I could chew.

When the last rock was smoked, I found myself wanting more. The high was impeccable. I couldn't compare anything to it. I couldn't remember ever feeling this good. I got up and started dancing to the songs that played in my head. Donna sat on the couch staring off into space.

"Bitch, sit down. You fucking my high up."

"Come on, Donna. Dance with me," I requested.

But Donna didn't want to dance. All she could do was think about Jay Baby. She knew that Jay Baby would surely leave her if he found out she was smoking crack. Donna decided that she wouldn't smoke crack anymore, or so she thought.

Emillio

I watched my phone light up several times. I had cut the ringer off when I walked out of the door. I knew Meaka would be calling. I hated that I couldn't trust my own wife enough to reveal to her what had been haunting me these past years. How could I explain the death of my first child to her? How could I get her to understand that by my saying I didn't have any kids was just a Band-Aid on a gunshot wound? Would she think that I was guilty or forgive me for the role I played in my son's death? I didn't know the answer to any of the questions that I continued to ask myself when I entertained the thought of letting Meaka in on why I was not ready to have any children.

It was unbearable watching my phone light up with Meaka's number time after time. I decided to go out to Mom's house. I hated bringing my problems to Mom's front door, but she was the only person that could advise me on what to do unbiased.

I entered Mom's home and was welcomed to the smell of greens, corn bread, homemade macaroni, and fried chicken. Mama was the chef around the house. She made sure both of her sons knew how to cook. She would make us sit in the kitchen with her while she whipped us up meal after meal. Mama used to tell me and Juan that she didn't want us having to depend on any woman to cook us our meals or for anything for that matter.

"Emillio," my mother called out to me as I walked into the kitchen.

Esmeralda was always delighted to see her oldest son. It was like looking at her late husband all over again. Emillio Sr. was shot down and killed cheating on Esmeralda. Emillio Sr. was often unfaithful to Esmeralda. She was aware of his betrayals, but she couldn't see herself leaving her husband. He was all she had.

Esmeralda was the child of illegal immigrants. When Esmeralda was born, her parents were deported back to Mexico. Her mother thought that it was a good idea to put their only child up for an adoption. Her parents genuinely thought that they had given their daughter the best opportunity there was to provide their Mexican daughter a United States citizenship. Each of them knew that her chances were better of becoming something in the States versus Mexico, even if that meant that they would never see her again.

But the night of August 16 of '93, Emillio found himself in the bed of another man's woman. He walked in on Emillio and his woman bumping and grinding in his bed. He shot them both with his sawed-off shotgun. Neither one of them saw it coming.

"Hi, Ma," Emillio greeted his mother with a kiss.

She returned the gesture, kissing Emillio on the lips. Esmeralda got up from the table and proceeded to fix Emillio a plate. Emillio smiled at his mother. She always knew just what to do. Esmeralda set

Emillio's full plate on the table after packing as much as she could on the plate. When Emillio didn't dig in the plate headfirst, she knew something was bothering him.

"That wife of yours must have learned how to cook."

Emillio cracked a smile. "She learnin', Ma," he answered.

"What's got you down, son?"

Silence.

Emillio looked Esmeralda in the eyes and told her, "Meaka wants a baby."

Esmeralda knew the day was going to come when Meaka wanted to have her son's baby. She would have been a fool not to.

"So what did you tell her?"

"I didn't tell her anything," Emillio stated as he stood up from his mother's dining room table.

He walked over to the window. He couldn't allow his mother to see how much the thought of having another child pained him.

"Emillio, you are my son whom I love dearly."

Emillio listened on attentively. He knew that his mother was going to give him the advice he needed. He hung on to her every word.

"I wouldn't be half the women. I am, let alone, half the mother I am if I don't let you know that you can't leave your wife out on what's happened to you. Your past is your past, and everyone has one."

"I know, Ma, but—"

"But nothing, child," Esmeralda interrupted Emillio. "There are no buts in dealing with the one you love. Have you ever wondered the same reason you don't want to discuss with your wife what happened to my grandbaby could be the same reason your wife wants your baby? Think about that, Emillio. You don't understand how, by you ignoring the very same matter that could make that girl feel unwanted or unworthy."

"Ma, she know how much she mean to me," Emillio tried to defend.

"And she might have, but how does she feel now, Emillio?"

Silence.

Emillio didn't take the time to try to understand that part of the dilemma. It was solely on how he didn't want to discuss the matter and didn't want to answer the questions that he was sure Meaka would ask.

"Emillio, that is your wife, and you need to let her know everything. You owe her that," Esmeralda stated sternly as she looked over her eyeglasses, just the way she always did when she meant business.

Emillio had had enough of the bloody truth, and Esmeralda knew it. She read her son like a book just the way she had with Emillio Sr. Each time Emillio Sr. would tell Esmeralda that he was staying over at work, she would laugh in the receiver of the phone; and before hanging up, she would simply state, "She must be special." Of course, Emillio Sr. would deny it and would cuss her out and call her out of her name. She never took it personally because she was aware of how the truth hurts. Some women would rather you tell them a lie than to give them the bloody truth.

"I'm out, Mom," Emillio stated as he grabbed his fitted cap off of the back of the chair he was sitting in.

"Emillio, promise me something," Esmeralda requested Emillio.

Emillio continued walking through the living room, acting as if he didn't hear his mother. Esmeralda knew he heard her, so she continued.

"Promise me you will tell that girl about Javiier," Esmeralda stated as she followed Emillio to the door.

Emillio turned around and planted a kiss on Esmeralda's forehead.

Esmeralda held on to her son's face and let him know, "You can't run from this, Emillio. I'm not asking you to do this for Meaka but for yourself. You can't keep carrying that around."

"All right, Ma," Emillio stated as he rushed out of the door.

Esmeralda sat in her rocking chair, looking out the window at her son as he sat behind the wheel of his black Range Rover. She thought for a second that Emillio had gotten over the tragic murder of his son. She thought that, with all the years that had passed, Emillio somehow found it in himself to let his son's soul rest.

221

Esmeralda's phone rang. She scrambled around trying to detect where the phone was from the tone of the ringing.

"Hello?"

"Hi, Mom, I was wondering if you had a minute to talk. I'm around the corner from your house."

"Yes, I do, Meaka. Come on over."

Surely somehow she and Emillio would have to run into each other, and if I know my son like I think I do, then I know now will be the time his burdens will be lifted.

Esmeralda took her place in her rocking chair and looked out of the window as Meaka pulled up behind Emillio.

Meaka

What is he doing over here? I thought to myself when I saw Emillio's truck parked outside of Miss Esmeralda's house.

I checked my face in the rearview mirror. I wanted know signs of having been crying my heart out on the drive over here. I walked over to the driver side window. Emillio opened the door and got out of the truck. We stood face-to-face for what felt like eternity. He walked me over to the passenger side of his truck and asked for my keys. I didn't resist. I handed Emillio my keys, and as he shut my door behind me, I could tell from the moment Emillio opened up the door on his truck that he had been crying. I had never seen Emillio cry, not even the death of Al brought him to tears. I wondered if Stormy put him up on the fact that I knew he had a child. I couldn't tell.

We rode down the street in silence, just listening to the sounds of Yo Gotti's *Cocaine Muzik 3.*

"I got something I need to tell you, Tameka," Emillo stated somberly.

"I already know, Em," I stated, trying to make it easy on him.

Emillio looked shocked that I told him I was aware of the fact he had a kid.

"But I don't understand. Why did you keep your child a secret from me? And what kind of father keeps his child away from his wife?"

Emillio realized that I didn't know his full story, so he had to fill in the blanks.

"I was going out with a girl by the name of Carmen Baker. We dated for about four years. She was all a nigga could want. She was smart, beautiful, and had ambition. She had her shit together. She was studying to be a psychologist. I loved Carmen, and she loved me. She got pregnant in 2000. She gave me my first son, Javiier Juan Ramos, on May 2. Carmen constantly complained to me that she didn't feel the same. She told me time and time again. Meaka, I was so busy out there in those streets that I didn't take the time to see just how having a baby had affected her.

"One night, Carmen had called me and told me that she had went out to a friend's house, and she needed me to come get the baby because he kept crying. She said that she feel like killing him and herself. Of course, I didn't think she meant what she was saying. I just thought she was crying out for my attention. By the time I had called her phone back, her friend had answered her phone hysterical. I couldn't make out what she was saying other than 'Em, it's blood everywhere.'

"'Where y'all at?' I continued to yell in the phone.

"'On Oxford.'

"I got over there, only to have been confronted with detectives and police questioning me about my acquaintance to the victim. I didn't know who they were referring to as a victim, so I asked, 'Who's the victim? I'm here to pick up my girl and my son.' I let the officer know. Just then, Meisha run up with terror in her eyes.

"'Where Carmen and li'l Em at?'

"'I left them only for a minute, Emillio.' Meisha began to cry. 'Lil Em just kept crying. We did everything to try to calm him down, but he cried and cried, then I saw tooth trying to break through his gums. I was shocked he was teething so soon, so I offered to go get some Orajel for him. By the time I came back, they were both lying in a pool of blood.'

"I couldn't breathe. I lost my will to live that second she told me my son and my girl was dead. Carmen was suffering from post-partum depression. She kept that from me. I later found out from her mother that she didn't want me to blame myself for her depression, so she made her mom promise not to tell me when the doctors revealed to her that she was suffering from postpartum depression."

I was speechless. I didn't know how to respond to what Emillio had just informed me of. I placed my hand on his thigh. It saddened me deeply to see my husband hurting, and I couldn't take the pain away. I watched tears flow freely from Emillio's eyes.

"It's okay, baby. I understand. It's not your fault though, baby."

Emillio pulled the car over and began bawling right in front of me. I pulled his head toward my chest to let him know that it was okay for him to cry on me.

"It was, Meaka. Do you know she was on Oxford all that time crying out for my help and I was around the corner on Grand? But did I take a second to ask her where was she? Had I known she was one minute away, I would have been there."

Lyric

The beating of my door was what alarmed me. I wasn't expecting for any company, it was nothing for me to put on a private show for a private customer. At the moment, I had just performed for my new regular. I had a pole built into one of my rooms in my two-bedroom condo. This was my favorite room in the house. This one room paid the bills and my car note, put food in the fridge, and oh so much more. I liked the art of seduction, and I was even more thrilled with the way a man stared on in amazement when I flipped and slipped my ass up and down on a pole. I wasn't into the whole dancing-on-the-scene thing, and for the ones who did, kudos to them. But I had an image to uphold. I couldn't be seen as Lyric the stripper. Hell nah, I would rather beat my feet in the street. I'd rather walk up and down Main Street in a tight red leather skirt and some Louboutins before I am stamped as a stripper.

I slid up and down on the pole all the while I put on seductive faces as I looked Juan in the eyes. I thought about how Meaka would kill me if she found out I was doing private dances for Emillio's brother. I was not sure why Meaka held me at such high standards when I never showed her any other signs other than I was a gold digger.

Juan was cool people. He requested my services at least twice a week. He paid well, so my only question was when. It turned me on, the way Juan stared at me. I stripped out of my La Perla lingerie, working my hips and ass to the beat. I shook everything my momma gave me. I submitted to the call of his finger signaling for me to come over. I sat my naked ass right on his lap. Juan's hands were all over me, the ecstasy pill I took before Juan came in the door did its magic. His every touch felt like ecstasy. Nothing ever happened with me and Juan other than me dancing for him. So when he pulled his dick out of his pants, I didn't know what to do with it. His size and girth competed with the best of them.

He asked, "Do you want some of this, Lyrie?" calling me by the nickname Meaka called me.

I wasn't one to turn down no dick, nor was I the one to stab my friend in the back. I knew, if I fucked Juan, then he would tell Emillio. Emillio wasn't blind to how I made my money. At least he thought he wasn't. Al tried to put him up on game; but I was sure I had him questioning himself, whether or not I just danced for niggas or I got down for the crown, as Al told him. Seemed all his brother had gotten was a dance.

I was a rock in a hard place. I wanted nothing more than to sit my pussy right on top of Darren's dick, but something inside the hoe in me wouldn't allow me to fuck Juan. As fine as he was, I had to turn him down.

"I only dance, Juan. That's it."

"Come on now, Lyrie. I done heard you got some of the best pussy in Dayton."

Juan pulled out a knot from his pocket. I was breathless.

"How much you want?" he asked.

It wasn't that I wasn't used to this question because somehow, someway, whenever I was in the company of a nigga, this question presented itself.

"How much?" I stood from Juan's lap and started clapping my ass in his face. "I told you I only dance."

If I could turn around and bite myself in the ass, I would, because it killed me to turn that money down.

Juan took a liking to me, and against his brother's request, he had been pursuing me weekly. Juan lived in Columbus with his wife and her daughter, but that didn't stop him from coming to Dayton twice a week to meet up with me. It wasn't the dance that turned him on to me. It was my determination that aroused him. For some reason or another, it was always the hood women that appealed to Juan. He fell for plenty strippers, but for me, it was much more chemistry than infatuation.

"Well, dance then," Juan stated.

He groped his dick right in front of Lyric and commenced to jack off to the provocative dance she was performing. After he got his nut, he went to the bathroom to clean himself up.

In the midst of Juan going to the bathroom, there was a knock at the door.

Who the hell could that be? I wasn't expecting anyone today or any day that I was in the company of Juan. I never wanted him to know that this condo had a revolving door with niggas coming in and out. I looked out of the peephole, and it was Jay Baby.

What the fuck? I mouthed.

I quickly opened the door and stepped out. I didn't care I was in my robe asshole naked.

"What's up, nigga?" I asked, trying to keep it as cordial as possible, all the while holding my robe together.

"I need to holler at you."

"That's cool too, but don't just pop up at my shit without an announcement, you know, a phone call or something. Give me a minute. I got to get rid of my company."

I knew Juan wasn't going to stay much longer. He never did.

"All right, but hurry up," Jay Baby demanded.

"Who was that?" Juan asked cautiously, gripping his 380 under his hoodie.

He had heard someone knocking on the door from the bath-room. He silently prayed to the heavens that it wasn't Meaka at the door. He didn't want word to get back to Emillio that he had gone against his brother's better judgment. But when he stepped out of the bathroom, Lyric was pulling the door up behind her. So he waited by the door, holding on to his pistol.

"That was my neighbor," I lied. "I wasn't sure if she knew you, so I stepped outside. I wasn't trying to fuck up your game." I put on a slight grin.

Juan wasn't buying it, and he hoped for my sake I wasn't playing with fire by trying to set him up to get robbed.

"What?" I asked when I noticed how Juan screwed his face up at me. "What's that look for?"

"Nothing." Juan snapped out of it. He had murder on his mind as he thought about Lyric setting him up. "Let me race up out of here."

"Well, not before I get what's rightfully mines," I said sternly yet with a smile as I held my hand out."

"Oh, yeah, yeah." Juan stuttered, completely forgetting to pay me for my services. "You just robbing a nigga blind, ain't you?"

"Fair exchange. Ain't no robbery, nigga. You know how the game go," I stated, pushing the knot of hundred dollar bills in the pocket of my robe.

There was no need to count it the way I had to do some niggas. Juan always came correct.

"Take care of yourself, li'l Lyrie," Juan teased.

"You know firsthand, ain't nothing little about me." I smiled, opening the door, letting Juan out the house. "Will I see you again next week?"

"We'll see," Juan stated.

I noticed his hesitation, and I didn't like it. It was never any hesitation with Juan. It was always a definite y-e-s.

Juan couldn't shake the feeling of being set up, so he held on to his pistol in his hoodie, ready to blow somebody's head off if he had to. It could have been the light Emillio saw me in. He warned Juan to not go near me. He was convinced that I was nothing more than a scheming gold digger, but something about me had Juan intrigued. From the very first time he saw me at Emillio and Meaka's engagement gathering, Juan secretly followed me with his eyes just as a predator stalks its prey.

Once he made it to the car safely and there were no signs of him being followed, he hopped on the phone and dialed my number.

"Hello?"

"We on," Juan stated in the phone.

I couldn't help but smile, I figured he thought it was some shit in the game when Jay Baby knocked on the door.

"I knew you would see things my way."

We shared a laugh, and I hung up the phone.

I then turned to Jay Baby. "So what did I do to deserve this visit?"

I smiled, but I really was bothered by Jay Baby taking the liberty to just pop up at my doorstep unexpectedly. Jay baby was starting to get too comfortable.

"Lyric, I think we need to talk about where this is going."

I stared blankly at the thin air. As much as I liked Jay Baby, I just couldn't get him to see that I was no longer that young girl he fell in love with in the Bass. Jay baby saw no wrong in me, and I didn't know why.

"What is it, Jay?" I asked even though I was sure where this was going.

But I wanted to make sure. I was hoping from the knapsack Jay Baby carried thtough the door with him that Donna didn't put his ass out and he was over looking for a place to lay his head. I had love for Jay Baby but not enough to let him come up and live in my space.

"Lyric, you know a nigga trying to be with you—"

"Jay Baby, why do we have to go through this? How many different ways can I tell you it ain't like that with me and you?"

"Well, what is it like, Lyric?"

"We cool, Jay Baby."

I didn't like the look Jay was giving me, so I got up from the sofa and proceeded to the bathroom to take a bath. Lord knows I needed one from the sweat I worked up dancing for Juan. For some reason, I wished that it was Juan in my living room confessing his feelings for me. But that would be too much like normal, and it ain't shit normal about my life. Just like me wanting something that I couldn't have, I was aware that Juan was married and had a child with his wife, but that didn't stop me from fantasizing about what it would be like to have him as my man.

I pulled the door up to give Jay Baby a hint that I didn't want to be interrupted. Just as I sunk my body under the bubbles in the tub, Jay Baby knocked on the door. I patted myself on the back for locking the door. I closed my eyes and tried to drown out the knocks.

"Lyric!" Jay Baby called from on the other side of the door.

I tried to ignore him in hopes that he would hop in his Park Avenue and ride out. But the next thing I knew, my door flung open. This nigga had went too far.

"What the fuck is your problem, nigga?"

Jay Baby had a confused yet terrified look in his eyes.

I hopped out of the tub. "Get the fuck out now, nigga."

"Lyric, my bad, man. When you didn't come to the door, I didn't know what to think. Why you ain't say nothin' when I was calling your name?" Jay Baby asked.

"Fuck you, nigga. Get the fuck up out of here!" I yelled.

"Look, Lyric, I'll pay for the door. That ain't shit. I'm trying to tell you I didn't know what was going on. I was just trying to make sure you were all right."

I heard the sincerity in Jay Baby's voice. As his six-foot-one frame towered over me, I felt like giving up and just giving in to him. He was the only nigga that was trying to be with me and only me. Yeah, he had Donna; but I knew, once I said the words, he would be done with her. But how would I live the lifestyle that I was accustomed to? I didn't have that much love for him to downgrade for him.

When Jay Baby grabbed me up in his arms, I felt secure, and I loved it. As much as I tried to fight, he wouldn't let me.

"Lyric, a nigga trying to be with you," Jay baby whispered in my ear.

I was speechless. "Jay Baby, I like the idea and all, but let's face it. You can't take care of me, and a bitch like me needs to be taken care of."

I hated to put it to him like that; but I thought for sure, if I did, then he would quit with this shit. Jay Baby put me down and pulled me to the living room.

"You know what? All you bitches are alike. It's always about a nigga taking care of y'all."

"Come on, Jay. You know me better than anybody. You know how I am."

"Nah, Lyric, I don't. I know what you were exposed to. I know what a mufucka showed you, but that ain't you, Lyric."

Tears welled up in my eyes. I couldn't help but think about the night Jay Baby was there for me, the night of mommy's suicide.

Jay Baby's mom and my mom had an agreement that I would come home from school and teach Jay Baby what I had learned; and in return, Jazzy, Jay Baby's mom, would get Mommy groceries every month. I was surprised that Jay Baby had never been in school. He was about as smart as me. I remembered how surprised I was when he told me that he had never been to school. Jazzy went to private schools, so she was smart. But as she got older, the work got harder, and Jazzy could no longer keep up in certain subjects, math not ever being one of them. No matter how many men I had to trick with, I never let it get in the way of me going to school and tutoring Jay Baby. It was as if that was the only time I had to be myself, the only time I didn't feel like I had someone breathing down my neck about the smallest things.

"Why you eating this? Why you drinking that? Don't nobody want a fat bitch," my mommy would say.

At Jay Baby's, I snacked and ate whatever I wanted without having to hear Jazzy complain about how much this cost and how much that cost. Jazzy left her door open to me. I could do whatever I wanted besides go in Jay Baby's room. Jazzy was hip to what Yolanda had her daughter doing, so hip that she pointed it out to her son the ills of Yolanda. Nothing surprised Jay Baby. He had seen and heard it all in his sixteen years living in the Bass. So what Jazzy had just told him went in one ear and out of the other.

I thought Mommy was drunk and passed out on the floor, but that didn't explain the blood I saw seeping from up under her. I got down on my knees searching for any sign of life. There was none. I screamed out for help several times. In walked Jay Baby. Jay Baby pulled me up and held me in his arms. He told me he needed for me to go outside and call the police. I walked outside. There were people crowded around our apartment building. It took the police forty-five minutes to come even though the police station was right across the street.

I actually thought somebody came in and killed my mommy until Jay baby handed me her suicide note.

"Did you read this?" I asked him.

He held his head down. "Yeah, man, I didn't know what it was. But I felt like you needed to see it."

I felt naked in front of Jay Baby after reading the letter. I held my head low. I felt so low.

"Lyric, I ain't here to judge you. Shit, look where we at, man. It ain't shit but A.........Story."

Jay Baby picked up the knapsack, and before I knew it, he threw what looked like fifty stacks on my table.

"This what you want, right? To know that a nigga got some paper? Well, do this prove that to you, huh, bitch?"

I was taken aback. At no time had Jay Baby ever talked to me like that before.

"You so muthafuckin' stupid, bitch, a nigga would have done anything for your trifling ass."

I done been called worse, but for some reason, the words stung deep coming from Jay Baby's mouth.

"Fuck you, nigga. You think, 'cause you throw fifty stacks on my table, then that mean I'm going to make you my nigga? I don't think so. Fifty stacks might be some money to you, but to me, I'll take pleasure in wiping my ass with that," I stated, staring a hole through Jay Baby.

I watched my words touch him just the way his did mine.

"Bitch, I should put my hands on you," Jay Baby stated as he balled his fist up in a fit of rage.

I stepped in the wider area of the living room so he wouldn't corner me and gave him an inviting glare. Jay Baby knew all too well that I was not an easy win, and if he was smart, he would leave defeated rather than dead.

"I wish you would, nigga, and I'll be the last bitch you put your hands on. Now all that tough-guy shit might work with Donna, but I ain't that bitch, nigga." And I wasn't. "I done took too many ass whoopings in my lifetime to be afraid of anybody, nigga or not."

I watched as Jay Baby scrapped up his stacks off of the table. I opened up the door for him as he began to try to reel me back in.

"You know, Lyric. I didn't come over here for this shit. This shit ain't for me, and you are better than this," Jay Baby stated, referring to the open door I was patiently waiting for him to leave out of.

"Go, Jay Baby," I stated, trying to ignore the tears that wanted to escape my eyes.

I blinked a couple of times to bring the tears back to wherever they were formed from.

"All right, Lyric, I'll leave. You got that, but for the record, that was a hundred thousand dollars. I stack my stacks on top of stacks, and this ain't even half of the money I'm seeing. What can I say, Lyric? You chose the wrong side," Jay Baby stated, laughing sinisterly as he walked out of the door.

I must be tripping, trying to change a hoe into a housewife. What the fuck is wrong with me? Jay Baby thought.

I was stuck staring at a horrible image in the mirror. I had just broken one of my best friends' heart. I knew that it took a lot out of Jay Baby to set aside his pride and practically go out on a limb to let me know that he wanted me for his woman. I respected him for that, and for real, I would always fuck with Jay Baby for that. I just didn't know how to tell him that I was not what he needed. I was not good enough for a man to be with. I was tarnished, and I was not afraid to admit it. Matter of fact, I embraced it. I was not the one to sugarcoat anything. I loved Jay Baby, and it pained me to know how I just trampled over his feelings.

Agape

I didn't like the way the young hustler was forcing his dick down my throat. He damn near had his nuts in my mouth. Had it not been for the plastic baggie he held over my head, I wouldn't even be in this position.

"You know, you too pretty to be a junky bitch," he kept telling me.

I was in the zone. His words went in one ear and out of the other. I could careless what he thought about me. Before I knew it, he was coming in my mouth. I reached for the baggie, and he began to tease me by placing the plastic bag full of my new drug of choice in the air higher than I could reach. But it didn't stop me from stepping on my tippy-toes and stretching my arms to no avail. He laughed on just the way a person does when they are teasing a child. I wanted to kick him in the nuts and grab the bag, but I didn't want to cause no problems at Donna's house.

"I shouldn't give you shit for spitting my shit out. Next time, you better swallow it."

I paid the young hustler no mind as I held my hand out for what was rightfully mines. I silently prayed that he would place the plastic baggie in my hands, and when he did, I ran downstairs to Donna.

"We got some candy. We got some candy." I danced around with the plastic bag full of rocks.

Donna was downstairs throwing stones at me considering to suck a dick to get some more crack. She told herself that she wouldn't get high anymore, but when she was face-to-face with the hard white, she found her mouth watering, and her hands began to tremble in anticipation.

I might as well get high. It's right here.

Donna convinced herself that it was her choice and not the monkey on her back.

Just as the hustler left out, Jay Baby was walking up the pathway to the door. Donna looked at Jay Baby like she had seen a ghost. She had become so accustomed to him not coming home she surely didn't expect him to come home tonight. Donna got up off of the floor nervously. She didn't know what to expect. Jay Baby had enough on his plate. He could care less what was going on with Donna. He needed out of the relationship, and this little incident gave him the excuse he needed to leave her. Jay didn't want to leave the mother of his children. But how he saw it, the kids were at her mother's more than they were home, so it didn't matter whether they were together or not.

Donna was well aware that, in the beginning, Jay Baby only came around to fuck her; but she was head over heels over Jay Baby. It didn't matter to her how he played her time and time again, only coming over to her place when no one was on the block. It didn't matter to her that, when he was around Lyric, he wouldn't even speak to her. Donna wished to this day that he would look at her the way he looked at Lyric. Everyone in the Bass knew that Lyric was a hoe, but Jay Baby treated her like she was something precious. Donna gave Jay Baby her virginity in hopes that he would come around, but he didn't. He continued to play, so she formed a scheme to keep him around. She provided every condom that they used but not before she secretly poked safety-pin holes throughout the packages.

Jay Baby ran up the stairs and began to pack up what little bit of shit that he had left. He was slowly damn near moving in over Lyric's, at least he thought. Every time he would leave an item of clothing, Lyric discarded each item in the trash. She was determined not to let Jay Baby move in on her. Jay Baby laughed to himself when he thought about how much he still cared for Lyric. He knew that she herself didn't. He knew that she was loyal, and to him, that was the most valuable trait a woman could possess. Jay Baby could care less about how many dicks Lyric done sucked or how many niggas she done fucked because, when he looked at her, all he could see was the lost little girl he held in his arms the night of her mother's suicide.

Jay Baby had a connection with Lyric that went deeper than what appeared on the surface. Jay Baby was a fatherless son who had a mother that had an addiction to the streets. His mother never did a drug a day in her life. She got high off of money, being in the streets hustling and clubbing every day of the week. That was her thing. Jasmine "Jazzy" Brooks did whatever she had to do to live the ghetto fabulous life that she had become accustomed to, and having a son at a young age wasn't going to stop her either. She wasn't happy that she was bringing a child into her bullshit, but she was pleased. To her, she was having a boy because she was more than prepared to teach him how to be one of the biggest hustlers that the Bass had ever seen. She named him Li'l Jasmine Brooks. Everyday of Jay Baby's life, Jazzy made sure she showed him the type of niggas to not be.

"Don't be no lame-ass nigga like him. Don't be no crackhead like him. Don't be no gay faggot undercover as nigga like him and him."

Jazzy made it a point to point out these types of people whenever they surrounded her. She didn't want her son to get shit twisted. These types of people came in all different shapes and sizes. Jasmine never sent Jay Baby to school. Everything he needed to know to be what she needed him to be, he couldn't learn in no classroom. She was never on public assistance, so to the school system, Jay Baby didn't exist.

Jay Baby never questioned his mother about the life she had taught him to live. Shit, he thought that it was normal for him to be up for days making runs for his mother. Jazzy would keep Jay Baby on the corner early mornings holding on to a book bag on his back half his size. To onlookers, you would have thought that he was a kid standing at his bus stop. Only if the police knew his book bag contained ounces of crack rock. The only thing he questioned was why she always made him wear dingy jeans to big shirts and run-over shoes and socks while she sported some of the latest trends.

"Jasmine, we in the projects, so we have to live like we in the projects. What bitch you see out here looking worser than they kids? Not one. Every bitch out here wearing Tommy, Guess, and Fubu, and what the fuck do they kids got on? High-water and hand-me-down OshKosh B'gosh. I look good because I have to. You look like a scrub because you have to. This shit is chess, son, not checkers. When a nigga get to flashing his shit, buying shit another nigga can't get, that's when your problems start. But you see, they see me in a three-hundred-dollar outfit, and then look at you. A muthafucka would swear up and down that I spent my whole welfare check on an outfit and just said fuck you, not knowing that I would never accept a handout, let alone a welfare check or some fucking food stamps. A person is not supposed to know what you have, Jasmine, unless you are willing to show them."

Jazzy knew her son was getting older and yearning for some female attention and not just any female. She knew that he wanted Lyric's attention. She loved Lyric like a stepdaughter; and despite the shit she did to get money, Jazzy knew that Lyric was beautiful, smart, and ambitious as well. Her mother taught her to look at a package and judge it, so she knew that Lyric would never be interested in her son, at least no time soon. But the night Jasmine came home confessing his love for her, she didn't know how to put it to him, but she rather broke his heart first before Lyric did.

"Jasmine, you don't know the first thing about love. I ain't never taught you about love. You love your mother and yo' money. You don't ever love no whore."

Jazzy almost chastised herself for calling Lyric a whore. She saw the disappointed look in her son's eyes, and it pained her, only because she knew the day would come when a female would strike her son's eye. It was times like this that she wished her father was here to guide him the way he needed to be guided. Only a man could tell a growing boy about women. Jazzy didn't want to steer him wrong just as she was about to do, so she did the only thing that she could. She told him how to handle a girl like Lyric.

"Jasmine, everything about Lyric does not meet the eye. She is a pretty little girl, but she has had to grow up faster than most..."

"Like me?" Li'l Jasmine asked.

It was then that Jazzy realized that she was so busy trying to build an empire that she was willing to take her only child's childhood away from him.

"Yeah, like you," Jazzy stuttered. "Look, Li'l Jasmine, I'm not sure, if I could do it all over again, I would. You have enough of money now at the age of fourteen that, if anything was to ever happen to me, that you could live life comfortably without me. How many kids—No, fuck that. How many people you know can say the same?"

"But why does it always come down to money with you, Ma?" Li'l Jasmine asked.

"So you think it's just me, Jasmine? You think that, that pretty little Lyric don't got money on her mind?" Jazzy questioned her son.

He was silent. Jay Baby was like that when he didn't know the answer to something. He was never foolish enough to pretend to.

"You can bet your last dime she do, and that's the type of girl you better go for. You don't want no woman who can't do shit on her own. I don't care what the girl do to get money. Just make sure she do something, and if she wants you and you ain't got shit, then that bitch don't want shit. But if you love her, show her what you have, and the look in her eye will tell you if she real or not. But don't ever judge her for not wanting a nigga that appears to not have shit. Don't ever judge any woman, Jasmine, unless she's disloyal. Loyalty is everything."

Jay Baby's ringing phone was what disrupted his thoughts. The caller ID displayed Lyric's number. Jay Baby told himself to not answer the phone, but something in him told him to answer the phone. Something in him needed to hear Lyric's unspoken words.

"Yeah…"

"You busy?" Lyric asked.

"Nah, I'm good. What's up?"

Silence.

"I was just thinking that maybe we should try to work something out. I mean, you are my friend, and I don't ever want to hurt you, Li'l Jasmine."

Jay Baby could feel his mother in the room. She was the only one who ever called him by his full first name. Lyric was the only female around him and his mom growing up. Ma never trusted women, not even Yolanda. Jazzy knew, a woman like Yolanda, she may appeared as if she didn't know much of nothing; but something told her otherwise she didn't like the company of Yolanda in her own home. She never let Yolanda in her house.

Hearing Lyric call him by his name let him know she was sincere.

Silence.

"Come on, Li'l Jasmine."

Jay Baby couldn't help but smile. And that's all he questioned.

"And I love you, and I'm sorry," Lyric confessed, meaning every word of it. "And…" Silence. "And that was enough of money," Lyric joked.

Jay Baby caught on to the joke and laughed along.

"We good, babe," Jay Baby stated as he continued to pack his belongings. "So tell me. Can I come home?" Jay Baby questioned.

"Yes, you can," Lyric stated as she let her talk do the talking and pushed her pride to the side just as Jay Baby previously did.

"You know I love you, right?"

Lyric was just about to respond when she heard Donna in the background saying something about "Who the fuck you in here talking about you love? You not shit, muthafucka."

"Bitch, you better get up out my way," Jay Baby stated as he grabbed up his Luie suitcases.

"Where are you going?" Donna questioned hysterically.

"I'm leaving!" Jay baby yelled at Donna, mad at the fact she was not only eavesdropping but she had the nerve to come at him like he had been fucking her.

Donna reached for one of Jay Baby's suitcases. The attempt failed, sending her crashing down the steps.

Jay Baby couldn't help but notice my bulging eyeballs as I sat on the chair, not the least bit affected by Donna falling down the flight of steps. I continued to twirl my hair looking like a psych patient. Jay Baby knew what it was. He knew that I had took the leap from powder to crack rock.

Damn. He shook his head, leaving out of the door. *Putting two and two together, if A on it, then Donna is too. Fuck, how I end up with a crackhead for a baby mother?*

Jay didn't know if he should turn around and try to beat some sense in Donna's head. He decided against that and hopped in his car heading home.

Donna yelled my name for the fifth or sixth time, but I was so high I felt like I was in the clouds. And when I heard Donna call out to me, I came down from my high.

"What happened to you?" I asked as I ran to Donna's aid.

"Jay Baby pushed me down the steps," Donna lied.

I had no choice but to believe the lie that Donna had just told me because I went in my car to smoke a few of the rocks. I remembered coming in the house, but everything after that was a blur. Donna remembered perfectly well, what had just transpired. After Jay Baby went up the stairs, she tiptoed up the steps and stood in the hall listening to Jay Baby's conversation he was having. It brought her to tears hearing him ask someone if he could come home. She didn't intrude because she wanted to find out just who this other woman was, but when Jay Baby confessed his love to the girl, Donna couldn't take it anymore.

I tried to lift Donna up off of the floor, but Donna yelled out in agony.

"What's hurting you?" I questioned.

"It's my back. This shit hurts," Donna cried out.

"Do you want me to call the ambulance?" Just as the question escaped my mouth, a light went on in my head. "I know what you need. Hold on."

I went in the kitchen and retrieved the crack pipe and rocks out of my jacket pocket. Donna hoped that I had a solution to this pain. When Donna hit the pipe, she was immediately sent into a sensational bliss that she didn't want to be disturbed from.

"Come on. Let me try to get you up now."

Donna got up from the floor, ignoring the pains that shot through her back. I cut the lights off, and we smoked up the quarter ounce together in Donna's living room on the floor.

As the days turned to nights and the nights turned to days, me and Donna's taste for crack had only intensified. I found myself renting my car out for crack and selling my cell phone for some rocks, as well as my soul in the process. Donna and I binged on crack for three days straight.

Meaka

I couldn't sleep last night. I found it strange that some guy was answering Agape's phone talking about he found it, and when I asked him where he found it at, he hung up. I couldn't think, for the life of me, why would A go off for three days and not think to call me and let me know that she was okay. This really bothered me, and the only thing I could do was pick up the phone and call Lyric even though I knew she got so tired of me going through bullshit with Agape. Sometimes I felt like we were in a relationship. Shit, my own man didn't cause me as many problems as she did.

"Hello…"

"Hi, Lyrie," I greeted, trying to sound like I was happy despite the disgusted taste I had in my mouth when I thought about how inconsiderate Agape was being.

"What's up, Meaka? You sure is up early, and jolly, let me guess. You and Emillio been trying to make that baby," Lyric joked.

"Not exactly. We decided to wait. I mean, Em has issues that he has to deal with. Anyways, his restaurant hasn't been doing well, so he has been dipping and dabbing in the streets here lately, running around with Juan more than I would prefer, but that's a whole 'nother story."

"Well, you know what they say. Ain't no money like dope money," Lyric stated.

I busted out laughing. "No, I've never heard that one."

Lyric couldn't help but laugh.

"I hate to ask, but I have to. Have you seen Agape around?"

Silence.

"Hello?"

"Girl, yeah, I'm here. Why do you keep asking me have I seen A? Why don't you just call her phone?"

I tried, but some nigga answered talking about he found the phone, then when I ask him where did he find the phone at, he hung up on me."

"Well, that sound a li'l fishy," Lyric had to admit. "Let me holler at Jay Baby and see if he heard anything."

I listened to Lyric talk with Jay Baby. He stated that he hadn't seen A and that he would let her know if and when he did. I couldn't help but worry. It wasn't like A to go off for days without calling me and letting me know something.

"Agape's a big girl. I'm sure she cool," Lyric tried to soothe her friend's nerves when, deep down inside, she herself wondered just what Agape had gotten herself in. "You want to go out and get something to eat?" Lyric questioned, trying her best to get A off of Meaka's mind.

"Nah, I'm good. Em downstairs cooking up a feast."

"Damn, you lucky girl, you ain't got to worry about cooking shit."

"How about you and Jay Baby come over for dinner?"

I had noticed that Jay Baby's been over Lyric's three days straight. Not that he hadn't been over there a lot here lately, but she usually put him out at checkout hours. I sensed Lyric getting serious about Jay Baby, and I hoped she was. Jay Baby was a good dude, and I don't think it mattered how much money he had. I really think he could make Lyric happy if she gave him a chance. They were made for each other, and my asking them over for dinner was a test.

"Yeah, we ain't got no plans for tonight. What time is dinner?"

I was shocked. "Um, do you have a cold or, better yet, maybe the flu? Did you just say that y'all are coming?" I asked to make sure I heard Lyric right.

"Haha, Meaka, what time is dinner?"

"Be here at eight."

"We'll be there."

Click.

I ran downstairs to let Emillio know that we were expecting company for dinner. I walked up behind Emillio from behind. I wished I could get Agape off of my mind; but just as I held on to my man, wrapping my hands around his waist and placing my head on his back gently, sadness loomed over me. If only I knew she was okay.

"She all right, Tameka," Emillio stated, reading my mind.

Emillio turned from the stove to face me. I didn't want to talk about Agape. Instead I let Emillio know that Lyric would be over for dinner.

"All right, that's cool. I'll set the table for three then."

"Set it for four."

"I'm about to shower. You think you can look over this baked chicken for me? I don't want it to overcook."

"Baby, but I want to shower with you," I whined.

I had no plans on showering again, but I didn't want to mess up dinner. Nine times out of ten, if Emillio left me down here with this food, something was bound to overcook.

"All right, that's cool. I'll just set the timer."

I loved showering with Emillio. I took pleasure in washing my man just as I would my child, and I loved when he cleaned me up as well. Emillio was always gentle with me. He always made sure that he washed every crease of my body. We dried each other off, dressed, and went downstairs. Emillio put his finishing touches on the food. I sat at the table, watching my man do his thing in the kitchen.

"You think you can set the table for me, babe?"

I immediately got up from the table to retrieve our good china. I set the table to the best of my ability, but of course, I put the spoon and fork on the wrong side of the table. I realized that when I asked Emillio how I did. He stated perfectly, but I noticed him rearranging the silverware. I smiled to myself and went to call Lyric. It was 8:15 and just like her to be fashionably late.

"Hello, where are you? Dinner is ready."

"Open the door," Lyric interrupted.

There they stood. Jay baby had a bottle of champagne and one single white rose. He handed me the rose as they entered the home. I walked in the kitchen to let Emillio know that our company was here. I introduced Jay Baby and Emillio. They hit it off well.

"I wish I had known that you were accompanying Lyric. I would have got us a bottle of spades, brah."

"Well, there's always a next time, and if not, pour some of that shit out for yo' boy!" Jay Baby exclaimed while stuffing his mouth.

"Aye, yo, Em, yo' girl put her foot in this food, my nigga? If you don't mind, I'll like to compliment."

"Nah, brah, go ahead."

"Meaka, this food right here," Jay Baby stated, pointing his fork at his plate, "is good enough to slap your mama," Jay baby joked.

I looked up at Emillio. He was always willing to give me the credit for his food when people who didn't know him automatically assume that I cooked.

"Jay, I didn't cook. Emillio did."

Jay almost choked on his food. "My bad, my man. No disrespect intended."

"And none taken," Emillio responded.

"Dinner was good."

Emillio pulled Jay away from the table so they could get better acquainted behind the PlayStation 2.

"I see you and Jay are hitting it off good."

"You don't know the half, girl," Lyric stated, rolling her eyes up in the air.

"Oh, bitch, don't front," I stated, noticing how Lyric was trying to brush things off.

"Okay, okay, okay. Jay Baby asked me to be with him, and you know, I'ma see how all that works out."

"How what works out?" I questioned.

"You know, the whole relationship thing. Meaka, I've never been in a relationship with nobody."

"Never?" I questioned.

"Never. I just don't know if I make a good girlfriend. At least I never thought I would."

"Well, I think you make a wonderful girlfriend, and I am happy for you. You deserve someone who wants to be with you. So what's up with Donna? How she taking this?"

"Fuck Donna. How I see it, she didn't know what to do with him. That's her issue."

We high-fived, and before we knew it, we had drunk the whole bottle of Moet. Time went by, and before we knew it, it was midnight. Emillio and Jay Baby came in the living quarters of the room.

"Aye, Lyrie, where you been hiding this dude at? You got a all right nigga right here. Don't fuck up," Emillio stated.

Lyric knew what he was saying came from a good place, so she nodded her head.

I couldn't help but put my two cents in. "And the same for you, Jay."

"Don't worry about that. I'ma make sure I do right by y'all, Lyrie."

"You better, my nigga. That's li'l sis right there."

Lyric was stunned at how much love Emillio had for her. He never showed her any love. He barely spoke to her, and if Meaka wasn't in the room, he wouldn't say one word to her.

We walked Lyric and Jay Baby to the door, and just as we got to the door, the locks on the door began to turn. Emillio reached for his pistol but realized he wasn't strapped. He kicked himself for that, but when he looked at the pat Jay had just given him and looked down to see a chrome 380, he grabbed it and aimed at the door. In walks Agape. The room was silent. She raised her hands up as if this was a stickup. She looked like she hadn't had any sleep.

"Come on, Jay. This is definitely our queue to leave," Lyric stated before she grabbed Jay Baby's hand and led him out the door.

The air was thick, standing face-to-face with Agape. I couldn't understand for the life of me why she was standing in my doorway after me not hearing from her in three days straight. Emillio must have felt my venom ready to release because he turned and walked up the steps.

"And where have you been?" I asked with much attitude, blocking Agape's way.

"What do you mean where have I been? I'm not your fucking child. I don't answer to you, bitch. Who do you think you are?" Agape stated with just as much attitude.

"You don't have to be my child for me to be up worried sick about your ass—"

"Worried?" Agape interrupted, laughing hysterically. "You didn't look worried to me. Shit, to me, it look like you carefree, you, your husband, and your best friend and, not to mention, her new boyfriend. Bitch, please," Agape stated, trying to go around me.

"Look here, Agape. We need to get some things straight. I'm not going to have you disrespecting me in my own home. That's for one," I stated, holding up a finger just so she could understand. I added another one before I said, "And for two, if and when you leave for days, just let me know because, whether you want to believe me or not, I was worried about you."

"Listen, Meaka. I don't answer to you or nobody else for that matter. I do just as I fucking please," Agape stated while bogarting her way through me without touching me. I looked on in disbelief at the nerve of this bitch.

How dare she disrespect me, the way she is in my own fucking house? I thought as I followed her up to the second floor.

As I hit the top step, I heard her slam her door. What the fuck was up with her?

"What is going on with you, A? Where have you been, and why is your hair and your clothes in a disarray? Did someone do anything to you?"

My questions went on and on. I desperately searched for a reason that she could possibly have to act the way she was, but Agape didn't want to make this easy. She stood in my face, staring me right in my eyes, saying nothing with her arms folded on her chest. Her stare was so cold that I couldn't face her any longer, too afraid of what might take place.

So I left the room but not before I stated, "You know what, A? You fucked up. You have real fucking issues."

Agape

I slammed the door so hard I tried to break it off of the hinges.

I don't know who that bitch think she is. Just because I live in her house, she think that means she has to keep tabs on me. She got me fucked up, I thought. *Talking about she was worried about me, that bitch wasn't worried about me. I don't know why she wanna act like she mad. The bitch is probably mad I came back. Yup, that's what it is,* I convinced myself.

I needed some much-needed sleep. I hadn't slept in three days. I shunned myself for leaving from over Donna's. I knew that was the only place I could keep a peace of mind at. Shit was too closed in over here for me. But I needed some sleep, and if I would have stayed, then sleep would have been the last thing on my mind.

Lyric

"Did you see that bitch?" I questioned Jay Baby.

"Yeah, I saw her."

It was evident to everyone but Meaka what had been going on with Agape. Jay Baby didn't know if I knew the extent of Agape's addiction.

"If I didn't know any better, I would say that bitch hitting rocks."

Jay Baby remained quiet. His quietness disturbed me.

"Jay, don't tell me that dumbass bitch hitting rocks?"

Jay Baby pulled the seat back while pulling his fitted cap down over his eyes. I knew this meant my accusations was correct, but for some reason, I needed to hear it come from Jay Baby's mouth.

"Answer me, Jay."

Silence.

Jay Baby was beginning to piss me off. I punched him lightly in his chest.

"Come on, Jay. Let me know."

"I can't say for sure, Lyric, damn," Jay Baby stated, trying to get off the subject.

"All right."

Me and Agape hadn't been on the best of terms, but I didn't like seeing her like that. That was for sure. I don't know how that happened to her, then I thought about it as I whipped my all-black Challenger in and out of traffic—Donna. See, that's why I don't hang around miserable bitches because a miserable bitch doesn't mind you wasting your life as long as you're doing it with them.

"So what did you think about Em?"

"He cool people. I remembered him from around the way. He couldn't believe that Jazzy was my mom. He and his brother used to hit the highway for her back in the day."

"Jazzy had her hand in everything, didn't she?"

"Hell yeah, she did," Jay agreed.

"So you don't ever go and visit her?"

"Nah."

"What about Tay and them?" I asked.

"You know, all my moms did for her people, they disowned her when they thought she was in the projects because she needed to be there, but when they realized that she could pay for their children to go to college, they wanted to make it seem as if they loved her. She put Tay, Meiko, and Dink through college, and neither one of them niggas ever write her a thank-you note, send her a card, or nothing. If I ever see one of those pussy-ass niggas, I'ma beat they asses close to death."

"Let's go see her, Jay. I miss Jazzy. I can still remember the first day I met her. She was so straightforward. She told me like 'Look, Lyric, I love you like a stepdaughter. Everything in my home is open to you. You don't have to steal nothing from me. All you have to do is ask, and if you ever do, then your mother won't have a daughter.' I knew she didn't take no shit."

We laughed sharing stories about Jazzy as we pulled up to our condo.

The champagne definitely was working a toll on me. I was more than tired. I was beat, but I knew sleep was not in the cards for me when I peeped how Jay Baby was staring at me as he undressed.

"Come here, baby, he demanded.

I complied and walked over to the bed where Jay Baby sat stroking his dick. I reached over in my party bowl. The party bowl was a bowl I kept discreetly decorated, and it contained condoms.

After retrieving a condom out of the bowl, I tore it open seductively with my teeth, staring at Jay Baby. I was tired, but I had to perform. When I went to slide the condom down on Jay Baby's dick, he objected.

"I don't think we need that, Lyric."

I looked at him like he was crazy. "Yes, we do. I ain't trying to get pregnant, Jay. Come on now. Let's just enjoy ourselves for the night. Can we do that?" I pleaded.

"Lyric, come get on this dick," Jay Baby demanded while he held the condom.

I complied for the sake of our relationship. I had never had any dick without a condom. I realized that I didn't even know what dick really felt like.

Jay Baby put me on my back, raising my legs over his neck. He commenced to make his dick disappear inside of me. It felt so good.

"Whose pussy is this?" Jay Baby asked.

I responded by telling, "This pussy is yours, Jay Baby."

"You bet' not give my pussy to nobody. You hear me?" Jay Baby asked as he stroked my insides. "You hear me?" he continued to ask.

"Yes, baby. Yes, I hear you."

The dick Jay Baby was giving me was crowned the best dick I had ever had before. We came together.

Before I knew it, I was waking up, not even remembering going to sleep. Jay Baby wasn't next to me. The dick was so good from the night before I got up searching for him, naked and all. When I stepped out of the door, I noticed that my moneymaking room door was cracked. I pushed it open. Jay sat in one of the red leather La-Z-Boy seats that I had built in the wall.

"What's up?" I asked, not knowing exactly how Jay was feeling about this room.

"Nothing. Just wondering why you ain't never did your thing for me in here."

"Shut up, nigga."

"How many niggas done been here, Lyric?" Jay Baby questioned.

"What difference do it make?"

"We moving."

"That's fine."

And it really was. I was tired of the condo and wanted a change of scenery.

"You want breakfast?"

"Breakfast like you-cooking-me-something breakfast or breakfast like we go get breakfast?" Jay teased.

"Breakfast like I'll cook breakfast."

"As long as you cook it just like you are naked," Jay Baby requested.

"We have a deal. Let me brush my teeth."

I heard Jay Baby's phone going off, and had it not displayed "Baby Momma," I wouldn't have answered the phone. But I felt like, if she didn't know, she needed to know that Jay was now my nigga.

"Hello."

"Who the fuck is this?" Donna asked.

Then I realized that it was too early for this shit. "Hold on. Baby!" I yelled for Jay Baby, making sure Donna heard me call him baby. I wanted to rub her the wrong way. "Your baby mama on the phone," I continued to fuck with Donna in my own way.

I laughed to myself when Jay Baby grabbed the phone out of my hands. I couldn't help but follow him into the living room.

"Donna, look, I ain't been there 'cause I no longer live there. When I wanna see my kids, then I'll go over your mother's just like I did yesterday and the day before."

"So what you saying, Jay? You gon' just leave me for another bitch?"

"Donna, I ain't fucked up with you or nothing. If my kids need something, then let me know, but as far as me and you, it ain't no me and you. It ain't about no other bitch."

Jay Baby heard the sadness in Donna's voice, and he couldn't find it in him to let her know that he left her for Lyric just yet.

"Who was that bitch that answered your phone then?" Donna tried everything in her power to gain control over her situation.

"That don't have nothing to do with what I'm telling you, Donna. If it ain't about the kids, then you need not call this phone."

"Oh, so if I needed something, then what?" Donna taunted.

"Then you need to find you a nigga or, better yet, a job." When Jay noticed Lyric in the room, he knew he had to bring the call to an abrupt end. "Take care, and I'll be to get the kids from your mom's and take 'em out, so don't go rushing over there to get them."

249

"You bet' not have my kids around no other bitch…"

Click.

Jay Baby couldn't promise her that because he knew eventually Lyric would be a part of his kids' lives.

Meaka

I hated living so far away from Lyric, but since Emillio had to take care of some business with Juan, I had to make the drive out here to keep from killing Agape. She'd been sleep for two days, and I couldn't find it in me to see how a person could sleep for two days straight. I hated bringing my problems to Lyric's peephole, but who else did I have to talk to?

I could hear music, so I knew Lyric was in the house. She must haven't heard me knocking. I tried calling her phone to no avail. What the fuck? I banged harder. Just when I was about to give up, I heard the music cut down, and I did a one-eighty and began knocking again.

"Who the fuck is it?" Lyric asked, walking to the door, desperately hoping it wasn't one of the many niggas that she had been ignoring since she turned over a new leaf.

"It's me, Lyrie. Open the door."

I was shocked when Lyric came to the door in what looked like a stripper's outfit.

"What are you doing?" I asked, laughing.

"Entertaining my man, bitch. Why are you not doing the same?"

"I thought to stop by and see if you wanted to do some shopping. My treat. I know those pockets of yours are hurting due to your newfound profession," I stated while spinning one of the pasties on Lyric's nipples.

"Bitch, if I show you how that nigga just made it rain for a bitch, you might want to put this shit on," Lyric joked. "Let me hop in the shower. Give me a minute."

"What's up with you?" I asked Jay Baby as he entered the living room.

"I'm good. What's up with you?"

"About to head out and go see my kids soon as I get out the shower."

"Kids?" I questioned Jay. "I didn't know you had kids," I stated.

"Yeah, I have two boys and a girl with Donna. Shut the front door."

"You and Donna have three kids together?"

"Yeah, man," Jay Baby admitted jokingly.

"You know what? I always wondered who was that in that picture with Lyric?" I asked, referring to the life-sized portrait on Lyric's wall.

"That's Lyric's mom."

"I didn't know that. I thought that was her sister."

"Lyric aint got no sisters, but she got a shitload of brothers running around."

We shared a laugh. I took note that Jay Baby knew a lot about Lyric. She was my best friend, and he knew her far better than I did.

"How long y'all been knowing each other?"

"I been knowing Lyric, shit, since I can remember. We grew up in the Bass together."

I didn't know what had hindered Lyric and Jay Baby from being together. I was just happy they made their way to each other. I was happy for Lyric.

"So how is the married life?" Jay Baby questioned with admiration in his eyes.

"Don't tell me that you are thinking about marrying my girl without my blessing?" I teased.

"You know, Meaka, if I only knew she would say yes."

"Yes to what?" Lyric asked, coming from around the corner in an all-white Juicy Couture jogging suit and a pair of all-white Air Max.

"Mighty nosy now, aren't we?" I spoke up when I saw she had caught Jay off guard.

"We about to go shopping, Jasmine," Lyric stated as she sat next to Jay on the sofa.

"I know. I know. I know," Jay Baby stated as he got up to go to the back room.

I eyed Lyric as she eyed me back.

What was that about? I thought until Jay Baby came around the corner with a knot slightly bigger than the one Em gave me.

He handed over to Lyric, questioning, "Ain't this how it goes?" he joked.

Lyric looked at the money unfazed and stated, "It's a start."

My girl was so hard. I smiled as we made eye contact.

"Come on. Let's hit the road."

"You good, Meaka?" Jay questioned.

"Yes, I am," I responded, patting on my Louis Vuitton.

"I see you, Meaka. I see you," Jay Baby joked.

I couldn't help but laugh. Before I walked out of the door, I looked on as Jay Baby and Lyric stole kisses. I had never seen my friend so happy.

"Aye, Jay, she would say yes," I stated as I pulled the door up behind me.

I waited for Lyic to come out.

"What was that about?"

"Nothing, girl. Let's ride," I stated.

I knew once I whipped the car out in traffic, Lyric's mind would hit the road. She loved to passenger side drive.

"Slow down, bitch. Why you always got to drive like a bat out of hell?"

It wouldn't be like Lyric to not roll up a blunt hitting the highway. When the potency of the weed got too strong for me, I cracked my window and watched the thick smoke leave out of the window.

"I don't see how you smoke that shit."

"Well, as long as it's this shit and not none of that hard shit, then we all right. You know that's right. So what's up with that sister of yours?"

"You know, Lyric, I don't know what done got into A. It's like she not the same person. But I do know one thing. She is really starting to get on my muthafucking nerves. You wouldn't believe she at the house 'sleep."

"What that mean?" Lyric asked, confused.

252

"It wouldn't mean shit if the bitch hadn't been 'sleep for two days straight."

Lyric knew her suspicions of Agape were true, but against her better judgment, she chose to keep it from me. It was obvious that I didn't know the reason for Agape's change, and she wasn't willing to let me know what it was.

"Ever since Al died, it's like she just hasn't been the same then. The shit with Chance didn't make matters any better."

"Speaking of Chance, I seen Amira the other night in the Trees. She vowed to beat the shit out of Agape on sight for getting her brother jammed up like that."

The sound of Amira's name brought a bittersweet sensation to me. I was happy she was finally released from prison, but to hear that she wanted to bring harm to someone I loved put a bad taste in my mouth.

"That don't make no sense. He beat her ass like she was a nigga. What else was she suppose to do?"

Lyric listened on to me defend Agape's actions and found it quiet funny.

"What's so funny, bitch?" I questioned.

"Nothing. It's just that somehow, someway, you find a way to justify that girl's actions," she said, referring to Agape.

"That's not true, Lyric."

"But it is! How is it that you and her both fuck with street niggas but don't know the code of the street? The police are not to be called at no time. She lucky all Amira talking about is beating her ass. Shit, some people kill for less than that."

"Well, like I said, he shouldn't have put his hands on her."

"That wasn't Chance's first time putting his hands on that girl, and not no other time did he beat that girl like that. Did you ever stop and think what made him beat her ass like that?"

"I hadn't, but I still didn't excuse him for what he had did to my sister."

From the looks of all the cars parked in the mall parking lot, I could tell that the mall was packed. Shopping was always fun with Lyric. Whenever we were at the mall, there was always niggas walking up to Lyric, requesting to see her or handing her over knots of money. A lot of niggas showed Lyric love, but today was different. I knew that when some nigga walked up on us as we stood in Kay Jewelers. He was a stocky dark-skinned Notorious BIG lookalike. He grabbed Lyric's arm as if she was his child and began his scolding.

"Why you aint been answering your phone, bitch?"

"If you don't get your muthafuckn hands off of me, muthafucka," Lyric warned between clenched teeth.

"Or what, bitch? I'll beat your hoe ass. You think I give a fuck about being in this mall?"

"I'ma ask you one last time, Xavier. Get your fucking hands off of me," Lyric warned as she looked from the arm he had on her to looking him directly in his face.

I stepped in between the two of them when I noticed security walking our way.

"Look, here come security. Why don't you go your way? We go ours."

"Oh, I get you a dike now, huh?" Biggie joked.

"And if I was?" Lyric responded.

"You know what? You ain't worth shit, bitch. You ain't nothing but a two-dollar hoe."

Biggie walked off, and Lyric and I kept walking in and out of stores.

"These niggas is crazy. I'll tell you the truth," Lyric admitted.

Her phone began to ring. Her caller ID displayed a name that she had been dodging for a few days now. It was Juan. As we stood at the perfume case buying our favorite True Religion for women, the Macy's worker was helping us when a guy called from across the stand.

"Excuse me, miss. Can I get a bottle of that True Religion too please?"

The voice sounded familiar. I just couldn't put my hand on who it was. When I looked up, I realized that it was Juan.

"Let's go say hi. That's Juan." I pulled Lyric around the counter. "Hey, brah," I greeted Juan.

"What's up, sis? How you doing?"

"I'm good. You remember Lyric, right?" I asked, gesturing toward Lyric.

"Yeah, how could I forget?" Juan stated. "How are you Lyric?"

"I'm good, and you?"

"Better now that I see you." Juan appeared to be joking, only thing was that he meant every word.

Lyric had been avoiding his calls. He thought about popping up at her spot a few times and dismissed the thought as stalkerish.

"Too late, playboy. Lyric here is now taken," I informed Juan playfully.

Lyric punched me lightly in the arm.

"How about Lyric tell me herself?"

"Tell you what?" Lyric questioned as if she hadn't been listening.

Juan walked up on Lyric and spoke to her eye to eye. "Are you taken? Are you married?" she asks.

Lyric always thought quick in on her feet. She wasn't about to give in that easy to Juan.

Juan then looked in my direction and asked, "Do you mind if I speak to your friend for a minute?"

I'm not one to hate, so if Lyric didn't have such a confused look on her face, then I would have simply obliged. But something was telling me that there was something that I didn't know about going on between the two of them.

"We all are grown, Juan. Whatever you have to say to Lyric, I'm sure you can say in front of me."

It was obvious that he wouldn't.

"Come on, now, sis. Don't do that."

Lyric looked over at me and smiled. "She right."

"Meaka is not your wife nor my nigga's, so I don't see why you can't just say whatever you have to say now."

Lyric knew that he wouldn't. That was the only reason she challenged him.

"You two are something else," Juan had to admit.

The sales clerk brought our cologne over to us. Lyric requested that she put all three on one tab, Juan's tab. We laughed all the way out of the store.

"So what was that about?" I had to ask.

"Trust me. You don't want to know."

"If I didn't want to know, then why would I ask?"

"You ready? My arms are beginning to hurt," Lyric asked, avoiding the question.

"Yeah, I'm ready, but my question still stands."

"And what is that?"

"Bitch, stop playing with me. What was that about back there with you and Juan?"

"Meaka, Lyric pleaded, "do I have to tell you?"

"Yes, you do."

Lyric

We looked for the car in the parking lot full of cars. I didn't know how to tell Meaka what had been going on between me and Juan. In a way, I felt kind of guilty for keeping a secret from her.

"Meaka, if I tell you, you can't be mad."

"Oh my God, you and Juan been fucking," Meaka assumed.

"No, not exactly," I emphasized. "We never fucked, but I have been putting on shows for him."

"Shows?"

"Yeah, every now and then, I would strip for him. There, you happy?"

Silence.

"How long you been doing that?"

"For a minute now."

"A minute like last week or last month?" Meaka went on to ask, apparently upset.

"Like a year ago. He first approached me the day we were getting fitted for our dresses and they were getting fitted for their tuxes. He walked me to my car and asked if he could get my number. I gave it to him, and since that night, he would call a couple times a week to get a dance."

"Did Emillio know?" Meaka asked.

"Nah, he didn't know."

Meaka didn't know what to believe. The thought of Juan and Emillio both getting dances from Lyric entered her mind. Had Lyric not told her, she wouldn't have ever thought that she would do something like that, but neither did she think that she would be doing private shows for Juan.

"So is that all you been keeping from me?" Meaka questioned in a way that I didn't like.

"What do you mean by that?" I looked at Meaka, trying to read directly where she was coming from.

"I mean, did Emillio ever join him for one of these shows?"

It pained Meaka to question her best friend's loyalty to her, but after Agape's tirade, she didn't know what to think.

"You have to ask me that, Meaka?" I asked. "Because if you think I was dancing for Emillio, then, bitch, fuck you too."

I didn't have time for Meaka's bullshit. *I don't owe this bitch every detail of my fucking life*. I thought to myself.

"I didn't say you were. I asked because Em and Juan has been spending a lot more time together, so—"

"Well, the answer to your question is no. No, Meaka, I didn't dance for your husband."

"I'm sorry, Lyric," Meaka admitted. "I should have never asked you anything like that."

Silence.

I didn't know how to respond, being the fact the question had already been asked.

"It's cool, I guess. I would have asked the same thing if I was you," I stated sarcastically.

"You wanna get something to eat?" Meaka asked, trying to change the subject, apparently.

"Nah, I'm cool. You can take me back to the house."

"You mad, Lyric?" she asked.

And as mad as I was, I couldn't deny I wasn't. Here, my best friend sat here and asked me if I danced for her man. She must have really thought of me what I thought of myself for so many years.

"Yep, I'm mad. Just to think, I didn't fuck him because of what you and yo' nigga might think. Shit, I thought, if word did get back

ASSATTA

to y'all that I was dancing for him, then, shit, y'all couldn't do nothing but respect my hustle. You feel me? I wasn't trying to keep nothing from you, Meaka, but you see how quick you were to entertain the thought of me dancing for yo' nigga just off of me telling you I was dancing for his brother? Then what would it be for your husband to accuse you of doing some shiesty shit cause you fuck with me."

"You got a point," Meaka had to admit.

I pulled breath from my stomach through my nose to try to blow off some steam. I hated living by other people's standards, and every time I attempted to, I hated myself for it.

"You okay?" Meaka asked sincerely.

"Yeah, I'm good," I stated as I got out of the car.

Meaka got out of the car to help me with my bags.

"You know, I didn't know that was your mom on that picture with you. She looks so young. I thought she was your sister."

"Who told you that was my mom?" I questioned on defense.

"Jay Baby."

"Oh, I don't have any sisters, Meaka," I stated as a matter-of-fact as I walked to put my bags in my room.

I felt how tense things were between me and Meaka, and I didn't like it. Meaka was my friend; but before our friendship could go any further, I needed to make sure that we were in the same lane because, if anything like this was to ever occur again, our friendship would be over.

"I need to talk to you, Meaka," I stated as I sat at my dining room table rolling a blunt.

"What's up?"

"I want to get something straight with you. I know I do some fucked-up shit, but before I met you and your sister, I had never befriended females, okay? I was fucking Chance while he was courting Agape, but as soon as I found out he was fucking A, Meaka, that nigga couldn't even sniff my panties. I was done with him. I didn't even know I was cool with A because, the whole time we were cool, I was using her to keep tabs on Chance. You feel me?"

I knew she did because Meaka nodded her head.

"But see, the difference between you and Agape is that you are my friend, bitch, and I would never do shit to fuck up our friendship. What bitch ever asked me to be her maid of honor? No one. What bitch you see coming up here kicking it with me? I have no friends, Meaka. Can't you see that? I never knew how to be a friend. That's why I never wanted any. If you knew the shit I was taught and shown, then you would know why I do half of the shit I do, but you don't, so that's why I forgive you for questioning me about dancing for Em."

I was not sure why tears were running down my face. But I continued.

"Meaka, the only way I know how to be to you is the way you are to me. I don't think for a second that you would do anything to jeopardize our friendship."

"Aw, Lyrie, come here," Meaka stated as she walked toward me with her arms out. "I love your crazy ass like the sister I never had. You know that," Meaka stated as she gave me a friendly hug.

I wiped my eyes carefully, trying not to mess up my mascara any worse than it already was.

"Well, some love, bitch. You have a sister."

"Lyric, I know that we are different and that there are things about you that I may not know, just like there are things about me that you don't know, but one thing that we do have in common is that neither one of us has a sister."

I didn't know if it was the weed I was hitting that had me tripping or Meaka tripping.

"A ain't your sister?" I questioned.

"Nah, we were foster sisters. We both had been through a lot of shit, so we considered ourselves sisters due to the circumstances. We always clicked. We always got along. That's why it's so hard for me to come to grasp with our relationship now. We promised each other that we would never do anything to jeopardize the family that we built amongst ourselves, and I meant that. That's why I was willing to take that charge."

"What charge?" I questioned.

"So you don't know why I was locked up?"

"Nah, shit, A never talked about it."

"Well, some shit went down between me and my foster mom. I got tired of the shit she was making me do."

I wanted to inquire about the shit she was making her do, but my own skeletons wouldn't allow me to.

"She then started threatening that she would make Agape do it. I was fed up with her manipulations. We started fighting. I guess we woke A up or something. She came in my room and jumped in the fight. We were getting the best of her. She was on the ground as we stomped on her with our bare feet. She tried to get up, then all of a sudden, Agape smashed her in the head with a lamp."

Damn, I thought but didn't dare say a word. I just listened, afraid to say something that would cause her to realize what all she was revealing to me.

"She came down on the edge of my dresser," Meaka stated, looking into the thinness of the air. "Then there was blood and lots of it," Meaka stated as she remembered the night she was speaking of.

I couldn't believe my fucking ears.

"Damn, Meaka, I didn't know that," I confessed. "That's some real-ass shit you did. You don't find bitches like that do a bid behind another bitch." I couldn't help but chuckle. "Now, don't get me wrong. I know a few bitches that will take a charge for a nigga but not ever for no bitch behind loyalty and loyalty alone. Nah, they don't make 'em like you no more."

"You see, that's why I get so upset with A sometimes because it's like she don't care about the promise we made to each other," Meaka stated between sniffles.

"I feel you, Meaka, but you know, people change. That's just like everything that glitter ain't gold. You have to realize everyone ain't in your life to be there for the remainder of your life. Sometimes people are placed there to build your character. But one thing for sure and another for certain. If a person shows you who they are, believe them, or you will regret it."

Meaka

"Look at me getting all sentimental on you," I stated, wiping my eyes. "You cool?"

"I think," Lyric admitted. "I think we both needed to get that out."

I never imagined Lyric crying. She was always so hard. I was happy the ringing of my phone distracted us both because, after what I revealed to Lyric, neither one of us could fix our mouth to form a word.

"It's Em. What's up, baby?"

"Nothing much. Where you at?"

"I'm over Lyrie's. You need something?" I questioned.

"Nah, babe. I'm happy to hear that you with Lyric because I got questions, so I hope you have answers."

"What's your question?"

"I want to know what your girl done did to my brother."

"What do you mean what did she do to your brother?" I asked in hopes that Lyric caught on that this call was about her, and she did.

Lyric hopped on the couch with me. She pulled the phone to her ear while she and I both held our ear to the phone.

"Yeah, this nigga over here tripping. He come over here on some sucka shit, babe, talking about he just saw y'all at the mall. Now don't get me wrong, babe. When he was checking for Lyric, I tell him like 'Leave that girl alone, nigga. She ain't shit but a gold digger.' But that's before I knew her. I was just going by what my nigga told me, you feel me?"

I saw the look on Lyric's face. I put my finger up to my mouth to silence her.

"Why would you say something like that about my friend though, Em?"

I had to defend Lyric at the moment even though this was my husband, but I didn't like how he put her out there. Even if she was a gold digger, what business of it was his to throw dirt on her name?

"Watch your mouth, Tameka, so I tell the nigga like 'Yeah, that's yo' girl, and she cool people.' Baby, the nigga flipped out on me. He talking shit. 'Aw, nigga, you told me she was a gold digger.' I'm trying to explain to the nigga like 'I didn't really know her then, my nigga, but she cool people.' The nigga gets to pacing back and forth, then the nigga tell me, 'A, brah, I think I'm about to have to leave Sharon.'"

My eyes got big. Lyric looked at me, as I looked at her.

"What?" I said.

"Baby, that's not it," Emillio continued, tickled by the situation. "I tell him like 'Brah, it's too late. She got a nigga.' The nigga storm out the door swearing up and down I'm a hater."

Lyric and I both were tickled pink.

"Baby, that's crazy."

"Hell yeah, it is. Ask that girl what she do to my brother."

"Lyric, Em wants to know what is it that you did to Juan. Girl, he was over there going crazy." I repeated what Emillio just had informed me of as if Lyric didn't already know.

"Tell him for me to know and he would never find out," Lyric stated, cracking up laughing.

After I hung up the phone, we continued laughing.

Things got serious when Jay Baby walked through the door. I noticed the serious face Lyric put on. I wasn't sure if it was because she didn't want Jay Baby to know what we were laughing about or if it was because of the kids he came in the door with.

I tried to lighten the mood by asking, "Are these the kids?"

"Yeah, they are. This is Jazzy. This is Jasmine, and this li'l one here we call her L," Jay Baby introduced his children.

Lyric got up from her seat and introduced herself to the children. Lyric reached down as she shook each one of the children's hands. "I'm Lyric. I'm your daddy's friend."

L grabbed Jay Baby by his pants leg. "Li'l Jasmine, I thought you said Lyric was your new girlfriend."

"She is, Mama. She was just trying to be respectful."

"Well, I'm happy you got a new girl 'cause I don't want to go back over Donna's house."

I listened to the li'l girl as she spoke beyond her years. I questioned myself why they referred to their parents by their first names. I found that weird.

"Shut up, L," the little boy who was just introduced as Jazzy stated. He appeared to be the youngest of the three.

"I don't want to go back home. Donna always make me clean up," L stated as a matter-of-factly.

"So y'all gon' do this right here, right now?" Jay Baby questioned.

He knew that his kids were a handful; but he thought that, if he brought them around someone that they never met that, they might be on their best behavior. But then he remembered that it wasn't wise to think. Better to know. And he knew that neither of the kids knew how to hold what they were feeling inside because of Jay Baby's own guilt that lay underneath his chest, deep down in the organ that pumps his blood.

"She better shut up talking about her," Jazzy demanded.

"Or what?" Jay Baby challenged.

"Nothing," Jazzy backed down.

Lyric grabbed Jazzy by the hand. "Hey, li'l man, you look just like your dad. You know that?"

"Nah, I look like my momma, Jazzy responded, looking Lyric directly in her eyes.

Lyric couldn't help but laugh. "Jay Baby, this you all over again."

How could she forget how protective Jay Baby used to be over his mother, questioning her like he was her man? "Where you going? When you coming back?" But what really tripped Lyric out was when he demanded to meet a guy that Jazzy was once going out with before she left with him, and if that wasn't enough, Jazzy came back in the door with the guy.

"My son wants to meet you." Jazzy stood at the door as her son gave the guy the once-over and then began to interrogate him.

"What's your name?" Jay Baby questioned the dude like he was the child and he was the adult.

Jay Baby couldn't begin to deny that Jazzy was a split image of himself. He never questioned anything that his mother did and anything she ever told him. To him, his moms was always right, and Jay

Baby never argued with him on that. He was cool with that because he had Jasmine and L on his side till the end. Looking at L was like staring at his mother. She had the same feisty attitude like Jazzy. She didn't take shit from nobody, and when she was mad, the only person who could calm her down was Jay Baby. Now Jasmine, on the other hand, he was the prodigy child. He was a straight A student. He could be found with his face in a book more often than not. He was quiet. You wouldn't know that he was in the room unless you were looking at him. Nothing moved him unless someone was messing with his organ that pumped his blood, and that was his sister.

"Well, I see your mother in you, but you remind me a lot of your father."

"You know my momma?" Jazzy questioned, shocked.

Before Lyric could answer, Jay Baby grabbed his arm and pulled him toward the back of the condo. "Come on, y'all. Let's go to the back and let Lyric have her space."

Jay Baby rounded the kids up and headed to the back room.

"Hey, Miss L, you want to chill in here with the ladies?" I asked.

I saw the hesitation written all over her face.

"It's okay, baby. We won't bite. You don't want to be cooped up in the room with boys, do you?" I joined in.

Immediately her hesitation vanished. "Nope, I want to chill with y'all. Is that cool, li'l Jasmine?" L turned to Jay Baby and asked.

"Yeah, Mama, that's cool. Y'all go'n in there. I'm right behind y'all," Jay Baby told the boys. I watched on as he kneeled down in front of L. "I need you to listen up to these two ladies. They're good people, and I need you to respect them at all times, understand?" Jay Baby questioned her.

"Understood."

I was taken aback. This little girl was very mature for her age.

"How old are you, L?"

L looked from her father back to me. I detected the same hesitation.

"That's Meaka. She want to know how old you are, L."

Then I saw a hint of shyness in her.

"You go'n tell her, L."

L then turned to me with the most beautiful hazel eyes. "I'm eight."

"Go'n over there with them. You all right."

L walked over slowly. Lyric got up from her seat and placed L on her lap.

"So what you want to do today, miss lady?"

"I don't know."

"Well, what do you like to do?"

"Li'l Jasmine takes me to basketball games at UD, and sometimes we go to Wright State or to the Dragon Stadium. We always do boy stuff," L confessed.

"Well, good thing you have me and Meaka now, huh?" Lyrics questioned.

"Yes," L stated with her eyes lit up, excited about her newfound lady friends.

"Let's go to the nail salon. My treat." Lyric hopped up with the quickness.

I was not sure if she was exicted for L or herself.

I chuckled to myself. *That girl is a mess.*

"Oh, can we?" L questioned with a skeptical look on her face."

"Of course we can."

"I have to go tell Li'l Jasmine. I'll be right back." She ran to the back, excited. She manuevered through the apartment as if she'd been there.

In the back, L stood in front of her father, smiling from ear to ear.

"Let me have it," Jay Baby stated, aware that L had something up her sleeve.

"Um...um..." L stuttered.

"Spit it on out," Jay Baby teased, patting L on her back as if she was choking.

"Lyric and Meaka want me to go get my nails done with them," L stated shyly, working her puppy-dog eyes she knew how to use.

"Just as Jay Baby was about to answer L, Lyric walked in the room.

"Come, L, give your daddy a kiss. We about to go."

L looked from Jay Baby to Lyric and from Lyric to Jay Baby.

Lyric was confused. She thought they had broken the ice with the nail thing when she saw how L's eyes lit up.

"It's okay if you don't want to go." Lyric tried to ease the tension she felt coming from the room.

"But I do want to go," L protested as her eyes started to tear up.

"What's the problem, Jay?" Lyric asked seriously, taking her attention off of L and placing it on Jay Baby.

He ignored her and looked at Jazzy and Jasmine play the PlayStation.

"I know you heard me. What's the problem? You don't trust me with your daughter?"

"It ain't nothing like that, Lyric. Come on now," Jay Baby tried to assure her.

As he grabbed hold of L, her tears began to slide down her cheeks.

"Come on now. It ain't no need for those," Jay Baby stated as he wiped L's tears from her face.

"But I want to go…"

"Quit crying like a pussy," Jazzy interrupted L's moment.

"Watch your mouth, boy," Jay Baby scolded.

He was stuck. He didn't know what to tell his baby girl. He had no problem with Lyric taking his daughter out to get her nails done. It was Donna that he was worried about. If word got out that Lyric had her daughter in nail salon, the one place she shunned L from going with her, it would really cause a problem.

"Well, come on then, L," Lyric stated. She reached for L's arm, and the next thing happened took her by surprise.

"You heard what Li'l Jasmine told her. She ain't going, so go'n back in there with your friend," Jazzy tried to dismiss.

L came right back to her defense. "Shut up, mutherfucker. Don't talk to her like that," L defended as she jumped out of Jay Baby's embrace.

"Hold the fuck up," Jazzy stated as he placed his controller on the floor and stood to his feet. "You know Donna don't let you paint your nails. And you get over here with her," Jazzy continued, pointing directly at Lyric. "And you talking about getting your nails done? You nasty," Jazzy taunted on.

Lyric stood speechless.

"Sit down" was all that came out of Jay Baby's mouth, and Lyric was shocked that Jazzy sat down and picked the controller up. Jasmine hadn't taken his eyes off of his game.

"Don't ever get in my sister's face like that again, Jazzy. Otherwise, I'ma forget that you my brother," the youngster stated.

"Y'all done?" Jay Baby scolded. "Come on. Wrap that shit up. Let's go."

"But, Li'l Jasmine," L pleaded. "I don't want to go."

"You don't have to." Lyric grabbed her arm and her jacket, and off they went to joining me in the car.

"It's okay," I assured. I could see the frustration plastered across Lyric's face. "What took so long?"

"We talk about that later."

"Li'l Jasmine didn't want to let me go to the nail shop. And then Jazzy's dumbass got up in my face like he was crazy."

I listen to the little girl talk as if she was one of our peers. "Did your daddy get him for getting in your face? You know, it's not okay for no boy to get in any li'l girl face," I said sincerely.

"He only pull that when Li'l Jasmine around. He don't do that when we by ourselves 'cause he know Jasmine will beat his ass."

"L, do your daddy know that you cuss?"

"Yeah, he knows I cuss. We all cuss," L stated like she was reciting her ABCs.

I didn't like her talking like that, and I sure didn't want her talking like that while she was in public with me.

"Well, listen here. You can go anywhere you want with me and Lyric. Anything you want, you can have. All we ask is that you stop cussing, okay?"

"Um...um..." L hesitated.

"What's wrong?"

"Well, I don't know if I can stop, especially if I'm mad," L confessed. "And what about when Donna tell me to call Jasmine a punk mutherfucker or a gay bitch?" L questioned but covered her mouth when she realized that she had just cussed. "I'm sorry," L stated with heavy eyes.

"It's okay," Lyric and I assured her.

Lyric

I been around some badass kids in my days, but I don't think none compared to Jay Baby's kids. And to hear that Donna had her daughter cussing at her brothers went beyond words. I thought as we pull up to Onyx's nail salon. Meaka signed the book, and I flipped through the nail book to see if I saw anything I liked. L sat next to me, flipping through a magazine. My attention was broken when I noticed the small Asian lady walking up to the sign-in sheet. I loved watching them try to pronounce their African American customer's names.

"Shikiaasha," she pronounced.

I muffled because I was more than sure the girl's name was Shakeisha. Then a male walked up to the sign-in sheet, and I prayed that he didn't call my name. I didn't like men to do my nails. All of my experiences with male nail techs were horrible, so if he called my name, I would be placing L right in front of me.

"Tammecca," the Asian man called out.

I had to wipe my brow. That was close.

L and I made small talk. I found out that she and I shared the same birthday. I didn't know how L was going to act when we got to the nail salon. I had to admit she was on her best behavior. She was the perfect li'l lady, telling me everything I asked.

"Let me see your nails," I requested to L as she sat under the dryer. "You like them?"

"Yes," she stated with a big smile on her face. "Do you think they are cute?" she asked.

"Yes, I like them." Even though I was not a fan of Mickey Mouse, the little Mickey Mouse faces on her nails was cute for her. "So you like Mickey Mouse, huh."

"Yes, that's my favorite cartoon. I'm dry, Lyric. Is it okay if I go over there and sit with Meaka?"

"Yeah, baby, go'n over there."

I called her baby. I thought I myself never thought I could be sensitive enough to know how to talk to a child. Shit, there were no babies running around in my house growing up, and the only kids I was around was badass project kids. There was nothing soft about them.

Leaving out of the nail salon, I asked L where she wanted to go next.

"Can we get something to eat?"

"You hungry?" I questioned sincerely.

"Yes. When Li'l Jasmine came to get us from over my maw-maw's house, we were about to eat, but he told her he would get us something to eat."

"Well, I must confess. I'm a li'l starved myself," Meaka stated. "What we gon' eat?" she went on to ask L.

"Um...um, McDonald's."

"We not eating that stuff. We gon' get us some good food. How about some Red Lobster?" I questioned.

"I like Red Lobster. Li'l Jasmine take us there all the time, but Donna don't. She say that only grown-ups eat at Red Lobster. She always make us get McDonald's."

Just like her dumb ass, I thought to myself. "Well, today you gon' eat like the grown folks do because we going to Red Lobster."

Jay Baby

I felt like my stomach was touching my back. I knew, if I was hungry, then my sons had to be as well, recollecting that they were about to eat when I went to get them from their grandmother's house.

"I want McDonald's," Jazzy stated as he looked out of the window of my black Cadillac STS Lyric made me purchase.

I didn't care what I drove as long as it got me from point A to point B. But Lyric insisted that I treat myself to a nice car, and I obliged.

"You always talking about McDonald's, man," I complained. "What about some Chinese food?" I asked, having a taste for some orange chicken.

"Nah," Jazzy said, giving it no thought.

"What about you, Jasmine?"

"I'll eat whatever you get," Jasmine stated humbly, leaving me wondering why Jazzy couldn't be a li'l more like his older brother.

"I knew that nigga was gon' say that. He never speaks what's on his mind. He a pussy," Jazzy taunted.

Jasmine gave Jazzy a look that said "Say another word." Jazzy wasn't stupid, so he knew that he tried his hand with Jasmine when I was around, knowing that I wouldn't let him beat him up too bad. But I was driving, so he declined to respond.

I would usually laugh at my son's sporadic outbursts, but something about the way Meaka and Lyric looked at my children in the middle of their tirade made me feel like I wasn't doing such a great job with my parenting.

"Watch your mouth, li'l nigga," I scolded Jazzy.

"What I say?" Jazzy questioned.

Even his young mind couldn't wrap around what he had said so wrong.

Sad, I thought. "Look, we going to Red Lobster," I informed my sons and turned the music up.

The waitress informed me that I was in luck because they had one table left before it was a half an hour wait, but the table was in the far back.

"That's cool," I assured her.

I couldn't help but notice how phat the waitress's ass was and laughed to myself when I saw my sons enjoying the view as well. When we sat down, Jazzy couldn't help but voice what he was thinking as the waitress went to get their drinks.

"Damn, she got phat ass," he stated slightly above a whisper.

My eyes peered over my menu. "Watch you mouth, boy."

"Come on, Li'l Jasmine. You know she got a phat ass," Jazzy continued on.

I once wanted friendship before anything with my kids, but it was up until now I realized how wrong I was. I didn't know if it was too late to correct my wrongs.

"What did he just say?" Jasmine questioned as if he was the father.

I watched on as Jasmine reprimanded his brother.

"You always acting like a bitch, Jasmine, just like Ma said."

"Get your son," Jasmine requested before excusing himself from the table.

After Jasmine was out of ear reach, I questioned Jazzy, "What's up with you, my man? Why you always putting your brother on blast like that?"

"That don't be me. He always got something to say," Jazzy whined.

"Well, look, that's your big brother. You need to start showing a li'l respect," I demanded with a stern look. "One day you might need him, and if you grow up with the same attitude that you sit at this table with, then that might change to a will."

"Yeah, all right," Jazzy dismissed and reached for the glass that the waitress had returned with. "What's your name, Ma?" Jazzy questioned as if he was the girl's peer when clearly she was at least ten years his senior. But that didn't stop Jazzy.

"Don't pay this little one no mind," I interrupted Jazzy before his next question rolled off of his tongue.

"That's okay. He's cute," the waitress responded with a chuckle but was clearly more interested in me. "You must be his father."

I could feel her attraction. "Yeah, he's mine." I chuckled.

"Well, I see where he get his good looks from," the waitress added, putting it on thicker for me.

Had Jasmine not walked up, I would have been at a loss for words because of the waitress's boldness.

"Y'all ready to order?" I asked my sons.

"I want what you get," Jasmine stated while Jazzy ran off a list of things that he was sure he wouldn't eat—coconut shrimp and lobster.

"Okay, I'll place you guys' orders. It will be out shortly," the waitress informed before walking away.

"Are we going back over Mawmaw's today?" Jasmine asked.

"Depends," I responded.

"On what?" Jazzy dipped in and asked, sipping out of his lemonade.

Jasmine looked across the table as if to say "Who was talking to you?" Jazzy caught it and stuck his middle finger up.

"You want that finger cut off?" I asked, talking to Jazzy, then turning to Jasmine. "That depends on whether or not you want to go back over there."

"I ain't trying to go back over there," Jasmine admitted.

"Why's that?" I couldn't help but wonder.

Shit, Donna's mom's house was like a second home to my kids. Anytime I left the house, Donna would take the kids to her mother. There would be often times I would have to practically make Donna go get them from her mother's house.

"No reason. You know Mawmaw do good by us. I just ain't trying to go over there."

But I knew better than to believe that; but I didn't press for answers because I knew, when the time was right, Jasmine would let me in on what's bothering him.

"What about you, Jazzy? You wanna go back over Lyric's?"

The mention of Lyric's name turned Jazzy eyes black.

"Naw, man, I wanna go home," Jazzy responded.

"Here you boys go," the waitress innocently interrupted as she placed Jazzy's and Jasmine's plates in front of them.

I wiped my brow. Thank yous were given to the waitress by us three. Jasmine blessed the food, and we three dug in our plates, not exchanging another word.

Lyric

"Refill, ladies?" the waitress asked.

"Yes please, and thank you," Meaka stated.

I didn't need a refill. I sipped my tea graciously.

"You want a refill, L?" I questioned.

"Yes please," she stated while handing her glass to the waitress.

She's so pretty, I thought to myself, admiring how she had changed up her etiquette with me and Meaka. I didn't think she was going to be able to, but she was handling herself perfectly.

"So what school do you go to, L?"

"I go to Wogomanly. It's okay."

"Just okay?" I badgered.

"Yeah."

"Well, do any of your friends go there?"

"I don't have any friends. Donna don't let us have friends. She say ain't no such thing as friends."

Figures. "What about your brothers?"

"Nope, and I don't like going to school with Jazzy because he always getting into fights, and if one of us fight, we all have to fight. So I stay getting suspended because of him."

"What your daddy say?"

"He tell me to quit jumping in Jazzy's fights, but if I don't, Donna a whoop me, so I just do what she say."

Sad. I was at a loss for words.

I looked up at Meaka to see her expression, and it was the same as mine.

The waitress came back with the drinks. "Can I get you anything else?"

"We're fine. Thank you."

Then out of nowhere, I heard, "Well, can I get something for you, miss lady?"

I turned my head to see Juan. I blushed a little. Big mistake.

"Who was that?" L questioned.

Just as night turned to day, I remembered that I was with my nigga's daughter, and I had lust in my eyes for another man. That was clearly obvious to L.

"Oh, L, this is Meaka's brother-in-law."

"What's up, brah?" Meaka interrupted, trying to get the heat off of Juan.

"Oh, I'm good. Your husband outside parking the car. I got out because I had to take a leak."

L busted out laughing, and we couldn't help but laugh along.

"So who is the new addition?" Juan asked, referring to L.

"This is L, my—" Meaka introduced. After noticing my hesitation, she said, "She's Lyric man's daughter."

Instantly Juan saw black, and I noticed it.

"I have to go the ladies' room. Do you have to go, L?"

"Yes."

Once in the restroom, I took a deep breath.

Damn, do that nigga have to look that good? Oh my God, what am I going to do? I thought, semi panicking.

I snapped out of it when I heard the toilet flush.

"You okay, Lyric?" L questioned, apparently concerned.

"Yes, I'm good, baby." I tried to sound confident enough to make myself as confident as I sound.

I lifted my head and twitched my hips right on out of the ladies' room, holding on to L's hand, but when I came back to see that Em and Juan had joined our table, my confidence went out of the window.

I saw the lust seeping through Juan's pores. He couldn't hide the fact he was into me.

"Do you mind if Em and Juan join our table? It's a thirty-minute wait."

I looked at Em's michevious smile, and I didn't know whether or not there was a wait. I thought quick.

"Well, that all depends on li'l mama right here."

She held on to my hand, and the energy I felt within sent silent shock waves through L. L didn't know the reason why, but she could feel that Lyric wasn't feeling the situation.

"L, baby, do you mind if my husband and his brother join us?" Meaka cooed, feeling like she had L on her hook.

L looked up in my eyes and only sensed uncertainty. "Miss Meaka," L began to say, and everyone hung on to her every word.

Of course she was going to say she didn't mind, everyone including Lyric thought.

"Li'l Jasmine only gave me permission to hang out with you and Lyric. I'm not sure if he would want me at the table breaking bread with your husband and his brother. I'm sorry," L went on to apologize while focusing on her sky-blue Air Force 1s.

"No, baby, it's okay," Meaka assured. "We just did them a favor. Now they don't have to wait for a table."

As soon as we were about to get in the car, I heard my name being called. Why didn't I go with my first instinct and got in the car? But instead I made eye contact with Juan. He called me over. I knew I had to put things to an end with me and him. As much as I loved the attention, I didn't crave it the way I used to. Jay Baby had been good to me, and I couldn't see past him at this point in my life.

Jay Baby

I had to squeeze my eyelids together because definitely my eyes had to be playing tricks on me. When I opened them again, only to reveal Lyric standing in front of the same guy I just saw her hugging, I knew I wasn't tripping.

Look at this fucking slut-ass bitch hugged up with the next nigga, and she suppose to be looking after my fucking daughter. I sat behind my Black tinted STS. "Lock the door, and don't get out the car," I demanded to the boys as I got out of the car. "Understand?" I questioned before closing the door.

Both boys gave a nod that they did.

I walked up on Lyric as her back was turned to me. The look of bewilderment was plastered across Lyric's face when I grabbed her arm and turned her toward me.

"Where the fuck is my daughter at?"

"She's in the car with Meaka."

I walked toward the car. Lyric followed behind me.

"What is your problem?"

I continued walking across the parking lot, ignoring Lyric as if she wasn't there.

"Jay!" Lyric called out.

I swiftly turned around about to snap on Lyric until I heard L's voice.

"Li'l Jasmine was..."

I calmly turned back around and whispered through clenched teeth, "Bitch, you bet' not ever look my way. Come on, L. Let's roll."

"But, Li'l Jasmine," L protested. "But why, Li'l Jasmine? She was so nice to me."

"But nothing. L, come on."

"She okay with us, Jay. She been on her best behavior," Meaka interrupted.

"It's not her I'm worried about," I jabbed, glaring at Lyric. "Come, L, and I'm not saying it again."

Her watery eyes were breaking my heart. I never wanted to bring her to tears, but the here and now was that I was not going to expose my daughter to Lyric's whorish ways. Then my mind chastised me.

I shouldn't have my daughter with the bitch anyway. All the shit her own mama had her doing, I'm sure she wouldn't mind turning my daughter. What the fuck was I thinking? I thought as I pulled L from the car.

"Jay Baby!" Lyric called out.

"Fuck you!" I fumed in her ear as I walked to my car. "Unlock the doors," I commanded the boys.

"Li'l Jasmine!" L called out.

But I was in a trance. I didn't see nothing but black at the moment, and I knew I had to get somewhere and calm down before I made a big mistake. I was lucky I had my three clovers with me because, had it not been for them, I would have been strapped up; and if that thang was on my hip, there was no telling how I would have reacted.

After riding around for hours with no destination, I noticed the boys had fallen asleep, but L sat in the back sulking.

"What's wrong, L?"

"I want to go with Lyric."

"Well, get that out of your mind because you will be nowhere around her ever again."

"But why, Li'l Jasmine? She was so nice to me."

Agape

"I got about three dollars," I informed the young hustler, shifting from one foot to the other, desperately holding out the three dollars in hopes that the hustler would take the money.

"Man, what the fuck am I supposed to do with three dollars?" he barked.

"I'll give you the rest of the money in a couple of hours. I promise you I will give you your money."

"And why would I believe you? You owe damn near every nigga over here, so I'm just supposed to believe you gon' pay me my money?"

I stood there dumbfounded. Of course he had a point, but the fiend in me allowed me to believe my own lies. I knew, if the hustler would have let me walk off with so much as a crumb, I would not come back with his money.

"Yes, I'm good, and I done paid off all of my debts," I continued to lie, knowing, the longer I kept the hustler talking, the better my odds would be in receiving my drug of choice.

"Man, get yo' lying ass out of my face. You owe damn near every nigga out her. Don't come at me with that bullshit, and don't come back with less than twenty dollars," the hustler hollered after me as I walked off with my head down defeated.

I had to walk the walk of shame all the way back to Donna's. I hated to reveal to her that I couldn't cop no dope. It was one thing that I didn't want to face, but just maybe she had a way of getting some.

"Bitch, you won't believe how that muthafucka just tried to play me."

"What happened?" Donna questioned.

"He wouldn't give me shit for the three dollars, then the nigga had the nerve to tell me not to come back with less than twenty dollars. Who the fuck do he think he was? He is some bullshit for that. Man, we need to come up on some money. What about Jay Baby?"

"Girl, that muthafucka ain't came back here. I tried calling him today, and his bitch ass didn't answer the phone. He lucky I don't know who the bitch is, or else I would have been at the bitch's door-step flat out."

Then it clicked to me as Donna rambled on about what she would do to the female that Jay Baby was messing around with. It clicked to me. I not only knew who Jay Baby was creeping with.

"He fucking with Lyric," I informed Donna.

"Bitch, you got me fucked up. He ain't fucking with that whore," Donna stated overconfidently.

"Yes, he is. Him and her was at Meaka's house the other night."

"Why you just now telling me this?"

"Donna, do you think I keep you and your man on my mind?" I dismissed. "You need to call that nigga up and threaten to go beat the brakes off of that bitch if he don't bring you some money."

Donna knew better than to threaten Jay Baby, but the fiend in her thought otherwise. Hearing that he and Lyric were together ate away at her soul.

"Aye, Mom, if Jay Baby comes by there, don't let him get the kids."

"Girl, what are you talking about? Jay came by here three days ago to pick them up. I told him to call and let you know that he came and got them."

"Ma, when was you going to tell me that, that nigga had my muthafucking kids?"

"Look here. You dropped your kids over here a month ago, you and that redhead bitch. I don't know what you think I am, a live-in babysitter or what, but Jay has been the only one calling checking on them, bringing money over to ensure they have what they need. Shit, he has every right to come by and get his kids. And I been meaning to talk to you about you and your kids."

Click.

"Who the fuck this bitch think she is!" Donna yelled. "I can't believe she gave that muthafucka my kids."

The thought of Jay having her kids around Lyric only added fuel to the fire that burned inside of her. After trying to call him several times, only to receive the voice mail, Donna decided to play a few games of her own.

"Agape, we need money. You trying to tell me that Meaka and Em don't have no money around their house."

"Nah, all they use is credit cards. Em don't keep no money in the house."

"Well, shit, I know they got something in that muthafucka worth some money. Shit, we done sold all of our shit. I bet they got so much shit that they won't even notice shit missing."

I never thought about stealing from Em and Meaka. That just wasn't me, but something in me told me that Donna was right. Shit, Em and Meaka had so many diamonds that they could build their own dynasty.

"You right. I need to take my ass over there and snatch up a few trinkets"

I could taste the crack in the back of my throat when I saw that Meaka and Emillio weren't home. I crept up the stairs. It wasn't until I turned the doorknob and saw pictures of me and Meaka I started to feel a little guilty for what I was about to do. So I decided not to touch anything of Meaka's. Instead, I went into Emillio's jewelry box. I saw a pair of yellow canary earrings and decided to put them in my pocket along with a medallion resembling Jesus with a few diamonds on the crown that was adorned on top of his head.

"He won't miss this," I convinced myself as I floated down the flight of stairs, stopping in my room in search of something valuable, and couldn't find anything. I had sold all of my jewelry and anything else I had of value.

Meaka

"It's going to be okay, Lyric. He's just upset right now," I tried to console Lyric.

"No, it's not. Did you see the way he was looking at me, Meaka? He not gon' ever fuck with me again. I know Jay Baby. I know how he is, and you can believe that he is done with me," Lyric cried.

"Come on now, Lyric. That nigga love you," I continued.

"I just want to be alone, Meaka. I'm sorry."

"It's okay. I'm here for you, Lyric, and if you need anything—and I mean anything—let me know. I'm only a phone call away."

"Thank you, Meaka. I really appreciate you."

"You don't have to thank me, Lyric. Just promise me that, if you need me, you will call me."

Lyric hesistated, not knowing if she could make such a promise.

"Come on, Lyric. You are my sister, my friend. I got your back, girl," I stated sincerely.

Lyric could tell that I was sincere, so she gave her word. "All right."

"I'ma let you go. Lay down. Get you some rest, and I'll lock the bottom lock for you."

"Thanks, Meaka."

I felt bad for Lyric after she explained to me how Juan practically cornered her into giving him a kiss, telling her that, if she could kiss him and walk away, then he would not bother her anymore. Lyric went in for the kiss and turned to walk off, only to be faced with Jay Baby. Damn.

I had to get Emillio on the line.

"What's up, babe?" Em greeted.

"I need to talk to you."

"You all right?" Emillio asked, startled by my response.

"Not really."

"What's up?"

"When are you coming home?" I asked.

"You need me there?" Em asked like yesterday. "I'm on my way. Let me tie these ends up."

"I'm waiting on you, Em."

"All right, baby."

The drive home was a somber one. I found myself thinking about Agape and how things had changed between us. I wasn't sure what was going on with her, but I knew that I couldn't keep coming up with excuses for her behavior.

Lyric

The ringing phone was what woke me up out of my sleep. The caller ID revealed a number I didn't know.

"Hello?" I answered with an attitude.

"Tell Jay Baby that he nor my kids better not be over there by the time I get there, or else it's going to be a muthafucking problem!" Donna yelled through the phone.

"Donna, I'ma tell you once, so listen clear. The next time you call my phone making threats, then it's going to be you with the problem. Your badass kids ain't here, nor is their father."

Click.

Donna knew to take me far more seriously than I took her. She was well aware of how I—Got down, she knew firsthand that I could be cutthroat. So she decided not to call back once I hung up on her. Instead, she dialed Jay Baby's number. She was shocked when L answered.

"Hello?"

"L, where the fuck is yo daddy?"

L was disappointed when she heard Donna's voice on the other line. She assumed the private call was from me. L passed the phone to Jazzy.

"Who is this?" Jazzy asked L before placing his ear to the phone.

"Your mother," L responded.

"Hey, Mom," Jazzy greeted Donna.

Jazzy was the only one of Donna's three kids that called her mom. L and Jasmine called her by her name.

"Li'l Jasmine in the gas station. Oh, here he come," Jazzy stated when he noticed Jay Baby leaving out of the gas station. "Li'l Jasmine, the phone for you," Jazzy informed, handing the phone over to Jay Baby.

"Yeah?" Jay Baby blared through the phone.

"You muthafucka! You better not have my kids around that hoe you got for a girlfriend, and how the fuck do you call yourself leaving me for a fuck bitch, you stupid mutherfucker? Bring me my muthafucking kids, bitch," Donna threw slur after slur at Jay Baby.

Never the one to disrespect a woman in front of his kids, Jay never wanted to give his only daughter the impression that it was ever okay for a man to disrespect her nor was it okay for his son to ever disrespect a woman, so he chose his words carefully.

"Donna, you left yo' kids"—Jay Baby stressed the *yo'* to make sure she was listening—"on your mother for damn near a month without even calling them, so don't ring my phone acting concerened."

"You son of a bitch, I hate you. Bring me my fucking kids before I call the police on you."

Hearing Donna threat to call the police, he immediately came to his senses. "I'll drop them off in a minute," Jay Baby gave in.

When Jay Baby pulled up to the Bass and saw the long faces on two of his kids' faces, he was torn.

"You coming in, Li'l Jasmine?" L questioned and pleaded all at the same time.

"Not today, li'l mama. Not today. Out y'all go," Jay Baby instructed. "I'll swing by and check on y'all tomorrow."

"I want to go with you, Li'l Jasmine."

"Next time, L," Jay Baby stated sternly so L wouldn't ask again.

She and Jazzy hopped out of the car while Jasmine sat up front in a daze.

"You gon' go back over Lyric's?" Jasmine asked.

"Nah, partner. I can't do that either." Jay Baby laughed to himself.

"Let me stay with you, Li'l Jasmine," Jasmine asked.

"If I do that, then who gon' look after your sister?"

Silence.

Jasmine gave Lil Jasmine a pound of his fist and hopped out of the car.

Donna

I wasn't happy to see my kids, and the smile that was plastered across my face didn't have anything to do with them being home. I figured, if my kids were there, then they would have some money. Or I might get lucky and Jay Baby come in and bless me with some money. My hopes were up when L and Jazzy came running in the door. I assumed Jay Baby would be coming in behind Jasmine. But when Jasmine came in by himself, my hopes were diminished.

"Where your daddy at?" I questioned Jasmine as if I hadn't gone the whole month without seeing him.

"He gone."

"Gone?" I questioned, visibly upset, marching in the kitchen to retrieve the phone. "Did he give y'all some money?" I questioned each kid.

They all shook their heads no and looked on at their mother like a stanger as she emptied their pockets.

"Come on, L. Let's go to bed." Jasmine grabbed L's hand, and she followed him up the stairs.

Agape

I watched a black STS Cadillac pull out in front of Donna's door. I wished that it was a dope man dropping Donna off some work. If not, I knew we were going to be able to get high all morning with the cross I lifted from Emillio. I knew that the Jesus piece was worth more than twenty thousand dollars. I swallowed hard. My throat acted as if it wanted to close up on me with the thought of getting high. I walked briskly toward the door, desperately trying to straighten out the wrinkles in my clothes with my hand.

"Hey, girl, what's up? Look what I got," I stated, sounding like a kid on Christmas.

"Oh, now that shit is nice. Where you get that from?"

"Now that's for me to know and you to find out. I'll be back in a second, so be ready to get higher than high." I laughed at myself when I thought about how serious I was.

The block was covered with dope dealers. I walked up to a young dealer. I hadn't been too fond of the older dope dealers that had been around the block a time or two. They had no patience for anything other than a quick money transaction; and at times, they were reluctant to exchange work for material possessions, knowing that, nine times out of ten, the items were stolen goods.

"Can I talk to you for a second?" I asked the young hustler.

"What's good?" the hustler asked, eyeing her hungrily, walking up on me.

"I was wondering if I could, um…" I hesitated.

"Spit it out, Ma. What you want to holler at a nigga fo'?" the hustler asked overconfidently.

This was one reason that she liked to cop her work from the older hustlers. They always knew the look of a fiend. Didn't matter how pretty, how thick, and how well put together, they knew off top what you wanted. Only question asked was how much.

"Can I interest you in a pair of canary diamond earrings?" I asked, holding out the two-carat earrings.

"Let me take a look at those."

I stood watching the hustler as he eyed the earrings. I saw the approval in his eyes.

"Oh, hell yeah, these shits is official. Damn, look at the clarity on these muthafuckas. How much you want for these?" The young hustler dug in his deep pocket and pulled out a fat knot.

I looked around cautiously. Something about the projects kept her on edge.

I grabbed the hustler's arm lightly. "You can pay me in work."

He looked shocked and disappointed at the same time. I didn't have time for no one throwing me a pity party, so I cut straight to the chase.

"Let me get a eight ball."

"Damn, baby, I ain't know you was rocking like that. Follow me."

I followed close behind the hustler. As we entered the apartment, I was taken aback by how well furnished the apartment was. There were two different furniture sets in the house; flat screens on the walls, even in the kitchen; china cabinet; and the list went on. I was not sure how it was legal for a person to live in low income with so many expensive things in their apartment. Then it hit me when the young hustler handed me the eight ball. Drug money wasn't a reportable income.

I was down the block by the time the screen door was completely shut. I didn't know how I didn't notice Donna's kids were home when I walked through the front door and saw Jazzy sitting in front of the television.

"Why you so close to the TV?" I questioned.

"Because I can't see on this little-ass TV."

"Where your moms at?" I asked, completely ignoring his rude ass.

"She upstairs."

"Donna!" I yelled upstairs for Donna.

"You got?" Donna asked, running down the steps.

"Yes, ma'am," I responded with excitement.

"Let me get rid of Jazzy's ass. Jazzy, go'n to bed."

"I don't want to go to bed, Mom."

"Boy, it's ten. You need to be in bed."

Who was Donna kidding? It was summer break. Jazzy didn't make it to bed by ten on school nights.

"Since when I got a curfew, Ma?"

"Since I just said so. Now go upstairs, Jazzy," Donna demanded, turning the TV off.

Jazzy looked over at me like I had been the one who sent him to bed.

"Bye, Jazzy," Donna demanded.

"You letting this bitch change you, Donna?" Jazzy stated as he took off up the steps.

Donna saw the hurt in her son's eyes. She had never dismissed him that way. She always gave in to Jazzy. She promised herself she would make it up to him. Now was just not the time to address his hurt nor him calling her Donna.

Donna and I sat up getting high on our drug of choice. We were so high that we hadn't even noticed Jazzy watching everything taking place right in front of his eyes. He was well aware what we were doing. His father had shown him, his sister, and his brother what a crack pipe looked like. He had shown them what powder and crack looked like just so that, if anyone was to ever offer them any, they would know exactly what to say; and that was no. He'd even went so far as to let a dope fiend smoke it in the bathroom while he made his kids go outside, and when the fiend was done, they came into the house and was then introduced to the potent smell of crack. Just in case someone tried to slip it in on them, they would be able to dectect the smell. All of these lessons went unknown to Donna. That was why she was comfortable hitting the rocks while her kids were upstairs asleep.

Donna

I felt like someone was looking at me, but my focus wasn't on whatever was watching me. I was more focused on the glass pipe in front of my face. The touch of the glass added confidence to my self-esteem. It seemed like the pipe gave me the happiness that Jay Baby was only able to give me. But he was nowhere around to provide me with that confidence, so this was the next best thing. As I hit the pipe, I told myself this was all I wanted. These white rocks were all I needed.

"Damn, bitch, that's all?" I asked Agape, visibly irritated that we didn't have any more rocks.

"Yeah, that's all, but I got the medallion. I can go out there and try to get something for."

"Well, what you waiting for?" I asked more aggressively than Agape liked.

"Hold up now, bitch. Don't go demanding shit," Agape argued.

I sensed Agape's irritation and decided to back down. "Come on, A. Go'n out there and see if you can get it off."

Agape went to retrieve the medallion and walked out of the front door. She peeped the scene to see if she could find the young hustler she had done business with earlier. Bingo. Agape practically ran over to the young hustler.

The young hustler was standing on the block with a few other guys that appeared to be hustlers as well. Agape walked up behind him and gave him a tap on the shoulder. The young hustler turned around and looked down at Agape as if he was her senior and she was the eldest.

"Can I talk to you for a minute?" Agape asked, a little over a whisper.

All the while, her best friend, paranoia, was egging at her; so she continued to look behind her and to the side of her, awaiting the young hustler's response. The young hustler let the guys he was talking to know that he would be right back.

"What's up, miss lady?"

"Um, um, I was wondering if you needed a medallion."

"You got it on you?" the young hustler asked.

Agape was in a trance, realizing how close she was to continuing getting high. She didn't even hear the young hustler's question. When he stopped walking, that's what brought Agape out of her trance.

"What's wrong?" the young hustler questioned. "Do you have the medallion with you" the hustler repeated.

"Oh, yeah, yeah," Agape stuttered. "It's right here," she said, still looking out for her best friend.

Agape pulled the medallion out.

"Damn, shorty, where you get this shit from?"

"You like it?" Agape asked, not knowing how to take his response.

"Do I? Shit, this look like some Don shit," the young hustler stated excitedly as he placed the medallion up to the center of his chest.

Agape smiled with relief. "It's going to look good on you," she had to add to ensure her transaction went through.

"Yeah, you're right. What you want for this?"

"Just give me another eight ball," Agape said, trying to not be greedy, too afraid of rejection.

"Follow me."

Agape's mouth began to twitch when her mind recollected that she was going to the apartment they were at earlier. Agape noticed that the hustler was taking awfully long and was asking a lot of questions.

"What you doing out here, miss lady? I mean, do you realize this shit gon' swallow you whole?"

"Come on now, Mr. Drug Dealer. I thought you were here to serve me, not save me," Agape joked, grabbing the work from the hustler, only he didn't find it funny but, better yet, insulting.

He had never pried into any of the fiends he served business, but Agape was different. He thought she could be saved. He felt that her addiction hadn't eaten her whole until she just sold him a thirty-thousand-dollar medallion for three hundred dollars' worth of work. He thought for a moment, when she came with the canary earrings, that she might have just came up on those; but even those were worth over ten stacks.

"Forgive me for having a heart," the young hustler responded, laughing sinisterly.

"Nice doing business with you," Agape stated before leaving the apartment.

The excitement that ran through Agape showed as she ran from one side of the Bass to the other.

Meaka

I sat in my car, waiting on Emillio to pull up. I dialed his number to see where he was at. Just as the phone began to ring, I saw his black Range Rover pull up. I noticed he and Juan were still together.

"What's up, baby? You all right?" Emillio asked.

"I just feel so bad for Lyric. I feel like it's part of my fault that her and Jay Baby broke up. I feel so bad, baby."

"Come on, baby, not out here," Emillio stated as tears began to flow from my eyes.

Juan noticed the distraught look on my face and vowed that, if anyone had so much as harmed a strand of hair on her head, then there would be repercussions for whosoever would try such a thing.

Once in the house, I spoke hysterically, "Lyric and Jay Baby broke up, and it's all my fault."

Juan interrupted their brief counseling session when he walked through the door. "Take my keys, brah. I need to take care of her. Is she all right?" Juan asked sincerely, noticing the tears streaming down my face.

"Yeah, she good. I got this," Emillio informed.

Once Juan left out of the door, Emillio took a seat on the sofa and called me over with a pat to his lap. I sat my 135 pounds down on him and placed my head on his chest.

"Put it on me, babe," Emillio requested.

"If I would have never texted you and told you that we were at Red Lobster, then it would have been no way that Jay Baby would have caught Lyric and Juan kissing."

"Now...hold up," Emillio interuptred. *Caught them kissing?* he thought.

"Yeah," Meaka confirmed what Emillio was thinking. "Juan done convinced her that, if she could kiss him and walk away, then he would leave her alone. She did, and Jay Baby saw the whole thing unfold from his car."

Emillio cursed himself. He, too, felt partly guilty for the demise of Jay Baby and Lyric's relationship. He warned Juan when Lyric and Meaka exited Red Lobster for him to let her go, but Juan insisted that he only wanted to relieve himself to go to the bathroom. But instead, he was outside practically begging for the same woman that he had told him was now off-limits. How could Juan be so ignorant?

"Don't worry. I'ma fix this," Emillio informed just before he planted a kiss on Meaka's forehead. "This not your fault, babe." He hated to see his wife cry, but her open vulnerability was a turn on for him. "But before I take care of that, I have to take care of you," Emillio confided.

He picked her up and carried her to the bedroom.

Jay Baby

The feeling of having to throw up was what had awaken me. I had chastised myself the night before for drinking a fifth of Privilege Hennessy. I couldn't have made it to the toilet quick enough. My whole meal I had consumed at Red Lobster was now floating in the toilet. I continued to throw up over the toilet until I had nothing left to throw up. The taste of bile sickened me even more, so I decided to grab up one of the complimintary toothbrushes and toothpaste and began to brush my teeth. The sound of 50 Cent's "Many Men" blared from my cell phone. I continued to brush my teeth as if my phone wasn't ringing. I was to consumed with the thought of my kids and Lyric to entertain any business or personal situations at the moment. My heart was on my sleeve, and I knew that when I found myself wishing that it was Lyric calling to apologize about her whorish ways. But when I grabbed the phone up, I noticed that I had five missed calls, all of which were from Donna.

I can't do this right now, I convinced myself. *I'll swing pass there and drop her off some money. That's all the bitch want.*

My thoughts were interrupted by "Many, many, many men wish death upon me..." The caller ID displayed Donna's number again.

Afraid that something may have been wrong with one of my kids, I decided to answer the phone.

"What!" he roared through the phone.

"Dad!" Jasmine called out.

"I'm on my way," I informed Jasmine before hanging the phone up and leaving straight out of the door.

The adrenaline within me started to pump throughout my body. I no longer entertained the hangover I was experiencing. The pit of my stomach knew that there was something that was definitely not right over at Donna's. Not one time in Jasmine's eleven years on this earth did he ever call me dad.

I never allowed him to. I knew that kids' deepest, darkest secret was always kept from the people they referered to as mom and dad. I didn't want that for Jasmine, or any of my children for that matter. I only hoped that, whatever the situation was, I didn't have to choose between the love for my children and my freedom.

I drove aimlessly to Donna's. Once I reached the apartment, I called from outside to make sure I wasn't walking into a setup. I became nauseous when no one answered. I reached for my 9 before exiting the car. My phone went off. It was Donna's number. A sense of relief came over me.

"Hello?"

"Dad, where you at?" Jasmine questioned.

"I'm on my way in. What's up?"

"Just come in and get us. Don't let Donna know I called," Jasmine whispered through the phone with urgency and hung up.

I looked at the cell phone awkwardly and decided to walk into whatever waited on the other side of the door. A twist of the knob was a failed one. I kicked myself for ridding myself of my key. I forcefully knocked on the door. There was no answer, so I knocked harder.

"Who the fuck is it?" Donna yelled from the couch after being awakened by my banging on the door.

"Open up the muthafuckin' door!"

When Donna realized who was on the other side of the door, she hopped up and lit a couple of incenses and grabbed up her and Agape's crack pipes off of the table. She hurriedly placed them under the pillow. Donna tried to run upstairs to coach her children to tell me that they already ate and, if I asked if they all want to go with me, to say no.

"Do y'all hear me?" Donna asked, stepping in front of the TV, distracting Jasmine and Jazzy from their game.

"Yeah, Donna, we hear you."

"And, miss bitch"—Donna glared at L—"I swear on your life, if you say anything outside of what I just said, I'ma put yo' ass back in the closet, and it ain't gon' be shit anybody can do about it," Donna warned, taking her stare from L and placing it on Jasmine.

Donna noticed how protective Jasmine was over L. She didn't know why all of her children couldn't be like Jazzy. To Jazzy, the sun rose and set on her. She could do no wrong in his eyes. Donna ran in the restroom and took a look at herself in the mirror. I continued to knock on the door, yelling obscenities. She looked like shit, but to her, she was on top of her shit. Donna ran down the stairs and pulled the door back forcefully. Donna turned to walk toward the kitchen, and I grabbed her arm and spun her around.

"What the fuck took you so long to answer the door? You got a nigga up in her or something?" I shot Donna a look that told her "Don't fuck with me."

Donna, at the moment, loved the attention that she was receiving from me, not realizing that I could have cared less if she fucked every nigga in the Bass as long as my kids didn't witness it. But somewhere, somehow, Donna perceived it as my finally coming to my senses and leaving Lyric alone.

"Don't come up in here questioning me about who I'm fucking. Shouldn't you be over at Lyric's making sure she ain't got a nigga up in the bed with her? She the whore," Donna tested.

"Look, I don't give a fuck about that bitch," I lied. My pride wouldn't allow for me to care for Lyric after what I witnessed.

Donna gleamed.

"Where my kids at? I don't have time for this shit. L, Jasmine, and Jazzy!" I yelled upstairs for the kids to come down.

"What's up, Li'l Jasmine?" Jazzy greeted.

I stood confused. Surely there had to have been a problem, I thought, but here, Jazzy stood with a smile on his face. Just as I was about to throw in the towel and admit that I was tripping off the fact my own son called me dad, Jamine and L came down the steps. The last time I saw the distressed look in either one of their eyes was when the feds came and took Jazzy away. Yet and still they had smiles on their faces. Something was up.

Donna gleamed at the kids. She was worried about L and Jasmine. She thought surely they would come down looking like the weight of the world was on their shoulders, but instead they all appeared happy. If Donna only took time out to pay them any attention, she would have seen that their eyes didn't match their smiles, and any real parent would have known that something just wasn't right.

"So what's up, blood?" I greeted Jasmine, playfully shoving him in the head.

"Nothing. Playing video games. I didn't know you were coming over today," he lied.

"You know yo' pops had to stop through and make sure his seeds are all right."

I took note that Donna was watching over my kids like she was a warden. I couldn't understand, for the life of me, what could be going on.

Maybe Donna was on some lazy shit and ain't want to cook for them, I contested. "Y'all hungry?"

"Nah," all three of them lied.

"L, baby girl, what you eat today?"

"Um…um," L tried to stall out before she had to tell her father another lie.

She hated lying. It was the one thing that her dad punished her for. "Nobody like a liar, L," she could hear her father telling her. "If you're going to lie, let it be to save you or your siblings' lives but never to kick it. Silence is better than any lie any day."

"Why you always gotta act so fucking stupid? I swear it's something wrong with that girl," Donna went off, visibly upset. "Jazzy, tell your daddy what y'all ate since the cat got your senseless-ass sister's tongue."

I shot daggers through Donna with my eyes at the insult she just casted upon my daughter. Through the slits in my eyes, I noticed that something was different about Donna. She seemed to have lost a few pounds, and the admirations she once held in her eye was as cold as mine was.

Jazzy ran off a list of food that he knew there was no way in hell Donna saw to it that they ate that good. "Breakfast, we had pancakes, eggs, and sausages, and lunch, we had salad and steak."

Now, had he said McDonald's, Wendy's, or Taco Bell, I would have went along with Jazzy's story.

"Is that right, big man?" I egged on.

"Yep! It was good too," Jazzy continued.

The disgusted looks of L and Jasmine didn't go unnoticed as Jazzy rambled on.

"Y'all trying to go with me?" I asked.

"Why, so you can have them up under that whore you have for a girlfriend?" Donna interrupted before any child could speak.

"Her name is Lyric," L butted in.

L liked Lyric, and she wasn't going to sit and let Donna talk about her.

"Who asked the ho's name, L?" Jazzy questioned, coming to Donna's defense.

"Don't say nothing, Jazzy. She the only one of my kids that's disrespectful."

293

I looked at Donna with disbelief. I was sure my ears were fucking with me.

"Jazzy, don't call her no hoe. You don't even know her."

"And neither do you. How you gon' take that bitch side over your own momma?" Jazzy got up from the love seat and walked toward the sofa where L was seated next to Jasmine.

"That's yo' momma," L responded, getting up from the couch, clearly not intimidated by Jazzy.

"Bitch, I'll—"

Just as Jazzy reached out for L, Jasmine intervened. Jasmine grabbed Jazzy up by the neck with the strength of two men and began to shake him just the way his father had taught him to do when a man violated or disrespected his sister.

"That's enough!"

And just as the words escaped my mouth, Jasmine let Jazzy go, dropping him to the floor.

"You punk muthafucka, don't put your hands on my fucking son, you son of a bitch!" Donna argued, charging at Jasmine.

I took a step in front of Donna, blocking her path toward Jasmine. Jasmine stood behind me with his feet planted in the floor, his chest heaved up and down, just thinking about how Donna made L get in the closet.

L had woke Jasmine up out of his sleep, nudging him on the back with her elbow. Jasmine woke up. Jasmine started to ignore her but forgot whom he was ignoring, realizing L wouldn't give up.

"Wake up, Jasmine."

"What, L?" Jasmine called out groggily.

"You smell that?" Jasmine sniffed the air.

It was evident what L was smelling, but to be sure, he didn't let the cat out the bag. He pretended not to know.

"What?" Jasmine questioned. "I don't smell nothing."

"You crazy nigga, it smell like crack."

She knew, he thought but didn't admit to what he knew she smelled. "Nah, you tripping, L. That ain't crack. Go'n back to sleep," Jasmine tried to dismiss, lying back down, hoping that L did the same.

He felt her get out of the bed, only to hear the steps creaking. He followed behind L, knowing there was about to be trouble.

Before Jasmine reached the steps, he heard Donna tell L, "Go'n back upstairs, L."

"I'm hungry," L stated.

"Well, you eat when I feed you."

"But I'm hungry, Donna."

Donna could care less about how hungry L was. Agape was back on her way with the work, and she didn't need L in the way of her getting high. Feeding her was just not in the plan.

"Bitch, if you don't take your retarded ass upstairs, I'ma know something."

L motioned for the steps but turned around and asked, "Why do it smell like crack in here?"

"Crack?" Donna taunted. "How the fuck you know what crack smell like? Get your grown-ass bitch come here." Donna grabbed L by the arm and dragged her up the steps.

jasmine hopped in his bed, not wanting Donna to know he was up.

"Since it smell like crack so much, get your ass in this closet." Donna placed L in the closet. "And don't get out until I tell you to."

Jasmine opened the closet and let L out. L's eyes were watery, and that pained Jasmine. He grabbed her up and placed her on his top bunk. As he and L lay in the bed, he listened to L tell him how much she hated her, Donna. In the midst of this, they both got quiet for a second as the smell of the crack filled their room. Enraged, Jasmine made L put the sheet over her head and turned the air conditioner on. After, he placed a towel under the bedroom door.

"I can't believe she got crackheads smoking in our fucking house," L complained whiningly.

Jasmine knew better. He just agreed.

Jasmine didn't have the respect for his mother that Jazzy possessed. As a matter of fact, Jasmine didn't respect Donna at all. He didn't respect the way she talked to L. He didn't like the fact that she was constantly feeding them bullshit. All of her lies and schemes appeared to be a mystery to Jazzy, and it disgusted Jasmine some-times how gullible Jazzy was when it came to Donna.

"We leaving," I dismissed the whole altercation that just played out in front of him. "Go put y'all shoes on."

L and Jasmine went flying up the stairs whereas Jazzy stood next to Donna.

"Go get your shoes, Jazz," I ordered.

"He staying here with his momma," Donna taunted me, giving Jazzy a kiss on the cheek.

"That's cool." I couldn't argue Jazzy loved his mom to pieces, but he needed to know what was up with Donna. "Let me holler at her real quick."

"Jaz, go'n upstairs, baby. It's okay," Donna added.

"What the fuck is up with you, Donna?"

"The question is what's up with you? Don't act like you give a fuck about me."

"You need to keep your face out of that plate. You ain't even looking like yourself no more."

Donna was offended completely. "Fuck you, Jay Baby. I'm a grown-ass woman. I do what the fuck I wanna do, but don't you forget that you're the reason I even fuck with this shit."

Lyric

Today is a new day. I will not call him. I will wait until he calls me, I coaxed myself as I stared down at my cell phone.

A picture of me and Jay Baby was displayed as my screen saver. I tried my best to not address the situation between me and Jay Baby, but the silence of the room and staring at us made me realize how much I really missed Jay Baby's presence in my home. I was getting used to waking up to Jay Baby every morning. I looked up at the picture that hung life-sized on my wall and couldn't help but despise my mother.

"You see what you did to me?" I cried out, talking to the image that displayed my mother in the portrait. "Look at me. I'm no good, Ma. Look at me!" I cried into one of the zebra throw pillows on my sofa. "Please, God, bring him back. If you do, I will be good to him. I love him, God," I cried out in attempt to connect with a higher being. "I love him."

Emillio

I knew I had to fix this whole ordeal with Lyric and Jay Baby. As long as my wife was upset, then I was sure that my home front wasn't going to be right. I hated to be the mediator in the situation, but I felt that it was necessary to play homage toward the circumstances. I knew I had to make the call quick. Meaka was upstairs asleep, and I wanted everything to be taken care of before she awakened. So I decided to give him a call. Just as I was about to hang the phone up, Jay Baby answered the phone.

"Yeah?"

"What's good, playboy?" I questioned from the living room.

Had it not been for Jay locking my number in his phone the night he and Lyric had dinner at me and Meaka's house, he wouldn't have known who was on the line.

"I can't complain. What's good your way?"

"Wondering if there is any way you could come by and let me holler at you, you know, face-to-face and not over the phone," I requested in a pleasant tone.

"About business?" Jay baby jabbed jokingly.

"Business, man," I somewhat lied. "You remember how to get out here?"

"Nah, man. Give me the address so I can plug it in my GPS."

I repeated the address back to Jay Baby, making sure he heard me right.

"Aye, yo, Em, you don't mind me bringing my seeds over with me? My nigga, it's a long story, but it's what's best right now."

"No need to explain. Your seeds are more than welcome in my home."

"I'll be there in a minute."

I thought that maybe I could get to Jay Baby through his kids. So I began to make an assorted amount of blueberry, strawberry, and pineapple cupcakes; sugar cookies; and chocolate cookies. I made homemade vanilla ice cream and a rum cake for Meaka, her favorite.

Just as I set the table of goods for Jay Baby's kids, hoping Jay didn't have more than five kids—otherwise, there wouldn't have been enough for everyone to take some home—the doorbell rang. I took off my chef jacket and opened the door up to Jay Baby and what I now knew as his daughter and son.

"Come on in," I welcomed Jay and his kids in my home by opening the door wider.

"This house is nice," L stated, walking in the door and running up to the table full of goods.

I couldn't help but smile how my plan was going my way thus far.

"L," Jay Baby called after her before she could take another step toward the table, "come on now."

"She good," I affirmed. "When you said you were bringing your kids, I thought it was only right to whip them up a li'l something."

Jay Baby chuckled because he knew good and well I went a li'l further than a little something.

L finally took a good look at me as if she hadn't paid me any attention earlier. She shouted out, "I know you!"

I searched the girl's eyes for some similarities, and I found something familiar about the little girl and begged that I had not bagged the little girl's mother or anything down that road.

"Where you know me from, li'l one?" I asked, looking toward Jay Baby, who looked as if he had the same question in mind.

"You Meaka's husband. I met you the other day when I was with my daddy's girl."

"Oh, yeah, my bad, baby girl. I remember you."

Jay Baby lightened up his mood, but the mention of Lyric's name brought him back to reality that he and I had business to attend to.

"The table is y'all's," I informed L. "And what's your name, son?" I asked.

Jasmine scowled his face up at me, unsure how to take my pleas-
antries. Jay taught him to watch out for a man that was quick to offer
him anything. *No one does something for nothing*, Jasmine thought.

"Go'n head and indulge. This man right here throw down in
the kitchen. I know firsthand," Jay Baby ensured Jasmine.

I watched Jasmine's face soften up when his father assured him
everything was cool. I looked on with admiration and couldn't help
but wonder whether or not me and my son would have shared the
same type of bond that Jay and his son shared. The look of admiration shone defiantly on the little boy's face could not be ignored.

"Let's go in the other room. They cool in here."

"L, Jasmine, don't touch nothing other than what's on that
table."

L and Jasmine was too consumed with all the sweets that lay
before them. Neither answered but instead hungrily stuffed a cup-
cake in their mouth.

"Did y'all hear me?" Jay Baby questioned loud enough to get
both of their attention.

Mouths full, they looked toward Jay Baby and chimed yes with
smiles on their faces.

"They good, man," I contested as I motioned toward the sitting
room. "You wanna drink?" I offered, pouring myself a shot of Patrón.

"Nah, I'm good. I got my hands full," Jay Baby admitted, nod-
ding toward his children in the other room.

I had to chuckle.

"So what's the business?" Jay Baby questioned, rubbing his
hands together.

"Look here, my man," I stalled, downing my double shot I
had just poured myself. I subconsciously let out an aah as the liquor
burned my chest. "I got something I need to let you know. I knew,
if I brought it to you' attention over the phone, then you could have
simply hung up on me, so I needed to speak with you face-to-face."

"Well, I'm here. Ain't no need to waste another minute. Let me
have it," Jay Baby stated jokingly, somewhat felling like this wasn't
about business.

"My brother, Juan, and your girl had a thing going on."

Jay Baby saw black. I noticed his demeanor and knew it all too well, so I chose my words carefully.

"Not nothing sexual or anything like that, but see, she cut my brother off when y'all got together on some ole, not answering his calls and shit. I'ma be one hundred with you. When brah told me he was feeling ole girl, I myself couldn't believe it because I had shunned him from seeing her for my own reasons. Now this was well before you came into the picture. But the two of them kept the shit away from me and Tameka. So when she cut him off—"

"Look, my man, yo people can do whatever they wanna do with ole girl. I ain't fucked up with that. She ain't my bitch," Jay Baby interrupted, clearly unmoved by what I was saying.

"Jay, what I'm trying to say to you is my brother was on some sucka shit the night we was out to Red Lobster. He followed the girl out after she told him she had a nigga, propositioned her to give him a kiss."

Jay Baby had a skeptical look on his face.

"Look, brah, he cornered the girl, came up with some ole shit about, if she could kiss him and walk away, then he would let her be."

A look of unbelief came over Jay Baby. He wanted to believe that Emillio was telling the truth, but then that would have to mean that he would have to forgive Lyric. For some reason or another, he wasn't about to do that just yet.

Meaka

I heard my doorbell ring. I got out the bed to check and see if I knew the owner of the vehicle that just pulled up. To my amazement, I saw the black STS Cadillac of Jay Baby's. I immediately hopped on the phone to call Lyric.

"Lyric…"

"Yeah?" Lyric answered.

"Hey, Lyrie," I greeted, trying to sound as normal as possible, "can I borrow your nude-color Louboutins? Me and Emillio are going to a play, and I have the perfect outfit to wear with them. Please don't say no," I purred.

"Girl, I don't care about them shoes. Jay Baby bought them shits, and as a matter of fact, you can have them bitches."

Lyric was immediately heated at the thought of Jay Baby. She hadn't heard from him since the altercation at Red Lobster, and as if getting rid of the shoes would rid her of the loneliness she felt now that Jay baby wasn't around, she hung up the phone and stormed out of the door with the red bottoms.

"Hi, kids," I greeted L and Jasmine.

"Hello," they both chimed, still stuffing their mouths with the delicious treats Emillio made for them.

"Someone's missing," I added, trying to remember the missing addition.

"Jazzy," L spoke up with a mouth full of sugar cookies. "He wanted to stay at the house with Donna."

"Where's your dad?"

"He and your husband is in the back, talking."

I smiled. Sure that, by the time Lyric got here, Jay Baby would be here as well.

"What's up?" I greeted Jay Baby as I entered the room.

"Up so soon?" Emillio jabbed, fully aware that his wife had to hear the doorbell and couldn't help but make my presence known, which could only mean one thing. *Let me get this nigga out of here,* Emillio thought to himself.

"Nothing much. Just kicking the breeze with ya mans," Jay Baby responded in a laid-back demeanor. "What you up to? I'm surprised you and your girl ain't somewhere tearing the mall down," Jay baby joked.

Emillio laughed as if the joke was on me. I didn't see the humor, but I surely hoped his spirits stayed up once Lyric walked through the door. I chuckled deviously.

Lyric

What the fuck is this bitch on? I thought to myself when I pulled up to Meaka's and saw Jay Baby's Cadillac sitting out front.

"I'm outside," I called Meaka to inform.

Surely I wasn't about to come in and be faced with what was my happiness I found in Jay Baby.

"Good. You made it just in time. Come in. Someone wants to see you."

"Meaka, quit playing with me and come out here and grab these fucking shoes."

"Okay, I'm on my way out."

When I saw L, I got a li'l choked up because I took a liking to L and I didn't know how she viewed me or if she liked me anymore for apparently breaking her father's heart. Damn, I hoped she wasn't mad at me. But when I saw that smile, I knew she was still my girl.

"Lyric!" she yelled after Meaka whispered something in her ear.

As she ran to my car, I had no choice but to get out and meet her halfway. L hugged me so tight a tear escaped my eye.

"Lyric, Li'l Jasmine in the house. I need you to go in there and make up with him right now because I want to come live with you and go get my nails done with you. I want you to—"

"Okay, okay, li'l one, take a breath," I recommended.

"I told you someone wanted to see you."

"Well, you should have told me it was my girl. I would have been over here."

Then, as if a ton of bricks had been placed on my heart, Jay Baby called for L, "Come on, L. Tell Em thanks for the treats. We about to be out."

"But, Li'l Jasmine, can we just stay for a li'l long please?" L begged, hanging on to my waist, never fully letting go of me since our hug.

"Come, L," Jay Baby demanded pleasantly.

L marched off, visibly upset.

"I could keep her here, if you don't mind," Meaka suggested.

"Nah, your husband has plans for you, and I wouldn't feel right ruining them. L coming home with me."

"Where's home?" I couldn't help but question.

Just two days ago, home was with me. Jay Baby looked at me with so much fire in his eyes I couldn't distingush whether or not it was hurt or love. I took my attention off of Jay Baby and placed it on Jasmine.

"Hello, Jasmine."

"Hello, Lyric, how are you?" Jasmine asked.

"I'm good. I miss you guys." I grabbed his hand so that he could feel that I was sincere.

Jasmine placed both arms around me and whispered, "We all miss you too."

A smile of satisfaction escaped my lips, not because Jasmine told me that they all missed me, but because he hugged me. I remember Jay Baby telling me that Jasmine was in no way the affectionate type, so I would have to excuse his abrasive personality. He claimed he'd always been like that and that he only ever remembered him hugging him once and couldn't remember him ever so much as giving Donna a hug. I didn't even know that Jasmine liked me. He'd never said any more than a hello to me.

It wasn't about liking me. Jasmine knew his father loved me. At this point, he was upset with me for whatever reasons, but he didn't want me to feel like his father didn't love me when Jasmine knew good and well he did. He saw the tear escape his father's eyes the night of their fight. Jasmine wasn't too sure what I had done to get under his father's skin, but he knew what his father always told him.

"Don't waste your time giving your heart to just any girl. You'll know when you have the right girl."

After years of hearing this from his father, Jasmine asked Jay Baby one day, "How would you know, Li'l Jasmine?"

"You'll know if you really love her the day you shed a tear for her."

Jasmine had never seen Jay Baby cry over his own mother, and she had taken him through hell and back. So as far as Jasmine knew, he loved Lyric; and she needed to know that despite their differences at the moment.

"Can I talk to you, Jay Baby?" I asked.

"You talking, ain't you?" Jay Baby stated aggressively. "Jasmine, take L, and y'all go get in the car. I'ma be there in a second."

Jay Baby and I looked on as L and Jasmine did as they were told.

"Jay Baby, you know that I love you, and these past days that I've been without you, I have realized just how much I love you. I miss you. Can you please come back home?"

I wouldn't allow a tear to drop from my eyes, but my eyes pleaded with Jay Baby.

"What's the deal with you and that nigga, Lyric?" Jay Baby questioned. "Give it to me one hundred."

"Look, I used to dance for him, Jay. That's it, and that's all. Now I was feeling the nigga, but that was way before me and you. That night, the nigga was pressing me, babe. He wouldn't leave me alone. It was like, everywhere I went, I was running into him. Then he came at me with some shit about, if I could kiss him and walk off, then he wouldn't bother me anymore."

She ain't lying, Jay Baby thought, remembering him and Emillio's previous conversation.

"I went for it because I knew the kiss didn't mean shit and I needed the nigga off of my back." I grabbed on to Jay Baby's arms, hoping that he believed me. "You got to believe me, Li'l Jasmine. I swear on my dead mother's grave I'm telling you the truth."

Jay grabbed me by the waist and lifted me up in the air. I grabbed on to his neck and wrapped my legs around his waist.

"You know I'll kill a nigga dead over you, Lyric," Jay Baby whispered in such a sexy but sinister way.

"And you know I wouldn't think twice about beating a bitch's head in over you," I responded as I held on to him tight.

"Come on," Jay Baby requested as he let me down gently.

"Where we going?" I asked, following his lead toward his Cadillac.

"Home."

I love this nigga, I thought as I climbed in the passenger seat.

"I'm so happy we home," L couldn't hold in her excitement.

"You's a buster," Jasmine teased, trying to put L in a headlock.

But as soon as Jay Baby put the car in park, she was out the door. Jasmine was on her heels.

"Hey, hey, hey now, I can't have you all up on my girl like that." I blocked Jasmine with one arm stretched out with L right behind me.

Jasmine wanted to show me how much fire L really had in her and that she was not as sweet and innocent as she appeared to be.

"You better get the fuck out my way."

As soon as *way* left Jasmine's mouth, L ran from behind me with a kick to the leg and a right hook to the left cheek.

"You muderfucker, don't disrespect her!"

Jasmine picked L up over his shoulder to try to calm her down a li'l bit. Jasmine teased as L fought to free herself.

These kids are off the chain, I thought to myself.

Jasmine's goal backfired when I grabbed L by the hand. A defeated look escaped, and L caught it and proceeded to stick her tongue out.

Jay Baby asked L, "What's that for, L?"

Unbeknownst to him, Jay Baby saw her.

Meaka

I watched from the window as Jay Baby and Lyric pulled off, with a big smile on my face. I was satisfied. Just as I was turning from the window, I was surprised to see Emillio standing behind me.

"Dang, babe, you scared me," I stated after I damn near jumped out of my shoes.

"Oh, did I?" Emillio questioned, grabbing my arm. "That's your girl, ain't it?"

"Yeah, I'm just happy that she could find her someone that makes her happy, and I would have hated for her happiness to end over a mistake, you know."

"Yeah, I feel you. Those two do deserve each other, only if I could find a way to bring some sort of happiness in Agape's life."

"Speaking of A, what she been up to?"

"Shit, I don't know. She ain't been home in over two weeks. She ain't called or nothing. Lyric told me to not keep stressing myself over Agape and to let her come around. So that's what I'm going to do. I just sometimes feel bad for A. It's like, since Al died, she hasn't been the same, you know what I mean?"

"Yeah, you know, everyone deal with death in their own way, but for some reason, I feel that A got other shit with her, you know, shit she gotta deal with. All this talk about making people happy, how about you tell me what will make you happy?" Emillio stated.

"Baby, you make me the happiest woman on earth," I stated even though I wanted to tell him that it would make me happy to carry his child, but I didnt want to kill the mood.

"Come on now, babe. I'm hardly ever home. I wanna show my appreaciation for your patience and love that you continually show a nigga."

"Aw, listen to you," I joked.

"For real, Tameka, what can I do?"

I pondered on the question. When I looked up, I guess Emillio could read my thoughts, or maybe it was the sadness in my eyes that told him how he could make me happier than he had already had.

"You wanna have my baby, don't you?"

I solemnly shook my head, not knowing what Em's response would be.

"Tameka."

"Yes, babe?" I focused on the fireplace and couldn't bring my eyes to meet his.

Emillio turned my head by gently grabbing my chin. "Tameka, I want to give you my seed."

A tear dropped, and a smile spread across my face. I couldn't form a word.

"I want you to have my babies, Tameka, all six of them."

"Hold on now. Six? I don't know about about no six kids, baby," I stated as I walked up to him real slow and seductively. "Show me," I teased.

As if he had been waiting for me to utter those words, Emillio wasted no time on fucking me for hours.

"He better got me pregnant," I thought when I woke up.

Meaka

"Hello, you've reached Baby Dolls."

Silence.

"Hello?"

"Yes, um, I was wondering. Do you have a Agape Lewis?"

"Well, it is our policy to keep all of our baby's information confidential, but Ms. Lewis came in. She wouldn't give us any emergency contact information. And so far, she has refused to provide us with her next of kin. Would you, by any chance, know who Ms. Lewis next of kin is?"

"Yes, this is her sister, Tameka," I stuttered.

"I didn't think I would ever refer to Agape as being my sister ever again in life, and here I was."

"Okay, Miss Tameka. Our director, Mama Meagan, will contact you later. You can expect to hear from her within the next hour. She's in group right now," the receptionist informed.

I thanked her before hanging up the phone.

Mama Meagan looked around the room, at the circle of drug-addicted females. Her heart went out to each and every one of them. She knew all too well what it was like trying to yank a monkey off of your back. Her eyes stopped at the newest girl in her rehab—Agape Lewis.

"Agape, it's your turn."

Agape cleared her throat. "My name is Agape Lewis. I am twenty years old, and I am a crack addict," Agape stuttered.

Everyone's in the room were locked on Agape. No one could believe that she admitted to being an addict. Each time it came time for her to admit to her addiction, she would always deny being an addict or simply get up and leave when Mama Meagan called on her.

Agape paused. MamaMegan stood up and went to Agape's side. She rubbed her back. Agape put her head in her lap and couldn't help but cry. She couldn't understand how her life had spiraled out of control the way it had. She couldn't believe all the pain she had caused to the one person she loved and cared for dearly—Meaka.

Mama Meagan continued to rub Agape's back as it heaved up and down from her crying hard. The other twelve girls looked on with tear-filled eyes; each one knew how hard it was to admit to being a drug addict. Mama Meagan was proud that Agape admitted to being a drug addict, being the fact that admitting that there is an addiction is the first step in recovering from an addiction.

"Group is over" Mama Meagan announced. She wanted to be alone with Agape. She felt her pain in between her sobs. Agape had come into Baby Doll's three weeks ago. With the weight of the world on her shoulders, MaMa Meagan didn't know exactly what was going on with the young lady; she didn't have anyone visit her. She didn't have anyone noted as her next of kin. Only information she knew about Agape was what met the eye. Even though she would never look Meagan in her eyes, she could feel Agape staring holes through her. But when she would turn in Agape's direction, she would simply turn away. Meagan understood the downfall with trying to face your addiction. You're stuck in between shame and the guilt of living life as an addict.

Meagan

"I just want to let you know I am so proud of you, baby. This is the first step to recovery, admitting your addiction."

The pain of what I'd taken myself through began to manifest. Agape focused her eyes on the tile on the floor of the room. As Agape's eyes began to water, I paid close attention to Agape, so close that, before the tear could roll down her cheek, I wiped it away. I then raised her head by gently placing my fingertips up under her chin. As soon as our eyes met, immediately down her eyes went. I got up and went over to Agape, reassuring her that she could do this.

"It's okay."

I rubbed her back as the tears flowed freely down her face, and just as the universe produces energy, I began to manifest my own. I could remember there was a time that I was in this very predicament, trying to confront the beast, the beast meaning heroin. I had been in love with heroin. I loved her more than I loved my own mother, my daughter, and my friends. No one or nothing could compete with the beast. I was not too sure what all Agape had done out there to maintain her status in the world of addiction. But I myself let my addiction take over my whole life.

I was a teenage mother who just so happened to get impregnated by my aunt's boyfriend. He took full advantage of me, constantly telling me my mother didn't love me due to her working day in to day out to provide for us. My young mind couldn't process what he was trying to do. I began to think that my mother didn't love me. Imagine that. I'd learned that the mind is a very tricky thing. You can convince yourself of believing anything. When I looked back on it, my mother loved me; and she sacrificed herself and her happiness so that I could be a happy child, only if she knew how leaving me with her brother, as she would refer to him as, wasn't a safe haven for me. Instead, it was a place that I held secrets and hidden hostility toward my mother.

The very first time Tommy touched me, it was in the kitchen. He touched my butt of course. I thought it was an accident, but he went on to ask me if I felt that, knowing he was going to apologize for touching me in such a manner.

"Uh, yeah," I shyly responded with a slight bit of a smile due to the embarrassment I felt.

In his sick, perverted mind, I was smiling because I liked it. Imagine that. His advances went from just touching on me to having my aunt leave the house on a hunt to have me with himself alone. He began to have sex with me, and he continued with his manipulations. He had me thinking that he was the only one who loved me, and since I shared his energy by allowing him to have sex with me, we became one. After I had my baby, Tommy swore me to secrecy. No one till this day knew that he was my child's father, the same as no one knew about Tommy's secret addiction to cocaine, in which he introduced me to before I got pregnant.

Agape

I found myself wondering if Ma D heard me confessing to being a crackhead as I lay down in my bed. How did I let this happen? I knew Ma D was turning over in her grave.

"I hope you can forgive me, Ma D. I never meant to spit on your grave. Ma, please forgive me," I begged and cried in my pillow.

I had so much guilt weighing heavy on my heart. If I had just kept her memory with me, it would have been no way that I could have disgraced her in such a manner. Then there was Stormy that kept entering my mind. What are the odds in the man who I gave my heart to end up being her baby's father? I don't know if it was a moment of clarity I was experiencing had to do with my system being cleaned, but for some reason, I felt the need to reach out to Stormy. When thinking of Stormy, I immediately began to think of Meaka. Poor Meaka, my sister, the only person that ever kept it all the way a hundred with me. This girl did time for me. I couldn't think of anyone who would be willing to minimize their life to three hots and a cot for another, and here I was holding on to a created beef that I had concocted up myself. Meaka had always been loyal. This I know for sure; but when she went ahead and got married and made Lyric her maid of honor, it kind of hurt me because I had just lost my man and I felt like, *How could they be planning a wedding*? I couldn't understand that, and it hurt like hell they could be so dismissive to what I was going through.

I really was being selfish because it really was a beautiful thing, but when I went to that hypnosis and I realized I had been sleeping with the man that was the cause of my nigga's death, I think that was what drove me overboard, let alone I was hanging with a woman who was battling her own demons. She could care less about anything or anybody when she would call me over to get high continuously, passing me a straw along with a plate, stating how she was just trying to look out for me. I couldn't believe I fell for that. Ma D always told me and Stormy to always be careful of those smiling faces. She said that a person doesn't care if you waste your life as long as you do it with them, and how could I've ever thought that Donna was looking out for me when she didn't have the decency to look out for her own children? Donna would light up her pipe not giving a fuck if her kids was there or not, so much for looking out for me.

Lyric

I could go over to Donna's and whoop that bitch's ass myself, I couldn't help but think as I pulled up to Meaka and Em's house. *That bitch,* I went on to think as I let myself in the house.

"She had the nerves to smoke crack with them babies in the fucking house. What's wrong with that dizzy-ass bitch?" I went on to ask aloud.

I turned my head when I saw Meaka balled up on the couch. Meaka sat with a dumbfounded look on her face, the same look she had on her face since I walked in the door.

I asked, "Why you look like you saw a ghost?"

She ignored me and just stared off into space. Had I not been so focused on what L had just revealed to me and Jay Baby, I would have noticed my girl had something serious on her mind. She was still staring off in space.

"Girl, you all right?" I went on to ask, waving my hand in Meaka's face.

"I just don't know where to begin."

"Well, let's start by getting some light up in here," I stated, all the while opening up the curtains. "Where's Em?"

That woke her up.

"Em? He rode up to Kentucky, his second home." Meaka went on to chuckle.

"That sounds like money to me. So what's up with you, Meaka?" I asked, knowing all too well it had something to do with Agape even though she'd been missing in action for years.

She was the only reason I ever saw Meaka stare off in space, the way she continued to float off in space.

"So what she do?" I went on to ask.

"Who?" Meaka questioned.

"Who else?"

"I don't know who she is," Meaka responded.

"Unless you know something I don't, it's only one reason you could be up in here looking like a lost puppy."

Meaka went on to drop her head. I was getting really impatient. She was sitting here playing the hell out of crazy.

"Agape. What she done did now?"

Meaka, looking so somberly, got up.

"What's up, Meek Meek?"

Then the tears.

What the hell? I thought to myself.

"Agape is in a rehabilitation center for women. She's been there for three weeks." Then she went on to crying hysterically.

"Don't cry, Meaka."

"What you mean don't cry? All this time, I done turned my back on my fucking sister, and she was out there. She probably felt like she didn't have anyone. I can't believe I allowed that nigga to make me choose between him and my fucking sister."

Well, damn, I didn't know Em made her choose, I thought even though I knew it had to be something the way Meaka chased Agape around like she was her nigga.

When she stopped calling me in the wee hours in the morning, I wondered why, but I just sucked it up as she was fed up with Agape and all her bullshit.

"Come on now. You ain't turn yo' back on that girl. She turned her back on her muthafuckin' self. She didn't give a fuck about her muthafuckin' self. That was her decision to run around like a chicken with her head cut off with Donna."

"So you knew?" Meaka went on to ask me like I was the one out there on the block serving her, her drug of choice.

"Did I know? Yeah, Meaka, I knew when her and Donna tried to proposition Jay Baby to a threesome. I walked in the house, and these two stupid bitches was in my house in they hoe wear wigs and fishnet stockings looking a mess. I hadn't seen A in about a year. I couldn't call you and tell you what I saw. I realized how hard it was for you to let her live her life without you. I know about the promise that you made to her, and I know how loyal you are to A, Meaka.

So I knew, if I had told you that she was up in my shit trying to sell pussy, then what would that have done for you? You would have been worried sick about that damn girl, so I kept it to myself in order to give you some sort of peace."

"Peace? You think that's what you gave me?" Meaka stated a li'l to defiant for my liking. "You didn't give me no peace. What you gave me was a guilty heart. I feel so guilty, Lyric. I can't even think straight." She went on to cry.

"I'm sorry, Meaka. That's not what I meant for you. My mother taught me that, if you know something about someone that could hurt them, don't be like every other bitch that can't wait to open up they dick suckers. Spare them that hurt, and how they find out is how they find out, but never break someone's heart without being the source of their pain."

Meaka couldn't help but chuckle.

"What?" I questioned.

"You know, yo' momma ain't said no shit like that, Lyric."

I couldn't help but laugh. "Girl, I would never put words in the mouth of the dead. Damn, give me some credit, Meek.

We continued to laugh, Meaka at the thought of my momma saying dick suckers and I reminiscing the day my mom put that jewel in my ear.

"Why don't you think my mom said that, Meek?"

"Come on now, Lyric. You know she ain't say no shit like that."

We both began to laugh, me at her because she was so sure that Moms wouldn't have said no such thing. I, on the other hand, could hear Moms as if it was yesterday.

Meaka got up from her seat. "You gon' go down to the center with me?"

"What center?" I asked, completely forgetting about what she had just revealed to me with thoughts of Mommy.

"I want you to go up to Minnesota with me to see A."

"So she up in Minnesota," I questioned, which wasn't surprising. Every addict from Dayton always ended up in Minnesota.

"Yeah, she been there for three weeks. I'm just grateful that she surfaced because secretly I thought A was somewhere dead after the first year of not hearing from her."

"I don't know, Meaka. Ask Em to roll with you. You know I wasn't rocking with A like that before she went on her little hiatus to keep it all the way real with you. I did know that Agape was running the city getting high with Donna. I tried to talk some sense into the bitch's head, but when the bitch start wearing that fucking pink wig thinking she was invincible, I was done with A. She told me all kinds of fucked-up shit, how I was jealous of her and I ain't shit but a whore and how she don't know what Jay Baby sees in me."

"Well, then you know that she was on that stuff, Lyric, and ain't no telling how that shit fucks with you. So it isn't like she meant a word of any of that. Y'all were best friends at one point in time."

I noticed Meaka's pleading eyes, and I couldn't find it in me to continue to reject her offer. So I did what any real bitch would do.

"All right, Meaka. When are you planning on going up there?"

Excitement replaced in Meaka's eyes.

"Thank you so much, Lyric." She then got up, hugging all on me, telling me how much she loved me.

I damn near had to pry her off of me. "Girl, get yo' hands off of me."

"Why you always acting like can't nobody hug on you?"

"Unless they got a dick in between they legs," I interrupted.

"You are something else, girl."

"You know, I get that a lot," I responded.

We both busted out laughing at my comeback. We both knew I was going to have a comeback.

"But I was thinking that we can go next week. I'm trying to surprise her. I didn't get to speak with her for whatever reasons. The owner, that bitch, was more interested in me than what I was calling for. The bitch had the nerve to ask me my fucking mother's name. She tried to act like she was trying to validate that I was A's sister. I simply gave her Agape's mom's name. Being locked up with A's mother, it wasn't hard to portray that she was my mother." Meaka went on to think. "It just felt weird."

"Meaka, that may be some sort of protocol that they have to do. With all these laws, I know it's something to protect their privacy or safety for that matter."

"It still seemed like she was more interested in me than what I was calling for."

"So what were you calling for?" I went on to ask.

"After not talking to A for damn near two years, I began to get a li'l worried about her. I was talking to one of Em's friend's wife, and she asked me why don't I look for her. I explained to her that Em made me choose between him and her and that I chose him. She ensured me that that was what I was supposed to do. She's a li'l older, about fifty, but she gangsta, and she know the game. She told me to call every hospital in the city. When I had no success with that, she had me check into rehab centers, which kind of took me aback. I looked at the bitch like she was crazy.

"'And what am I checking in rehabs for?' I began to ask.

"But then, she goes on to say, 'Well, Meaka, I wanted to tell you that from jump, but I didn't want to offend you, but when you mentioned Em was missing jewelry, I had my suspicion about her then, and when I asked you who all be in yo' house and you told me nobody comes to y'all home, that was a dead giveaway.'

"'So you telling me that, that bitch was stealing from Em?' I asked.

"'Well, I'm not sure if she stole anything.' She was just speculating."

"That's a li'l more than speculating, don't you think? Here it is ole girl running the city getting high, and yo' nigga's shit come up missing don't sound like speculation to me. Sounds 'bout right. Em probaly knew that bitch was stealing his shit. That could be why he wanted you to choose. You ever think of that, Meaka?"

"But don't you think that's a li'l extreme? Besides, he don't even wear that shit anyway."

"But it's his," I interrupted before she could go any further. "And I know you like to think A's shit don't stank, but she just wasn't who she used to be. Them drugs will turn you into a completely different person, so no, I don't think that was a bit extreme. I thank

God that bitch ain't bring that thieving shit my way because I would have hated to send A to the morgue over some petty shit like that."

"So you saying you would have killed her if she stole something from you?" Meaka went on to ask.

"Nah, it wouldn't have been about the stealing. If it came down to her stealing my shit, then obviously the drugs had her. I would have just taken her life because she was allowing that shit to take her life in the same breath, so in a way, I would have been saving her life all in the same breath."

She always acting like she don't have no feelings for nothing, Meaka began to think. "Well, good thing she didn't make that mistake because she would be dead and you would be in jail. So there is no need to think about that."

"So you say," Lyric stated.

"So what's up with you, Lyric? Everything all right?" Meaka asked, completely forgetting I came over here to discuss what L had told Jay Baby and me.

"Oh, man, with all this talk about A, I forgot my purpose for coming over here. Girl, you wouldn't believe what L told me and Jay Baby."

"Try me," Meaka stated, thinking that it was something other than what was said. Meaka thought she might have started cussing freely.

"Girl, she told us that, that raggedy bitch Donna had her stashed in the closet while her and her friend was downstairs smoking crack." I put emphasis on the *her friend*, insinuating that it was Agape.

"Oh my God, are you serious?" Meaka questioned. "Crack?" she went on to question.

"Crack," I confirmed. "You know, with all this drug talk, I must admit I thought that it was the pills. I never thought for a second that it was crack."

Here she go, I thought to myself when Meaka began to cry. *Why would she do that to herself?*

"Well, how I see it, Meaka, birds of a feather flock together. Had she stayed down with the team, she would have never been puffing on that and fucking with that glass pipe, and them dizzy bitches in the house getting high not even realizing that Jay Baby done already hipped his kids to the game. He told me, soon as his kids turned five, he introduced them to the smell of crack, so when L smelled it, she went downstairs telling the bitch, 'It smell like crack in here,' and she makes that girl get in the closet after telling her not to get out since she wanna be grown, yelling at her, asking her, 'How the fuck would you know what crack smell like? And you bet' not get out of that closet until I tell you to.' Girl, I had to get up out of there. I came straight over here when Jay Baby went to the back room with Jasmine. I started to pull up in the Bass and give that bitch a piece of my mind, but then I remembered Jazzy was still with her."

Jay Baby

As soon as I walked through the door, Donna went in.

"Where the fuck my kids at, muthafucka?"

"Yo' kids, huh? Yo' kids?" I repeated. I couldn't help but taunt Donna. "Your kids, bitch?" I asked, walking toward Donna.

"Bitch?" Donna questioned. "Who the fuck you think you talking to?" Donna questioned.

As soon as I got my hands around Donna's neck, Jazzy came down the steps. Not one to disrespect a woman in front of my kids because I never wanted my sons to ever lose control of themselves in that manner, and as for L, I never wanted her to feel it was acceptable for any nigga to put hands to her. But at that moment, I couldn't get past this bitch smoking crack in the house with my kids. I snapped out of the trance I was in when I felt Jazzy on my back.

He went on to punching me in my head, yelling, "Get the fuck off my momma!"

I flung that li'l nigga off my back and went back to the matter at hand. "So you up in this muthafucka getting high with my kids under the roof, bitch?" I hollered off and smacked her.

Donna hit the floor. She stumbled to get off the floor. I smacked the shit out of her again. She fell back to the ground.

"What are you talking about, Jay Baby?" Donna tried to play crazy.

317

Boom, I punched her in the nose. Donna saw the blood and immediately started screaming, not that it hurt. The crack she had been smoking had her numb. She was devastated that Jay Baby had done what he vowed never to do—hit her with a closed fist. Despite his accusations being true, Donna couldn't let Jay Baby know that she was smoking crack, let alone with the kids in the house. Seeing the blood brought out the savage in Jazzy. He ran up the stairs and looked under the pillow that was previously mine and pulled out the Chrome .45. He ran down the stairs. Still in a trance, I kicked Donna in her face. All the while I kicked, she screamed, desperately trying to grabbed my foot before it came crashing down on her face.

When I heard the gun cock, I turned around to see my seed holding a gun to me. Knowing that he was trained to use the .45, I didnt know what to do. My instinct was to pull my .357 from my hip and open fire at his li'l ass, but this was my seed.

"What the fuck are you waiting for? Shoot this muthafucka!" Donna muffled from the floor.

Pow!

Aw, shit. I grabbed my side. I couldn't believe my seed had just shot me. I don't know what hurt more, the pain from the bullet or who was behind the trigger.

"You dead to me, li'l nigga. You hear me? Dead to me!"

"Shoot him again!" Donna muffled.

But after the first shot, it sent Jazzy to the ground, knocking some sense in him because it was as if he was having an out-of-body experience when he came to. He couldn't believe what he had done.

"I said shoot him again!"

I fought the pain of the bullet hole in my stomach. I had to get up out of there. Blood continued to pour out of my side.

"You okay, Jay Baby? My nigga, you need some help" were some of the questions I heard as I headed to my Navigator.

I had no time to entertain their questions. I had to get to Miami Valley and fast. I could feel myself getting weak. I went to grab my cell phone. It felt like I could barely lift the phone. My adrenaline wouldn't allow me to give in to what was trying to stop me.

This bitch, I thought when Lyric didn't answer my call.

I swerved in and out of traffic recklessly, desperately trying to make it to the hospital.

Lyric

I was frustrated after agreeing to go with Meaka to visit Agape. If I could turn around and bite myself in the ass, I would have. She thought I vowed to let go of ties with Agape after I walked in on her and Donna trying to offer Jay Baby they pussy. Even though Jay Baby thought the shit was hilarious, I myself thought it was disrespectful, not one for tolerating any form of disrespect. Jay Baby pulled me off Donna, and I swore Agape was dead to me. After hearing my phone, it broke my thoughts, which was actually a good thing because it was making me want to call and decline my already confirmation that I was going to come along with her.

"Hello?"

"What's up, Lyric?"

"Nothing much. What you doing?" I went on to ask Mar.

"Girl, word on the street is Jay Baby just got shot."

I saw black. "Look, Mar, is this just some hearsay, or is this word on the street, which is completely different?"

Hearsay wasn't reliable, but the word on the street was different. This is something someone witnessed.

"Word on the street. You know Kia that lives next door to Donna? She said she heard the gunshot. She looked out the door, and she saw Jay Baby running to his car holding his side. She said there was blood everywhere, Lyric."

Click.

That was all I needed to know. I proceeded to call Jay Baby's number. After the fourth attempt, I proceeded to call Miami Valley.

"Thank you for calling Miami Valley Hospital. How may I help you?"

"Yes, I was wondering. Do you have a Li'l Jasmine Brooks?"

"Hold on one moment...I apologize. We don't have a Li'l Jasmine Brooks."

Click.

319

After calling every hospital in Dayton and surrounding hospitals, getting the same results, I began to worry. Did he not make it to the hospital? Had he driven off the road and in some ditch? Where was he? I called any and every one I could think of. After calling one of the niggas that be in the Bass, he informed me that, when a person got shot, sometimes the hospital had them down as anonymous, especially if the patient was not willing to cooperate; and that for sure had to be the case because I knew for certain Jay Baby ain't a cooperating kinda guy.

"So have you heard who shot him?"

"Nah, I ain't got word of who did it. All people keep saying is that only Donna and Hell was at the house."

"And who the fuck is Hell?" I went on to ask.

"That's his young son."

I immediately began to think Donna had to be the culprit. I felt so lost as what to do, so I called Meaka. She was always my voice of reasoning.

"Hey, Lyrie," Meaka answered.

"Meaka, can you please come down here?"

Meaka wondered what could be going on. I never called. This had to be serious. But I had the tendency to play games, so she had to make sure before she had Emillio turn the car around.

"What's going on, Lyrie? You all right?" Meaka questioned.

"I feel lost, Meaka. I don't know what to do." Then the tears started.

"What's wrong, Lyric? Let me know. We gotta turn around, baby. This Lyric. She crying."

Em knew this had to be serious. He'd watched me long enough to know that I wasn't shedding tears behind no bullshit, so he busted a U-turn in the middle of the divider on the highway.

"It's Jay Baby. He got shot, and I don't know what hospital he at or even if he made it to the hospital. Meaka, where are you!" I yelled out hysterically.

"I'm here. I'm on my way. You hear me, Lyric? I'm on my way. Drive this car, Em."

Em followed orders. This was more serious than he thought. Meaka had never been so demanding with him, so he hit the gas.

"Move out the way, muthafucka!" I yelled out of the window to some young teenaged boy not paying attention to what he was doing and walked out in front of my car.

"Lyric, you need to pull over right where you at. Where are you?"

"I'm pulling up to BP on Salem."

"Pull in BP," Meaka stated with urgency. "You don't need to be driving. Just pull in BP," Meaka pleaded. "We'll be there in ten minutes. I'ma talk to you until we get there."

"Meaka, please hurry up. I can't just be sitting here, Meaka," I cried.

"Em, Jay Baby got shot."

Emillio was now doing eighty on the highway.

Meaka

When we pulled in BP, I was relieved to see Lyric's Mustang. I knew how headstrong Lyric was. It was hard to get her to do anything she didn't agree with. I could only imagine how perplexed she had to be feeling because I couldn't imagine being in her shoes. We pulled up next to Lyric. She had her head down on the steering wheel. She looked up, and my heart went out to her when I saw her tearstained face and her red teary eyes.

"Let me get her," Emillio stated, getting out the car. "Come on, Lyrie. Wipe them tears. Jay Baby can't get word you out here like this."

Lyric felt the strength of Emillio, and the energy definitely transferred just as Emillio expected. He opened the door for Lyric. She hopped in; and Em walked inside of BP, letting a young cashier know that he couldn't get his sister's car to start up and that they were on their way to get their mechanic and would be right back.

"Just make sure nothing happens to that car," Emillio stated with authority after peeling off five one-hundred-dollar bills.

The young cashier had an attitude with Emillio, not knowing who he thought he was, coming in there demanding that someone watch his sister car; but when he peeled the hundreds off, the young cashier's attitude changed up quick.

"Is there anything else I could do for you?" the young cashier said, stressing *anything* all the while looking seductively at Emillio.

Rat, Emillio thought to himself as he turned his back.

I hopped in the back seat as soon as Emillio walked into BP. I consoled Lyric to the best of my ability. I could feel how tense she was when I tried to wrap my arms around her.

"It's gon' be okay, Lyric," I consoled.

Emillio flew through downtown going toward Lyric's house.

"Where we going?"

"To Lyric's," Emillio stated as he called a couple of numbers and spoke as if he was talking in code.

There were no sentences formed, just "Uh-huh" and "Get it done."

When we pulled up to Lyric's, I questioned, "I didn't know what we were doing here. Shouldn't we be looking for Jay Baby?"

"Y'all go'n in the house. Just give me a minute."

I could feel Emillio's urgency, so I got out the car and proceeded to walk around the car to the driver side. Emillo rolled down the window.

"Everything okay, Em?"

"Everything gon' be okay. Let yo' girl know."

I reached my head in the car and thanked Emillio. "You know I love you, right?"

"That's understood. Don't have to be explained, baby. You know I love you, right?" he went on to ask.

"Without a doubt, baby."

*****

"You want something to drink, Lyrie?"

"Grab me a 7 Up."

We both had to laugh because Lyric loved 7 Up and she knew I hated 7 Up. She claimed clear pop is better for you than dark pop.

"I got Pepsi, Dr. Pepper. Which would you prefer?"

"You got some Kool-Aid?"

I couldn't tell you the last time I drank Kool-Aid or even heard a person requesting Kool-Aid, I thought.

"Kool-Aid though, Lyric?" I taunted.

"Yes, bitch, Kool-Aid," Lyric responded.

"Oh, I know what you would like."

I went in Em's cabinet and pulled out a bottle of Moët.

"Ching-ching," Lyric agreed with the Moët.

Once the Moët was good in our system. Lyric hopped up. "Where the weed at?"

"Um, I don't know."

"You don't know?" Lyric questioned.

Just as her interrogation was about to begin, the phone rang. I was relieved to see Emillio's number on the caller ID.

"Hey, baby, I'm 'bout to be pulling up. Come on out," Emillio informed us that he found Jay Baby. "Y'all gotta get up to Miami Valley Hospital. That's where he at. There was no question as to who he was."

"How did you find him?" I went on to ask.

"Ask me no questions. I tell you no lies."

"What's that supposed to mean?" I butted right in because I knew that could have only meant one of two things.

Emillio got the info from someone he used to talk to, or it was someone he still had ties with.

"Damn, brah, I forgot all about Missy," she said, referring to my Mustang Emillio pulled up in.

"Yeah, she all in one piece?"

"I don't know what you would have done if Missy right here had so much as a scratch on her."

"Nah, brah, all you done for me today, I couldn't even charge you for any damages."

We all busted out laughing.

After getting in, I rolled down the window and asked Meaka if she was riding with me, as if she was waiting on me to ask. She went on to tell Em she'd give him a call once we got up there.

"All right, that's cool. Y'all be careful. Matter fact, Tameka, why don't you do yo' girl the honors of driving her up there?" Emillio stated all the while he proceeded over to the driver side and opened up the door. "Come on, li'l lady. Let Meaka drive you."

Lyric, to my surprise, didn't object. I hopped in the driver seat, and off we went.

Lyric

"I can't believe someone shot my nigga," I thought but stated out loud.

"Who you think did it?" Meaka went on to ask.

"I don't have a clue, Meek. Jay Baby ain't got no enemies. I can't began to think which one of these hoe-ass niggas could have did some shit like that to my nigga," I responded.

Our fifteen-minute drive seemed like a minute. We followed Emillio's directions precisely—elevator B, fourth floor. As we walked down the hall to get to his room, I pulled back the tears that were trying to fill my eyes.

I guess I focused too much on keeping the tears back when I heard Meaka, "Lyrie, where you going?"

I done walked pass Jay Baby's room.

"It's okay, baby. Jay Baby need you, Lyric. Come on." Meaka all but pushed me through the door.

Immediately tears began to flow from my eyes seeing my man hooked up to all of these monitors. I stood there in complete shock.

Meaka came over and rubs my back. "It's gon' be okay, Lyrie. Jay Baby strong. Just give him time. Just trust the process."

I wiped my eyes, put my game face on when the nurse walked up to us and asked, "Have he been sleeping since the medication?"

"Honestly we couldn't tell you. We just got here."

"Okay, that's no problem. Let me check the chart. By the way, I am the nurse in the intensive care unit. Do you mind me asking your relationship to the patient?"

As we came to the realization that we were in the worst unit possible, the shock must have been plastered across my face.

"I am his close friend, and this is his fiancé, my best friend," Meaka said.

"Nice meeting you, ladies. Li'l Jasmine came in about 9:00 p.m. from a gunshot wound to his abdomen entering through his side. He attempted to drive himself to the hospital but lost consciousness, causing him to have an accident. He didn't have a seatbelt on, so he hit his head on the windshield."

"That's why he bandaged up like that?" I asked.

"Yes, ma'am."

"So how is he doing?"

"Li'l Jasmine is a fighter. I can tell you that. I've seen injuries like Li'l Jasmine's. I just never seen anyone able to live to tell about it."

I began to cry, hearing the severity of Jay Baby's situation. Meaka was right there at my side. She went in to give me a hug. All I could do was accept it. I tried with everything in me to control myself. The nurse walked us out of the room when Jay Baby began to squirm in his sleep.

"Li'l Jasmine is out of the battle, but he is still in the fight. I need for you to know that. You have to stay positive about this. After a li'l TLC, Li'l Jasmine will be back to normal," the nurse let us know.

"Thank you." Meaka said.

I couldnt help but follow up. "Thank you for that. I really needed to hear that," I admitted somberly.

"He will be fine. Li'l Jasmine is a very strong man."

"Have he been up at all?" I asked.

"Lil Jasmine is on some pretty stong medication, so therefore it would be kind of hard for him to be up. Just give him some time. He will come around."

I felt so lost. I'd never been this unsure. Then we heard beeping coming from Jay Baby's room. We entered his room, and there Jay

Baby was ripping his heart monitor off. I toughened up as soon as I locked eyes with Jay Baby. I rushed over to his side. I grabbed Jay Baby's hand, not knowing what to say. I just rubbed his hand.

"Go'n somewhere with all that soft shit?" Jay Baby joked just above a whisper.

I couldnt help but smile. *That's my nigga*, I thought to myself and couldn't help but kiss Jay Baby right on the lips.

He pushed his tongue in my mouth. I gently grabbed the side of his face, and returning the favor, gently I slid my tongue in his mouth. My pussy instantly got wet. I had to slow this down. I removed my tongue, and Jay Baby reached for me, letting me know he didn't like the way I removed my tongue from his mouth.

"Give me back my tongue, bitch. Don't play with me."

I looked Jay Baby in the eyes. I may have been sick to be turned on standing at the side of his hospital bed, but I was. I had no choice whatsoever but to put my lips on Jay Baby's, along with sliding my tongue in his mouth. Jay Baby began to squirm. As soon as I felt his discomfort, I removed my tongue and backed away, noticing Meaka and the nurse, whom I forgot was in the room coming on the other side of the hospital bed. Jay Baby held on to his gunshot wound. He began to yell out in pain.

"Uh! Uh! Shit!" Jay Baby screamed out in pain.

I took a step back, careful not to look Jay Baby in the eyes as my eyes began to water.

"Okay, Li'l Jasmine, this may hurt a li'l on three. One, two, three," the nurse counted, and on three, she stuck Jay Baby with a needle.

I walked up to Jay Baby's bedside. As much as I tried to conceal how saddened I was, I couldn't hide that from Jay Baby.

He turned to me and asked, "Where all that tough girl shit at, Lyrie?"

I couldn't help but smile. It cracked me up every time someone referred to me as Lyrie. Whatever that was the nurse put in Jay Baby had to be some powerful shit because he was out of it cold.

Meaka and I tiptoed out of the room and into the hall.

"You know I'm here for you, Lyrie. Whatever you need, I got you," Meaka stated while putting her arm around me.

Surpisingly I let her. "I do need something, Meek," I admitted.

"Just say the word, Lyric."

"I need you to go pick the kids up from Janice."

"Janice?" I questioned.

"That's Donna's mom. I took the kids over to her house when I got word that Jay Baby got shot."

"All right, Lyrie. Just send me her address, and I'm on my way."

"All right, thanks, Meek."

"All right, girl. Get on in there with yo' nigga. He need you. I love you."

We gave our hugs, and off to my nigga I went.

Meaka

"Who at my muthafuckin' door?" Janice yelled as I knocked on her door.

"It's Tameka, Lyric's friend. I am coming over to pick up the kids," I yelled through the door.

"What kids?" Janice opened the door, asking with much attitude.

"Hello, my name is Tameka. I am here to pick up L, Jazzy, and Jasmine."

"Hold up. Wait one minute," Janice stated while holding her finger up, then closing the door.

I waited as I heard her call for L and Jasmine.

Jazzy must be right there, I thought.

I put on a fake smile when Janice opened the door with L and Jasmine standing behind her.

"Who is this?" L came around Janice, attempting to open the screen door, which made me, in return, go to pull the door open.

Janice immediately pulled L back behind her, all while pulling the screen door out of my hand with much force.

Well, damn, I thought to myself, careful not to even look at Janice the wrong way. I could tell she was not to be played with.

327

"Now who the fuck is this?" Janice turned her back to me, facing Li'l Jasmine and L.

L spoke up first, "That's Li'l Jasmine's lady friend. She be taking me to the nail shop with her killing two birds with one stone."

L knew for sure Mawmaw wouldn't let them leave with Tameka if they had never been anywhere with Meaka.

"Oh, so she took you to the nail shop?"

"Yes, Mawmaw, she had to get her nails done. Uh-huh, and that's it." L avoided eye contact with Janice.

I saw how Janice was interrogating the children. I was immediatly reminded of when correctional officers would go around abusing their authority. I began to knock on the door. L was relieved the knock distracted Janice. Janice turned around and looked me in the face.

"What!" she yelled.

I stood there like a deer in headlights.

L ran behind Janice. "Mawmaw, Tameka good people," L stated while grabbing a hold of Janice's hand, putting her puppy-dog eyes on strong.

"Okay, girl. Hell. Take y'all asses on," Janice stated. "Yo' momma dont give a fuck, then I don't either. Shit." She walked off, leaving L standing there unfazed.

"Come on. Let's go," I stated while Jasmine and L exited the house.

L ran down the steps. Jasmine followed behind her.

Once I started the car up, Jasmine went on to ask, "Did he get caught?

"Who is he, Jasmine?"

"My dad. Is my dad locked up? Don't play games with me, lady."

I was taken aback by Jasmine's demeanor. Here he was a small boy in my eyes, ready to know what was going on with his father.

"No, Jasmine, your father is not in jail."

"Well, is he alive?"

"Alive, Jasmine..."

Again, I was taken aback by his response.

"It's two ways my father would leave us, and that's dead or in jail."

I knew I was talking to a child, but Jasmine was far ahead of his time.

"What you trying to say, Jasmine?" L butted in and asked.

"Look, L, I ain't trying to say nothing. Some shit ain't right. I can feel it…"

ABOUT THE AUTHOR

———————•◦•———————

Assatta was born in Dayton, Ohio. She was a teenage mother who finished high school and went on to obtain an associate degree. She likes to spend time with her daughters Shaniia and Shavone, as well as her goddaughters Nunu, Myracle, and Chanel. She has eleven brothers and sisters. She came from a big family with strong women. Her grandmother was from Fort Deposit, Alabama, as well as her mother, aunts, and cousins. She was diagnosed with MS in 2016. She couldn't get you to understand how everything is so different and how the challenges are unbearable at times. This is her new normal. She is capable. She did it. She always wanted to write a book since a little girl. This is a dream come true.